ELIZABETH CORLEY was born and brought up in West Sussex. Married, with a step-daughter, she manages to balance her passion for crime-writing with a successful position as Chief Executive, Europe for a global investment company, dividing her time between London, Germany and France. A one-time committee member of and vice-chairperson of the Crime Writers' Association, Elizabeth is an active member of the organisation yet still finds the time to pursue her outside interests of travel, gardening and music.

a&b

REQUIEM MASS

ELIZABETH CORLEY

This paperback edition published in 2007 by
Allison & Busby Limited
13 Charlotte Mews
London W1T 4EJ
www.allisonandbusby.com

Copyright © 1998 by Elizabeth Corley

First published in 1998 by Headline Publishing Group.
Published by arrangement with Headline Publishing Group.

A CIP catalogue record for this book is available from
the British Library.

10 9 8 7 6 5 4 3 2

ISBN 978-0-7490-8002-0

The paper used for this Allison & Busby publication
has been produced from trees that have been legally sourced
from well-managed and credibly certified forests.

Printed and bound in the UK by
CPI Bookmarque, Croydon, CR0 4TD

To my parents, Robert and Yvonne Trown, with love.

This book could never have been written without the support and understanding of my husband, Mike, who variously cajoled, encouraged and fed me!

I would also like to thank Philip Wharton, for his invaluable input on police procedures, and Tony Heath, whose original invitation to a performance of Verdi's *Requiem* started it all.

REQUIEM

Requiem aeternam dona eis, Domine:
et lux perpetua luceat eis.

Rest and peace eternal give them,
Lord Our God:
And light for evermore shine down
upon them.

The old man was dying. He lay in a stark white cot in a private room far removed from the incidental noises of the busy hospital. Around his bed a hush had descended, as if he was already separated from the world by a giant, invisible bell jar.

Fierce Australian sunshine leaked around the edges of tightly closed Venetian blinds, exposing the lack of colour in the room – white walls, white floor, white blinds, white sheets, white skin, white hair, white lips, bleached white fingers. Only the shadows made any sense of the man's features. He was weaving in and out of a dreamlike state: one moment a young man, the next already dead, looking down on the decrepit, cancerous body with a mixture of pity and contempt, failing to find the man he had been in the skeletal limbs and ballooning gut.

For days he had been hovering painfully on the point of death, refusing the numbing drowsiness of a full morphine dose. The doctors and nurses had been trying to increase the dosage daily – but he had the money and the will to resist their efforts, appearing to prefer agony to insensibility. They couldn't understand why. He wasn't really old, only sixty-two, but he looked ninety. An immigrant away from his homeland, on his own, no family, his wife long dead. The hospital staff had no idea what drove him. Still he clung on to his delirium, resisting the temptation to slide into one last, comfortable sleep.

In his mind the man was held fast in the past of nearly twenty years before. In a recurring nightmare he relived the same week of his life over and over again. Each time he was a silent witness to the events – paralysed and dumb – unable to intervene. Every time he had to watch as his daughter walked along an idyllic cliff path to her death.

She would turn and wave, not to him but to her friends, and walk on down the dip and out of view. Then his perspective would change: he would be hovering like a seabird above her, his squawking cries unregarded, trying to swoop across her path, to head her away from what awaited her a few yards ahead.

In his semi-drugged state, the pain of his cancer became the ache in his arm-wings as he dived again and again over her head. The relentless dryness in his throat became the hoarse cawing as he screeched his warning. Every half-sleeping hour he followed her down the same path, to the same fate; his attempts to warn her weakening each time but the cold dread that accompanied her last moments growing stronger and darker with repetition.

Down the dip, around the bend and there was the other one waiting for her, watching silently as first her golden head and then the rest of her delicate figure appeared from below the rise in the path. He couldn't see the other's face; the waiting assailant was visible only from a bird's-eye view. Dark, slim, athletic – he could make out nothing else – but his daughter knew who it was. From the top of the rising path she ran down laughing, arms wide, into a wiry embrace. The look on her face as she gazed upwards was one of love and trust.

The man-gull screeched frantically, beating wings, desperate to warn her. Instead she closed her eyes and raised her face for a kiss. In one smooth motion the dark stranger lifted her off the ground swinging her around, like the father-bird had done when she was a little girl, but then let her go. She flew, sailing over the edge of the sheer chalk cliff. For frozen seconds her eyes stayed closed, her smile simply puzzled. At the final moment she opened her eyes and looked upwards and around in confusion. Her arms flailed in empty space, utter fear washed over her face. She twisted downwards, bouncing on ledges of unyielding chalk before breaking her back on a jagged outcrop to be thrown by the impact outwards, paralysed but conscious, to fall another two hundred feet on to the broken rocks below.

The father-bird plummeted down on folded wings, to grasp his daughter before a wave could claim her. His talons hooked into her white T-shirt, spattered crimson now; his beak gently touched her cheek, to turn her head. She stared at him sightlessly from flat blue eyes. Her head rolled back to settle at an odd angle, leaving blood and grey matter on the rocks. She lay unmoving except when a wave from the incoming tide broke over her, stirring her shattered limbs into a semblance of life. She was dead, always dead.

Ten nights after the patient had been admitted into her care, Nurse Sarah Evans was startled by a summons to his bed. He had previously defied them all; saying nothing, resisting medication to the point where it had been less distressful for him to let him be. By rights, he should have been dead by now. Instead, he was suddenly sitting upright in bed, his skin flushed not by fever but by excitement.

If his alertness surprised her, his next request astonished her. He was demanding a priest – a Catholic, no less – to attend him straight away. Fifteen minutes later, the young priest was running to deliver the last rites. Only when he was in the dying man's room, with the door securely closed, did he start to doubt the reason for the summons.

Yes, there was a soul here for the young cleric to rescue; yes, the man would confess his sins, repent and deliver himself into God's hands, but there was a small condition. The priest was to take down a letter, a very important letter, which the man would dictate. He was to swear on the Bible to see it was delivered to his nephew in England. It seemed a small condition. The intensity in the man's eyes as he insisted that the priest place his hand on the Holy Book and swear to dispatch the letter, swear to keep its contents as secret as the confessional, should have warned him.

5

'I will take your letter, my son. But tell me why it is so important.'

The old man's stale breath smelt of decaying things under floorboards. He gave a ghastly smile.

'I have seen the face! I have seen the face! I know who it was and he must be told – at once. He'll know what to do.'

It sounded harmless enough to the priest – almost a spiritual revelation. With an open and simple heart, he swore his oath and started to transcribe the old man's final words.

The house was exactly as he remembered it: a concrete path leading to a cheap painted front door, once determinedly buttercup yellow, now aged to the texture and colour of sour milk.

As he put his key in the lock he was hit by a crippling sense of grief so strong he had to wait, head rested on his raised hand, whilst the almost physical pain passed. It was followed immediately by a customary anger that spurred him on, over the threshold and into the dark, neglected hall.

The interior was familiar, even in the half-light. He walked straight through to the kitchen where occasional sunlight from the westering sun filtered through heavy clouds, grimy windows and the dust of decay, revealing an oilcloth-covered table and broken chair. Sitting down wearily, he pulled from his pocket a dog-eared black-and-white photograph and ran his fingers lightly over the image of four smiling faces. Beautiful faces, happy smiles lost in the past, and one, the most beautiful, was gone for ever. She had died still innocent and unaware of his love for her.

Whose fault was it that she had died? Not his! For years he had thought that the blame lay with him. For years he had worked, fought and killed in a vain attempt to quieten his conscience and appease her memory. Now he knew it hadn't been his fault. Unlooked for, unwelcomed, the letter had made everything so clear, so obvious. There was nothing he could have done to save her – because someone had wanted her dead.

Who that was he could not yet be sure but suggestions had been made and they were enough to bring him back. There could be only a short list of suspects. He didn't know which of them it was, it could even have been more than one. Thinking of their stricken faces as they had brought news of her death back to this house, realising for the first time the hypocrisy that was hidden behind the pitying, tear-filled eyes of at least one of them, brought him lurching to his feet with a roar of uncontrolled rage, turning over the table as he leapt up, blindly searching for something to hurt or destroy.

He stumbled over to the sink and rammed his fist into the window above it, straight through the glass, taking obscene pleasure in watching the blood swell slowly from the gouges along the back of his knuckles. Only when there was a danger of it falling softly on to the photograph did he lift his arm free and wrap it in an old roller towel from the back of the door. The feeling of blind fury passed slowly, leaving him, as it always did, weak, empty but momentarily at peace. He picked up the photograph, stroking it gently, and made his way back to the kitchen chair. One thought blew slowly through his mind – it wasn't my fault. And with that thought he was filled with an icily clear sense of purpose.

Someone had wanted her to die and had brought her to a twisted, broken death. When he was certain of his facts he would do what little he now could for her and for her memory. Once he would have died for her. Now he rejoiced in the knowledge that he could at last do something real for her: he could revenge her; he could kill for her – once, twice, three times – as many times as proved necessary – to avenge her death and finally let her rest in peace.

At that moment the sun broke through the clouds in its last seconds before falling behind the distant hills. Its light fell softly on the quietly smiling face of a man sure of his destiny and at peace.

PART ONE

DIES IRAE

Dies irae, dies illa,

Day of anger, day of terror,

CHAPTER ONE

'Thank God!'

Deborah Fearnside closed the front door and leant back on it heavily, closing her perfectly made-up lids over delicate blue eyes. It was Monday and the children had finally gone, taken early to nursery school by the ever-obliging Mavis Dean. Now all she had to do was finish getting ready and leave herself.

She opened her eyes and glanced at her watch nervously. Now that it was so close she had butterflies in her stomach. She desperately didn't want to mess things up at the last minute. She was completely ready, had been since quarter to seven that morning. Now all she needed to do was collect her coat and keys, lock up and go. Her natural high spirits returned as she rushed through the house.

Deborah Fearnside had always liked Mondays. She knew that this set her apart from most other people but she rather liked the idea that she was different in at least one aspect of her life. She was the only person she knew who looked forward to Monday, the day when time briefly became her own again. On Mondays Derek went back to the office, reversing out of the drive in his new, silver-finished Audi at 6.55 a.m. precisely to catch the 07.12 to Victoria, and the children went off to school promptly at quarter to eight. Noreen, the cleaning lady, would arrive at 8.15 in time to clean up the breakfast things and tidy away the debris of the weekend.

And this spring morning was even more special than usual. Today, Deborah would be going up to London to sign papers that would launch her into – what? Excitement, challenge, fame? It didn't matter; into something new at last. She was desperate for something new.

Four weeks previously, she and a number of her friends had answered a quarter-page advertisement in the local newspaper for young mothers interested in part-time careers as mature models for a new catalogue. The advertisement had explained that the catalogue was aimed at those families who liked to buy 'quality clothes at their convenience, to suit their busy, active life-styles'. Further, it said, research had shown that 'the response rate among our target audience is significantly better (up to three times in some instances) if the fashions were modelled by *real life* mothers and their children.'

The requirements for the models were exacting and there was a four-stage selection process. In addition, there were strict limits on the mother's height and weight and on the ages of the children. The rewards for successful models were, in the words of the advertisement, 'excellent'.

At first Deborah and her friends had been sceptical. At least six of them matched the height and weight limits specified and had children in the right age group. Three of them, in Deborah's opinion, were really quite attractive. Deborah could not help admitting to herself that perhaps she was the most attractive. She still had the naturally crinkly gold-blonde hair and light blue eyes that had driven the boys wild at school and, despite two children, her figure was firm and shapely. At thirty-three, some stretchmarks and the start of cellulite seemed inevitable but the advertisement had made it clear that all the shots were to be clothed, with professional models being used for swimwear and lingerie. But it felt risky, they might look foolish, and at first they had reluctantly decided that the opportunity was not for them.

Then two things happened that led Deborah to be setting out for the 08.12 to London and her appointment.

The first was Derek. She could accept that he was not the most demonstrative of men, he had been brought up that way, but she had expected at least *some* reaction when, on the

Saturday following the appearance of the advertisement, she had glided out of their en-suite bathroom in her latest purchase from the Naughtie Nightie party she had been to earlier in the week. The sheer, turquoise chiffon two-piece had been chosen amid much joking and envious innuendo from her friends. The flimsy garment had a daringly cut top that plunged almost to her navel, with trimmings of ivory lace softening the cut-away arms and upper-thigh-length hem. There were matching French knickers and the whole outfit made the most of her still firm breasts while minimising the slight spread around her hips that remained despite twice-weekly step classes.

As she had walked into the dimly lit bedroom, pink and warm from her shower, with traces of Derek's favourite perfume drifting from all the right places, she had expected some reaction from her husband. Instead, he merely glanced up from *The Economist* and asked her to switch off the bathroom light behind her. She had left it on deliberately to light her progress across the room, hoping for a seductive silhouette.

Not deterred, Deborah slid on to the bed and pulled away the top of Derek's magazine, believing that by now he must have noticed that something was different. Far from it. He had snatched the magazine from her hand, turned, plumped up his pillow and noisily flopped down under the quilt before turning off his bedside light with a frosty, 'For heaven's sake!'

The argument this precipitated was one of their worst. It ended with Deborah, warmly wrapped in her candlewick dressing gown, sipping tea in the kitchen at two in the morning and vowing to prove to Derek, somehow, that she was still an attractive woman. It wasn't until later, when she came to tidy away the Friday papers, that the modelling advertisement caught her eye again. On impulse she tore it out and put it to one side.

Even then, it is unlikely Deborah would have done anything had it not been for the fact that Jean and Leslie, two of her closest friends, changed their minds over the weekend and decided to answer the advertisement after all. Leslie's husband, Brian, concerned about his wife's growing interest in the advertisement, had telephoned the number given. He had left a message with a very well-spoken and reassuring secretary and was called back within the hour by the executive responsible for the new venture. The man had been professional and had been able to answer every one of Brian's questions. Two days later a glossy brochure on the firm, together with an interim financial statement from their parent company, arrived at the Smiths' home address. Brian, an accountant by training, checked out the main company at Companies House. It existed and, sure enough, there was a subsidiary responsible for the wholesale distribution of fashion accessories. Comforted but still determined to be absolutely sure, Brian rang a friend in the trade who confirmed that the parent company were expanding heavily into catalogue distribution.

Leslie was reassured by her husband's comfort and encouraged her friends to apply. Her husband even agreed to accompany them to their interviews if they got that far. This decided Deborah, and in the end six of the mothers on the school run agreed to apply together. The advertisement specified that they should supply name, address, telephone number, height and weight, details of the children's ages and sex, and a selection of good-quality family and individual photographs (which would be returned if a stamp-addressed envelope was enclosed).

Of the six friends that eventually applied, four were invited for interviews in London within a week. Deborah had travelled up with Leslie and the two others in a state of apprehension and excitement. Their interviews were arranged at the Carlton Hotel (four star, as Deborah proudly informed Derek) near Trafalgar Square. In the end, Leslie's husband had not accompanied them; four women travelling together was considered safe enough.

The interviews were conducted in an executive conference room by a woman in her early thirties, stunningly attractive and elegantly dressed. She asked probing questions and entered their nervous answers on to a laptop computer, which, she explained, already held information from their applications. Her enquiries focused on their backgrounds; any previous modelling or acting experience (Deborah remembered a charity fashion show at college when she was nineteen and some acting at school); their children, particularly their characters and whether they were likely to enjoy and cope with the experience of modelling clothes; and finally, apologetically, on whether their husbands approved of their potential involvement.

At the end of two hours all four women had been interviewed and each was told that she would be contacted within a week to be notified of their success or otherwise. They were given a leaflet containing details about the agency and catalogue. As the friends left the lift and crossed the marbled lobby, they were disconcerted to see two very attractive women ask for the agency's conference room at reception. Deborah secretly felt with competition like that they would be lucky to reach the next stage.

Within three days Leslie and Deborah were telephoned and told that they had been successful. They were asked to a test photo session the following week. Times had been arranged to allow them to travel together. They were also asked to have photographs taken of their children at a local studio, at the agency's expense, where arrangements had been put in hand. This, it was explained by the very pleasant lady on the telephone, would avoid the children having to travel until the selection was finally confirmed. Both Deborah and Leslie felt this was particularly professional and sensible.

The test session in London went well, and both women were told later that they were being invited up to London to sign contracts. They had been successful; they had been chosen, along with two others, from over a hundred applicants. This time, instead of making their own way to the studio, they would be picked up from the station by a chauffeured car.

Thus it was that with a decidedly light heart, Deborah Fearnside closed and carefully locked her front door for the last time on a bright April morning. She carried with her no troublesome conscience and only a light overnight bag in which she had placed a few necessities for the trip, a rather strange good luck charm and her chequebook in case she had time after the session to visit the West End.

* * *

Deborah had agreed to give Leslie a lift to the station and turned up promptly to collect her friend. She was not prepared for the sight that greeted her arrival.

'Deborah. Oh God, I'm sorry.' A distraught Leslie, her hair still in heated rollers, answered the door. 'I'm not going to make it. I've had a disastrous morning. First of all we've lost the cat – heaven knows where the daft thing is! She's never gone off before and I've had crying children wandering around looking for her since seven o'clock. Then Julie, who was going to take them to school today, has just rung to say she can't get her car to start. And finally, to cap it all, Jamie's headmaster has literally just called insisting he sees me when I drop the children off over a "serious matter" he couldn't go into over the phone.'

Leslie looked close to tears. From behind her Deborah could make out the sounds of tearful children and a dog barking frantically.

'Leslie, I'm so sorry. What do you want to do?' Deborah was full of sympathy but she still had to get to the station, park the car and buy a ticket. 'I'll tell you what,' she volunteered, seeing her friend at a loss, 'I'll let them know you've been delayed. As soon as I reach the studio I'll call and see if you're back from the school and what your plans are for the day, OK?'

'Oh thanks, Debs, that's great. I should still be able to make it, provided things go all right with the headmaster.'

'I'm sure they will, don't worry. And the agency won't mind you being a little late after all the trouble they've gone to finding us. I'll see you later.'

Deborah turned to go without waiting for her friend's reply. With luck, she might just make the train if the traffic was light.

Fifteen minutes later she sank thankfully into a seat as the 08.12 pulled away from the platform five minutes late. If the traffic had not been so kind, if the train had been on time, if she had waited for Leslie, maybe, just maybe, she would have made it home again safely that evening.

CHAPTER TWO

He waited calmly and quietly behind the wheel of the hired 5-series BMW. All the planning and preparation had led to this moment. As on previous occasions he was completely at ease and totally absorbed with the details of the performance he was about to give. He had raised his craft, his killing craft, to an art form over the years. He planned, casted and rehearsed until he was performance perfect; he was creator and artist combined.

In this case, he had been faced with an apparently insoluble problem: how to remove a woman from her daily routine without causing alarm *and* give himself time for a leisurely interrogation without an obsessive police operation dogging his steps.

The easy part had been finding her and the others. Their names had been traced from a school yearbook and an old girls' magazine had provided the rest. Then it had been a question of deciding on the order in which to approach them. He needed more specific information and he could only hope to extract the full truth from the first one of them.

He had chosen this one because she would be easy to crack. He doubted her resistance would be high in any event, and vanity and concern for her pretty face would increase her sensitivity to his threats. He disliked interrogations – they were invariably messy and time-consuming. He took no pleasure from them, unlike others he had met from time to time who appeared to derive sexual satisfaction from inflicting pain and wielding the power of the blade over a helpless victim.

The difficult challenge had been creating a plan which would provide sufficient opportunity for abduction without immediately raising a hue and cry. Taking her directly from the village would be a non-starter; he knew this type of community too well. Even though they were populated largely by commuters and their families, everyone knew everyone else's business as it related to mothers and their children. Worse, their daily routines and rituals were so intertwined that a variation would be spotted within a few hours – in some instances, less.

There had been a chance that she did not fit the normal mould but during his surveillance of her it had become clear that she was pathetically of a type: part of the school run; exercise classes twice a week; helping out at the old people's home once a week; shopping and visiting friends too frequently for her husband's comfort. There would not be one day in her self-styled empty life when she would not be missed too quickly for his purposes.

Even more problematic, there were very few occasions when she could be picked up from home without the risk of someone seeing him, as her house was overlooked by not one but two neighbours of the curtain-twitching variety.

The first glimmer of a solution came to him during one of his surveillance trips, when he had followed her with a group of friends into a restaurant where they had coffee. They had been complaining of their hollow lives, how unfulfilled they were, how much untapped potential they had which was rapidly going to waste. He had automatically filed this away for future reference.

Later on they had been poring over a mail-order catalogue. Mixed with various derogatory comments about the clothes had been remarks about the artificiality of the models themselves; one of the women had remarked that they simply did not look like 'real people'.

He had been sifting through the facts he had gleaned when the two separate conversations fused into an idea in his mind. Like all good ideas it was surprisingly simple: do not abduct her in her home environment, take her in one of your own making. She would have to become one of the dozens of people who went missing every week. She would simply have to disappear in London where it was commonplace, not in leafy Sussex where it might still be remarked upon. Even better, if she is bored, give her an excuse to do something different, legitimise it and reinforce it with an idea or prejudice she already has. Real-life models for a mail-order catalogue pulled all the threads together.

Of course, the execution of the idea was rather more complex – 'overworked' his old CO would have said. It was his one failing, a tendency to make the execution of his plans too intricate. It grew out of his love for, obsession with, detail and the desire to prove himself more clever than his opponents. But no part of his plot was irrelevant. Planning the advertisement was easy: a letter and cheque to the local newspaper enclosing copy but allowing them to set the advertisement for a fee meant that he had no need of a design studio. The chequing account had been opened by post from his 'business' address – a serviced one-room office in a run-down part of North London, paid for with cash and no questions asked by the seedy landlord.

He had researched the clothing and catalogue industries quickly: the relevant trade magazines and a few personal investment weeklies had provided him with a list of clothing manufacturers and retailers based in the UK. He chose the most appropriate one, bought a few shares and was rewarded with copies of their report and accounts and interim statement. It had proved just as well that he had them as they served to reassure Leslie Smith's husband at the right time.

Thus prepared he had placed the advertisement to run fortnightly for eight weeks and had used printed stationery from a local print shop with the same business address to add weight and legitimacy to the ad. He had been concerned that perhaps the newspaper would try to check the firm placing the advertisement, but he need not have worried; his cheque was taken as a matter of routine.

The advertisement had been drafted to appeal to her person- ally. He knew that she received that local paper and he had seen her pause over the classified ads. She had some social pretensions and the copy was written to pander to these. She obviously thought she was attractive and probably felt she could have been a model when younger, and he suspected she had reached that time of life when opportunities to prove her attractiveness would be particularly seductive. Of course, he had also heard her join in the criticism of professional models.

Finally, the advertisement would allow a team response – suggesting that this was something the girls could all do together. There was always the risk that she would not reply, in fact he viewed this first attempt as something of an experiment to test her reactions to some obvious bait. When he'd developed the plan, he had deliberately not placed great hope on it; if it failed he would lose a little money, but he had plenty of that, and he would waste some time. So what? Time was on his side; he had waited nearly twenty years already.

He had been slightly surprised when the woman had replied to the first advertisement, but relieved that the group of them had written in together. What had followed had been a simple process of elimination, done convincingly with style and reassurance at each stage, just as the marked sheep is extracted from the flock and isolated with minimal alarm.

Thinking back over the detail of the elimination process he allowed himself some pride in the simple ways he had built in double-checks to encourage her to continue to the next stage. The hotel was typical of the type in London that did as much business by day as by night; large enough for his single booking to be unremarkable and smart enough to appeal to his target.

Finding an attractive interviewer had been easy. He had called a staff agency with explicit requirements as to the physical impact, keyboard skills and style of the person he wished to hire for three weeks. He had then arranged to interview the candidates at the agency's offices, selecting the one who was looking for money from one last assignment before she set off on a round-the-world trip. He briefed her, gave her the laptop, details of applicants and a small supply of brochures, printed by a different high street firm from the one that had produced his stationery. He paid in advance, and had given his accommodation address to which to send a daily print-out of interview notes and any commentary on the candidates. The temp had been delighted with an interesting job in a smart hotel for generous pay. He promised her a success bonus if they found good-quality candidates quickly. She had asked no questions and seemed incurious about this latest job in a long and varied stream of engagements.

He handled all the correspondence himself, picking up replies from the North London address and typing the appointment letters. He had worried that the temp he used might notify the police of her involvement if she recognised the name when it eventually appeared in the press. With this candidate, though, the risk was minimal. She should be long gone before the police ever became involved.

He sent her more than a dozen interviewees and then telephoned shortly after contact with the target and her friends to say that the search was over and her success fee was on its way. He asked her to return all the materials and the laptop to the agency where it was collected by one of the less reputable mini-cab firms. A week later, he left the PC, erased of all data, in a builder's skip at a site near Aldgate.

The laptop hadn't been strictly necessary but he had found in the past that putting information in a computer conveyed authority and respectability. It was unlikely the police would ever be able to trace the purchase of the laptop – supposing that they ever made the connection with it in the first place. He had bought it from a PC warehouse on a busy Saturday, for cash; it was one of their most popular models.

Thinking of detail his lips compressed into a rare smile as he considered the two beautiful, high-class escorts he had arranged to turn up at the hotel to coincide with his target's interview. He had insisted over the telephone when finalising the arrangements that they make a great show of asking for the suite – emphasising that there would be a number of people he wanted to impress in the lobby. The escorts, professional women, had agreed – used to humouring their customers' whims – and had arrived promptly. Unfortunately, the interviews had run over time despite his precise instructions, and from his observation post in the lounge by the reception desk, he had watched with frustration as the two escort girls went through their extended enquiries, only to finish as the other women left the lifts. He couldn't be sure that they had caught the show, in fact he was almost sure that they must have missed it, which caused him some annoyance. He had been relying on beautiful competition to make the women feel envious and nervous about their ability to be selected. He knew that one of the most effective ways to overcome any lingering reservations would be to make them really want the job, to make it an aspiration they would be reluctant to abandon.

Despite this small setback, he felt that step two had gone well. Step three, the photographic session, which he had anticipated would be the most difficult part of his plan, had been the easiest to arrange. He had found an addled junkie with the remnants of a good speaking voice to make the appointment phone calls. The addict had been so surprised at the money that she had asked no questions and performed her part with a pathetic desire to please. Then the studio. He had not realised just how many studios there were in London. He had hired one not too far from the centre of town with a good address, through the simple expedient of looking up telephone numbers in Yellow Pages and confirming with the lucky photographer that it would be a legitimate deal. He had sent the money and brief round by courier, explaining at the last minute that he found himself abroad and would be unable to supervise the shoot himself. The studio performed perfectly, he knew, having listened to the whole thing with the assistance of routine surveillance equipment – a transmitter concealed in a double socket.

The final stage required delicate manoeuvring. Like a collie circling and separating the marked sheep he finally needed her alone. He wanted her away from the other woman whose only purpose had been to make the whole enterprise feel safe. He had to make her confident enough to come along finally on her own, without giving her the opportunity to get cold feet. By allowing her to believe right up to the last minute that this experience was still going to be a shared one, he felt he could lull her into a sense of security.

He was aware that the whole plot could fall apart at this stage – the phoney call from the headmaster might have been ineffectual; she might have decided to wait for her friend. He would know soon enough. He waited calmly, immune to any concerns about future disappointments, schooled to keep his eagerness to the minimum. Now totally controlled in his emotions and betraying no anxiety, he gently moved the hired car to a halt alongside the kerb by a side entrance to Victoria Station.

CHAPTER THREE

The train drew into Victoria Station virtually on time. Deborah roused herself from a happy daydream in which she had taken Derek on a romantic holiday for two, thanks to the proceeds of her modelling assignment. She handed the outward part of her ticket to the collector at the gate, giving him a radiant smile that made his day and could later have given him the role of vital police witness if only there had been a police investigation. Walking purposefully, she left by a side exit as instructed, to make her way to the promised chauffeured car. By now, Deborah could feel the butterflies in her stomach again and she had to take several deep breaths to calm herself.

As she stepped out into the heat of the unseasonably warm April day, the dust and noise of the busy London street did little to aid her composure. She squinted against the bright sunlight, fighting a growing sense of disorientation, and looked around almost desperately for the driver they had said would be there to meet her. It had sounded so simple on the phone, but here, in the press of people and traffic, she realised that she could conceivably miss the car altogether.

Increasingly panicked she started violently as a dark, garlic-breathing man came up to her and touched her elbow lightly.

'Are you lost, madam? You look a little dazed.' He spoke with a heavy accent.

'No, no, I'm all right, thank you. Just a little bit dazzled by all this sunshine. Thank you, really I'm OK.'

'But, forgive me for saying so, delightful madam, you do not *seem* OK – and I should never forgive myself if I left you looking lost like this.'

His attentions were vaguely threatening and Deborah was desperate to shake him off.

'No, really I am all right. I'm meeting someone here. They'll be along in a minute,' Deborah answered abruptly, belatedly softening her tone with a half-smile that did not reach her eyes.

'But it is wrong to leave you here unescorted, lady. And I have a nice restaurant just over the road there, where you could sit comfortably and watch for the person you await.'

The man was now insistent and his touch on her elbow changed to a firm grip. He started to move her to the kerb as if to cross the road.

'It's all right, the lady's with me,' said a voice from above and behind the man.

Deborah and her unwelcome guardian turned together. They could make out little of the man's features for his back was towards the sun, casting his face into half-shadow. He was tall, well muscled without being brawny. Something about his bearing immediately made Deborah think of the police, but she dismissed this almost at once and put the impression down to the effect created by his peaked chauffeur's cap.

'Mrs Fearnside? I'm your chauffeur from Happy Families, the catalogue people.'

'Yes, yes, that's me.' Deborah responded quickly, keen now to have the pestering restaurateur removed, and then in a manner she felt more becoming, 'How kind of you to escort me.'

'Not at all, madam, it's my job. But we must go at once. I'm on a yellow line and I don't want us clamped.'

The restaurateur had not relinquished ownership of her elbow and seemed reluctant to let her go but then something in the driver's eyes and his manner made him back down quickly. He sketched a faint bow to Deborah before leaving to cross the road.

'*Au revoir, madame.* I hope our paths may cross again.'

Deborah ignored his retreating back. 'Thanks again. He was becoming a nuisance.'

The driver said nothing but smiled at her, and in one fluid movement, took her small overnight bag in which she had brought her make-up things. He gently placed his palm under her elbow and almost lifted her across the road to the waiting car, avoiding the busy traffic. Unlocking the doors he placed her bag and jacket on the rear seat and opened the front passenger door for her. Deborah hesitated slightly.

'Unless you'd prefer to ride in the back, madam? I just thought you'd be more comfortable in the front; people usually are.' For the first time he looked her full in the face and smiled. With a small flutter Deborah realised that he was extremely attractive: older than she had first thought – but very good-looking and with a younger man's physique.

'Thanks. I'll ride in the front with you. I prefer the front too.'

She slipped into the warm, leather-scented interior as he made sure that her dress was well clear of the door. The car nosed into thick traffic and he switched on the air conditioning. Soon the air was down to a pleasant temperature that did not rely on the recirculation of the fume-filled atmosphere outside.

'As we have to go through one or two rough spots, Mrs Fearnside, do you mind if I lock the doors?'

'No, that's all right. I always drive with my doors locked these days; there are so many horror stories, I honestly don't feel safe any more if I'm driving on my own.'

He smiled reassuringly and all four doors locked automatically with a satisfying, synchronised clunk as the car purred its way slowly through the tightly packed cars around Buckingham Palace. Most of his concentration was on driving smoothly through the late rush-hour traffic. At all costs, he wanted to avoid any sort of accident that might draw attention to them. Some of his awareness, however, was still focused on the woman beside him. The next half-hour was the most dangerous and difficult part of his plan. If she became suspicious or upset in any way now, he had few non-violent options for dealing with her. He did not believe that she knew London well, so he thought he had at least another ten minutes before the signposts started to hint that they were heading away from the direction she had taken previously to reach the 'studios'.

In the meantime, he needed to build up her confidence in him. His intuition told him that gentle flirtation would be the easiest way to create a relaxed and intimate atmosphere between them.

'Are you quite comfortable, Mrs Fearnside? Is the temperature all right for you?' He treated her to a sidelong glance from amber eyes which, he calculated, should convey a hint of attraction and definite approval of what he saw, though in truth, he had no sexual interest in her whatsoever. In a purely academic way he was aware that she could be described as very attractive – a factor which would be a hindrance from now on as there was an increased risk she would be remembered by potential witnesses.

However, he had learnt to respond to his targets when necessary in the way they expected him to. This even extended to subtle modulations in voice, accent, and mannerisms. They'd had a behavioural psychologist in once who had explained that most people gained comfort from the subtle repetition of their normal behaviour by others in their company. Apparently he had a natural skill. Deep down, he felt nothing for her – no compassion, no pity – only a calculated interest in her likely reactions and a finely tuned sensitivity to her mood. There was no way that she would have been able to sense this, so polished was his performance.

'I'm fine, thank you.' Deborah thought she caught a hint of interest in the glance he gave her from deep tawny eyes – like a tiger, she felt. There was something slightly predatory in his manner, in the way that he looked at her, but his obvious interest in her transformed this into an exciting hint of danger. A warm feeling grew in the pit of her stomach. She felt no trace of alarm. 'And it's Deborah, please, not Mrs Fearnside.'

'Right. Deborah it is. That's a nice name. My sister had a friend called Deborah when she was at school; I always secretly fancied her. Do you know what the name means?'

She shook her head.

'It comes from the Bible, somebody's nurse, I think. Anyway, it's the Hebrew word for bee – which can mean one of two things, diligence or sweetness. I learnt all this to impress that earlier Deborah but it didn't do me much good!' He laughed, the comfortable, relaxed sound of a man who could poke fun at himself without being worried. 'For what it's worth, I think the name suits you.' He treated her to another of his sideways smiles.

To her consternation, Deborah found that she was blushing and hoped he had not seen. She was finding him increasingly attractive. For the first time she noticed that his voice was quite cultured, softly middle class, and she wondered why he had a job as a chauffeur.

Most of his attention was now focused on the traffic, which was typically heavy at that time in the morning. She looked at his hands on the wheel, long-fingered and strong in light-weight driving gloves. Her eyes travelled down until they reached his legs, sleek and athletic in dark navy trousers. Deborah realised with a start that she was staring and that her idle interest in him could be taken as serious unless she was careful. Naturally romantic and deeply frustrated, she recognised the danger signs in her behaviour. She waited impatiently for him to speak again.

After a few minutes of silence she ventured a comment of her own.

'You mentioned a sister, do you keep in touch with her?'

'Not as much as I'd like. She works abroad, in Brussels, so I see her only rarely. How about you – do you have brothers or sisters?'

'I'm an only child. My father died a few years ago. My mother lives close by so I see her quite regularly – duty visits really as we don't get on particularly well. My family life really revolves around my own family. I have two children, a girl and a boy.'

Deborah could hear herself wittering on and stopped abruptly. She was not sure why she had revealed so much of herself to a perfect stranger and she felt exposed. He was the sort of person, though, who seemed to invite confidences,

28

someone who appeared genuinely interested in her, despite the need to steer them through a mêlée of aggressive black cabs and suicidal courier bikes. Inevitably, she thought of Derek, who rarely displayed any interest in her conversation at the best of times and certainly not when he was driving.

He was aware of her growing interest in him and delighted in the additional power it gave him. She was perceptibly more relaxed and had inclined her legs towards him in an unconscious gesture of acceptance. More importantly, she was paying scant attention to the streets through which they were passing.

'I have to stop for a moment and pick up some clothing samples to take to the office. I hope you don't mind but I didn't want to risk collecting them earlier and making myself late for you. It's on our way and'll only take a moment.'

'That's fine. You seem to be making good time despite the traffic and we don't need to be there until ten o'clock, do we?' Deborah returned his grateful smile and settled back more comfortably in the leather seat.

He pulled slowly into a side road off Kensington High Street and then turned carefully into a small mews that ran down from it at right angles. He had picked the spot a few weeks earlier and visited it a couple of times since to confirm the choice. Most of the residents would, by this time, have left for work and it was too early for the few that remained to be setting out for the shops. He drew up in front of a double garage on the shady side of the street where two ornamental bay trees in tubs provided screening on the passenger side of the car.

He opened the driver's door, which automatically released the other locks and the boot. Leaving his own door open, he walked around to the boot and unzipped the small black holdall he had left there, taking from it a prepared hypodermic. In the shadow of the boot lid, screened from both the street and the occupant of the car, he carefully checked the measured dose in the syringe, then concealed it along the length of his open left hand.

Speaking just loudly enough for his voice to reach her inside the car, he called out: 'Mrs Fearnside, I'm sorry to trouble you further but could you just give me a hand with this, please?'

Deborah roused herself from an idle daydream and undid her seat belt. She moved to open her door but realised with a smile that he was there already, the perfect chauffeur, ready with a hand to assist her from the car. He was standing with his back to the rear passenger door, his right hand outstretched ready to help her from the car. Still in her seat, she lifted her own left hand to him, experiencing a small thrill as their flesh touched. He gently turned her hand, as if to kiss it. She looked up expectantly into his eyes and was startled by the intensity of his gaze.

Deborah felt a sudden shudder of fear as she realised she knew nothing about this strange, compelling man bending over her with such sense of purpose. She tried to remove her hand from his. In that instant, his grip tightened. His left hand came over and he smoothly inserted the needle into the soft vein on the back of her hand. She had time to murmur a soft 'No', before the fast-acting tranquilliser hit her nervous system and plunged her into semi-consciousness.

He had given her the maximum dose he could based on her height and weight, so obligingly provided in her application. The whole episode had lasted less than a minute. He gently redistributed her unconscious body, reclined the seat and refastened her seat belt. From the back seat, he took a small cushion and placed it behind her neck, supporting her head and preventing it from lolling to the side. His peaked cap and chauffeur's jacket went into the holdall in the boot of the car.

As he drove back out of the mews, they looked a perfect couple; she tired and solicitously cushioned for the journey, he smart in a white shirt and dark tie, perfectly in control of the steady, stately BMW. He had originally contemplated carrying her in the boot but had dismissed the idea. With the random road blocks in London and police stop and search powers, there was always the risk, however remote, that he could be pulled up by a routine patrol. A sleeping wife whilst he responded to questioning would not be unusual; an unconscious woman in the boot of the car would be hard to explain.

He calculated that he had six to eight hours before she started to come round, ample time to reach their destination. Driving quickly and confidently on the speed limit, he continued along Kensington High Street, out past Olympia and on to Hammersmith. He took the M4 west and within two hours was well past Reading. Deborah was still unconscious when he left the motorway and Severn Bridge behind and was making his way down a rutted track in the Black Hills beyond Monmouth. After a few more miles, a small holiday cottage came into view.

During the ride west, the sky had clouded over and darkened to a storm grey in front of them. The first heavy drops of what promised to be a sustained downpour fell on his bare head as he unlocked the cottage front door.

Returning to the car he replaced his leather driving gloves with thin, skin-tight latex ones and then put a similar pair on to Deborah's hands. He lifted his passenger out gently and carried her into a small downstairs bedroom at the back of the cottage, laid her on the bed, and returned to collect the remainder of his supplies before concealing the BMW in a nearby barn.

Within an hour, he had completed all the necessary arrangements with an economy of effort natural after years of training. The bed had been stripped and large, thick plastic sheets spread on top and underneath it. Deborah's inert body had been stripped naked except for a shower cap on her head and the rubber gloves on her hands. Her wrists and ankles were secured to the heavy iron bedframe with nylon ropes. The curtains were drawn and what little light there was came from a 40-watt bulb inside an incongruous frilly pink shade hanging from the centre of the low ceiling.

On a solid, crudely crafted chest of drawers, he had laid out commercial paper towels, a fresh pair of gloves, an apron, a gag in case it was needed and a large jug of cold water. There was no heat in the room and the rising storm wind whistled through cracks in the wooden window frame. On the bedside table, where her waking eyes would see them, he finally placed his instruments – scalpels, a filleting knife, a thin piece of cheese wire with wooden handles, pliers.

When all was ready he settled down to a strong mug of fresh coffee in the pretty country kitchen and prepared a light meal from his stock of provisions. About now, she should start to come round. She was completely secured, the door was locked and she could scream her head off without there being any danger of her being overheard. The cottage was isolated. True, he had seen on the Ordnance Survey map that even this remote tract of land had its footpath which might tempt a particularly ambitious walker, but on this increasingly stormy and grey evening, he doubted he would be troubled. He would be left alone to his work.

CHAPTER FOUR

Shortly after five o'clock, when the storm outside was gusting around the cottage shutters and howling down the chimney, he heard a different low-pitched moan, emanating from within the house. He waited patiently, knowing that shortly it would rise to a shriek to rival the most fearsome wailing of the storm. Part of him, deep inside, was aware that he would find the next few hours unpleasant. He suppressed the thought as soon as it started and schooled himself to his normal state of calm. She was only a woman but they could be more cunning and deadly opponents than men.

With care, he put on his disguise. He hadn't bothered with one before but after some deliberation, he had decided that she would be more co-operative if she felt that there was a chance of life. And she was clever enough to realise that any kidnapper who revealed himself to his victim would never let her go alive. The idea of a disguise also comforted him. He would find it hard enough to do what he needed to do, but to reveal who he really was, and to see her recognise, despise and hate him was more than he could stand. It was important that she did not see the chauffeur in him now.

The minimal disguise was prepared quickly; light body padding under a loose black shirt and two pairs of jogging trousers made him look at least fourteen pounds heavier. Coloured contact lenses – a dark brown was needed given his deep amber eyes – and a hint of shading in the sockets changed his expression completely, making him expressionless yet sinister. A heavy gold chain around his neck and a tight-fitting Balaclava completed the transformation. He still wore his gloves; they had not left his hands since he had entered the house. When he glanced at himself in the mirror over the kitchen range he was satisfied with the bullying figure that stared back at him.

He heard her first real shriek of terror as he pulled the Balaclava under his chin. It was quickly followed by short, panting cries which made him shudder. Without warning the sounds reminded him of a vixen he had once found caught in a trap on a friend's farm; the animal's agony and fear had produced pathetic, urgent yelps that had sent him running, so fast, to find help. He had thought in his childish innocence that his friend's father would know what to do to save the maimed animal. He could still remember running back with the man, pleased with himself for playing the rescuer and eager to see how he would save the fox. And he could still remember standing with a frozen 'No!' in his throat as he had watched him raise his gun and shoot her where she lay, helpless in the gin. He had seen many worse deaths since but none with the same power to shake him with its recollection.

It was an unlucky twist that the woman's screams should vividly recall those of the injured fox when he had been impervious to previous human cries. Hardening himself to her unexpected appeal he abruptly unlocked the door to the little room.

'Shaddap!' He deliberately coarsened his voice, eliminating the middle-class vowels she had found so comforting earlier. Deborah screamed even more at the sight of the menacing, dark stranger on the threshold.

'Shut the fuck up now, or I'll come over and sew your fucking lips together.'

The threat was real and her cries subsided into pathetic whimpers, terror robbing her of all coherent protest. She had been struggling against the cords that bound her to the bed. The knots had been designed to tighten with resistance and the ties had bitten into the soft flesh of her wrists, deeply scoring the

34

skin and drawing blood with every test of their strength.

He took a few short steps towards the bed and stared down at her. She tried to shrink into the mattress and draw away from him but there was nowhere to go. His proximity threw her into further paroxysms of terror as she flung her head away from him. In a final desperate attempt to shut him out she screwed her eyes up tight like a child pretending that the monster does not exist if it can't be seen.

His quiet, dead tone cut through her denials and compelled her to complete silence.

'Listen to me very carefully. Be quiet, be a good girl and no harm will come to you. I don't want to hurt such a pretty girl now, do I?' He ran a gloved finger lightly over her cheek, stroking her eyelids and brows gently as he passed. 'No. I'm sure that you can be a good girl, if you want to be. Because if not,' his hand moved like a viper to cup her jaw in a dreadful, constant pressure, 'if not, then I'll have to kill you, won't I – but not before I've had me some fun first.' He tightened his grip even further until he could feel her jawbone creak and tears of pain ran down her contorted face. Abruptly he let go.

'Now look at me.' He waited with his fingers loosely on her neck to see if she would obey but her eyelids remained tightly shut, her face angled away as far as he would allow. With no warning, he raised his hand and brought it down with a hard crack against her cheek. Her whole head jarred with the force of the blow and she moaned as a slow trickle of blood dribbled from the corner of her mouth. He clenched his hand tightly around her jaw again and jerked her face roughly towards his own. His voice was oily and cold.

'Debbie, dear, I said look at me. Open your eyes now! Do it!'

He squeezed tighter, feeling her teeth grate. 'Do it,' he whispered.

Deborah opened her eyes and looked up into his. He could read no resistance now, just abject terror. She was close to the very thin line dividing reason from escape into imbecility; he would have to coax her away from it or risk losing too much

35

time in order to learn what he needed to know.

'Debbie,' he crooned, 'dear Debbie. You don't need to be so frightened of me. I don't want to hurt you – in fact I would much rather not.'

He let the truth of those words enter his eyes and was rewarded with a look of bafflement. 'Listen to me very carefully. The reason you're here is because you know something that I need to know. It's a secret you're going to have to share with me if you want to get out of here alive.'

Again, he could see the confusion in her face and for the first time, a glimmer of spirit. He had deliberately given her hope as a line to pull her back from the edge of terror-induced madness.

'What . . . what is it you want from me?' Her voice was rusty and dry, cracking around the edges at her attempts to hold on to reason. '*Tell me*! I want to know. I don't know anything important; you've got the wrong person. Please let me go. It's not me, it must be someone else, you—' Her voice was cut off as he clamped his hand once again tightly around her jaw.

'Just be patient, luv. It'll come to you soon enough. And I know it's you, see, because I've done my homework and I'm *very* sure that you're the one I want.'

'But I told you, I don't know anything. I'm just an ordinary woman. Please, let me go. I can't tell you something I don't know.' Her voice was growing stronger as she became more certain that she was the victim of a frightening case of mistaken identity, and with that conviction came a defiant sense of outrage. 'You just can't hold me here!' She saw the darkness beyond the curtain. 'My children. They'll be home from school. They'll be worried! You must let me go. I'm not the one you want!'

The man simply ignored her protests, released the last of his grip and turned to leave.

'Listen to me,' she shrieked. '*Listen to me, why don't you?* Damn you, come back.' The last words were shouted in angry desperation. With a catlike swiftness, he was back on the bed, kneeling over her and hitting her hard with the flat of his hand, again and again on both cheeks, with enough force to knock her head from side to side with each blow.

'Shaddup! I've told you, you're the one I need. Any more noise and I really will sew your lips together. I've warned you once. You'll be able to write the answers I need as ready as speak them.'

She stared up at him dully, beaten into obedience once more. In an instant he was gone, slipping softly off the bed and leaving the room in darkness.

Deborah lay shivering with cold and fear, tears of pain rolling down bruised and swollen cheeks. She was utterly frightened and close to complete panic but deep inside her a small voice reasoned that her only chance of survival was to keep thinking clearly. For long moments she just stared blankly into the grey, silent room. Then slowly, as the minutes passed, she forced herself to think about what was happening to her.

Her memory of the day was vague and confused. She could recall the train journey and the charming chauffeur who had collected her. Her last memory of the drive was of the car moving slowly in heavy traffic and her heart leapt within her chest as she wondered whether he had been killed during her kidnap. Then, more chillingly, was he in on it, the two of them together? She could not bring herself to believe he was dead, but it was equally impossible that he would associate with her tormentor. Deborah's mind shut down again. It would not let her think about *him* yet, nor what he might do to her. The first objects she had set eyes on as she regained consciousness had been knives and scalpels and the precise shape of them was burnt into her memory. She could imagine him picking them up, holding them delicately and flaying small pieces of skin from her. Or would he stab and gouge? She had such knives in her kitchen – razor sharp, capable of dicing steak, filleting fish, slicing hard raw vegetables into tiny thin strips. She knew what knives could do.

There was a strange whining noise in the room and she strained to work out what it was. Then she realised it was her own moaning and, with a desperate sob, she gave in to hard exhausting tears that tore through her throat leaving it even more bruised and sore. Eventually the fit subsided. There were no more tears, no more energy. Always, though, pictures of the scalpel and the knife remained in her mind.

To divert her thoughts Deborah tried to work out what the secret was that he wanted from her so badly. There had been that brief affair between the births of her first and second children. Derek had known nothing about it; it had been over virtually as soon as it had begun, a classic tennis club dalliance that culminated in a momentarily exciting, and subsequently embarrassing, sticky mess. But that was nothing. Nobody could seriously be interested in that.

Her mind drifted back further, to her job that had been relinquished willingly as soon as she had become pregnant. Try as she might she could think of nothing in those four years as a dental nurse that was in the least clandestine or tragic; nobody had died under anaesthetic, no bodies had been named because of their dental records.

She pushed her thoughts back further until they passed university and reached school. At the first touch of memory she froze. No. It could not be that. It was too long ago, so long ago she had almost forgotten it and half persuaded herself that it had nothing to do with her. It had taken a long time to forget. For years she had suffered nightmares, lived in dread of going to sleep. Then with time, and with Derek, the dreams had grown infrequent, stirred only now and again when the children wanted to go on school trips.

Her mind picked around the edges of that most sensitive memory, gradually working towards the heart of it. She went back over that day, forced herself to relive all of its terrible detail, ending with the frightening climb back, then waiting at home for news of the body. Fresh tears rolled down her chin and dripped on to the plastic sheet. Never again, until today, had she been so frightened, so helpless, and so desperate to rewrite history.

It had started out as such a beautiful day – 15 June. They had finished their exams and the Upper Fifth geography class was

38

going on a celebratory school trip. They had set out for the Dorset coast early in the morning with no cares, relaxed and happy. The party was made up of thirteen girls plus the geography master and the gym mistress in the school's minibus. Much of the early talk had been about how terribly everyone had done in this or that exam, with everyone agreeing that the Physics papers had been compiled by an evil genius from hell.

The five of them had sat on the bench seat at the back – well, four really, but Leslie always tagged along however lukewarm the welcome. Small for her age, with glasses and permanent braces, she was not the person to be seen with and had no close friends in the class. The other four, in the same netball team, the same choir, the same form, were inseparable friends – confident, boisterous Kate; stunning Octavia who was sure she would become a professional musician: quiet, athletic Carol, who sang like an angel and was fast rivalling Octavia for the lead soprano parts; and Deborah, the prettiest and least venturesome – not as clever but whose looks and surprisingly sharp sense of humour earned her a place in the select group.

They had arrived at Durdle Door at eleven o'clock, in time for the first walk along the cliffs before a picnic lunch. The weather was glorious and they were soon stripped down to T-shirts and jeans. The sun burnt into spring-white skin and they relished the feel of its power reaching beneath the surface and starting the tanning that would occupy most of the long, idle weeks of the summer vacation.

After lunch they set out on their second walk. As always, it had been Kate who had taken the lead, deciding which footpath to follow and striding out at a pace that soon left the shorter-legged Deborah far behind. At the top of one cliff, they flopped on to springy, cropped, coarse grass, flat on their backs, hypnotised by the gulls that wheeled above them against the cloudless sky. A light breeze whipped wisps of hair about their faces, tickling eyes and noses. For once, no one talked as they absorbed the atmosphere.

Into the pure silence, Carol's voice floated on the first notes of the Barcarole from the *Tales of Hoffman*. Instinctively Octavia picked up the harmony, as her hand reached out to hold Carol's, and perfect crystal drops of sound rose up into the limitless sky like larks' song. When they finished, the silence returned. All of them realised they had shared a moment that would become a life-long memory. It did not need to be remarked upon.

A gull's raucous cry shattered the silence and they laughed, embarrassed as people are when emotions are shared unexpectedly. Deborah, always the first to venture words into silence, turned on her side to face Carol.

'You know, with a voice like that you should be thinking of taking up music as a career too.'

'D'you think so? As a matter of fact, I've been wondering about that and I think I've finally decided that I'm going to.'

They all looked at her, surprised. Until that moment, Carol had seemed hellbent on becoming a doctor.

'What?' It was Octavia who seemed most amazed, though she and Carol were the closest of the four, always together, so close, Deborah thought, that were Carol more physically mature, she would have questioned the nature of their relationship. 'You've never mentioned it before. Where did that idea come from, for heaven's sake?'

'I don't know. It's been growing on me this term. And, well, it just seems right. I've suddenly realised that music is probably the most important thing in my life and I have to do something about it.'

Carol looked embarrassed. She was naturally modest and found it hard to discuss her musical ambitions when she already excelled at sports and was expected to get straight top grades in her exams. Seeing that her closest friend still stared at her mutely, she tried to explain further.

'I think what finally did it was singing Verdi's *Requiem* with the County Youth Choir before Easter. Suddenly, during the 'Offertorio' when the soprano comes in above the other voices, so sweetly, so quietly, I knew *that's what I've got to do*. I looked above me to the roof of the cathedral and I just *knew* I had to go on singing and performing as far as my voice would let me.'

The four of them had been in the Youth Choir that year. The

performance had received excellent reviews. Deborah started to understand why Carol had changed her mind so dramatically and firmly. Not only did she have a beautiful voice, but when she sang she sang from her soul. More than once, Deborah had been moved to tears as she listened. It was a glorious gift, which they'd all somehow just accepted; Carol was such a special person. Octavia, though, was still struggling to understand.

'But what about being a doctor? You always said you wanted to help people – and earn decent money to look after your family. And singing, well—'

'Look,' interrupted Kate, 'there's someone waving to us from over there. I think it's Sticky.' She glanced at her watch. 'Good grief, look at the time. It's nearly 3.15 and we were due back at three o'clock at the latest. They'll have been worried sick. Come on!'

All five leapt up and started back at a run – all except Octavia who walked at her own pace, increasingly falling behind. When Carol glanced back over her shoulder, she broke her stride and turned to rejoin her friend. Together, they started a slow jog along the cliff top.

Deborah, the least fit and slowest, found herself panting with a stitch between Leslie and Kate, way ahead, and Octavia and Carol behind, but close enough for her to hear some of their conversation.

'You're crazy, you know. Music is an awful career. I should know, look what it's done to my mum and dad.' Octavia's protesting voice carried all the concern of a worried parent. 'You don't know what you'll be getting into. It's a cut-throat world – you're just not tough enough.'

'I can toughen up.'

'Oh, come on, you're little Miss Softie. Even in games you only win because of skill and speed, you've no aggression. And anyway, what do your parents think? And your aunt and uncle – what about them?'

'They're all dead against it, of course. Can't understand me, think I'm crazy. Auntie even blamed you at first but I told her

41

you didn't even know. No, they're still convinced I should take up medicine. Apparently they'd even started saving against the time I would go to university but they've made it clear they won't be wasting money on music!'

'What, you mean they won't support you? How on earth are you going to be able to study then?'

'I'll think of something. I already have one idea. Please try to understand, Octavia, this means a lot to me.' Carol stopped and grasped her friend's hands. 'We both have the same problems – parents who have no money and ambitions that are beyond us. But it hasn't stopped you being determined so I don't see why I should give up without at least a damned good try.'

'You're mad. I've been planning this and working towards it for years. I know you've got talent but you're basically untrained. Have you spoken to Miss Sharpe yet? She'll be bitterly disappointed – she had you marked out as her star of the form.'

Carol's reply was lost in Deborah's panting breath as she plodded her way to the top of the final rise and, with a yelp, ran pell-mell down the long slope to the waiting minibus.

The gentle reminiscences lulled Deborah into a fitful doze despite her acute discomfort. Wherever her skin rubbed against the stinking plastic sheet it was starting to get sore and her lips and throat were parchment dry. The muscles in her upper arms, stretched by the angle at which her wrists had been pulled and tied to the bed were locked in a spasm of pain which no twisting or arching of her neck could relieve. The smell in the room was disgusting. Outside the noise of the gale reached a crescendo. Gusts of air found their way through minute crannies in the window frame, billowing the flimsy curtain into spectral shapes that danced in the dim light from under the door. Howls of wind drowned the fitful animal whimpers of her sleep, providing a fitting accompaniment to her torture.

At about three in the morning – in the dead zone of night when spirits fail and hopes die – the storm wrenched a slate tile from its pins and sent it crashing into the stone yard, waking Deborah. Startled, disorientated, chilled to the bone and conscious only of a desperate thirst, she lay with staring eyes, trying to remember where she was. The room was in pitch darkness. For long moments she remained confused, convinced that her nightmare was continuing. There was now no feeling in her restricted arms and legs, only a slow-burning pain running in rivers from fingers to toes. Then a manic gust sent the curtain flying from its rail, letting in the faintest of storm light to create grey shadows in the room's darkness.

She caught a glimpse of the white binding on her ankle, which secured her leg to the bed. The sight brought immediate and total recall. A pathetic scream rose from her parched throat and was forced out through cracked lips. Once it had started she was powerless to stop it. It went on and on, forming itself into cries for help.

'Oh God, help me. Please. Oh Mummy, Oh God, help me, please help me. Help me. What have I done to deserve this? Dear God, have mercy on me, please have mercy on me. Don't let me die. Please God, don't let me die. Mummee . . .'

He sat comfortably outside the door, relaxed yet alert despite having had no sleep for twenty-four hours. The sounds of her waking distress crept through the keyhole and door frame to his waiting ears. Now he knew he had her. In a few hours he could begin his work.

CHAPTER FIVE

In Harlden, at number 24 Meadow Gardens, life continued with little amiss until 6.30 and Derek Fearnside's return home. He was mildly perplexed to find the house quiet and dark in the fine spring evening but reassured to see three messages on the answerphone.

Beeep . . . the high-pitched whine always annoyed him. 'Hello, Debbie, this is Mavis. It's 5.30. You could at least have called to let me know you were going to be late!' The tone was amused to take the sting out of the words. 'The children are starting to ask what's going on. If you do pop in at home first, please ring to tell me when you'll be here. Thanks.'

The bemused tone of Deborah's friend filled the hall as Derek browsed through the day's post and the tape played on. He only half listened as it continued, waiting impatiently for the message from his wife he was sure would be next on the machine.

Beeep . . .

'Hello, Debbie, this is Leslie. Just thought I'd let you know the trip to the headmaster was a *fiasco* – you wouldn't believe it. I won't spoil the story. Give me a call when you get in. By the way, you did say you'd try to get them to pick me up later. I guessed because I didn't hear from you, that wasn't possible. Call soon. 'Bye.'

Derek stopped reading the latest bank statement and really listened for the first time. Wasn't Debbie meant to be with Leslie? What did that last message mean?

Beeep . . .

'Hello, Debbie, it's me again, Mavis. It's gone six o'clock and the children are getting restless. I hope everything's OK. Give me a call, love, as soon as you can. 'Bye.'

Derek pressed the replay button as soon as the last message finished and listened intently to all three messages. It was nearly quarter to seven. His wife had been due back more than two hours ago and it was clear her friend was getting worried. Where was she? He had encountered no problems with the trains and the second message was from Leslie; he had been sure they were meant to be together today.

A cold sickness churned his stomach as the first flutterings of fear touched him. His rational mind was busy telling him not to worry, there would be a perfectly logical explanation for this . . . it was just that he could not think of one for the moment. He noticed that his hands trembled as he reached for the address book and he cursed himself for being stupid, suddenly, superstitiously concerned that his nervousness would add substance to his fears.

'Don't be so bloody stupid,' he told himself out loud. 'She'll turn up any minute with some feeble excuse about late-night shopping,' (but it was Monday his brain insisted), 'or drinks with the photographer. Stupid woman.'

But even as he told himself this it felt false. Whatever her faults, Deborah would never forget the children. She would at least make contact with them to explain her delay. The overloud ring of the telephone echoing in the empty hall made him jump and drop the address book. He snatched up the receiver and was rewarded by the sound of a woman's voice.

'Debbie, is that you?' he bellowed, a contradictory mixture of anger and relief tightening his voice and making him breathless. 'Where the hell are y—'

'Hello, Derek, no, this is Mavis Dean. I was hoping Debbie was home. I take it she isn't there.'

For many seconds Derek stood dumbly staring at the handset. A nausea of disappointment crushed his voice and fear leapt back unrestrained in the pit of his stomach.

'Derek, are you all right?'

'Yes, Mavis, I'm fine. I – I thought you were Debbie, that's all. I was – I was about to call you; sh-she's not home yet, you see and I thought she might be with you.'

'No, she's not. I haven't heard from her all day and I'm starting to get concerned.'

'I'm a bit worried too. You see, there's no message from her on the machine.'

The woman's words of reassurance filled his ear, echoing his own previous attempts at rational explanation. Disgusted with his own weakness and lack of control, he strove desperately to sound calm as he replied: 'Mavis, I can't think where she is. There were no delays on the trains. Have you any ideas?'

'Have you tried Leslie Smith? They were going up together, you know. She could be there. Do you need their number? I've got it right to hand, it's 232496, got that?'

'Yes thanks, I've got it. Look, I don't like to ask but could you—'

'Look after the children? Yes of course. You just get on and sort this all out. I'm sure there's a perfectly sensible explanation and that she's fine. Give me a call later.'

Derek replaced the receiver absently. He was furious with Deborah for making him so worried. For long moments he stared dully at the hall wallpaper, light beige and cream Georgian stripes. He could still remember the awful row they had had whilst choosing it. He had insisted they buy something ready-pasted and forget the design; Deborah was adamant that this was *the* design for the hall, even though it would be difficult to hang. The trivial domestic squabble in the car park outside the DIY store (having bought nothing) deteriorated into an indictment of their marriage; Deborah criticised his pragmatism, lack of imagination and stifling contempt for anything stylish that, she claimed, had robbed their whole marriage of excitement. He had retaliated in kind, bringing up the effect of her latest extravagances on their delicate bank balance and her basic lack of common sense – a gloves-off fight with no winners but plenty of emotional lacerations and deep bruises.

In the end he had stormed back into the store. She had driven the children home where, two hours later he turned up with the contested wallpaper. It turned out that he had bought too much and the dye numbers did not match, making hanging it a nightmare. Neither of them had referred to the incident again but they both secretly hated the resulting décor. Now, as he focused blankly on the maligned and unappreciated stripes, he wished the whole incident away. What did it matter if it had taken longer to hang the bloody stuff? Once, he believed he would have done anything for her; now he realised with sudden self-loathing that for years she could justifiably have felt he had done as little as possible to disturb his routine.

He dialled Leslie's number, offering up a silent prayer as he did so: please, just let Debbie come home.

Leslie couldn't help him. Their plans had gone awry, she explained. She told him of the problems that morning, adding that the irony of it all was that the headmaster had not even wanted to see her and had disowned the phone call. In the quiet that followed her indignant explanation they both realised the possible implications of the hoax. It was a nightmare thought but once even the remotest suggestion of conspiracy had been admitted, it would not go away.

'I'm not sure what I should do. D'you think I should call the police?'

'I don't know, I really don't. It's only 7.30 – ever so early to trouble them – and what would you say?'

'I've no idea, but I've got to do something! I can't just sit here and I don't know what else to do, short of going up to London. Do you have the address of the studio, by the way?'

'Only the one we went to for the first photos and we were told we would be going somewhere different today. Look, before you go off after her, are you sure she actually got the train? Is her car at the station still?'

'I didn't notice.'

'We're only a short walk away from the car park. I'll get Brian to look if you like and call you back.'

It was some action at least. While Leslie's husband made the

47

brief journey Derek searched in vain for any information on the modelling studio or catalogue. Deborah had apparently taken the folder she had been using with her and there were no stray papers anywhere. He searched his memory for any clue as to where she might have gone. There was none. He had been deliberately indifferent to her adventure and anyway, he told himself, there had not been much detail to discuss.

Upstairs in the bedroom he noticed that her make-up and her favourite perfume were not there. This made him curious to find out what else was missing. It was impossible to know whether any clothes had gone; certainly nothing obvious was missing. Her toothbrush was not there, neither were her hairbrush and hairspray. All this was consistent with a modelling assignment so he was not unduly surprised.

Then he noticed that the photograph from beside the bed was missing. It had been a family group in an antique solid silver frame, a bequest from Deborah's maiden aunt. Without doubt it was her favourite possession. And it had gone. For the first time he wondered whether she had left him but he immediately rejected the idea.

He went back downstairs. Her passport was still in the bureau but her chequebook had disappeared. She had saved up quite a bit over the years and its absence worried him; it would mean that she had money to rely on. He went completely cold for a moment and had to sit down on the sofa. It just didn't make sense. He couldn't see her leaving after all the years they'd had together; she had always been so dependent on him. And then there were the children. She might just contemplate leaving him if she was really angry but she would never abandon them.

The phone call from Brian resolved nothing.

'Her car's still there, old man, securely locked up, but no sign of her, I'm afraid.'

'I've got to call the police then, haven't I, Brian? The longer I leave it the worse it could be.'

'Well, if it will make things easier for you, why don't you? They've got masses of experience of this sort of thing. I expect they'll tell you that in ninety-nine per cent of cases the woman turns up straight away and that those that go off come back a few days later looking sheepish. Think of Agatha Christie – she did it, didn't she? And there are all those cases of missing people on the television; they turn up more often than not, don't they?' Brian was trying to be reassuring but they both knew his words rang hollow. He made a final attempt to introduce his own brand of hope to his friend. 'Look, you know what women can be like at this age. Turning thirty does something to them – they can go crazy. That could explain a lot.'

Brian's bluff remarks were of little comfort to Derek, who was now floating isolated in a sea of apprehension. The cold knot of fear was locked in place near his heart, reminding him of the dark side every time he breathed and swallowed. Brian had been right about the police, though. A woman missing for at most three hours didn't rank high in their priorities. Under-resourced, distracted by other problems, they found Derek Fearnside's concerns somewhat premature.

Derek knew he had become angry, even abusive, in his conversation with the desk officer at the local station, driven on by a sense of impotence and frustration. He had eventually been chastened by the patient, weary tone of the duty sergeant, who sounded as if he had to deal with over-anxious, irate husbands, wives and parents every day.

'If she's not back by midnight, Mr Fearnside, give us another call. In the meantime, I suggest you relax and make yourself a nice cup of tea. This happens nearly every day, sir, believe me. In virtually all the cases I've known the missing person turns up alive and well.'

The words, coming as they did from someone in authority, offered a modicum of comfort to Derek as the evening dragged on. He rang Mavis and asked her to look after the children. He said good night to them briefly over the phone but bungled the answers to their innocent questions so badly that they started to cry in confusion and he had to ring off before he did the same. He paced the house, a bear out of place in his pen. He tried driving to the railway station and even contemplated getting the address from Leslie and going up to London to the photographic studio, but thoughts of the empty house and the potential of a ringing phone drove him home. In every room there were a few odd jobs he could have started, but each time he sat down to mend this pan lid or put a new fuse in that plug, his attention drifted back to the last time he could recall it being used or touched by his wife. Eventually, he gave up and sat in front of the television, distracted but in no way diverted by its noise.

At midnight, he telephoned the police again and the duty sergeant promised someone would call him back. The phone eventually rang in the early hours of the morning. Derek picked it up, bleary-eyed, still in his crumpled suit, his jaw grey with stubble. A Detective Sergeant Blite announced himself.

'At last. You took your bloody time! It's nearly eight hours since I first rang your station.'

'I appreciate your concern, Mr Fernshaw—'

'Fearnside!'

'Mr Fearnside, but as I think the sergeant explained, this is still, technically, very early in a missing persons case involving an adult. But I'm here now and perhaps you could give me the background to your wife's disappearance.'

'It's just not like her to be late like this. She went up to London today and had to make careful arrangements for her return because of the children.'

'Right. Could you tell me more about this trip, sir, starting right at the beginning?'

'The beginning? Well, I suppose it all started when Deborah and a few of her friends applied for this part-time modelling job that was advertised in the local paper.'

'What job was this, sir?'

'You must have seen it. The advert's been running for the past few weeks. Debbie cut it out and put it in her file.'

'Do you have a copy to hand?'

'No, she's taken the whole file with her. I looked earlier in case she'd left something behind but there's nothing.'

'Do you have a copy of the local newspaper to hand, sir? In case the advert is still in it?' Derek obediently left to look.

Muted sounds of his search reached the detective at the end of the line. Derek returned moments later, his search frustrated by the cleaning lady's thoroughness. 'No, no, I haven't got it. All the rubbish has gone, you see.'

'Never mind, sir, we can easily get a copy from the local paper. Perhaps for now you can tell me roughly what it said and how it came to lead to your wife's disappearance.'

Derek explained about the opportunity that had eventually attracted Deborah and her friends, and the selection process in which she and Leslie had been successful. As he spoke he realised how vague and ill-informed he must sound.

'Do you have the address of the photographic studio?'

'No.'

'Any correspondence of any sort?'

Derek shook his head wearily. 'No.'

'There must have been some sort of correspondence, sir. You must have discussed the whole thing.'

'No. We didn't. It was a source of some disagreement between us. I didn't really approve of it, you see.' And so it went on, the policeman's questions becoming more and more cursory.

'So, Mrs Fearnside applied with a number of her friends to an advert from a firm whose name you can't remember, for some family models.'

'Yes.'

'Your wife and a few others – you can't remember who apart from Leslie Smith – then went to an unknown hotel in London for an interview. Then she and an unknown number of her friends went to a local photographic shop and had pictures of themselves and their children taken. That would have been expensive; would your wife have had the money to pay for that herself or did she ask you for it?'

'No and no. She obviously had money of her own but not enough, without going to her building society, to pay for anything significant and she didn't ask me for any.'

'I see. Then she went off to a photo session, again in London, but you don't know the address or the name of the firm. Is that correct?'

'Yes.'

'Excuse me for asking, but were you close to your wife, sir? It's just that, if mine had become involved in something like this, I think I would have looked into it a bit more.'

'I don't see that that's any of your damned business, Sergeant!'

'You called us in, Mr Fearnside, and your wife is missing. That makes this our business. I repeat, were you close to your wife?'

'About the same as any couple that have been married for some time and have two demanding young children, I suppose. With the best will in the world, it is pretty hard to stay really close – life had a way of coming between us. Surely you must have found that yourself.' Derek waited hopefully, but the policeman was quiet for some time.

Eventually he broke the silence: 'So, you weren't very close. You realise that I have to ask you the next question, sir. Was your wife having an affair?'

'No! That is, I don't think so.' He paused, then finally: 'No! Of course not. The whole suggestion's ridiculous.'

'I see.' The detective's tone indicated that he did not see it the same way as Derek at all. 'When she left today did she take anything with her that might indicate that she was not intending to come straight back?'

Derek paused uncertainly before answering.

'Not really, no.' But even he could hear the falsehood in his voice.

'What *did* she take?'

'A small case, her make-up, some toiletries – the usual things.'

'Nothing else? Like money, passport, chequebook, credit cards, those sort of things?'

'She didn't take her passport. I came across that when I was looking for the papers earlier. But she did take her chequebook . . .'

'And?'

'That was it; that's all.'

'So, if she were staying away for the night for any reason, she would have sufficient money in her account?'

'Yes.'

'Exactly how much does she have?'

'I'm not exactly sure. About a thousand pounds, I think. She'd just had a small legacy left her and was deciding what to do with it.'

'That's rather a lot of money. It does rather change things, doesn't it, sir?'

'I don't see why at all, Sergeant. She's still missing, I still have no idea at all where she went or where she might be. Her friend, the one she was meant to be with today, was prevented from going in the most peculiar circumstances and Deborah hasn't even called to make sure the children are all right. I know my wife, and I can assure you that none of this makes sense!' Derek's anger and concern exploded in a tirade at the policeman. As he paused for breath, the detective intervened.

'I understand all that, sir, but this is all very vague. Now if you'll just calm down and tell me the names and addresses of your wife's friends I'll be able to get someone on to this in the morning.' Derek could hear him turn to a clean page in his notebook.

The policeman advised Derek to go to bed and try and get some sleep. He would make sure there was a full briefing for the day shift and if there was still no news from Deborah by the following afternoon – twenty-four hours after her disappearance – they would start investigations.

Derek replaced the receiver and stood forehead pressed against the wretched cream-striped paper. Tears smarted his eyes and he blinked them back. He understood, with some surprise, that he still loved his wife deeply, had never stopped loving her. Things would be different when she came home. He would suggest that they go away, just the two of them. He would indulge her and treat her to make up for lost time. Derek locked up mechanically, made a pot of tea and poured a whisky to take to bed. He was exhausted, not thinking straight, and when, halfway up the stairs, he saw that he had automatically made tea for two he sank to his knees and wept like a child.

CHAPTER SIX

By eight o'clock in the morning he had all the information he needed. Towards the end she had become incoherent; thirst, sustained terror and measured but constant pain had finally robbed her of her reason and hence her usefulness. It was irrelevant. He doubted she knew anything more.

The mention of a diary had intrigued him. Not hers, a friend's; that could be helpful and it tied in with the letter he had received, the instructions he now followed. The woman's confession had been revealing. The final twist, Octavia's love affair, angered him. Part of his mind – the emotionally underdeveloped adolescent that he kept locked away and out of sight – refused to believe her speculations, but the remorseless adult in him knew it could be the truth, however odd and unsuspected.

Of course, she had denied the death was anything but an accident, even when the pain had been at its worst. Even under the pressure of the scalpel and the whisper of the filleting knife she had held to that part of her story but it did not matter. He had confirmed the truth amongst her twisted ramblings and he knew more than enough now to move on to the next stage.

He had only one immediate problem: what to do with her? She had pleaded with him to spare her life; had offered to do anything for him for the privilege. Some of her more exotic suggestions had stimulated his curiosity but not his desire. He was amazed that a middle-class, county-town housewife should have such a fund of ideas. At one point he had almost found himself tempted despite his best intentions; he was curious to see what she would do given the opportunity. But the risks were too great and her stinking, bruised and bloodied body did not arouse him.

The question now was, should he kill her? He knew he had little option and how would not be an issue – he had an embarrassment of choices. The problem, to his surprise, was that he did not really want to. Despite himself he had warmed to her and she had not, after all, been directly involved in the killing. She had spirit. Beneath the obvious vanities he had seen the caring mother and fond wife. Even at the worst point of her humiliation and torture she had carried on pleading with him to contact her husband to make sure that her children were all right. Part of him insisted she wasn't a bad woman. She hadn't committed the murder, although she'd admitted she had done nothing to prevent it. Could she have, though? It was a moot point.

Perhaps he could let her go, eventually. She would be unable to identify him and, with his contacts, he planned to leave the country once the final killing had been done. He remembered the vixen, and his determination to kill the woman wavered even more.

His musings were interrupted abruptly by a knocking at the front door. His immediate thoughts were – Police! Where was his gun? Had he regagged her securely? He smoothly picked up his weapon and tucked it into the back of his waistband. He removed the Balaclava and checked his face in the kitchen mirror; most of the simple disguise was still intact. Lastly he removed his gloves and looked at his hands for signs of blood – they were clean. Then he calmly went and opened the front door.

The rain had subsided to a thin drizzle but the yard was a swamp of muddy puddles. In the middle of one stood a short, profoundly ugly woman in her late fifties with a muddy dog attached to a length of rope.

'Ah good, you're in.' She had a plummy English voice with no trace of Welsh lilt. 'I'm Miss Purbright from Lee Farm. I

56

promised to keep an eye on the cottage for the rental agency, check on any problems and such like, y'know.'

He clearly did not know and his silence disconcerted her.

'Yes, well, after last night's storm and what have you, I thought I'd better check you were all right, had power, phone, that sort of thing.' She paused to tap the fat, smelly retriever on his haunch. 'Better check the new tenant's all right before we do anything else, hadn't we?'

'I see. I'm fine, thank you.' He moved to close the door as she tried to peer over his shoulder into the hall.

'On your own here, are you? A bit remote for a holiday, isn't it?'

'I'm a writer. I like to get away for the peace and quiet.'

There was a distinct emphasis on the final words.

'Yes, well, I suppose that explains it.'

'Yes, I'm sure it does. Now, if you don't mind, I really do have a lot to get back to.' The dog, now showing distinct signs of life, was sniffing the air greedily and trying to move between and around his legs. Given the interesting smells that must be reaching his nose from the small back bedroom the man was keen to close the door on the prying hound as soon as possible.

'Right, well, I'll be off then. If you do happen to fancy popping over for tea sometime, some tenants do, y'know . . .' She could read in his face that his appearance at her kitchen table would be highly unlikely. 'No, well, I doubt you would if you're a writer. Like to be alone, I suspect. But if anything does go wrong, or if you need something, my number's by the phone, you can't miss it, 2813. I'm only a couple of miles away, further down the track on the way to the village, and I can be over here within fifteen minutes in the Jeep if it's important.'

'I'll be sure to remember that. Goodbye.'

'Goodbye.'

He shut the door on the valediction and the dog's probing nose.

'I'll bet it's no problem for you to pop over here,' he said out loud to himself as he walked back to the kitchen. 'I'll bet you do it all the time, poking your nose around, just to make sure everything's all right, of course. Know where the spare key is too, I expect!'

Her knock at the door had decided him. He couldn't risk an intrusion, couldn't rely on the occupant of the back bedroom going unnoticed for any length of time. He would have to act now. A strange, alien emotion moved through him, disturbing him deeply. He searched his mind in vain to try to identify what it was, like an amnesiac hunting the vital clue to bring recall, but recognition remained out of reach.

The feeling remained with him as he made his preparations. It was only at the last moment, as he found himself pulling on the unnecessary anonymity of his black mask, that he realised what it was. It was sadness; knowing he had to kill her had made him sad. It was unbelievable after all these years that he could experience such an emotion. Mild regret, anger, hate, relief – he had felt all these as he had prepared to kill in the past, but never sadness. The feeling stayed with him as he made his way to the small back room.

PART TWO

LIBER SCRIPTUS

Liber scriptus proferetur,
in quo totum continetur,
unde mundus judicetur.

> Open lies the book before them,
> Where all records have been written,
> When creation comes to trial.

CHAPTER SEVEN

'It's good to see you back, Andrew. Take a seat.' The Assistant Chief Constable radiated a kindness and concern that his visitor would happily have done without.

'Thank you, sir.'

'How are the children?'

'They're well, thank you.'

'Good, good.'

There was a pause in which Detective Chief Inspector Andrew Fenwick could see the ACC worrying over whether he should probe further into his family life and personal circumstances. It would be inappropriate – the two men had never got on, particularly since the ACC had quietly failed to back Fenwick's last bid for promotion. Fenwick wasn't supposed to know why he hadn't been put forward, but he did. These things had a way of becoming known within the force.

'Now that you're back, we need to make sure that you're busy – but not too busy, eh?'

'There is no reason why I shouldn't resume my full workload, sir.'

'No, no, of course not, but I don't want to see you overdoing it. You've additional responsibilities now at home, after all, and we need to be sensitive to that.'

'I can assure you that my home life is in good hands. My mother is living with us now and has everything under control.'

The ACC looked surprised but was too skilled to show disappointment.

'I've assembled a number of interesting files for you. Some of them are cases that have gone a little cold but I doubt that will be a problem for you. I want to continue your attachment to HQ. The Division's doing fine without you and we have more than enough here to keep you busy.'

A desk job, thought Fenwick. 'I'd really rather be back at Division, sir. I've missed it.'

'You're needed here, Detective Chief Inspector, and they have their full complement.'

'But I've been reading about this spate of car thefts around Harlden and the Weald. They've been going on for a long time; it's obviously well organised. I could give it a good go.'

'Inspector Blite already has that well in hand, Fenwick, and I need you here.'

Inspector Blite. That explained it all. The weasel's promotion had come through at last, just when Fenwick had been hoping there was some justice in the world after all. He should have known better.

Back in his cramped temporary office, Fenwick started to sort the files he had been given. Some were even dusty. In the middle there were two red-foldered complaints. Both had been logged but neither was deemed serious enough to involve a Police Complaints Authority follow-up. That was one relief at least, but inspecting the force's dirty linen was nobody's favourite job.

The Chief Constable still hadn't set up a central complaints department but expected the ACC to ensure there was no hint of any complaint not being followed through effectively. The force had received forty-eight complaints the previous year, all logged and notified to the PCA. Nearly half had been dropped in the end; complaints and accusations often went away when tempers cooled. Many of the others had been resolved informally, members of the public reluctant to go through a time-consuming formal process. The remainder, though, received the full works.

It was hell for the force officer put in charge of the investigation either way. If you screwed it up, and that was found out, your career was finished. If you found there were genuine grounds for complaint you had the difficult choice of blowing the whistle and finding it hard to live with your colleagues or keeping quiet and it becoming impossible to live with yourself.

Fenwick was known to be scrupulously fair, so black and white they had nicknamed him the Zebra at HQ. He was diligent enough to be relied upon to do a thorough job, tough enough to take the crap and sufficiently intelligent to see through the deceptions that would be put his way. In other words, the perfect fall guy.

At least there were only two complaints. Fenwick scanned the rest of the files quickly. Half of them could be ignored straight away. They were cases so old, and more importantly so trivial, that they had obviously been added to make up the weight of the pile. The rest was paperwork, statistics for reports to be completed by the end of the month. Cursing the ACC he settled behind the scarred desk in the cramped cubicle and thought almost affectionately of his old office at Division, in Harlden.

Fenwick opened the first complaint file later in the long, dull day and consoled himself with the thought that at least he would be home before the children were in bed. Half an hour later he was still reading, oblivious of the time. He then tried to telephone around the area to talk to the various officers involved and spent over an hour tracking them down and taking notes. His luck was in as he discovered that the duty sergeant he needed to talk to was about to come off shift and he drank two cups of tea in the canteen whilst he confirmed the main details and filled in the blanks.

It was nearly six o'clock when a casual 'good night' from someone in the corridor reminded him that he had been planning to leave early. One of the many disadvantages of working at HQ was that it added another forty-five minutes to his journey home. He reached for the telephone to make his guilty apology.

The receiver was picked up within three rings.

'Hello, 526592, whospeaking please?' A breathy falsetto

told him that his call had been answered by the brightest star in his personal constellation.

'Hi, Bess, it's Daddy. Why aren't you in bed yet?'

'Daddy! I'm waiting up for you. Nanny says I can 'cos I didn't see you much yesterday.' She paused. 'You *are* coming home soon, aren't you?'

'Not for a while yet, sweetheart. I'm afraid I'm going to be at work a little longer.'

'Oh.' The disappointed whisper spoke volumes. He strained to hear whether there were tears there too.

'What have you done today then? Was being back at school fun?' Normal conversation helped Fenwick even if he doubted it would work on his five-and-a-half-year-old daughter.

'No, school was horrid, really, really horrid. Mrs Goss was cross with us all day and we weren't allowed to play outside 'cos of the rain, and smelly Jimmy Barnes hit Christopher over the head with a spade when they were playing with the sand, and made it bleed, and I got told off and it wasn't even *fair* 'cos *I* didn't do anything. Just 'cos I gave Chris my hankie for the blood. It was horrid!'

Fenwick was immediately concerned for his younger child. 'Is Christopher all right, Bess? How bad was his head?'

'Well, he's gone all quiet – like he does when you don't like it, Daddy. He'll talk to me but he won't eat his tea and he's not talking to Nanny.'

'Oh dear. I'd better speak to her then and try to talk to Chris. But are you all right, little one?'

'I'm fine . . . I miss you, though, Daddy, *lots*! Nanny's very nice and she gave me a lovely tea but, well . . . she's not you.' Again the final words emerged as a whisper, almost lost in the static of the line.

'I know, but look, don't worry. Only one more day to the weekend and, remember, I don't have to work this Saturday.' He crossed his fingers and hoped.

'I know but, well, things happen, don't they, and you can't help it – something always comes up in your job – doesn't it?'

He couldn't help smiling at a five-year-old copying his own

lame excuses exactly; she not only knew them backwards, she believed them too!

'Put Nanny on now, dear. Night-night and God bless.' He blew a kiss down the line quietly, hoping no one was still around to hear, and was promptly rewarded with her return blessing. Thank heavens for Bess. Without her over the past few months he didn't know to what depths he might have descended.

'Hello, Andrew. Late already?' His mother's tone delivered as sharp a slap as her hand used to.

'Yes, Mum. Sorry. Things are impossible here. Look, how's Christopher? What's all this about him being hit at school?'

'Yes, he was hit, but to be honest it was nothing out of the ordinary for boys of his age. Mind you, I think Bess delivered more damage. Apparently she really laid in to the lad that hit Christopher and he was either well-mannered or frightened enough not to hit back! You know what a tiger she can be over her brother. They had to pull her off the other boy and she was made to sit in the corner for the rest of the afternoon.'

'So that's why she was told off. The little madam! I'm glad I didn't know earlier – I'd have had too much sympathy to tell her off myself. And what about Chris?'

There was a pause in which he could hear his mother closing the door. 'Well, it's not good. Oh, the bump on his head is nothing – he's had worse. But I'm really worried about him, Andrew. I can't get a word out of him and he's started that rocking again. He hasn't done that since he lost his mother.'

'Should we take him back to the doctor's, do you think?'

'We'll have to. There's no way he can go back to school tomorrow. They can't keep an eye on him all the time.' She paused to draw breath. 'In fact, Andrew, I don't think he should go to that school any more. We really need to consider finding a proper school for him.'

'Hang on a minute! We've been over this before. It's a big decision. Give Christopher more time to settle down – he's only been back a day. He was happy enough there before.'

Fenwick squared his jaw firmly, ageing and hardening his face. Christopher had never been an emotionally robust child and his father had attached great hopes to the steadying effects of his attending a 'normal' school now that he was just old enough. He was convinced that the boy needed to be in the real world of the village and that the rough and tumble of the other children would do him good. Privately, he thought that too much mollycoddling had contributed to the boy's sensitivity in the first place.

'Andrew, we've been over this before, time and again. I know he's your son but it's time to face facts.' She lowered her voice further. 'You must accept that Christopher is not a well little boy. He's deeply disturbed and he's nowhere near recovering from the loss of his mother; he still misses her deeply.'

'But he's near Bess now, Mum, every day, don't forget that.' Fenwick could hear an acknowledgement of defeat nibbling at the edges of his words. He knew what his mother would say next before the sentence was out of her mouth.

'Bess's not yet six years old, Andrew. It's totally unfair to rely on her. We need expert advice and help. You're being unfair to all of us with your pig-headedness, me included and Christopher most of all.'

'Look, we can't discuss this now. Take him to the doctor's tomorrow and get his opinion by all means, then we'll talk again.'

He cleared his throat to recover his normal tone of authority. 'I'll have a word with Chris now, if I may.'

'I'll see if he'll come to the phone. What time are you coming home, by the way?'

'I'm not sure. Looking at this lot it could be an hour or so yet.'

'Give me a call before you set off then and I'll put your supper on to warm.' The muffled clunk of the handset on the table announced her departure before he had a chance to say thank you. It was amazing the way she could always maintain the moral advantage. She really was an exasperating woman but he would not have been able to keep his children at home without her.

Fenwick stared blankly at the half-screen opposite his desk.

The dark brown material was curiously empty – devoid of the usual clutter of photographs, maps and notes associated with current cases. He had no open cases, he reflected ruefully. No cases, bugger all career. That was what extended compassionate leave did for you. He looked darkly at the pile of files on his desk.

One of them might yet present a hope of rebuilding his reputation. As he waited on the line, he was tormented again by memories of the previous six months. How could he have missed the signs, first with Monique and now with Christopher? After all these weeks he still cursed his myopia over his wife's steady decline. Perhaps if he had been more attentive, had been at home more often, he would have been alert and they would have been able to do something. He was a detective, for God's sake; it was his job to detect, to spot clues, to create whole pictures from a jigsaw of evidence. And he had failed on his most important case – his wife's health.

The doctor and their friends had tried to comfort him, of course, when the prognosis had been confirmed. They said there was nothing more that could have been done, so little he could have achieved; she had covered it up so well. She'd had them all fooled for a while but she couldn't cheat nature. Now it was too late and he was faced with a growing dilemma over his son. The sense of helplessness and inevitability threatened to overwhelm him again.

He had vowed that he would never, ever again allow work to drive a wedge between him and his family, nor compromise his commitment to them. But he had only been back at work a day and was already faced with choices. As he listened to the empty static on the line he promised himself he wouldn't let it happen again. If Christopher needed him then he had to be there.

The silence at the end of the line thickened. With the unique sensitivity of a parent, he was aware that his son was suddenly there.

'Hello, Chris, it's Daddy. How are you then? How's your head?'

Silence.

'I hear from Bess that you got a bit of a bump on it today.'

Nothing. An aggressive silence echoed in his ear.

'Well, the good news is that Nanny and I have agreed that you don't have to go to school tomorrow. That'll be fun, won't it?'

Incidental static tickled his ear, masquerading as a preparatory intake of breath.

'Chris? Chris, look, I know you're there. Talk to me, tell Daddy something – like what've you done today? Please?'

'Clouds. Clouds and clouds and more clouds. I saw them today.' The boy's voice was distorted, strained, without character. Fenwick had to swallow down the hard lump in his throat.

'I see. Were these nice clouds, Chris? Were they friendly?'

'They're *my* clouds, Daddy. I've brought them home with me.'

Fenwick fought a growing sense of panic as his son's nonsense words continued.

'Where do you keep these clouds, Chris? What does Nanny think of them?'

'She can't see them. Not sure you could either. They're my clouds. Bess can.'

'What colour are the clouds? Are they pretty, like at sunset?' Fenwick just wanted to keep his son there on the line.

'They're my clouds. If I don't look after them they'll go.'

'Look after them? What do you have to do?'

'They're always changing shape and splitting into bits. If I don't know how many there are, I'll lose them.'

The stone in Fenwick's throat was threatening to choke him again but he talked on in a desperate attempt to move his son's conversation on to firm ground. It was no good. He heard the receiver being replaced on the table and the sound of Chris's retreating steps. The phone was off the hook and, unless his mother returned to the room, there was no use shouting down it. For a few moments he fought a strong impulse to ignore the papers on his desk. In the end, he compromised and decided to work on the complaints at home. He bundled the files into his briefcase and left.

Two hours later he was sitting in the lounge, more relaxed and enjoying a blazing log fire. He had seen the children off to bed with long cuddles, eaten an excellent supper and was relaxing with a stiff whisky and warm water, ready to tackle the two complaints. The name on the first file seemed familiar – Derek Fearnside from Harlden – but the case had arisen back in April whilst he had been on leave so he couldn't think why it should mean anything. Then he remembered. Bob Fearnside had been one of his best friends at school and he'd had a brother called Derek. In a small town, it was highly likely that it was the same family.

Fenwick flipped open the file. A pool of light from the desk lamp flowed over a 6 × 8 inch colour photograph clipped to the cover. A happy family group had been captured for ever in a microsecond's exposure. His eye was drawn automatically to the woman, who appeared to be the focus of the picture.

Blonde, stunningly pretty, blue eyes alive and gazing through the shutter of the camera to hold the attention of the observer. Her intensity and beauty were, literally, captivating and for a moment Fenwick allowed himself the pleasure of simply looking at her.

He wondered who the photographer had been. Her look was intimate and confiding – the cameraman must have felt it, and enjoyed her attention. He found himself drawn into the photo, invited to share the intimacy of the little group. He guessed, with an uncanny insight, that she had been on intimate terms with the unknown photographer and that the poor man would never forget her. Was it her husband? If so, who was the man with her in the picture?

The woman was holding a small child in her arm, balancing its weight on a forward thrust of hip, protecting the neck and head within a sheltering elbow. The child was about twelve months old, sexless, asleep. Another, older, child clung to her leg and skirt. The woman's left hand rested gently on his head. He could see the way her fingers were entwined in his auburn hair, caught in a moment of stroking reassurance. The young boy's eyes were soft and distant, unaware of the photographer. He was relishing one of those unremarked but fundamental moments of childhood when a mother's body heat, smell and solid physical presence, provide a bubble of absolute safety and contentment.

The three of them, mother, child and baby, formed a tight trinity at the heart of the picture. So strong was their image that he almost overlooked the man to one side. He was distant from the group, a silent witness to it, like a shepherd at the cradle. He was avoiding the camera. Fenwick felt profoundly sorry for him.

Looking closer, he recognised the man's face. It was the Derek Fearnside he had known. The picture opened an old memory. He had attended his wedding; Bob had been best man and Fenwick was a close enough friend to warrant an invitation. Which meant that this radiant – possibly unfaithful – mother had been the young bride on that occasion. He couldn't remember her name, nor anything about the day except that he had managed to seduce one of the bridesmaids later on, thanks more to champagne than to any skills of his.

The coincidence of encountering some of Bob's close family put his own domestic worries out of his mind. He deliberately set the Fearnside file to one side to return to last, as a small incentive to keep him going. The next complaint related to police handling of a domestic incident. A six-foot-three father of four, Mr Baxter, was complaining that the police had used unnecessary physical force when attending a domestic incident at his home. Apparently, a five-foot-eight, *female* constable had physically restrained the man, bruising his arm and wrist in the process. The man had been off sick for over a week and, being self-employed, he was threatening to sue for loss of earnings. The amount he was claiming made him significantly better paid than the Assistant Chief Constable!

The account from the constable's notebook provided some clarification. Apparently the aggrieved gentleman had been in the process of delivering a 'lesson' to his live-in companion. During the incident the constable had had to wrest an old-fashioned marble rolling pin from his hand. She had, in her own words, 'employed the minimum of force and restraint necessary to prevent potential injury to the other person present, myself and the dog.' The dog?

The incident was less than a week old and Fenwick was puzzled as to why it was being taken so seriously. Then he noticed the ACC's note to him, clipped to the file: *AJF, Baxter is one of Councillor Ward's regular private-hire drivers. AHB*. It might just as well have been a large, red 'Handle with care!' notice. Ward was one of a large minority of militant left members of the local council and had decided to justify his minority position by taking the police to task, with monotonous regularity, on any and all points of issue.

Fenwick realised that he would need to spend hours investigating and making sure the paperwork was perfect before reporting back. It would be a waste of his time, the constable's and inevitably the ACC's.

It was with a compensating pleasure that he saw a recent note had been added to the file from an RSPCA investigator, called in by the enterprising constable. Concerned about the condition of the dog in the kitchen, she had asked the RSPCA to make a visit. Baxter's female partner might in the eyes of the law have sufficient self-determination to drop charges of assault and put herself at his mercy for another time. Fortunately for the dog, as a dumb animal, the law allowed others to intervene on its behalf. Baxter was to be prosecuted for neglect and ill-treatment of the animal.

Councillor Ward was unlikely, after all, to protest too strongly on his driver's behalf. There were a lot of animal lovers in Sussex!

It was after eleven when Fenwick finally found himself looking again into the too blue eyes of Deborah Fearnside. He spent time over Derek Fearnside's letter. It was depressingly familiar. Even in a relatively rural area such as this, missing persons cases were quite common. Usually they were troubled teenagers, depressed wives or disturbed husbands who simply could not cope any more. And usually the person turned up within a few days, if they were to turn up at all, apologetic, tired, sometimes in need of medical care, but grateful for the affection they found waiting for them at home. Occasionally, they were never seen again, except in ageing photographs in missing persons specials in the press or on TV.

Mr Fearnside could not understand why there was no police investigation into his wife's disappearance, now nearly four weeks old. A standard letter had been sent to him in reply to his initial enquiries, explaining that it was not normal procedure to investigate adult disappearances unless there were circumstances that were cause for particular concern. They had even quoted some helpful statistics to prove why it was impracticable and usually unnecessary to follow up, in a mixed attempt to reassure and quieten the anxious husband. It had not worked.

Mr Fearnside called every day and had written finally to state that he was considering a formal complaint. He insisted that there were peculiar circumstances, that his wife would not have simply walked out on him and their children. And now the file sat on Fenwick's coffee table waiting for him to decide the next course of action. He was mentally composing a polite but final note of reply as he read through Fearnside's letter.

But his half-formed reply was abandoned as he read on. He found himself agreeing with the husband, not his colleagues. The man had compiled a list of 'peculiar circumstances':

- She had left a note for the cleaning lady to take some chops out of the freezer to defrost for Derek's supper that she would cook on her return.
- She had not taken any clothes with her.
- She had not taken her passport.
- No significant amounts of money had been drawn from their joint account in the weeks leading up to her disappearance and none at all at any time since.
- A friend at the bank had unofficially confirmed that no money had been taken from her private account before or after her disappearance.
- Their credit card statement had just arrived and showed

- no entries since she had disappeared.
- She had not taken her car.
- She had bought a return ticket.
- The modelling agency she was visiting had not called or written once since her disappearance.
- Nor had they called Leslie Smith, who was also due to work for them.
- Leslie Smith had been unable to make contact with the agency despite constant attempts.
- He had visited the studio where the photographs had been taken during their selection, to find it deserted and available for hire.
- She had missed her mother's birthday – that had never happened before.
- She had missed her son's birthday – unthinkable.
- She hadn't called once to find out if the children were all right.

Nowhere on the list did the man mention himself! It was a peculiarly inverted inventory, starting as it did with the material 'evidence' against the routine nature of her disappearance and ending with the emotional and real. Glancing again at the photograph, Fenwick wondered just what sort of man Fearnside was; perhaps his prosaic detachment was enough to drive a woman away but he clearly loved her. Or was it guilt?

The photo haunted him. There was no date on it. It could have been taken many years before but he doubted it, given the ages of the children on the file. The mother in the picture could never abandon her children – her husband perhaps, but not them. It convinced him more than any of Fearnside's arguments, and inclined him to ignore the fact that she *had* taken an overnight bag with her, full apparently of the things she thought she would need for the shoot.

He reread Blite's notes on his interview with Fearnside – a basic piece of paperwork intended to close the file. Fenwick was not a fan of Blite's despite the man's arrest record.

He knew what Fearnside was going through and why he

made daily complaints against the police. With himself, it had been constant calls to the doctors, venting his anger, frustration and despair. One moment, he had been moving through life with his goals clearly defined, details organised, and the next everything was shattered into a kaleidoscope of change and pain. Each day brought a new shift, a new pattern, making less and less sense. But it would be difficult and unpopular to reopen the case, despite his suspicions, and there were no legitimate grounds for complaint. Depressed, he started to draft a reply.

> . . . Thank you for your letter . . . As my colleague has already explained . . . standard procedure had been followed . . . details are on the Police National Computer . . . If you would like to proceed with a formal complaint you should follow the guidelines in the leaflet enclosed . . .

His work was interrupted by the sudden arrival of a damp, warm, dishevelled bundle that tottered across the room and landed firmly in his lap. Tough little Bess was in tears, sobbing hopelessly for her mummy, her brother and the father she had grown used to seeing every day during her mother's final decline.

After he eventually put her to bed, reading her story after story in a whisper until she was too deeply asleep to hear him leave, Fenwick returned to the study. He tore his letter to Fearnside into small pieces.

Every man had the right to a second opinion before being forced to acknowledge the ruin of his life.

CHAPTER EIGHT

A late bout of spring flu had swept through Harlden Division, leaving the CID team desperately short of men. Reluctantly, the ACC called Fenwick and told him to take up his old post again. There was a nasty spate of organised car theft going on and it was about time someone sorted it out.

But Fenwick's thoughts were on another case entirely and he knew he had to choose his moment with the ACC carefully, and make his request appear as casual and routine as possible. He bumped into him on the stairs as the ACC was sprinting to a regular meeting with the Police Authority, keen to arrive exactly at the appointed time. The man hardly listened to his request and nodded him away with the instruction: 'Take who you need from the Division, one man will be enough. And don't drag it out.' Fenwick knew exactly the man he needed and where to find him. He set off for his old office at Division with a lighter heart.

Thursday started routinely enough for Detective Sergeant Cooper. He breakfasted early with his wife – eggs (poached these days because of all the worry about fat and cholesterol), some nice smoked back rashers (only two now, though), a tomato (vitamin C), the butcher's special sausage (one, small) and a piece of fried bread (a man had to have one indulgence) – and was in the office to catch up on endless paperwork by eight o'clock. The message from DCI Fenwick came as a surprise. He knew he had returned but had been told he was stuck at HQ.

They had worked together in the past and each time it had been a significant case: a child abduction and an apparently motiveless murder, both solved by a combination of dogged police work and timely intuition. They were successes that had brought a thrill of achievement to Cooper, unexpected this late in his career. He and Fenwick worked together well. Divisional CID didn't stretch to the luxury of employing an analyst of team behaviour. Had they done so their expert would have observed that Fenwick and Cooper were a natural team, their strengths were complementary, and one's weaknesses brought out hidden depths in the other. Despite their radically different appearances and careers, they shared beliefs and values that allowed them to trust each other fundamentally. They were a winning combination.

Prosaic as always, Cooper wouldn't have seen it like that. He respected Fenwick, didn't understand the half of what the man said, of course – the words he used, his daft ideas that led to unexpected results – but he would rather work with him than any other DCI.

He had been disappointed by Fenwick's increasing preoccupation with his wife's illness, hated to see him lose his sharpness and to watch the natural toughness deteriorate into a bullying, vindictive spite that had alienated many of his colleagues, some of them probably for good. But Cooper had realised, with an insight Fenwick would have found surprising as well as disturbing, that his sometime partner had needed to lash out in order to survive. Cooper was curious to see what was left of the original man as he headed for Fenwick's old office.

'Morning, sir.'

'Morning, Sergeant.' Fenwick barely looked up from a slim brown file in front of him but at least waved Cooper to sit down. The burly, heavy man eased himself into one of Fenwick's notoriously uncomfortable metal-framed chairs.

'Coffee?' He didn't wait for an answer but shouted out to the group secretary: 'Anne. Coffee, please – one for me and one for Sergeant Cooper – white, two sugars for him.'

He turned to Cooper. 'It'll be a while. She's still got the old machine – takes an age but makes the best coffee around.'

Cooper reflected that it might take an age but for most other people at Division the delivery of palatable coffee would be a miracle. Some old habits died hard.

'Now, about this complaint.'

As usual, Cooper found himself trying to keep on top of the DCI's rapid speech and staccato sentences, surfing from one topic to the next with few clues as to where they were heading.

'Yes, sir. I thought you might want to discuss my report on what's been happening at the Dell. I've got it with me.'

'The Dell?' Fenwick looked surprised for a moment, as if interrupted in the middle of a puzzle for which Cooper was expected to supply a different answer. 'The Dell? Don't know anything about it. That's not the reason I wanted to see you. Read that.'

Fenwick threw him a complaint file with a family photograph on the front cover.

'Sir?'

'Just read it, Cooper. I want an unbiased opinion.' He left Cooper to it as he wandered off to investigate his old territory in the minutes before the coffee arrived.

Cooper tried to settle himself more comfortably into the visitor's seat. There seemed to be no way he could arrange his bones to fit the chair's angles despite his ample padding. Fenwick's own, old-fashioned chair was very tempting but he didn't dare. At least the coffee would offer some compensation.

Ignoring Fenwick's instructions to reach his own, unbiased opinion, he turned to the first page, written in the Chief Inspector's familiar, slanted scrawl. There were a dozen questions listed, half of them heavily underscored. He read the notes twice, slowly and deliberately. Then he turned to the rest of the file, his deeply lined face creasing further as he worked through the few pages. By the time he had read through those twice, the frown had been replaced with an expression his friends would have recognised as a smile of grim satisfaction.

He had the answer to his biggest question: Fenwick was back in style. Who else would have spotted the innocuous but curious set of coincidences that should have transformed a routine missing persons case into a suspected abduction? He doubted whether he would have picked up all the loose ends himself without prompting.

Cooper looked afresh at the list of questions. It was the modelling agency that troubled him most, that and the fact that Deborah Fearnside had apparently set out to an unknown destination confidently and without a worry in the world. As he waited for Fenwick, he started routinely to try to contact the agency. The local paper would be the first step. As he lifted Fenwick's phone he noticed the familiar scrawl again on a clean white desk blotter that wouldn't last the month.

BIG QUESTIONS:
- Does the agency exist?
- If not, what was behind the charade? (Did D. F. make it all up? Highly unlikely given his constant demand for serious follow-up!)
- If it was real, is there a conspiracy?
  - to attract provincial housewives to London?
  - to attract *a particular* housewife to London?
- What is/was so special about D. F. ?
- Is this an abduction or murder
  - local?
  - London?

He left a careful message on the answering machine for the local paper's archive department (they didn't open until nine o'clock) and thought about Blite, an ambitious young upstart, more ruthless than talented, who had just been promoted to DI. Why hadn't Blite become suspicious and probed further? If Deborah Fearnside hadn't simply walked off (it had to remain a possibility) she had been abducted in a way designed to remove suspicion from her disappearance. She might just have been an unlucky dupe but they couldn't discount the possibility that she was a targeted victim.

Fenwick spent some time wandering around Divisional HQ,

stopping by the front desk to pass the time of day with the duty sergeant before poking his nose into the room which housed Divisional CID. Nearly all the desks were empty, including the one in the airy office that Detective Inspector Blite had moved into on promotion. A plastic, brass-effect nameplate with a self-adhesive backing had been stuck on to the door. 'Detective Inspector' had been spelt out in full, as had all of Blite's initials, 'R. A. C.' Fenwick wondered whether Blite had bought it himself or whether it had been a gift from his adoring wife. It confirmed his assessment of the man, a complete lack of taste and style compensated for by limitless ambition and ruthless self-confidence.

His meanderings around Division confirmed that he was lucky to have kept his office. He'd have Superintendent Beckitt to thank for that, and for keeping Blite out of it. The old man wasn't an advocate of the new DI despite the ACC's endorsement.

Detective Constable Walters was glad to see Fenwick, standing up automatically when he entered. Fenwick brushed his welcome to one side, not unkindly but sympathy was still difficult to take and he had become practised at warding it off before it started. He asked Walters about the latest car theft.

'Taylor and Peters are out now, three more last night.'

Fenwick made a mental note to check with them when they returned; he'd need a quick result.

'You back then, sir? For good?'

'For now, Walters, for now.' He continued towards the door.

'Well, it's good to see you, sir. A number of us'll be relieved, I can tell you.'

Fenwick did not want compliments that verged into petty politicking. He lifted his hand in tacit farewell and left.

As he was walking back towards his office Superintendent Beckitt's secretary dashed out of her small cubbyhole and almost grabbed his arm.

'Chief Inspector Fenwick! Thank goodness, I've been searching for you everywhere. The ACC wants to talk to you, urgently. He's on the Superintendent's line. Wanted to talk to him really but I can't reach him at home.'

The ACC was furious. He had just arrived for the Police Authority meeting, confident that he would be able to keep Counsellor Ward in his place for once, only to be confronted by him on an even more sensitive matter than the incident involving his driver.

The Assistant Chief Constable could barely contain himself as he recounted the story to Fenwick. During an incident at an unofficial travellers' encampment, the Dell, one of the travellers had suffered a serious heart attack. Residents were blaming police harassment.

The ACC had immediately called the officer in charge at the scene. His story was that his officers had been pelted with stones and broken bottles. They'd been searching for suspected car thieves reportedly in the camp. The volley of stones that greeted them was fierce. Both constables confirmed that they saw a woman open her caravan door and look out. Seeing a bolt hole the man they were chasing had dived for cover in her van. The officers had followed hard behind.

The woman had collapsed and been taken straight to hospital, and all the officers involved had been ordered to HQ. The ACC had promised an immediate internal inquiry. There was little public sympathy for travellers but even so, the story would make the local paper's front page and from there could become syndicated to the nationals if they were unlucky. There was the real risk of a formal PCA investigation.

Fenwick's heart sank. He was being ordered to head the inquiry, reporting direct to the ACC. His hopes of devoting the next few days to tracing Deborah Fearnside vanished but he would still try to do what he could.

'Who are the officers involved, sir?'

'Taylor and Peters entered the caravan.'

'And the officer in charge?'

'DI Blite.'

'I see.' Fenwick's tone was perfect in its neutrality.

* * *

'Right, Cooper. We've a lot to do and we need to do it quickly. Do you agree?'

'Yes, sir. Definitely.'

'Well, come on. Tell whoever you need to that you won't be around for a few days.'

'Done that, sir.'

'Good. Well, it's two cases we're working on and there's a lot to do on both – quickly.'

Cooper refused to look confused.

The Dell case needed urgent attention for it not to get out of hand. Fenwick worked up a full list for Cooper, starting at the county hospital. Fenwick would need to interview Peters, Taylor and Blite, which meant returning to HQ almost at once. But he also left Cooper with the copious list of actions from the front of the Fearnside file, starting with a hunt for the catalogue company and modelling agency. The local advert seemed their only lead. As always, he had overprepared, but Cooper knew any instructions from Fenwick took none of the initiative away from him and that, if anything, even more would be expected.

Cooper disappeared to collect his coat and hat. He was back inside five minutes, during which he had also telephoned his sympathetic wife and issued a gloomy prognosis for their weekend. Inside though, he could feel the adrenalin starting to flow. Working with Fenwick, being trusted by the man, had motivated him more than he had thought possible. He should be counting the years to retirement, carefully managing his time and energy. Instead, he was happily prepared to overturn the prospects of a weekend's late spring gardening and a visit to his new granddaughter, to work on two complaints. Carrying a fax from the local paper and his report on the Dell, he joined Fenwick in his car.

He was dropped at the hospital with a curt reminder to be back at the station by four o'clock.

The county hospital was a long, four-storey, concrete and glass building, flanked on two sides by car parks, with access for visitors and emergency vehicles at the front, facing the road.

Cooper disliked the building intensely, partly for what it stood for, as both his mother and father had died in there, but mainly because a negative, deadening power seemed to emanate from the place, such that any individual, however healthy and positive, was reduced as they came within its shadow. They were forced to conform to fit a mould of anxiety, obedience and eventual selfishness as they drew near to its doors.

Cooper begrudged the hospital its power. As he entered the main reception area, Cooper felt his face set. His step became a purposeful march.

'Police. Detective Sergeant Cooper,' he announced to the receptionist. 'I need to see the doctor in charge of one of your patients; a recent emergency admission. I expect she's in intensive care.' His tone was brusque, authoritative because of his own inner tension. Too late, he realised that his customary courtesy would have served him better.

The receptionist was slow and unhelpful. She told him to take a seat whilst she told the duty sister there was a constable there to see her. She turned away before he could correct the rank.

He was left to cool off for ten minutes before the sister arrived.

'Detective Constable Cooper? You're enquiring after Mrs Carla Evans?'

'Detective Sergeant, and yes I am, Sister.'

'Would you come with me?' She walked over to a quiet corner of the waiting room, tucked to the side of an ancient tea and coffee dispenser.

'I'm sorry to tell you that Mrs Evans died an hour ago. She had another major heart attack and there was nothing we could do.' The sister's pinched monkey face stared at him dispassionately.

'I see. Thank you, Sister . . . ?'

'Barker.'

'Right. I need to ask some more questions about her medical history and condition on arrival.'

'Well, she was a very sick lady and her condition deteriorated rapidly. As far as her history goes, you'll need to speak to her GP.'

'Her GP? She has one? I would have thought she travelled around too much.'

'Dr Rogers, in Woodside Surgery. And you're wrong about the travelling. Until five weeks ago Mrs Evans was comfortably settled in an official council-run site. It was only because her son-in-law, Degs I think they call him, insisted that she go and join them that she moved. Very much against her will, if you ask me.'

'How do you know all this, Sister Barker?'

'I was on shift in the IC ward when she was admitted. I heard her daughter talking about it. She blames herself for her mother's attack, because it was she who finally persuaded the old lady to move to the Dell to please that husband of hers. Typical.' Her face reflected a view that any woman who so compromised her good sense for the sake of a man deserved whatever she got in return.

'I thought they were throwing blame in other directions, not at each other.'

'At the police, you mean?' Sister Barker smiled ruefully. 'Oh, the men will do, of course.'

'But not her daughter?'

'No, Sergeant. You'll find that women are usually more honest with themselves, even to the point of accepting blame, whereas, it is my experience that men are more interested in finding a scapegoat.' There was no reply to that.

'Thank you, Sister. If I need to talk to you again I'll be able to find you here for the next few days?'

'I'm not going anywhere, Sergeant.'

Cooper set off to find Dr Rogers with a hopeful heart. Inevitably, Degs and his acquaintances would pursue their accusations vehemently – and inevitably Counsellor Ward would be roped in and be tempted to give his support. But with the possibility that Mrs Evans had been too ill to move in the first place – and the prosecution of Ward's driver by the RSPCA looming as extra leverage – Cooper felt that they might have the start of an agreement to keep everything under control after all.

Fenwick's plan to cram in a couple of interviews on the Fearnside case before returning to HQ failed. Derek Fearnside had already left for work and was not due home until the evening. Leslie Smith was out and, according to a curious neighbour, was unlikely to return before teatime. Her son's headmaster was tied up in a meeting with the Governors and wouldn't be free until well after lunch. Fenwick accepted that luck was not to be with him that morning and turned the car round.

The interviews with Peters and Taylor were arranged for neutral territory at HQ. They went predictably. The former was cocky, sure of police support, and not prepared to say much at all. The latter was nervous, defensive and resented Fenwick's intrusion. His interview with Blite was difficult and one that neither of them enjoyed. The ACC, returning at last from his protracted Police Authority meeting, joined them but left quickly. Fenwick met him in his office half an hour later.

'So you think there might be some substance to the travellers' allegations? I thought as much but I'd hoped for a different opinion.'

'Possibly, sir, but Cooper's called in with some hopeful news. I've got him to work with me on this one.' He ran through it quickly.

'It's important that you confirm the facts as quickly as possible. Go ahead and dig. Make it your top priority. I don't want the bleeding hearts forcing us into a corner, and I don't want any secrets left to bite us later.'

Fenwick was surprised. 'You think there's a real risk of that?'

'You've been out of it too long, Andrew. Have you forgotten? It's local elections in May. Ward would love this to run until then.'

'Yes, but travellers; siding with them is hardly a vote-winning platform around here.'

'You've overlooked the ward he's in. Hockley North. I can

see him making a frail, grey-haired old lady a symbol for all the malcontents around, that's the *majority* vote where he comes from. Do what you must, Chief Inspector. I just want it sorted.'

The ACC was blessed with a vivid imagination when it came to politics. Fenwick was struck again by the man's mastery of probable moves in the local game. He could see why he'd made Assistant Chief Constable despite a curious lack of similar sparkle in his police work.

'Right.'

The ACC was already turning to the next pressing matter but Fenwick had other business. It had to be handled delicately if he was to keep the Fearnside case open. He turned back as he reached the door. 'Oh, the other complaint, sir.'

'Yes?'

'I mentioned earlier that one needs some more looking into.'

'Really? I'm surprised.'

'Well, as you said, sir, we don't want any loose ends tripping us up, do we?'

'Quite, quite. Well, get on with it. It's your judgement, I'll leave it to you. Just don't disappoint me on this Dell business. It's your top priority, get that clear in your head.'

Fenwick had time for one more interview before he met Cooper at four o'clock back at Division. He looked down his list. It was still too early for Fearnside, the headmaster or Leslie Smith so that left him the other two aspiring models that had gone to the interview with Deborah Fearnside in London.

There was no answer at the first house he visited so when he rang the doorbell of Deirdre Holt, the would-be model who had been eliminated at the final stage, he had little expectation of finding her at home. To his surprise, the door was opened immediately.

'Come in, come in. Thank goodness you've arrived. It's in here.'

He was shown into a elegant cream sitting room by an even more elegant brunette wearing faded 501s, a tight white body-hugging T-shirt and embroidered ethnic waistcoat.

'Over there.' She pointed imperiously towards a large, flat-screen television set, tucked discreetly in one corner.

Fenwick looked down at himself to check that he was wearing his customary suit and realised that the woman had not even looked at him. His satisfaction at finding her at home was immediately undermined by her apparent lack of any observation skills.

'Mrs Holt? It is Mrs Holt, isn't it? I'm afraid you've mistaken me for someone else. I'm Detective Chief Inspector Fenwick, Harlden CID.' He showed his warrant card in confirmation.

'Yes, I'm Deirdre Holt. Who are you then, if you're not here to repair the video?'

Fenwick's spirits sank even further. Not only could he not rely on her powers of observation, the woman obviously didn't even listen.

'Do I look like a TV repair man, Mrs Holt?' He reintroduced himself and the woman ran an appraising eye over him. She made it obvious that she liked what she saw: a tall, slim man, probably in his mid-forties. Were it not for the lines of worry around his eyes and etched from his nose to the outside of a wide, generous mouth, he could have passed for at least five years younger.

There was a latent power about the man that was compelling. She liked strong, physical men, such a contrast to her rather effete solicitor husband. But he was not a happy man, despite the carefully neutral countenance, and he looked at her in a quiet, penetrating way that told of past confrontations taken without compromise.

'No, you don't look like a repair man. Sorry.' She tried a coquettish smile.

'I'm here regarding the disappearance of Deborah Fearnside. I believe you're a friend of hers.'

Her smile faded and a small frown line appeared to mar the smoothness of her forehead.

'Oh, I . . . well, yes I was, *am* a friend of Debbie's. Why? What's happened? Have you found her? Why are you here now?'

She was lying. They hadn't been friends and there was no masking her disquiet at his announcement.

'No, there's no more news, good or bad, but there are some loose ends we're keen to clear up. So I have some questions for you, if you have a few minutes.'

'Yes, of course. Sit down. Would you like a drink, a cup of coffee or something?'

He thought of the untouched mug that would be sitting on his desk. 'A cup of coffee would be lovely, thank you. Black, one sugar.' For the first time he rewarded her with a smile. Fleeting, it didn't reach his eyes, but it warmed his face and made him seem younger.

'I'll only be a few minutes; make yourself comfortable.' She paused at the door. 'But there's one thing I don't understand. Derek, that is Mr Fearnside, told me you don't follow up missing persons cases, not routinely, unless there's something suspicious.'

'That's right, but these questions aren't yet part of any full inquiry. They won't take long.'

Deirdre Holt looked sceptical but said no more.

Over coffee, which was surprisingly good, Fenwick ran through routine questions.

'When was the last time you saw Deborah Fearnside; can you remember?'

'It would have been on the Friday before she disappeared. It was a Monday, wasn't it, that she went off to London? I saw her on the Friday afternoon when she dropped off my two children – we shared the school run, you see.'

'Was there anything unusual about her, would you say?'

'No, not really. Well, she was a bit excited, I suppose.'

'But she didn't say anything to you at all?'

'No. Well, she wouldn't have, would she – not to *me*. Not in the circumstances.'

Mrs Holt met his eyes for the first time since the questioning began. Behind her slightly faded blue gaze there lurked a touch of self-pity and a demand for sympathy.

'What circumstances, Mrs Holt?' Fenwick instinctively softened his voice and his gentle Scots tone became stronger. Mrs Holt knew more than she was admitting to. He wanted to know what and why she was so reticent.

'Well, you see,' she hesitated. 'I went with them – Leslie and Debbie – to the photographers, only I didn't get through.'

'I must say, I'm surprised at that, Mrs Holt, if you don't mind my saying so.'

'Thank you.'

'But, Mrs Holt, there's more you want to tell me, isn't there? You see, I know that's not the only reason Debbie didn't confide in you on that Friday.'

'You know? But how could you? I thought no one did but I suppose . . . oh God, does it all have to come out?' Her eyes filled and she blinked rapidly to preserve her mascara.

'Yes, at least to me, to the police. It may not need to go further, that would depend on how the case evolves, but you must tell me.'

What followed was a sorry little tale of suburban infidelity. Apparently, she and Derek Fearnside had been conducting an on-off affair for about seven years. It had started during Deborah Fearnside's first pregnancy and had then resurfaced on odd occasions ever since. She would make a trip to London and they would meet at Fearnside's company flat.

'Why did the affair start in the first place, Mrs Holt – and why has it continued for so long?'

'Why did it start? Oh the usual reasons. He was frustrated, I was bored silly, we bumped into each other in London one day, went for a drink – which became several – and ended up like a couple of sex-starved teenagers in a hotel near Victoria. Not the most romantic start to an affair!' She had warmed to her tale. It was a relief to talk about it at last and she handled each twist in the story with a raconteur's flair.

'And why did it continue?'

'I'm not sure, really. I think initially because Debbie went right off sex the first time she became pregnant. She wasn't very well and he doesn't like pregnant women anyway. And on my side, well, I enjoy sex, Chief Inspector,' she met his eyes frankly, 'and my husband isn't overly keen. Once a week and he's happy – whereas I'm decidedly not.'

She looked at him sideways from under heavy lashes lowered over her light eyes. Her lips were parted and she licked the tip of her tongue along even white teeth. Despite the obviousness of the practised gesture, Fenwick found it surprisingly alluring. He was conscious of the well-filled, tight white T-shirt and the flesh it hugged snugly. He realised, with a sudden shock, that it had been a long time since he had made love. The agony of Monique's illness and the stress of holding the family together had driven all thoughts of pleasure of any kind from his mind.

Deirdre Holt's open invitation had re-awakened in him needs he had assumed had atrophied along with so much else in his personal life. He was compelled to look away from her for a moment to hide the desire he knew would show in his face. An overdose of hormone surged round his body, reminding him of teenage discomforts long left behind. He made a show of looking back over his notes, appalled at his reaction.

Deirdre Holt, practised and sensitive in her way, was not fooled. She sat down next to him on the settee, placing her hips close enough so that their thighs touched. He noticed she had long, slender legs and that she was wearing perfume – a soft musky scent more suited to warm nights than a cold spring day.

'Chief Inspector, forgive me but I'm a very sensitive person. I can often tell what someone wants without them saying a word. You don't have to speak or do anything. Just sit there and stay still a moment.'

Her fingers stroked the back of his neck gently, enjoying the sharp bristles below his cropped hair. Her nails traced a light, intimate pattern across his skin, brushing his ear lobes, stroking his jaw and chin and now, delicately, beautifully, tracing the outline of his mouth.

Fenwick fought to maintain his concentration and resist the blatant sexuality of the woman. His heart rate increased, blood pounded in his temples, making it difficult for him to think. He became aware of every nerve-ending on his skin and acutely conscious of her touch wherever their bodies met, her fingers, the underside of her arm where it rested on his shoulder, the softness of her breast as she leant against him and the long, hot pressure of her thigh.

He could feel the heat and heaviness in his groin grow. For a few precious seconds he gave in and relished the tight, breathless pleasure as it saturated his body, gloriously reminding him that he was alive and healthy. Then with a fixed determination that had characterised his whole life he rose to his feet and crossed to the picture window on the far side of the room, keeping his back to the woman still seated on the couch. There was a silence.

'I have two final questions, Mrs Holt.' He addressed the small ornamental fish pond and budding lilac beyond. 'When did you last meet Derek Fearnside?'

Behind him he heard a smothered sniff and a soft rustle as she rose, and when he turned it was to find himself alone. With a soft expletive he stalked into the main hall where he heard a faint, muffled sobbing from the back of the house.

Mrs Holt was sitting at the kitchen table, a crumpled tissue clenched against her mouth. Fenwick walked to the sink and poured her a glass of water.

'Thank you.'

'Deirdre, you must answer my questions. What happened in there – forget it.'

'It was pathetic! My God, what must you think of me?'

'I think no less of you, really. Now come on,' he gave her a lopsided smile, 'I'm relying on you.'

'OK.' She cleared her throat and took a sip of water. 'The last time I saw Derek was the week before Debbie went off, on the Tuesday lunchtime. I went up to the flat.'

'Was there anything unusual about that occasion?'

'Not really. It was all rather rushed. Derek had an unexpected meeting in the afternoon and couldn't stay. We didn't discuss Debbie. We never did much.' She wouldn't meet his eye.

'But something was said – then or at an earlier meeting.'

'Derek thought Deborah was acting strangely, volatile. One minute all over him, acting the coy temptress, the next storming off. He thought – well, he thought she might be having an affair.'

'Do you think she was?'

'Yes. She'd had one once before – the worst-kept secret at the time, although I don't think Debbie realised that. She wasn't, isn't, the sort of person you would want to upset or confront, you see.'

'Who was the affair with?'

'Another Derek – Derek Neigby – but he can't be involved in all this. He went off to Saudi and is still there.'

'You said you met before "Debbie went off" – not went missing or disappeared, but "went off". Why did you say that?'

'It's obvious, isn't it? Surely she must have run off with this new man of hers – just escaped.' Sudden concern flooded her face. 'But you don't believe that, do you?'

'I, we, don't deal in belief, Mrs Holt, we work with facts.' Why did he always become pompous when he tried to lie? Even as he said it, he knew she was right. He did believe something had happened to Deborah Fearnside, something dark and grim with no trace of love in it.

In the car, on the way to meet Jamie Smith's headmaster, Fenwick was filled with an unfamiliar regret for the lost opportunity with Deirdre Holt. He regretted it happening, he regretted his response, but worse, he regretted that they had not seen it through. Despite her obviousness and desperation she had woken in him an urgent sexual appetite, all but forgotten in months of stress and tension. In his forties, a father, single to all intents, he had no idea what to do about it.

CHAPTER NINE

Fenwick was late meeting Cooper and after sorting out the paperwork they adjourned to a pub half a mile from Fearnside's house. They compared notes on the day, starting with the Dell, as Fenwick was to visit the ACC later to give him their final report.

Cooper settled one leather-covered elbow on the chair arm and took a good swallow of best bitter. Fenwick didn't rush him, despite his impatience.

'The people on the Dell site aren't talking, and I couldn't get to see the old lady's daughter, she's too upset. But I had more luck at the council site. I spoke to three of Mrs Evans's friends. They started reticent, each one, but when I told them the old lady was dead they couldn't contain themselves. They were furious and not at the police either, but with the son-in-law; said they had advised her not to move, pleaded with the daughter to let her mum stay put. One of them even said she knew the move would kill her, given how poorly she was.

'One of the friends was so mad she gave me a formal statement – and she'd been there when first Degs, and then the daughter, were trying to persuade the old lady to move. And the old lady's doctor has confirmed she had a serious heart condition and that he had advised her not to move. Best yet, he'd visited her the previous afternoon because she was feeling so bad and had advised her to go back home at once. Her son-in-law refused to allow that.'

'Well, that's promising. What about the allegations of

overdue force against Peters and Taylor?'

'It looks like the idiots went into the camp a bit hard. But, we've good evidence to show entry to the site was reasonable, it's just entry into the van that's tricky.'

'We need more, Cooper. You need a statement from Degs's wife. Ask him to the station for an interview and get a woman round there to try and get her to talk. She might be emotional enough still to tell us the truth.'

'I'll use WDC Nightingale, sir. You won't know her, she was only transferred about two months ago, but I hear good things. What about the ACC? He'll need a further briefing, won't he?'

Fenwick passed him a scribbled note he had been sketching during Cooper's account.

'Here's an update for him. Get it typed up, would you? My advice to him will be to make no comment to the press yet. We don't want them hassling the relatives or we'll have no chance with them. We'll drop this in for typing on our way to Fearnside's and I'll pick it up later. Now we need to be off. I'll brief you on what I've found out today on the way.'

Fenwick collected his jacket and turned to the door in one fluid movement. Cooper was left sitting in the cool draught as it swung shut behind him.

That morning, he had been concerned that the driving, tough-minded boss of earlier days might have disappeared for good. As he contemplated the evening, he realised that he was already having to perform the balancing act between conflicting priorities that Fenwick expected from anyone working with him. Something had fired the Chief Inspector and Cooper wondered whether there wouldn't be a point at which he would regret Fenwick's complete return to his obsessive, workaholic state.

On the way to Fearnside's, via Division to deliver the Dell update for typing, Fenwick brought Cooper up to date on his interviews with Holt, the headmaster, O'Brien, and Leslie Smith.

O'Brien had been helpful and friendly, calling his secretary in to confirm his recollection of events and checking back through both their diaries. He was absolutely sure that neither he, nor anybody in his office, had called Leslie Smith to ask her to come in on the day of Deborah Fearnside's disappearance. The previous day had been a Sunday and calls to parents were hardly ever made over the weekend.

He could confirm though, that Mrs Smith had turned up at the school first thing Monday morning and had taken a lot of convincing that she hadn't been summoned. Her little boy, if not a model pupil, was a long way from the worst they had to deal with; there had simply been no reason for them to invite her in. She'd left within minutes.

Fenwick was satisfied that the headmaster and secretary were efficient, sensible people who were telling the truth. If somebody had phoned Leslie Smith the call hadn't come from the school.

The interview with Mrs Smith was far less satisfactory. When he'd arrived at just after three, a neighbour told him she was probably on her way from the shops to pick her children up from school. He'd decided to wait, even though it would make him late for his meeting with Cooper.

The interview had lasted less than half an hour, despite Fenwick's best efforts. She had allowed her children to interrupt constantly, then the dog needed to be let out but its barking meant that five minutes later she was trying to coax it back in. When it eventually bounded in, it upset one of the children's glass of orange juice and a large part of the questioning was spent with Leslie on her hands and knees scrubbing at the sticky orange stain before it ruined the carpet.

Fenwick found her evasive and vague, constantly distracted from his questions and unhelpful in her answers. The noise in her household gave him a headache and in the end he was glad to leave, despite being no further forward from this interview with a key witness.

She saw no connection between Deborah's disappearance and the modelling agency; had been unable to recollect anything about the person who had called purporting to be the headmaster; and could give no explanation as to why her friend had suddenly vanished.

The Fearnside house was illuminated by a modern coach lantern to the side of an oak-panelled door with half-moon window. Early dusk on a greying late spring day had triggered the light sensor prematurely. The yellow bulb glared sickly in the twilight. An echoing yellow flush from the back suggested occupation, otherwise the house stood silent and unwelcoming.

To one side of the path which led in a meagre curve to the entrance, a formal lawn had been allowed to grow too long in the wet chill approach to summer but there were no signs of moss, no dandelion nor daisy had yet had the temerity to take advantage of recent neglect. To the left side of the path, bordering the drive, a long, thin flowerbed was full of a profusion of spring bulbs, their backs broken by wind and rain – late-flowering narcissi, pugnacious muscari fighting for light, tulips, some still in tight bud in the reluctant spring, interspersed with the swelling green seed heads of snowdrops and the spears of blind iris – choked in patches by tufts of rampant wild grass. The garden was silent, the birds having given up on the day and retired to an early rest.

As Fenwick walked to the oak door he saw further signs of recent neglect – a child's toy, still bright, lost under a faded rhododendron, a milk minder encrusted with grit and splashes of stubborn Wealden clay. Ornamental tubs flanking the door had been cleared of their spring glory but lay empty with no promise of a summer show.

A curtain twitched in the front downstairs window, releasing a beam of light, smothered quickly. The door was opened before Cooper had a chance to press the bell and, obviously pre-announced by the message Fenwick had left on the answer-phone, they were motioned into an elegant pale cream hall. From above came the muted sound of children's voices. Fenwick instinctively looked upstairs.

'The children – I thought it best they be out of the way when you arrived.'

'How are they?' Fenwick regretted the question at once.

'How do you think?' Fearnside's tone was contemptuous.

'I'm sorry.' The policeman stifled the desire to tell the man that he understood, to stand for a few minutes in the true comfort of shared pain.

The sitting room was a comfortable size, wider than it was long. The walls were covered in co-ordinating papers of cream sprigged with tiny sage-green abstract flowers. Cooper recognised the design at once, remembered the long hours spent matching joins in paper that stretched, and removing bubbles that appeared magically as soon as one strip was finished. The joins and finish here were perfect and he wondered whether Fearnside had done it himself; if so, he was a perfectionist. It was obviously a family room, slightly worn but clean and gently relaxing, the only jarring note the black television and video stacked prominently in one corner. It had been designed by someone who refused to let wear and tear and practicality start a slide through compromise away from standards of co-ordination and care. It worked.

Fenwick and Cooper seated themselves opposite Derek Fearnside, who continued to stand by the fireplace. Fenwick cleared his throat in the uneasy silence that had developed since their initial greeting. Cooper glanced at his boss, surprised by this unexpected show of nerves.

'Mr Fearnside, thank you for making time to see us.'

'Well, it's about time you lot turned up and took some proper interest in my wife's disappearance.'

Fenwick embarked on the painful process of coaxing Fearnside over old ground, being more tolerant of the criticisms and abuse than he would normally have been. Cooper took copious notes, as always.

'I know that this might be painful, Mr Fearnside, but I want to go back over events in the weeks leading up to your wife's disappearance. You might like to sit down and make yourself comfortable.'

'Comfortable! I haven't had one moment of comfort for the past four and a half weeks, Chief Inspector, so don't start patronising me now.' Fearnside paced the room. 'And I thought that you were here to investigate my complaint, *not* to cross-examine me on facts I have already submitted to your station at least twice.'

'I appreciate your feelings, Mr Fearnside, really, but in order to investigate your complaint I have to review the earlier interviews. It will help me to have a separate discussion with you first.'

Cooper, who had been told on more than one occasion that his face could be read as easily as a book, looked down and busied himself in his notes.

'I see. Well, in that case,' Fearnside sat down, 'let us proceed.'

Fearnside recapped everything he knew about the modelling opportunity and his wife's activities in the weeks leading up to her disappearance.

'Were you in favour of her application?'

'No.'

'Why not?'

'It was a nonsense. A middle-aged woman preening herself in front of the cameras and then, assuming she avoids the indignity of rejection, facing the worse humiliation of having herself ogled by the general public with, one supposes, some prurient interest.'

'I see. So you thought it was beneath her?'

'Yes. Obviously it was, but that was Deborah all over. A strongly warped sense of judgement. Remarkably sensible where the children were concerned but betraying her lower-middle-class origins in all other matters.' Fearnside looked Fenwick in the eye. 'You see you must understand, Chief Inspector, Deborah was, I mean is, a paradoxical woman. A butterfly on the surface, practical about home and family matters, but deep down she was intensely insecure. I think she was desperately unhappy as a teenager.'

Fenwick was surprised by the depths of the man's sensitivity. He hadn't expected it from the reserved, tense individual sitting opposite him. He wondered briefly if Deborah Fearnside had known it was there.

'And so the modelling advertisement presented an opportunity for her to be the butterfly?'

'Yes exactly, Chief Inspector.' Derek Fearnside smiled, a taut grimace. 'Would you like a cup of tea or coffee?'

'Yes, coffee, please. Black, one sugar for me.'

'And a white, two sugars for me, thank you, sir,' added Cooper who, after Fearnside had left, turned to Fenwick and whispered: 'This is a bit slow, isn't it, sir? We're not getting anywhere.'

'Of course we are, Sergeant. We now know several things. Fearnside loves his wife, despite his affair, and he feels helpless and guilty that she's gone off into the unknown whilst he raised disinterest to a fine art. It's obvious he's had nothing to do with his wife's disappearance.'

A rattle of cups and a smothered oath over the sound of a stubbed toe announced Fearnside's return.

He set down a tray on which there were three bone china mugs – white with a fine gold rim, silver teaspoons, a cafetière, brown crystal sugar and warm milk. There were biscuits. The policemen looked surprised.

'Debbie's influence,' he explained.

'This is splendid, Mr Fearnside, thank you. I always enjoy proper coffee.'

'I suggest you wait until you've tried it before you volunteer compliments, Mr Fenwick.' For the second time, Fearnside smiled.

'Right. I'd like to spend a little more time on your wife's background, if I may. It helps to build up a picture of her. When did you meet her?'

Fearnside no longer seemed to find the questioning strange. 'When we were at university – Exeter – I was a year ahead of her and I helped her through her first year. For all her prettiness and glitter, she was a frightened young thing.'

'Frightened? Why?'

'Oh, I suppose because it was all new to her. She had never been away from home; and she was surprised to have made it to university, particularly Exeter. She told me she did nothing but study in her sixth form years and I believed her. She certainly couldn't maintain the pace during her degree. When I graduated, she left – with relief, I think.'

'Why was she so keen on studying and on getting away from home do you think?'

'I don't know, Chief Inspector. In fact, I can remember her mother telling me they'd expected Debbie to marry early, straight from school, but she changed, suddenly.'

'When was this change?'

'I'm not sure but according to her parents, its effect was to turn Debbie from being a happy-go-lucky, uninspired girl into a swot; she passed three A levels much to everyone's surprise. Her parents put it down to her realisation that she had to *work* to get on in life but I'm not so sure. Debbie has always been popular and her mother's stories of her staying away from her circle of friends and studying at home, even during the summer holidays, don't ring true to me.'

'What was she like at university?'

'Initially quiet, withdrawn even. She was timid in company and seemed nervous of being hurt but that only lasted a few months. As she made the acquaintance of new people and joined a couple of clubs, she blossomed. I have to admit I was one of several people who became enchanted by the change in her.'

'Which clubs did she join?'

'Um, drama and a music one – a choir I believe.'

'And her A level subjects?'

'Oh heavens. Let me see if I can remember – English, History and the other was Music, I think.'

'I'd like to come back to the present if I may, Mr Fearnside, and ask you again to try and recall the events in the weeks leading to your wife's disappearance.'

'I'll try. More coffee?' There were no takers. 'As I mentioned, it all started with that wretched advertisement. A gang of them – Debbie and her friends – decided to apply. I think at one point Brian Smith said he would go with them but then they decided there was safety in numbers.'

'How did your wife find out she had been successful?'

'I don't know – a letter, I suppose. I never gave the matter any thought.'

'Did you see the letter?'

'No. I've already told you, I never saw any correspondence. My wife had a file, a blue cardboard folder that she used, and I think everything associated with the affair went in there. I think she took it with her, Chief Inspector. At least I've searched and cannot find it. But, returning to your earlier question, I must say that my overall impression was that most of the arrangements were conducted over the phone.'

Derek Fearnside completed his story of the events leading to his wife's disappearance but nothing was added to the detail already in the files. The names of friends who had joined her at various stages were confirmed and Fenwick prepared to leave.

'You've been most helpful Mr Fearnside. So far as your complaint is concerned, I can assure you that we are and will continue pursuing the limited lines of inquiry open to us. Unfortunately, these are very few and, as you know, an adult missing person case is not normally investigated unless there are suspicious circumstances; even then, they may remain unresolved.'

'I appreciate that, Chief Inspector. But all I want to know is that you will do whatever you can. You see, I know something has happened to my wife. She just wouldn't stay away this long without some contact – nearly five weeks, and it's Katie's birthday soon. She'd never leave the children this long voluntarily. *Please* do what you can. I need to know that everything is being done that could be done.'

'I understand, Mr Fearnside. We'll look into this until we've followed up everything – even if we end up with dead ends.'

'Thank you, Chief Inspector, thank you. For some reason I trust you – you seem to understand what I'm going through.' He paused and thought for a long moment on the doorstep. 'I won't be pursuing the complaint now that I know you're on the case – but keep me informed, won't you?'

As Fenwick and Cooper made their way down a now darkened path, they both instinctively looked back beyond the dim glow of the light sensor. In the brighter light through the half-glazed door, they could make out the silhouette of Derek Fearnside as he watched them walk away.

CHAPTER TEN

The rented house was simple yet comfortable, sandwiched into a mews block in a fashionable but private part of the city. The white-painted front door at the top of a set of rising steps opened into a narrow marble-tiled hall, giving access to the downstairs rooms and stairs to the upper level. Two reception rooms, tastefully if clinically furnished, were ranged on opposite sides of the hall. At the end of this narrow passage, decorated with mirrors to create an illusion of breadth, was the kitchen, fitted out in black, white and stainless steel, and every appliance possible. A small cloakroom had been tucked under the stairs.

Upstairs, the whole of the front of the house was taken up with the master bedroom and, running back from this, a dressing room and en suite bathroom. A boxroom with ladder access to a small loft overlooked a paved square at the back of the house. All the furnishings were distinctly male, tasteful but impersonal. There were no photographs, records or CDs, no ornaments. The only art on the walls had obviously been placed there by the interior designer. The whole house was scrupulously clean, as if someone obsessively polished and removed all signs of occupation every day, which they did.

A single light was on in the study-dining room to the left of the front door. Inside, a man stood looking down at a large-scale Ordnance Survey map into which small coloured pins had been stuck, spearing the paper and penetrating the green baize board underneath. The man stared intently at a single orange pinhead and then opened a street map, the cover of which read 'Harlden and Surrounding District'.

From the dense grid of streets and grey hatching for houses it appeared that Harlden was a sprawling dormitory town with little remaining of the sensible market village it had been until it was discovered between the World Wars. The momentum of urbanisation had been so great that it had sprawled to absorb surrounding villages in successive waves. Even now, pseudo-pods of development were sketched in on the map, proof of the failure of local residents to preserve Green Belt and local identity. Belated attempts at character had involved intense planting of trees and shrubs in geometric lines along the new roads. At least the new-home dwellers appreciated them.

It was along several of these recently tree-lined roads that the man started to trace a route in green highlighter pen. It ran virtually straight west, from a grey shaded block marked 'Downland Comprehensive School' to a perimeter bypass. Just before the green line crossed this road it dog-legged north, ending in a small red circle on the map. The route resembled a long, inverted tick, which was somehow appropriate as it traced the daily path of school teacher Miss Katherine Johnstone.

His extremely unwilling but reliable source had provided enough details for him to find Miss Johnstone easily. The far more complicated task of tracking her and planning her death was taking more time. Preparations had so far consumed most of the spring and he was concerned now to complete the job quickly before school closed for the long summer holidays when her whereabouts would become less predictable.

So far, the facts he had gathered from his meticulous surveillance had revealed a remarkably straightforward and self-contained life. Kate Johnstone, as she was known, was responsible for the fourth year at Downland Comprehensive School. In addition to taking various mathematics classes, she helped to run the school orchestra and the surprisingly good sixth form choir. She was friends with the Head of Music, Mrs Judith Chase, but otherwise appeared to have few close acquaintances.

The extra-curricular activities required her to work late at the school on Tuesday and Thursday evenings. On Thursdays she also took responsibility for locking the music rooms. These were housed in a brick-built block, separate from the main school at the back of the original school hall, now only used for aerobics, self-defence classes and other fiercely twentieth-century activities that would have bemused the founding board of governors.

He had found the music rooms laughably insecure and a possible fire hazard. There was a steep flight of steps immediately inside the single door to the block, leading to three rooms on the first floor, large enough for choir or chamber orchestra practice and also used for music lessons for individual pupils.

On the ground floor there were two rooms. To the right of the entrance, the piano room housed a surprisingly good baby grand, a bequest from one of the founding governors. On the left, incongruously, was a changing room used by the various aerobics and other sports classes, which had about it the unwholesome odour of school changing rooms everywhere – a potent combination reminiscent of damp flannels, old socks and stale tinned tomato soup. On damp or airless days the unpleasant but compelling smell pervaded the music room – forcing a choice between fresh but cold air or a warm fug.

At times, particularly after the judo class, the smell was so bad that Miss Johnstone (who was blessed, or as it turned out cursed, with an excellent sense of smell) had taken to leaving deodorant sticks and aerosols on the benches. The gentle hint went completely unnoticed by youths who were still several years away from developing any sensitivity to their own body odour.

On leaving the music rooms, Kate Johnstone took a fifteen-minute walk home to number 1 Hedgefield, a house on the perimeter of an early eighties in-fill development between the town bypass and the original London road.

All of the routines of her life were known to the man patiently stalking her. The problem now facing him was where and when to kill her. As his pen traced her regular route on the map, his mind ran sequential pictures. He had already decided he should act at the end of the school day, as this would both delay realisation that she was missing and provide him with an opportunity to search her house. For what, he wasn't sure. Perhaps she might have further information which would confirm the guilt of his final victims, or provide more detail of the original tragedy.

Thursday looked the most sensible day. She was likely to be the last person at the school apart from the caretaker, who rarely left his snug next to the boiler room. On Thursdays, she had responsibility for locking and checking the music-room windows and door. Unless she stayed to play the baby grand piano, which she had done twice since he had started watching her, she locked up at about quarter to six, a full hour and a half after the main school had finished. Netball practice was already over and there was no cricket on Thursdays.

From painstaking observation he knew that her departure would be signalled by the lights going off on the top floor. Even approaching summer, the small windows and overhanging trees, which clustered thickly to the back and sides of the hall, made electric light essential for reading music.

Waiting deep within the trees he had heard her clump down the steep wooden stairs in her fashionable but impractical heeled court shoes, and then pause as she checked the rooms downstairs before locking the door. She always stooped to lock the door, peering into the shadowy darkness around the lock. On the threshold, she would pause, slip out of her heels and put on sensible shoes for the fifteen-minute walk home, placing the other pair in a school shoe bag.

Miss Johnstone then walked down a narrow, overhung path between bushes until she reached the side of the school car park. Cutting across the deserted square of tarmac, she would leave the school by the main entrance, placed directly to the rear of the school grounds. It was in this short walk across school grounds that she occasionally encountered the caretaker, though they rarely exchanged more than a few words before both going separate ways.

Miss Johnstone then turned left along the London Road,

crossed at the first set of lights opposite the White Lion public house and made her way due north along Elm Drive, continuing straight on when it became Copse Lane. The only variation in her otherwise predictable routine occurred at the local mini-market, the Handishopper. Sometimes she would pop in and emerge ten minutes later with a thin plastic bag containing several square-shaped tins. There was no pattern to her visits to the Handishopper and this element of her routine remained a mystery to her silent watcher.

He had followed her at a careful distance along Copse Lane. As one walked further north the buzz from the bypass increased until it detached itself from the middle distance and assumed a constant, full-throttled whine. The noise stopped just short of oppressive for visitors, and residents became inured within days of arrival. A close-boarded fence and an unbroken line of sturdy conifers screened the view of the road and cut down most of the fumes.

Copse Lane stopped abruptly in a T-junction 150 yards from the bypass. To the right lay Hedgefield and the house of Miss Johnstone, spinster of this parish, mathematics mistress of Downside Comprehensive School and intended murder victim.

Few places along her route presented opportunities for an unnoticed murder, and the assassin concluded that only her house or place of work were realistic options. This was unfortunate as he would have to work hard to establish a randomness for the killing with no suggestion of premeditation.

Now he removed a hand-drawn sketch from a buff folder, prepared during one of his early visits to the school's music rooms, pacing out internal and external distances whilst the choir and orchestra practised above. He knew every foot of the school grounds and could, if necessary, have manoeuvred his way through the shambles of tracks and concrete paths in total darkness. Perfect planning: the essential habits didn't leave him even though he felt isolated without the usual company of team support. He had found operating as a single-man unit over the past three months irksome and inefficient. To his great surprise he was also lonely; he missed the teamwork. Years of training and an inner self-sufficiency sustained him but he had started to look forward to the completion of his self-imposed task and to this artificial isolation.

He now knew the names of his intended targets. One had been dealt with, perhaps the least guilty of the quartet. He had found it difficult at the end to complete the job, an unexpected compassion confusing his hands. But her confession had confirmed the guilt of the other three; he couldn't yet be sure which of them held *ultimate* responsibility but his instinct told him his next victim was not the main one – had perhaps only performed a minor role. Nevertheless, she owed him a life and he was about to call in the debt.

After studying his plan of the school, he concluded that the music room offered neutral territory, the best prospect for a murder which could remain undiscovered for many hours. It was private, he knew it better than her home and there would be more opportunity to make it appear a random killing. The location decided, he finally sat down to complete the detail of his plan.

PART THREE

KYRIE

Kyrie eleison.
Christe eleison.
Kyrie eleison.

Lord have mercy on us.
Christ have mercy on us.
Lord have mercy on us.

CHAPTER ELEVEN

Kate was generally content with her life. At thirty-four, she had a responsible and still enjoyable job which allowed her to indulge in her three great passions – music, gardening and cats. She cared for four of the latter, all rescued from miserable past lives by the Cat Protection League, of which she was a dedicated supporter. The tabby tom was the oldest and, had she admitted to such inequality, her favourite. Blind in one eye, with virtually all his right ear missing, he was the man about her house and acted with proprietorial interest in the unfolding of all its affairs. Next in age was a blue Siamese cross, intelligent, suspicious, affectionate; and then there were the twins – brother and sister tortoiseshells with identical markings.

All had a fierce attachment to their mistress and an ingrained mistrust in the rest of humanity. They were allowed free rein of the house but instinctively obeyed the expected rules of behaviour in the garden, much to the annoyance of Miss Johnstone's neighbours. Her garden was special and the cats sensed that should they set paws in its deep, immaculate, herbaceous borders, they could jeopardise their comfortable shelter.

Although Kate could see the flow of constant traffic from her upstairs windows, there were compensations in being the end house with a good stout fence to screen the street and a large triangular garden, which in the early summer was her particular delight.

She shared a stout party wall with her neighbours at number

3, a newly married couple. Friendly and generally perfect neighbours they would have been distressed, not to say embarrassed, to know that shortly after they had moved in, Miss Johnstone had changed bedrooms, switching to the smaller one at the back of the house to escape the nocturnal (and occasionally diurnal) groans, sighs and laughs of passion that penetrated her house, threatening to spoil her carefully secured state of contentment. Miss Johnstone considered their activities rather excessive but as a member of a relatively rare species – an unmarried virgin in her thirties – she was acutely aware of her ignorance of the mysteries on the other side of the wall.

On June 7th, Kate was up shortly after dawn, eager to spend at least an hour in the garden before school. She had chosen to work among a massed drift of lupins and delphiniums that ranged against the west-facing fence – dead-heading, staking and squeezing to death the greenfly that were infesting the lupins this year. The dew washed her long bare calves and soaked her canvas shoes as she stepped delicately among Butterball delphiniums, planted randomly between old favourites of Mullion and Pink Sensation. The rich creaminess of the Butterball was working well among the blues, mauves and pinks. Along the front of the border she had let candytuft and cornflowers self-set, beside the gently fading blues and pinks of the forget-me-nots. She stepped among them carefully, avoiding the mists of flowers and the tight green shoots of sweet william and physostegia, that promised a continuing show for the summer.

The weather was beautiful, the sun already glaringly hot on the south-facing beds, leaving her working space to the west of the house in cooler dewy shade. She was dressed in her normal summer gardening clothes – cut-off jeans, an old cotton shirt and professional, thorn-resistant gardening gloves. Her open, round face was free of make-up and short golden-red waves of hair were pushed back out of her eyes with an Alice band. Her pupils would have been unlikely to recognise their orderly, prim maths teacher in the nimble and youthful woman who stooped and bent with a graceful monotony among her flowers.

Kate was moving fast to stake the growing stems firmly in an attempt to beat a threatening change of weather, forecast for later in the week. The promised rains and strong winds could ruin her display – snapping the heavy, flower-rich stems, some over six foot, and breaking the tender plants beneath. She took off her glove and bent to crush a glistening new leaf of bee balm, rubbing her stained fingers to release the heady scent that would drench this corner of the garden in months to come.

It was time for breakfast. Today, she decided, it was warm enough to eat outside, sitting on the south-facing cast-iron bench she had tucked into a small paved area amid the borders, next to a green-painted ornate iron table. The cats were already stretched on the warming metal and, for only the third time that year, she felt she could join them in shirt sleeves with no risk of a chill.

The breakfast tea was strong and refreshing, the sun hot on her face. Bees were already hurrying among the promiscuous blossom, one cat lay curled up against her, snoring gently. The others had found sun or shade according to their taste around her now naked feet. In the distance, the hum from the bypass provided a gentle counterpoint to the purring and the buzzing. As one of the twins toyed with a spring of unripe green-grey lavender in a terracotta pot by Kate's side, the spicy scent wafted up and over her. She was, she reflected, incredibly fortunate. She may be single and childless – the last hurt more than the first – but she had so much, and whilst contentment rather than happiness could best be used to describe her normal state of mind there were moments, such as that early morning, when she would change nothing. She was healthy, comfortably established, had loving parents and a sister who was also one of her best friends. She had interests that absorbed her, hobbies that thrilled her and faithful companions. She could not, all things considered, complain.

Katherine offered up her normal morning prayers and thanked God for all he had given to her and, most of all, for her recent renewal of faith. She viewed all of life's pleasures and good fortunes as God's gift and knew herself to be well blessed.

As she worked mentally through her daily prayers – the Lord's prayer, prayers of thanks, requests for the protection of her family and friends and the hope for guidance during the day – she came finally to her prayer for forgiveness.

'Dear Lord,' she prayed, her heart contracting painfully in her chest, 'please forgive me. Do not let me forget what I have done, let remembrance serve as my penance and a constant warning of my capacity for sin.' Her eyes as she opened them were wet, the view of her glorious garden blurred as she looked around. It was always worst in June, this sense of guilt, of not deserving any of her happiness when others – one in particular – had nothing.

In an outward demonstration of contrition she fell to her knees and rested her head on her hands against the edge of the table. 'Please, God. Please forgive me for what I have done. Please let there be no retribution. I do earnestly repent what I have done and I know I do not deserve my current happiness. But please, dear God, do not take it away from me. Do not punish me.'

In the fragrant semi-silence, as the sun fell on the back of her bowed neck and a cat's tail caressed her calves, Katherine gradually felt the love of God surround her once again, and His compassion enter her bruised heart. After long moments the cold of the flags penetrated her bones, making her alert to the passing time. Laughing rather self-consciously at herself she walked, refreshed and reassured into the house, ready to start the week.

By Tuesday evening, Katherine's pangs of conscience had retreated in the face of glorious news. That day, in the teachers' common room, she had received the call she had been waiting for. Octavia Anderson, an old school friend, had telephoned to confirm that she would be prepared to take the soprano lead in the County Youth Choir's performance of Verdi's *Requiem*. As one of the organisers of the autumn performance, Miss Johnstone had mentioned to the committee that she might just be able to secure Octavia's services as they were old friends but until the call came she hadn't allowed herself to believe it could be true.

Octavia Anderson was, belatedly, becoming a well-known opera singer, working her way slowly but consistently into the centre of attention as a potential new star. Strangely beautiful, and with a powerful soprano voice that was maturing as she aged, she was the local celebrity who had attended Downside School. As a pupil she had been awarded the De Weir scholarship which took her, via the Royal Academy, into the chorus first of the Welsh National Opera and then on to some junior roles. But her appearance and voice were suited to the heavier classics and she had to bide her time, waiting for the right opportunity to use the advantage of experience. About four years previously she had surprised audiences and critics alike when she had stepped in, as understudy, to perform Tosca when the performer slipped and broke her wrist during the battlements scene on the first night. Octavia had taken on the role with assurance and skill, and although not yet thirty, her voice had been sufficiently developed to prompt several of the critics to mark her as 'someone to watch.'

Since her Tosca understudy days, she had been given more prominent roles in her own right, working hard, touring the world receiving consistently improving reviews. For her to agree to perform in a county programme was a real coup for Kate and she couldn't believe her good fortune.

As luck would have it, Judith Chase, the Head of Music, had been in the common room after the call came through and the two of them had disappeared for a celebratory drink at the White Lion at lunchtime. This had proved a difficult moment for sixth former Melanie White, who was standing in the saloon bar with her biker boyfriend, Ron, as Miss Johnstone and Mrs Chase ordered their drinks in the lounge bar. She had to spend the next forty minutes standing out of sight round the corner, perilously close to the dart board.

Katherine stopped at the local Handishopper on her way home after choir practice. It was customary for her to do this for one of two reasons: either because she had had a particularly good day, in which case she gave herself a treat to make it even better, or because it had been a particularly bad day, when she treated herself anyway by way of compensation. Today it was obvious to Sandy, who served on the checkout in the evenings, that Miss Johnstone had had an excellent day.

'Good day then, Miss Johnstone?' said Sandy, who had left Downside at sixteen with three GCSEs – a failure for the school, which had a good academic record, but an extraordinary success for Sandy.

'Yes, Sandy, excellent. You'll never guess what, but Octavia Anderson has agreed to come and take the soprano part in our performance of Verdi's *Requiem*.'

Sandy looked blank; she had not been gifted with an ear for music.

'You know, the opera singer who used to go to Downside School, in my year as it happens.'

'Oh yeah! I think I remember now – we did something on her in music when I was at school. That's good then, innit?'

'It's excellent, Sandy. Couldn't be better – and a cause for celebration. Now, do you have the latest delivery of Sheba in yet?' This was the cats' favourite food and Miss Johnstone had seen the new flavour advertised at the weekend. A generous and good-hearted woman, she wouldn't have dreamt of indulging on her own without the cats benefiting too.

'Ooh. I'm not sure, miss. I'll go check, boss'll know.'

Whilst Sandy went off to investigate, Miss Johnstone searched the shelves for inspiration for her own indulgence. She was tempted by the luxury ice creams but the weather was already changing and the thought of the chilled dessert made her shiver. In the end, she bought a small rump steak, a mixed green salad, a pre-packed slice of lemon cheesecake and as decent a bottle of claret as the shelves would furnish. To finish off, she picked up a box of shell-shaped pralines and placed them on top of the basket. By this time Sandy had returned.

'No luck, I'm afraid, but we're promised some Thursday.'

Miss Johnstone decided that the cats could wait until Thursday to share in her good fortune.

'I'll pick them up Thursday evening then, Sandy. Could you be sure to have some put by for me – say half a dozen packs? I don't want to disappoint them.'

'Rightyera, then, miss. I'll do that. That'll be twelve pounds sixty-two pence, please. Looks quite a treat!'

Miss Johnstone said goodbye to Sandy, confident that the cats' food would be there for her later. She may not have been a bright girl but Sandy was diligent and thoughtful and would not disappoint. As Miss Johnstone left the shop and walked along Copse Lane, she was shocked to see Melanie White on the back of a large black motorbike.

By Wednesday, the weather had changed completely and raincoats and jumpers were pressed into service by pupils and teachers alike. As she left the staff room after the last period, not even the weather and the fact that she could do little in her garden could dampen her spirits. A letter from Octavia was due any day confirming her commitment to sing and there was a meeting of the Organising Committee that night. Downside School had significant influence in local musical events and in the annual cathedral concerts of the county.

The committee meeting, held at the school, went on until nearly 7.00 p.m. This year, given the reputation of the soprano, the organisers were confident of attracting other excellent soloists and part of the reason for the long meeting had been a discussion on whether the other soloists should be 'upgraded'. The matter remained unresolved, as was the idea of having the performance recorded, which Kate Johnstone agreed to pursue with Octavia Anderson.

CHAPTER TWELVE

The storm broke during Thursday. By mid-afternoon Kate was regretting her decision to ignore the early signs of a chill that morning and come to school. She should have stayed at home and nursed her cold but the thought of choir practice spurred her on. Now in her final lesson, the same thought prevented her giving in and returning home at once.

At the end of class Kate hurried to the common room in search of the various remnants of cold remedies that usually haunted the coffee station along with herbal tea bags, branded sweeteners and indigestion tablets. She had just about given up hope when she spotted a sachet of lemon cold relief half hidden by a tray. It's my lucky day after all, she thought, remembering at the same time that she had to stop later and pick up the cat food.

'Kate, you look awful; what are you doing still here?' Robbie, the deputy head, entered the room with a stack of exercise books.

'Oh, dodn't,' she sniffed, 'I've god de choir todnight.'

'Well, let Judith do it, she can cope. Go home and look after yourself.'

'Perhaps I will.' Katherine wandered over to the large cork board to which were pinned notices to members of staff and any personal messages. There was one for her, in Judith Chase's handwriting. *Kate, sorry*, it read. *I've had to go home. I've got a stinking cold – can't stop sneezing. I know you'll be able to cope. See you tomorrow (I hope). Judith.*

'Oh no, Judith's god it doo. I'll have do go.' Kate's shoulders sagged.

'Never mind. Make it a short one, then go home and wrap up. See you tomorrow – I hope.'

His words echoed those in the note. Kate shuddered involuntarily. Outside the rain lashed the windows, splattering broken twigs with fragile new leaves against the glass, leaving them there marooned until the next gust whipped them away. No piano playing tonight!

The choir clattered off early, before 5.30 p.m., leaving the school deserted except for Miss Johnstone and the caretaker. In the music block Kate diligently collected and stacked the music and checked that all the windows were secure. They were all locked upstairs and she switched off the lights. From the semi-darkness of the upstairs room she glanced down on the shrubs that were being tormented by the storm winds. It was amazing, she thought, how, as soon as you looked at shadows, they took on real shapes. There, out in the bushes, that could be the shape of head and shoulders behind the nearer rhododendron, losing the last of its fading flowers to the wind. The more she looked, the more she became convinced it *was* a person, a man, hiding in the bushes, waiting for her. She was not a fanciful woman but the thought refused to leave her mind and began to assume the weight of reality.

She froze perfectly still and stared at the spot with eyes that dried as she tried not to blink. The shadow didn't move. It became neither more nor less of a man. In irritation she blinked and shook her head. When she looked again it had gone.

'Stupid woman,' she said out loud. 'Just get home and get to bed.' She walked boldly down the steep wooden steps, her high heels clattering on the bare boards. At the bottom she checked first on the changing room, making sure that the door to the old assembly hall was locked. It was, the key sitting securely on a peg by the side of the door. She walked back into the piano room, noticing a chill draft as she did so. Not bothering to switch on the light she crossed to the small window and found it ajar. Strange. Kate closed it firmly and secured the latch.

Finally, she walked back to the foot of the stairs, head, neck and shoulders aching with cold. She sneezed twice, violently, jarring her whole body. Sluggishly she changed into her walking shoes and put her smart courts into a shoe bag. Finally, stepping outside, she made sure she had her umbrella ready and sorted out the music-room keys.

Outside in the holly bush by the door he waited. Dressed completely in black, even to blacking around his eyes, he blended totally into the shadow. There had been a moment, minutes before, when he was sure she had seen him. He had frozen as her pale face seemed to stare right at him from the upstairs window. Then she had looked away and he had taken that moment to flit to the next dark pool of cover. Now he waited calm but alert, poised for action, the charge of adrenalin focused and controlled.

He had decided on a simple plan: kill her on the threshold of the door and drag her inside, locking the door after her. The weather was in his favour. He had been prepared to knock out the caretaker during his rounds, to be sure of no interruptions but when he had checked on the old man he had found him wrapped up snugly in his den with a Thermos and radio, obviously settled for the evening. There was no one else around.

He heard her steps on the stairs and mentally followed her through the downstairs rooms. He had hoped she would not play the piano tonight; he was eager for the deed to be done. His hands would suffice, they were his deadliest weapon. He had a knife for backup, just in case, but he doubted it would be necessary. He would break her neck with one simple blow; the spinal column would snap, and she would die without uttering a sound. Then he would do what was necessary to make this look like a random robbery and sexual assault gone wrong, perhaps perpetrated by an addict. Remembering this detail, he took the syringe out of his pocket and dropped it to the ground beside his feet.

The lights went off and he heard her sneeze, twice. He tensed, ready for action.

Kate walked out of the doorway and bent down to the lock. As she did so, she felt rather than heard a rushing noise behind her, and at exactly the same moment, was taken by a huge sneeze that rocked her body, nearly doubling her in two. In a nightmare of horror and confusion, the sneeze took shape, an arm went about her middle, another missed her neck by inches as her head jerked in the sneeze. She couldn't understand what was happening to her as a heavy weight crushed into her back, knocking her into the doorframe and jerking the door open. Her mind refused to work, numbed in terror and shock, but a basic primitive instinct urged through every nerve and muscle. On her knees on the muddy step she remembered her umbrella, still in her hand.

Lashing out and back, a lucky blow caught the man in the groin and she managed to tear herself away from his grasp. He kicked out at her, missing her head but catching her hand against the stone of the step. She heard the crack of bones but no sense of pain penetrated her adrenalin-soaked mind.

Whimpering she shuffled, half crouching, half crawling, into the changing room. She remembered the key on the nail by the door to the assembly hall and lurched forward, arm outstretched, to find it and so open up a possible escape into the room beyond. Kate had forgotten her shattered hand. As she tried to close her fingers around the key, pain spurted up her arm, setting her shoulder on fire, breaking her momentum. For a precious second, she fought down the sickness in her throat and fumbled for the key with her left hand. Just as her fingers closed on the cold metal he rammed into her from behind, throwing her on to the floor, bruising her knees hard on the concrete.

She tried to hide under the slatted benches, among the discarded socks and dirty boots, but he grabbed her ankle and yanked her back into the middle of the room. She struggled harder, realising now that she was fighting for her life. She twisted away from him, trying to break his grip on her ankle and grab hold of a bench, anything that might become a weapon.

The bench was bolted to the floor, immovable. Kate hung on to the iron frame, jerking her leg in a last desperate attempt to rid herself of his fixed hold on her ankle. It was useless: he was impossibly strong. He ignored all her struggles and silently flipped her on to her back on the cold concrete floor. There, exposed and looking up into a wild, inhuman face she finally started to scream. He put his hand over her mouth and forced her head back. All that she saw of the blade was a thin flash from the corner of her eye as it fell down in a tight arc. Warmth flooded her body, then an icy chill.

He held her tight as her screams became a low gurgle and she started to drown in her own blood. Her body went into spasms, arms and legs thrashing around. He held on to her mouth and head, avoiding the flailing limbs.

As her consciousness faded, she found herself praying, asking God why. Then, he bent and whispered a name into her dying ear and she knew that retribution had come.

CHAPTER THIRTEEN

At the Handishopper, Sandy became increasingly concerned about Miss Johnstone. The half-dozen cans of cat food were there, ready and waiting, but by six o'clock, her customer still hadn't arrived to collect them. In her slow and steady way Sandy knew that something had to be wrong. It was completely out of character for her ex-teacher to forget an arrangement or go back on plans she had made, and the unlikelihood became unthinkable where her cats were concerned! Sandy consulted her boss, the store manager, but he dismissed her fears, assuming that the teacher had been given a lift home from school because of the bad weather. He was irritable and short with Sandy, miserable at the unseasonally low level of takings and prepared to blame anything on the appalling storm.

In the White Lion, Ron, Melanie White's boyfriend, was becoming increasingly amorous. The heated couple only had one problem, where to go to allow their hormones full rein.

'You must know somewhere, Mel. This is ridiculous, I can't go home like this.'

'What about your mum and dad's? That's been OK before.'

'Yeah, but my brother's home tonight, with his football mates. There won't be a moment's peace there.'

'Well, where else can we go? All our usual places will be no good in this rain.'

'That's what I was asking you, you daft cow. I'm randy as hell and I can't take another night of not doing it just because the bloody weather's bad.' To prove his point, he grabbed her hand, which was resting on his knee, and thrust it against his swollen crotch, painfully constrained by his skin-tight jeans. Melanie, who still thought of herself as a good girl really, looked around quickly; she was almost sure nobody had seen them.

Withdrawing her hand she responded with an acerbity unusual in their relationship. 'Well, I *can't* think of anywhere just now. Why don't you get us another drink and cool down?'

'I'm not walking over to the bar like this. You go, it's your round anyway.'

Handing over the last of her dinner money in exchange for a pint of best and a large vodka and tonic, Melanie tried hard to put the open downstairs window of the music room out of her mind. It had seemed such a clever idea a few hours ago when she had anticipated the very scene that had just been played out under the disinterested but observing eyes of the Thursday night regulars. There was somewhere dry they could go but she wasn't really in the mood any longer. She was disappointed in Ron now that the macho mystique had worn off and she felt used, abused and decidedly unsexy.

In the darkened changing room, he glanced at his watch; 18.00. Still early, with plenty of time ahead of him to make the killing appear motivated by robbery and sex in no particular order. He had not enjoyed the killing, he rarely did, but it was necessary and she had deserved it. At the end, as he had whispered those words in her ear, he had seen her eyes focus and try to find his. There had been an acknowledgement in her gaze. She had accepted his violence for what it was, delayed execution for past crimes.

Now he was faced with the need to desecrate her body and he resented it. She didn't deserve that. Still, he worked methodically and silently to rip open her clothes with his knife. No point in mutilation – he knew that forensics would realise the injuries had taken place after death and he wanted to appear an accidental killer, desperate for money and sexual gratification.

He sliced her skirt away and inserted his knife beneath the elasticated bands of her tights and knickers. There was a lot of blood on the blade. He ripped them, leaving the ragged material lying on her naked stomach, her pubic hair curling round the folds. From the small knapsack on his back he took out a cigarette packet, opened it and withdrew a used condom, gathered from a local lovers' lane that morning. If they did more than routine tests, they would discover the age of semen inside but he doubted they would. They would be more interested in determining blood group and any other possible matching from the sample. He squeezed the contents over her bare thighs fastidiously.

There was blood everywhere in the room. In her death throes she had spattered the floor, benches, walls, even the ceiling, a bright arterial red. He was covered too, but he had dressed to avoid leaving any traces. When he had finished he would peel off the black latex suit he was wearing and put on the compact woollen jumper and soft jacket from his pack. The overshoes would come off as well, leaving trainers underneath. It was best to play safe. Even though he was completely covered from hood to overshoes, he knew that there would be a slight risk of contamination to his normal clothes as he changed and they would be burnt later along with the rest of the kit.

His final task before leaving was to rifle her handbag; he took purse, credit cards and keys, of which only the latter were of any value to him. He intended to go straight to her house once he had changed to search for further evidence from the past. It was unlikely he would find anything but the scent of the chase was on him so strongly now that he couldn't turn away from any opportunity to find out more.

Outside the gale continued, which was in his favour. Few would venture out on an evening like this. Already, the sky was darkening, hours before sunset, and the sheets of rain reduced visibility to almost zero. If he changed outside, as had been his original intention, he would be soaked to the skin before he could put on his cyclist's cape and hood. So he peeled off his blood-coated latex suit in the tiny vestibule at the bottom of the stairs, starting with the hood. He rolled it back and down on itself, peeling the Velcro fastenings at the sides, careful to avoid spattering the blood more than was necessary. Keeping the skin-tight black gloves on, he bundled the suit and overshoes into a plain plastic bag. Then he peeled off the gloves, placed them on top of the bundle and put the whole lot into a bin liner; underneath his hands were sheathed in another pair of latex gloves, preventing any trace of fingerprints.

He felt bitterly cold out of his suit and shivered involuntarily as he extracted his clothes and a bright yellow cycling hood and cape from his rucksack. Suitably dressed, he walked out of the music block, carefully pulling the door to behind him. Too late he remembered the music-room keys. The lock was empty; they were nowhere on the ground. She must have grasped them reflexively when she ran. He couldn't go back into the slaughter room now. The door would have to be left unlocked. His bike, a sleek racer bought second-hand two weeks before, was hidden in the shrubbery. In moments he was cycling through the school gates and out on to London Road. It was almost deserted. Ahead a 250cc Honda roared out of the car park of the White Lion pub. It swerved past him as he turned right, soaking him with a wave of water. He ignored it, which was to be his second mistake of the night.

Six minutes later he was cycling down Hedgefield. He scanned the roads and paths and checked the windows of the next-door houses. Nobody was around and the windows were blank, sightless eyes. He turned round slowly and cycled up the path to the front door of number 1. He used her Yale key to open the door. There was nowhere to hide the bike so he wheeled it through the house and into the kitchen. The house was silent at first but then from behind him he heard a scratching and high-pitched crying. His cleaned knife was out of the sleeve sheath in a flash and he sank into a crouch. The lounge door nudged open, and he tensed for attack. A tiny brown and black face peeked round, nine inches from the floor, to be followed quickly by two others. The cats regarded him suspiciously, backing away with a low hiss at the back of their throats.

The intruder laughed softly, a surprisingly normal sound in the silence of the house. 'Go away,' he whispered to them. 'I'm busy and I don't have time for you.' They were only the second set of words he had spoken out loud for three days and he was surprised at how rusty his voice had become. Pushing carefully past the cats he looked around the lounge for likely places of interest. Nothing looked hopeful. It took less than five minutes to rifle through the small chest of drawers in the corner without success. He pocketed a few small valuables automatically just to confuse the police. There was a partly written letter on a desk under the window with a rough draft to its side. He noticed the addressee's name with interest and picked the papers up, tucking them into his pocket for later scrutiny.

The dining room contained nothing of interest but as he walked into the hall he noticed the day's post lying on the carpet. He bent down and picked it up, looking at each item quickly. There was an expensive hand-written envelope among them, with writing that pulled at his memory. It was a beautiful italic script, every letter perfect and he had seen it before. The envelope was only lightly sealed and he pulled it open, taking out the single sheet of creamy vellum inside. He read the letter slowly once, then again. He dropped everything else back on the floor but put the letter in his pocket alongside the other papers.

There were two bedrooms upstairs. One was obviously a large guest room with a double bed, wardrobe and bedside table. It held nothing worthy of his attention. Her small bedroom looked out over the back of the house and was decorated in quiet good taste. There were two built-in wardrobes, a chest of drawers with a mirror on top, a bedside table and a small covered table in the far corner with a plant on it. There was no chair; she must have been in the habit of doing her hair and make-up whilst standing.

His hopes rose as he looked around the room. There would be something here; this was the heart of her house. He started on the chest of drawers, working methodically from the bottom up; there was nothing to see beyond the usual women's clothes.

He tried the bedside table drawer – nothing except a well-thumbed Bible and an erotic book on Parisian society in the 1920s. A search under the pillows revealed a used handkerchief and a nightie; the wardrobes – neat and tidy, clothes arranged by colour and type – held no secrets. He started to become annoyed, he felt the woman was toying with him from beyond his reach. There had to be something, his instinct was usually so accurate.

His fist slammed into the cupboard top – startling a large ginger tomcat from behind the long curtains by the radiator. Seeing a stranger barring his way to the door, the angry feline slid under the bedspread that fell to the floor. The man started to turn, to resume his search, and then stopped halfway. Under the bed – that would be a logical place to hide secrets.

He lifted the bedspread and peered under the springs. There, in the middle was an old dusty brown suitcase. He reached in – and was rewarded by ten pounds of angry cat attacking his hand, running up his arm and taking a side swipe at his face. The claws connected and the man experienced a burning pain as three parallel gouges were ripped from his cheek and chin. He swore but the cat was gone in an instant and he was left cursing the animal for the mess it had made of his hand and face. His fight with the woman had left him unscathed but now the bloody animal had marked him for the world to see. He checked the mirror. He was not a pretty sight. Blood leaked down his chin and spotted his jumper where it showed beneath his cape; the back of his right hand was raw. Blood ballooned out from three straight scratches which had torn his surgical gloves and left them flapping.

The pain of the wounds was a minor inconvenience but he did not want to leave traces of himself in the bedroom. Using tissues from a box by the table, he blotted his face and hand until the blood stopped. He slipped the used tissues into his cape pocket and opened the case with his good hand. Inside was a mix of papers, photographs and books. Opening an album at random, he was disappointed to find family snaps, but at least she had been methodical. Neatly printed on the front facing sheet were the words. *Family Christmases from 1988 (and counting!)*.

The next album covered various holidays, weddings and family gatherings, all dated, from 1985 onwards. Opening a page at random, he was startled to see Deborah Fearnside's face staring back at him from an anonymous wedding group. He lifted the plastic sheet and removed the photograph to study later. Similar albums, less glossy but with pictures somehow more garish, traced Katherine Johnstone's past back to the late 1970s. A graduation photograph was lovingly preserved in its original mount. He tossed it to one side.

His frustration grew. Half a dozen albums had revealed nothing but a photographic coincidence and all that was left in the case was a paper wallet of loose pictures and a shoe box. He opened the wallet first and smiled. Inside were school photographs: long line-ups of girls in grey sweaters and striped ties; portrait photographs of Johnstone from the ages of about eleven to eighteen; prize-givings, speechdays, school choirs – the pile of discarded photos grew on the floor. And then he stopped.

Five smiling faces looked up at him, one of them unmistakably that of a teenage Katherine Johnstone, grinning confidently at the photographer with her arms loosely thrown around the shoulders of her nearest companions. On her left, Deborah's blonde head rested on her shoulder – lips pouted seductively, eyes daring. To her right, two familiar, barely remembered faces. He knew their names now but could no longer remember which applied to which. And at the end, slightly apart from the group, beautiful and aloof, one face stared out at him, smiling at him knowingly.

His eyes dimmed. No matter how distant the memory, nor how many times he looked at his own photograph of this face, it always affected him. She was no different – so lovely, so irretrievably dead. But so were two of the others now, and it wouldn't be long before he had obliterated the whole group of lying, scheming bitches. Confident now that there would be more here to satisfy his thirst for knowledge, he opened the shoe box, inadvertently tearing the old cardboard where it proved weaker than the atrophied Sellotape.

Inside were several diaries, their dates embossed on the cover, with little gilt clasps or padlocks for which the keys were missing: '1973 My Diary'; '1976 Kate's Diary'; '1977–81 Five-Year Diary'; '1982/83 Diary'. 'Secret keep out' had been Dyno-taped to the outside of the shoe box, a show of adolescent independence. He glanced at his watch. It was still only 18.30. There was just enough light to read by as he settled down with controlled curiosity to find the date that lay at the heart of his search.

Ron had finished his second pint – two in half an hour was a considerable feat, even for him, but it had done nothing to stop his growing sexual frustration. This was the second night bad weather had prevented them finding a secluded spot in nearby woods.

One of his mates had already left the pub, bored by the weather and the commuter chatter. Ron was having another go at Melanie about finding a place to go.

'Mel, that's it. Two pints is enough. I'm not risking driving with more on a night like this. Come on, Mel – I'm either taking you home or somewhere I can screw the living daylights out of you!'

The last thing Melanie wanted was to go home. She had three pieces of maths prep waiting for her, a French essay from last week that had to be in on Friday morning and a sulk to continue against her mother. She thought of the music room and the open window. It didn't seem such a bad idea now. The two large drinks had warmed and relaxed her, making Ron seem quite attractive again.

'We could try the school, Ron. Sometimes they leave the doors or windows open in the music block.' She did not want to make it sound too explicit.

'Why didn't you mention it before?'

'I didn't think of it.' Another lie intruded into their relationship.

Ron eased his 250cc machine off the main road and through

an open side gate into the school ground, tucking it out of sight behind a late-flowering rhododendron. Melanie led their way along a narrow path through shrubs to the back of the music block. It stood silent and deserted in the early dusk.

'We can start by trying that window over there,' she said, pointing reluctantly to the one in the piano room.

A combination of the weather and his attitude had changed her mood completely again since leaving the pub and she was starting to find maths homework quite appealing.

The window was shut fast; even Ron's attempts to open it were unsuccessful.

'No good, then. You'd best take me home.' She huddled under the eaves, damp and cold.

'I'm not giving up that easily now we're here. Anyway, you said a door might be open.' He walked off round to where the door to the music block was just visible in the fading storm light.

'It'll be locked!'

'How d'you know?' He turned the handle and the door opened, screening the entrance to the changing room on the left as it swung back on the hinges. 'Come on – it's open.'

Melanie peered over his shoulder and up the gloomy stairs. 'I'm not sure we should do this, you know. The rain's easing off now – what if the caretaker comes round?'

'Don't be bloody stupid. If we close the door behind us, he's not gonna know – and anyway, we can nip upstairs. I bet he doesn't go that far.'

'Oh, all right, but come on then. I've got to be home by half seven; I've got homework to do.'

The couple clambered up the stairs and into the choir room, which was still warm from the earlier rehearsal. Ron threw his jacket on the ground and instantly threw Melanie on to it. A disappointing ten minutes later he was dressed again, sitting on one of the metal chairs, satisfied and on his second cigarette, having ignored Melanie's instruction not to smoke.

'You can do that downstairs. Look, it's gone half six already. We need to go.'

Melanie sounded peevish. The events of the past hour had turned her previous unease into clear disappointment and distaste. Ron sensed something was wrong and was sulking, partly because it felt good and partly because it was a test of the strength of his power over her. She wouldn't go without him. At the very least she needed a lift home.

'Ron, come on. I'm cold and Mum'll kill me if I'm late.' It was a feeble lie and Ron knew it, but he was bored and cold too. Without speaking he got to his feet and loafed downstairs. Melanie bent to pick up her overcoat and noticed the smudged outline of their footprints on the wooden floor. In the heavy twilight she took it for rain but it didn't look like water – it looked like paint – dark cherry red. Ignoring it she started down the stairs.

Ron was standing at the bottom, motionless, staring through the right-hand door into the changing room. He was leaning heavily on the door frame as if ill. Something about him made Melanie freeze by his side.

'Ron, Ron, are you OK?' There was no answer. He turned to look at her and his face became the thing of Melanie's nightmares for months to come. It was a blank, white oval with black pits for eyes and a gaping hole for a mouth. As she reached his side, she could hear a sickly gagging at the back of his throat – as if he were trying to speak or scream but kept swallowing his tongue. His breath was tainted and foul.

'Ron, what is it? For God's sake, tell me. Are you ill?'

As if they were words of command, Ron's cheeks filled and he started retching. He just managed to reach outside before he lost the contents of his stomach in a coughing, splattered mess.

Alone, Melanie turned and looked into the dark changing room. Her first thought was that somebody, probably the judo team, was going to have hell to play for leaving it in such a mess. There was a pile of clothes on the floor and some idiot had thrown paint around the walls. Then she noticed the smell and the hand on top of the bundle of clothes. Instinctively she moved closer. The sickly sweet stench, mixed with vague smells from the chemistry lab on a very bad day, filled her nostrils.

There was an iron tang at the back of her throat that reminded her of nose bleeds but still her bemused brain refused to put the clues together. It was only when she saw the face, with its ghastly second smile, staring up from beneath a bench in the middle of the room that the truth slammed into her head.

'Miss Johnstone? Miss Johnstone! Oh God, nooooo.' Her words became a repetitive cry as she fled from the music block. She ran wildly towards the main school and then stopped, realising it would be deserted. Then she remembered the caretaker, with his office by the boiler room, and she veered round to find him. She could see the light through the rain and threw herself at the door.

'Mr Yardell, Mr Yardell. Call the police – quickly, there's been an accident, a terrible accident. I think Miss Johnstone's dead.'

Two police cars and an ambulance were on the scene in ten minutes. The caretaker was there to meet them, white-faced and silent; he simply pointed in the direction of the music block and stood back gratefully to let the authorities take over.

The scene-of-crime officers turned up quickly and started to erect white plastic tents around the door. Donning white, hooded suits, overshoes and gloves they started a meticulous search of the block and surrounding grounds. A WPC went to find and comfort Melanie.

Fenwick was putting on his raincoat when the call came through. Despite his return to Division there hadn't been much of interest to occupy him recently and he had got into the habit of leaving in time to read the children a bedtime story. He was a little later than usual but stopped to take the call. The local constable at Harlden, responding to a 999 call, had reported a suspicious death at 18.45. Fenwick checked his watch, told the duty sergeant to make sure Cooper met him at the school, and called home to make his excuses.

The journey would only take him fifteen minutes at this time of day, as the school lay on the outskirts of town. He drove in a fast practical style that cut through the traffic without the need of a flashing blue light. He could feel the familiar mixture of curiosity, anger and, yes, excitement. Adrenalin pumped into his system, sharpening his thinking and creating a state of alertness.

By the time he arrived, blue and white tape already cordoned off a wide area stretching from the car park gates to the old assembly rooms. A white plastic tent was being stretched from the doorway to the bushes. It was clear from the buzz of activity that the scene-of-crime officers were already at work. They had been fast off the mark, which gave Fenwick a sense of optimism as he parked his car, then dashed quickly through the rain to the uniformed constable on duty by the door.

'Evening, Constable. Were you the one who responded to the call?'

'Yes, sir.' Constable Nolan recognised Fenwick and was pleased at the opportunity to impress a Division legend. 'I arrived at 18.43 in response to a 999 call from the caretaker, Mr Yardell. He was waiting for me in the car park and brought me straight here. I observed the body of a woman, clearly dead, and immediately notified the station. The SOCOs arrived a short while ago and the pathologist is on his way. DS Cooper has radioed to say he will be here shortly. The body was discovered by a pupil, Melanie White – she's in the caretaker's room with a WPC. The caretaker is back there with them now.'

'Thank you, Nolan.'

The constable straightened his shoulders in pleasure at the recognition. As the DCI turned towards the assembly room he spoke out again. 'Excuse me, sir. This is just a hunch but . . .' When he came to it he found it difficult to presume to make a suggestion to the DCI.

'Go on, man. What is it?'

'Well, sir. I don't think she's been dead that long – can't have been. My eldest is in the school choir and they rehearse here. He normally doesn't get home himself until well after six. If she's one of the teachers – and Melanie White says she's Miss Johnstone – she must have been killed within the last hour. And

I've been thinking, sir, waiting here – if he's taken her bag or her keys we might be able to trace him to her house.'

'Good thinking, Nolan. I'll speak to the SOCOs.'

Within minutes Fenwick had confirmed that the victim was indeed Katherine Johnstone, identified from her driving licence, and that there was no trace of house keys in any of her bags. Her address was on a gas bill in her handbag – less than five minutes away by fast car.

A startled Cooper was ordered back into his car just as he climbed out of it as Fenwick shouted instructions to follow him and call for backup en route. This time they would need all the blue lights.

Within the blue and lilac bedroom of number 1 Hedgefield, the man was engrossed in a large five-year diary. He had prised open the puny brass lock with a small screwdriver and was reading through her entries for the month of June 1980. It appeared that Johnstone had kept a lengthy, conversational diary; every day there was a chatty description of events with a reflective summary at the end. She had been a thoughtful and considerate girl and in other circumstances he might have read the entries with mild amusement.

Now, however, he was engaged in a search – for information, confirmation, details to conclude the construction of his case for the prosecution. He flicked impatiently to June 20th, a day scratched deep in his memory. It was blank. The entry for the 19th was there, hopeful, excited, but then nothing. Weeks passed with no entries, and then, in late August, she had started to write again.

August 29th. I must try to put the past behind me – but I can't. Every day I think about her, and her face as I last saw her. When I go to sleep she sings in my dreams but it's the screams in my nightmares that wake me. Dear God. I want to forget – but I can't. She's always there. Perhaps if I write it will help me. It has in the past but that's been over silly trivial things. It's school soon. How can I face it? Somehow, I've got to go on. Maybe this will help.

There were no entries for August 30th or 31st. Then, in September, she started writing again. The theme was similar to that of the 29th – no facts, just a stream of tortured consciousness. He skimmed through quickly, irritated by the schoolgirl drivel and self-pitying prose. Then an entry, just before Christmas, caught his eye.

December 16th. Carol Service. Beautiful, truly beautiful. Octavia took the soprano lead, of course; she was wonderful. But the duets weren't the same. The other girl tries her best but she just doesn't have the range or quality. Oh, how we all miss her. I came home in tears – we were all saying, 'Remember, this time last year.' She took us all by surprise. The sweetness of her voice and its richness. We'd all known she could sing, of course, but somehow we hadn't noticed her mature, what with Octavia and others around. And then, during that last year as she and Octavia became closer and closer friends, she was suddenly *there*.

I'll never forgive myself, as long as I live. If I had only done *something*, said something, I could have saved her. We all knew about her and Octavia – but no one else guessed just how *much* she loved her. I did. I knew. And I could see where they were heading. But she couldn't cope, of course she couldn't. Jealousy. It's the deadliest sin.

The writing stopped abruptly at the end of the page, the final sentence crammed between the last feint rule and the bottom edge. He turned to the next page and carried on, reading avidly, lost in the unfolding story of an affair he could never have imagined until Deborah Fearnside had planted the seeds of suspicion. As he read further, he could feel the denials building inside him. Day after day, the stupid girl wittered on about a love that had to be a figment of her imagination.

He started to hate the stupid bitch and her warped, adolescent preoccupation with unnatural sexual attraction. Every page built upon the last in creating an edifice of teenage infatuation, underpinned by her abiding sense of guilt, but there were no *facts*. In his fury, he threw the book across the room. Its weak spine burst against the wall, spraying old pages all over the carpet. One drifted back to lie at his feet. As he stared at it disconsolately, a scrap of writing caught his eye: . . . *why is she saying it wasn't an accident? Trust Leslie to make up the past. Let the records show the truth . . . inquest was clear. Why start all o—* He bent to snatch up the page, scanning its full contents. Feverishly he scrabbled on the floor, picking up page after page from the carpet and stuffing them in his rucksack.

At the edge of his hearing he caught an insistent whine and was momentarily distracted. A siren screamed past on the bypass, which he ignored, but it reminded him of the length of time he had been in the house. He cursed himself for his preoccupation and hurriedly scanned the room for any further pages. He couldn't risk waiting to tidy up. Downstairs he stepped over one of the cats and made his way to where he had propped his bike. A minute later he was cycling east down Copse Lane, away from the bypass when a black saloon car rushed passed him in the opposite direction, showering him with water. There was a glimpse of a dark, tense face, concentrating on taking the corner too fast – that was all – but his instincts screamed at him to get away.

A short time later another unmarked car and a police patrol vehicle drove into view, following the course of the black saloon. Without a doubt they were heading for Hedgefield. He forced himself to be calm and to keep pedalling. He turned right along Waycroft Avenue towards the town centre on roads too deserted of traffic to be comfortable; it would be too soon for roadblocks, surely. He hoped the weather was the cause of his solitude as he pedalled on. With a pricking between his shoulder blades he continued, disappearing at last into a multi-storey car park.

CHAPTER FOURTEEN

'The doors are locked, sir, front and back – no signs of forced entry.' Cooper was peering into the kitchen through the window over the sink as Fenwick joined him.

'He had the keys, Cooper. He may have been and gone or still be working his way here. I want to get inside without leaving any signs.'

Cooper stretched up and felt inside a hanging basket by the back door – the obvious place. People could be so predictable. The spare key was in a small freezer bag. He opened the door cautiously and took a step into the kitchen.

'I think he's been here and gone already, sir – look.' Muddy water puddled on the floor and fresh footprints faced towards the door.

They both moved cautiously through the house, touching nothing, to confirm that it was empty. As soon as they had, Fenwick gave instructions.

'I want a constable on the front door and as soon as the scene-of-crime boys have finished at the school, I want them cleaned up and over here. They're to go through this house from roof to floor. They should treat it as if the killing took place here. He might have relaxed and got careless.

'Next I want house-to-house enquiries in this road, neighbouring streets and all along the routes between here and the school. Concentrate on the direct route and immediate vicinity first. We're on his heels and if we move fast we might overtake him. I want road blocks around the town at once. Every car, every vehicle to be checked.'

'Every bike, I should say, sir. Look at these tracks out of the kitchen and across the beds. They're fresh.'

'Right, every bike too. I'm going back to the school – you take control of things this end. Call me if anything turns up. I'm interested in loose ends, inconsistencies – anything that makes you even think of thinking twice.'

At the school the SOCOs were still at work in the music block, but at least the pathologist had arrived.

'Bob – what's the verdict?' Fenwick poked his head around the changing-room door. The pathologist, a grizzled fifty-five-year-old veteran with a chronic ulcer and temper to match appeared to ignore him. Then words were flung back over his shoulder from an unseen mouth.

'Too early to say. She's obviously dead and it's obviously not from natural causes. There is no weapon in sight and the state of the body suggests it wasn't suicide but I can't rule that out until we've done the full autopsy.'

Fenwick bore the offhandedness without comment, knowing that interested silence would work where questioning would fail.

'She was killed within the last two hours – at least an hour ago. Died from one wound to the throat – sliced through both the carotid and jugular in a single, deliberate action that went through the full 180 degrees. My guess, and it is a guess at this stage, is that she put up a bit of a fight – ran in here to get away from him perhaps. There are contusions to face and arms, damage to her right hand. I can tell you more when I've examined her fully.

'The sexual assault might have happened after death – can't be sure until we've had results from forensics. There's lots of blood on the edges of the cuts in her skirt, tights and panties which suggests that he had cut her throat and then used the same knife on her clothes.'

'Sexual assault – are you sure?'

'Early indications are yes. There is fluid, probably semen,

across her thighs and her stomach.'

Fenwick still waited. Bob Pendlebury straightened slowly and turned to face him for the first time. 'I don't like this one. I don't like it at all. It looks messy but the death wound is precise and neat. She would have died in minutes, drowning probably before shock from loss of blood.'

'Result of the autopsy?'

'I'll do the PM tonight. Full report will be twenty-four hours.'

'Any chance of completing it sooner?'

Pendlebury looked at him with derision. 'Come on, Fenwick, you know I do eighteen holes minimum every Friday. But, I'll see what I can do. No promises.'

The man in charge of the scene-of-crime investigation was hovering.

'Yes, give me the highlights.'

'Well, she was attacked on the threshold. Despite the later trampling by the girl White, and the caretaker, we can still make out what we think are her footprints in two places. He was waiting for her probably. We haven't finished looking out here yet but there are some footprints behind that bush over there. We'll be analysing the shape of the prints and comparing them with those inside. And someone was sick on the threshold. We need to find out if it was the attacker.

'She escaped the first assault and went into the building. I'd rather you didn't go further in there straight away, sir. We're lucky, there are still footprints all over the place in mud and blood and we're taking detailed measurements. It looks like she tried to make it to the far door, which leads into a hall. He got to her in here and finished her off.'

'Presumably the attacker's likely to be heavily bloodstained?'

'Unless he had a change of clothes, yes, sir. But I think he might have done. There's been a clear pooling of blood in the space at the bottom of the stairs – enough for two sets of footprints to be tracked upstairs. I don't know whose they are – one set are too small for our attacker or the woman – probably the girl's, but we need to check.'

'Anything else?'

140

'Not at this stage, sir.'

'Why are you so sure it's a he?'

'Shoe print size mainly. It could be a woman with size elevens but it's unlikely.'

'Or someone wearing overshoes to disguise their foot size?'

The SOCO looked disconcerted. 'That's a possibility yes, but they wouldn't be very agile and this attacker was.'

'OK, I want you to finish here and then clean up and go over to her house. I've a feeling he's been there. Someone has – there's fresh mud on the kitchen floor. Check it out *fully*, will you, and I mean fully, as if it were the scene itself. If anyone wants me, I'll be with the girl – what's her name again?'

Melanie was huddled by the two-bar electric fire, her hands around a mug of sweet tea which had gone cold long before. The caretaker, feeling important but at a loose end, fussed over her to the point that she wanted to scream at him to go away. A WPC was with her and indicated to Fenwick that the girl had said nothing since raising the alarm. Fenwick dispatched the caretaker to find out the headmaster's phone number and addressed his attention to Melanie.

'Now, Melanie, listen to me very carefully.' He spoke in the soft low tones one uses to pacify nervous animals. 'You have been a very good and very brave girl so far. Now you're going to have to be brave again because I need you to tell me every little thing that happened this evening, all right?'

At the start of his sentence, her head started to rock slowly left to right in silent denial. It was the only motion in the silence of the room. Fenwick stared at her, trying to gauge her mood and how best to make her respond. She was obviously deeply shocked but she didn't appear unhinged. He had two routes forward – gentle coaxing or firm insistence. Having started with the first he decided to continue softly.

'Melanie, what you know is very, very important. It may not seem so to you but you might hold information that is vital to helping us catch the person that did this. You must try.' His words and his attempt at a familiar Sussex lilt seemed to get through to her.

'She's dead?'

'Yes, I'm afraid so.'

'She must've been lying there, dead then, whilst Ron and – whilst we . . . Unless,' a look of horror crossed her face, 'unless he chased her in there and killed her while we were upstairs. Perhaps, we could have stopped him.'

'I don't think it's very likely, Melanie, but to be sure tell me what happened, step by step, and we'll find out.'

'From the beginning?' She took a deep breath and put the mug to one side, tucking her hands into her armpits for comfort. 'Ron and I were in the pub.' She caught herself up short, remembering suddenly that he was a policeman and she was under age, the minor infringement momentarily forgotten in the immensity of the crime.

'It doesn't matter. I won't tell. I've got bigger worries than you drinking at your age. Go on.'

'It's embarrassing. Can't I just get to the bit where I find her?' Fenwick shook his head, adamant.

'Ron was cross with me. Well, with the weather really. We've not been going out together long and . . . well . . . he, he . . .' Fenwick refused to help her out, 'he gets excited, you see, and with the rain we can't go down Pixts Lane like normal.'

'Pixts Lane?'

'The local lovers' lane, sir,' the WPC chipped in.

'I see, so you thought of the school rooms, did you?'

'The old assembly rooms yes. I'd left a window open, you see – today, just in case, though I went off the idea in the pub – but Ron was insistent, he kept on at me.'

For the next half-hour, Fenwick went over her story until he was as sure as possible he had the times and details correct. Despite several attempts Melanie refused to give her address and phone number to allow her parents to be called and Fenwick was becoming concerned on their behalf.

'So let's be sure I'm straight. You were in the pub from about twenty past five to past six with Ron Jarvis. You left on his bike and drove straight to the school. You didn't see anyone or anything on the way here or in the grounds? You and Ron found the window closed but the door open. You went in, straight upstairs. Were up there for about ten, fifteen minutes or so and then came down. Ron must have noticed the body, was sick and ran off. You don't think he went into the room but you can't be sure. You went in a few paces and found the body. Then you came straight here and called the police.'

Melanie nodded.

'You did the right thing, Melanie and you've been very brave. I'm going to ask the constable to get you home now. If you remember anything more, anything at all, call me at the station. Here's my number. What you think of might seem trivial to you but it could be important.'

'It's the smell I'm going to remember.'

'The smell?'

'Yes, of the blood, and . . . everything else, sweet and sickly. I'll never get it out of my head.'

'You will eventually, you know. However horrible, these things do fade with time.' But as he watched the small, retreating figure, shuffle away through the rain he doubted she would ever completely forget. Tragedy in childhood could leave abiding wounds and warp the spirit. He hoped her natural courage would be enough to see her through.

By 11.30 that evening Fenwick and Cooper had returned from the post-mortem leaving the pathologist and his assistant to finish off and close up. Pendlebury's examination had simply confirmed his assessment at the scene. Forensic reports would not arrive until late the following day at the earliest. The cork board in Fenwick's old office was starting to accumulate the usual souvenirs of a serious crime. An 8 × 12 inch black-and-white portrait photograph was pinned top left, donated from personnel files by an appalled school secretary.

Underneath, a street map was highlighted in red pen to show the route from the school to Katherine Johnstone's home, with a green track from the White Lion pub to the school gates. The two lines overlapped along the whole length of London Road, running almost due south from the school to the pub, where it terminated in a T-junction with Elm Drive. At this point the red line turned east and continued alone.

To the right of the map was tacked an A1 flip chart page on which were written tentative timetables and a series of connections.

The middle and right of the board were still blank, awaiting SOCO photographs. An incident room had been set up at the school but for the time being Fenwick was happier using his old office at Division. It was always his bolt hole at the end of the day; he thought better away from the din of the investigating team.

Cooper sat dejectedly on the bone-aching visitor's chair while Fenwick paced back and forth in front of the pinboard.

'Right, let's go over this once more.'

The sergeant sighed.

'At 17.20 Katherine Johnstone was last seen alive by Steve Right, a member of the choir. We can be pretty certain of the time, he was just home in time to miss his favourite children's programme and was upset. His mother has confirmed this and we know the fastest time he could make it home.

'The murderer might have attacked at any time after that. *But*, let's suppose he didn't and that he waited for her to leave the building – there's enough initial evidence to support this.

'The caretaker told us Johnstone was always careful to lock up – and the headmaster tells us she was a diligent woman. So how long does it take her? Five minutes, no more than ten, to check everything, get dressed for the weather and leave. That means she was outside about half five, perhaps a little earlier.

'It would have been over quickly – he probably took more time defiling her than killing her, even with her struggle. Now it's 17.40 plus. He gets changed – we think – and leaves. You realise, of course, if he *did* change it was premeditated, despite how it looks. It's essential that we establish whether he did or not.'

'How are we going to do that?'

144

'I'm not sure, but the SOCO report on her house will help. If we find none of her blood there, he must have changed – he didn't have time to wash thoroughly.'

'Unless he had an accomplice, of course.' Fenwick acknowledged his sergeant's observation thoughtfully, then moved on.

'Where was I? Melanie White and boyfriend, Ron Jarvis, leave the pub after six – we don't know when exactly but the landlord's fairly sure they were gone quickly. We haven't found Jarvis yet? It's vital we do – is there someone trying to track him down still?' Cooper nodded.

'Then later, as we went to Hedgefield, there's a possibility – remote – that we passed him as he got away. His route's pretty clear – we need a sighting. First thing in the morning I want to complete the house-to-house along the whole route.'

'It was pouring with rain, sir. It's unlikely there were many people about – or looking out.'

Fenwick carried on, oblivious: 'And it's a bus route – have checks on the stops at the same time tomorrow. Now, take me over again what was found at her house.'

'It looks as if our murderer was there – or at least there are definite signs of a search by someone who didn't have to force an entry. It looks like the intruder was searching for something specific. Downstairs it's all very orderly but upstairs it's a mess. He either lost patience—'

'He or she, Cooper, not just he, not yet.'

Cooper was tempted to ask from which part of their anatomy women secreted semen but resisted. Sarcasm at this time of night was a certain loser.

'. . . He or she lost patience – or was interrupted in the search, which is a possibility. I think he found something there.'

Fenwick stopped pacing and paid obvious attention for the first time.

'There was an old suitcase open and a load of papers appear to have been rifled.'

'Take me through the list.'

'There are photo albums, mementos and diaries.' Cooper consulted the list in the preliminary report. 'Diaries, five: 1974,

1975, 1976, 1982, 1983 – the first three written in detail, the last two a series of notes on her final terms at school and early time at university. Some old letters—'

'What about years 1977 to 1981. Why the break?'

'No sign. Perhaps they were embarrassing and she threw them away.'

'Hmm.'

'The letters all dated from 1979 to 1985. Old photographs in albums, mainly school and family. Some certificates: O levels, A levels, Queen's Guide, flute practical grade eight, a dried bouquet of flowers.'

'Anything from 1976 onwards – for those missing years?'

'Perhaps some of the photos, sir; we'd need to check.'

'And the diaries aren't somewhere else in the house?'

'Well, I can't guarantee it . . .'

'Guarantee then, please. He was searching for something and so far the only items missing are old diaries. It doesn't make sense, but let's at least make sure that they *are* the only thing.'

'SOCO were still checking when I came back. We've been promised a full report for the morning.'

'Can you get the suitcase and contents over to forensics and then straight to the incident room when they're done? And any photographs they can lay their hands on. I want to know what he was searching for – and whether he found it. We'll need a relative or someone who knew her well to check out the house for us too.'

'It wasn't valuables, if that's what you mean. There was some jewellery, about £75 in cash in a pot in the kitchen, TV, video, CD player – a very nice one too – none of it touched.'

'It doesn't make any sense. An apparently random killing, followed by an orderly search – why?'

'Unless we did disturb him. Perhaps he had no intention of letting us know he'd – sorry, he or she'd – been there. It was very unlikely for her body to be discovered until the morning, given the weather.'

'Well, we can't know for sure and there's nothing more to do now. Sort out the rotas for the morning, will you, Cooper? I'll see you at seven.'

Cooper stumbled into bed in the early hours of the morning. Ron Jarvis, Melanie's boyfriend, had finally been found drunk and disorderly but he was drying out in one of the cells at the local station.

Efforts to locate the dead woman's relatives had been unsuccessful. Her mother and father were away in the Lake District according to a neighbour, and the sister was not at home. An urgent call was due to go out on the radio in the morning. Meanwhile the dead woman's name would not be published despite the undoubted front-page status of the story.

The post-mortem facilities were housed discreetly in a wing of the county hospital. As Fenwick returned, Pendlebury was just leaving.

'Still here?'

'Complaining? I thought you were desperate for my written report.'

'What have you got for me?'

'My full report will be with you in the morning—'

'Come on!'

'Don't interrupt. Now y're here, do you really think I'd keep you waiting that long? Come into the office, I've some whisky there.'

Fenwick looked doubtful.

'It's purely medicinal and you look as if you need some.'

When they had settled as comfortably as possible in the cramped office, with two generous doses of medicine in tumblers kept for the purpose, Pendlebury started without preamble.

'There's not a lot to go on, I'm afraid, no more than you heard earlier, really. She was a healthy, athletic female. Virgo intacto – yes, it still happens. Technically, she died by drowning. It would have taken several seconds before she lost consciousness. There are superficial protection wounds on her hands – not many, she appears to have tried to run rather than fight. Bruising to her back and left sides was probably before death, which suggests she was initially attacked from behind. At one stage she fell, damaging her knees quite badly.

'Interestingly, her right hand was badly fractured, crushed across the back. It was a fierce blow. No obvious traces so I can't tell you what it was made of. Skin samples will go to forensics. It's the only other wound of that type on her body, which is odd. Normally there would be several if a weapon had been used in the principal attack.'

'Could it have been crushed in the door?'

'Possible – worth checking for traces. It would have to have been slammed very hard.

'She was killed by a single wound to the throat, sliced left to right, probably whilst her chin was pulled back, exposing the veins and artery. It's probable, therefore, that the attacker was right-handed. Hard to say, from the wound, what length the blade was but we found some interesting damage to her coat. Looked like long jagged tears, could have been made by a saw or a serrated edge. I've sent it to forensics. I suggest you ask SOCO to check whether there was a possible source of the damage at the site. If there *isn't* then it may be that the upper edge of the blade was serrated. That's consistent with, say, a survival knife – very sharp-edged weapon, ideal for cutting but could snag clothing. I should get forensics to do some tests on identical material.'

'I'll do that. Who in your experience could have a weapon like that?'

'Anybody really – they're on sale in huntin' 'n' fishin' shops all over the country. And, of course, they're standard military issue. The US aircrew survival knife is a popular one. Ideal for this sort of killing.'

'Have you seen anything like this before?'

'The killing or the defilement or both?'

'Both.'

The pathologist rolled the last drops of whisky round his glass for a few moments, drained them in a sudden movement and looked Fenwick in the eye.

'The defilement of her body – no. It's odd. Something about it doesn't ring true. It was done post-mortem, that's clear, but without passion – no viciousness there. Where he cut her clothing away there were no marks on her body beneath. I would have expected some nicks and scratches at least but there's nothing, not a scratch. That means two things.' He counted them off on the stubby fingers of his empty hand. 'One, the person who did this was in full control – no shakes, no sexual urge to get at her body. And two, they were an expert with a knife. And that's consistent with the main wound by the way – neat, efficient, exactly in the right place to cause rapid, certain and virtually silent death – particularly with a hand over her chin and mouth.'

'And you've seen that sort of killing before?'

'Oh yes, I was attached to the army in the years when you were still playing in Glasgow backstreets. It's a classic silent killing technique.'

'That's your hunch then – a service man?'

'I don't have hunches, Fenwick. You know that by now. There are merely points of similarity. Go away and detect the rest.'

CHAPTER FIFTEEN

At 7.10 the next morning a bleary-eyed, inadequately fed, detective sergeant walked into the situation room at the school, fully expecting to be first on the scene, only to find Fenwick there already. Worse still, several fresh-faced uniformed and detective constables were there too, grouped around a large Ordnance Survey map, working out details of the house-to-house. After less than four hours' sleep Cooper had been feeling comfortably virtuous as he turned down his wife's sleepy offer of a cooked breakfast. His mood shifted radically on entering the room to one of sulky martyrdom, which was wholly unjustified.

Fenwick looked up as his sergeant slipped into the chair by a desk in a partitioned space at the end of the room.

'Sergeant! Good. They've started planning the house-to-house. Make sure they've got it right, would you, and then come back and help me go through these SOCO reports?'

Cooper's mood was transformed yet again.

The first few hours passed in a blur of activity. Cooper organised a schedule of interviews with staff, pupils, friends – highlighting the ones that he thought required Fenwick's presence. As part of the large team they'd been given Cooper spotted a detective constable he recognised, a graduate on the Accelerated Promotion Scheme on her first murder assignment.

WDC Nightingale listened intently to the briefing. Her dark brown hair was tied back in an uncompromising plait down her back, leaving her face bare and clean of make-up; she looked seventeen. She put a pair of steel-rimmed glasses on briefly to read the report in front of her but then tucked them away again as if embarrassed by them.

Fenwick went through the detailed scene-of-crime reports in gaps between interviews. The one from the school confirmed with more precision the initial conclusions of the officers at the scene. It appeared that someone had waited for Katherine Johnstone to leave, had chased her back inside and, after a struggle, killed her in the changing room. The sprays of blood from her throat and position of the body, all pointed to the fact that she hadn't been moved after death.

The semen had been blood typed – her attacker was type O – and sent off for full DNA analysis. The forensic lab had worked at once on the samples sent but despite the early analysis none of the spermatozoa was still alive. This marginally increased the probability that the attacker was infertile.

The photographs were excellent quality. Fenwick selected two to have copied for his office back at Division and passed the rest over to go on the display board. Johnstone's handbag and belongings had been examined and sent back to the incident room, together with a list of contents: pocket diary, lipstick, two tissues, three handkerchiefs (she was suffering from a cold), a half-pack of Tunes, a crumpled phone message, an emery board.

He extracted the message: 'Call Octavia – she says it's good news' and then a London number and a squiggle of a signature, which could have been 'RJ'. Fenwick dialled the number, to be greeted by an answering machine and one of the sexiest voices he had heard on the end of a phone: 'I cannot answer your call right now, but *please* try again, I wouldn't have wanted to miss you. If it's really urgent leave a message after the tone – which is a poor B flat, by the way, but I couldn't find a better one.' Fenwick duly left his urgent message, asking her to call him on a major, not minor, matter. He regretted the weak pun immediately but that was the problem with answerphones – once said, instantly recorded.

He turned his attention to the diary – only to be interrupted by Cooper.

'The press, sir. They've started to arrive. Two locals and three nationals – not even eight o'clock yet and it's started.'

Fifteen minutes later Fenwick had delivered his brief statement, polite, the bare facts, no speculation. He didn't know how much he might need the press as the inquiry progressed so courtesy and an attempt at co-operation were key. Still, he regretted the need for the additional officers on duty around the school.

He returned to the diary from Kate Johnstone's handbag. The entries were short and practical in a square, open hand. He saw that she had a dentist's appointment for lunchtime and recalled that the body had yet to be formally identified. Katherine Johnstone appeared to have been a woman of neat and precise habits, even regular appointments were written out in full each week, with start times and estimated finish times. It was orchestra and choir mostly, the occasional theatre trip or dinner with friends, and family visits ringing the changes. Unremarkable – according to her diary the day of her death had been another ordinary day. Yet something had marked her out.

He flicked forward into June: a horticultural show; a brief note – 'Drinks' – under a reference to the last GCSE examination; open day; end of term. July was completely blank except for two references to 'Rehearsals'. August had a firm line ruled through the first two weeks with only a '?' to indicate that perhaps a holiday had not been finalised. And then, towards the end of summer things started to change.

In mid-August there was a note: 'Planning meeting – combined choir and orchestra.'

Thereafter there were twice-weekly rehearsal dates and a weekly 'organising committee'. On August 31st he found 'First combined rehearsal'; on September 5th 'Full Rehearsal' and on the 6th, 'PERFORMANCE!' It did not take a genius to work out that these were notes and plans for some sort of event, a concert perhaps, given her musical interests.

'PERFORMANCE!' was awarded the only exclamation mark

in the whole diary. It was the only remarkable event, other than the brutal and abrupt manner of her death, in an unremarkable life. However, it was unlikely to provide any insights to her murder. He made another note, to ask Cooper to find 'RJ' and question him about Octavia.

The second SOCO report was slimmer and accompanied by another set of clear photographs. Fenwick looked at these first, laying them out one by one in progression from her front door to the bedroom. It appeared that his strict instructions to touch nothing had been obeyed – even her post lay undisturbed on the doormat. He studied the bedroom photographs carefully. Unlike the other rooms there were clear signs of search, with a suitcase lying open on the floor by the bed.

The SOCO team had completely changed their clothes and showered in between sites to ensure no errors, no contamination. There were few traces downstairs but wet foot marks confirmed that the intruder wore size ten-and-a-half shoes and the length of stride suggested a tall person.

The bedroom report had Fenwick sitting up and poring over every detail. They had found tiny traces of blood on the carpet and two of the larger spots appeared still to be damp when discovered; they had been sent to forensic for analysis. There was a scrap of rubber just under the bed. Fenwick looked at the photo; it was about the size and shape of a hard contact lense – that too had been sent off. And, a real prize, they had found three partial fingerprints – not the victim's – on the staircase and four further on the diaries and a scrap of paper left on the floor. Everything had been sent off to forensic. It looked as if the partial prints were too small to be of any help in identifying the criminal but they could be valuable in completing a prosecution case. He would have to wait for further forensic reports, which despite all pleadings were not due until the end of the day because of holidays and illness in an already depleted team.

Having briefed the Superintendent over the phone, Fenwick joined Cooper in the main school building. The able sergeant was looking jaded.

'Bad morning?'

'More harrowing, sir. They're all very upset, understandably, but I'm on my second of those already.' He gestured towards an economy-size box of multicoloured tissues.

'Anything useful?'

'No, just confirmed what we'd suspected already. She was a popular, quiet, orderly spinster. Her pupils liked her – apparently she made maths fun, if you can believe that. That's what she taught, by the way, and she was a main-stay of the music department. Did a lot there. But this is a very musical school, long traditions, so they try to look for musical ability in all their teachers – the Head told me.'

'You've interviewed him already?'

'Yes, briefly, and I've mentioned that we may ask him to identify the body if we can't track down her relatives. He'll do it if necessary.'

'Who're her close friends – anybody here?'

'The music teacher, Judith Chase, I think. But she's very upset and has gone home. She wasn't well anyway.'

'I still need to talk to her – fix it for this afternoon, would you? And which of the teachers or staff has the initials RJ? There was a phone message they'd taken in her handbag. I want to follow it up.'

'There's no RJ, sir.' Cooper was consulting a computer listing of all staff. 'There's an Anne Jeffries, Julia Jones – no Rs. As for Christian names, there's a Ruby Andrews, Robin Hove, Richard Stevens . . .'

'That could be it. It might have been an S. Have you seen him yet?'

'No. Give us a break, sir. We're up to the Ps on the staff list and I've been fitting in some of her form pupils as well.'

Richard Stevens was a fifty-something gentleman with a receding hairline and small features stamped on to a large, round face. He wiped constantly at a drip from a button nose and was clearly uncomfortable in the presence of the police. He had little to add to their general sum of knowledge until Fenwick asked him about the message.

'Oh yes. I remember that clearly. It was from Octavia Anderson, our most famous old girl. I taught her, you know – taught them both, in fact, though neither of them took to physics.'

'Both?' enquired Fenwick.

'Well, yes, Katherine Johnstone is, er was, an old girl too. She and Octavia were in the same year. That's why Octavia agreed to the engagement. She'd never have agreed to appear in our little concert otherwise. But the school was an important stepping stone for her and, fortunately, our date fitted a time she was in the country.'

'Take me through that again, sir. You're saying Katherine Johnstone and Octavia Anderson were at school here – when was that?'

'Twenty or so years ago. The secretary will have the records.'

'And Octavia Anderson. Am I right in thinking that's *the* Octavia Anderson, the soprano?'

'The same. The school's crowning glory really. Of course, we've produced some notable musicians but no one near Octavia's level of achievement. And she's agreed to take the soprano part in our anniversary performance in September. We asked her rather late but she's agreed. It was Katherine who put it to her and the message I took was confirmation. She said she'd sent a letter, agreeing in writing, but wanted to be sure we knew straight away.'

The secretary was all efficiency. She apologised for the fact that the records were still manual but produced the details and dates for Fenwick immediately.

'Kate joined us in 1975 at eleven and left at eighteen. According to these records Octavia Anderson joined three years later. She was bright so she leapt a year and joined Kate's class. She won a music scholarship after she got here. She joined us after her musical skills were recognised by a teacher – decent thing to do really, give your star pupil a chance at another school.'

'Could you produce me class lists for all the years Miss Johnstone was here?'

The secretary smiled lightly at the challenge; she enjoyed any opportunity to prove her efficiency. 'I'll get them to your incident room by this evening, Inspector.'

'Why do you want those, sir?' Cooper and Fenwick were walking down the long corridor that joined the old and new school buildings.

'I don't know, to be honest. Gut feel maybe. Or perhaps I'm running out of ideas for the present day. So far, let's face it, we've found nothing that hints at motive. There may be a crazed would-be lover – I'm going to ask the music teacher when I see her – but we've found no evidence of a secret life at her house. It might be random, as you said last night, but I don't think so. There was definite premeditation – no fingerprints or traces, which implies gloves and protective clothing, all that suggests planning. So I'm in search of a motive and if I can't find one in the present I'll go back into the past as far as I need to. Let's face it, the only unusual thing about her so far is that she was at school with an opera star and has been in recent contact with her about this concert. Do you know what it is, by the way?'

'Haven't a clue sir, but I can find out.'

They were walking along row after row of long school photographs arranged in date order. Cooper stopped abruptly and pointed at one of them.

'Look, this is a year both Anderson and Johnstone should be in the picture.' He scanned the lines of faces – serious, smiling, the inevitable tongue sticking out in the cross-legged front row of juniors. 'Can't see her, though.'

'No, neither can I. I doubt we'd recognise her anyway. But I know that face from somewhere – I can't think where.' Fenwick pointed to a pretty blonde head in the third row. Tiny though her face was in the long picture she caught the eye with her direct gaze and inviting half-smile.

'I bet she broke some hearts,' said Cooper. 'What a looker. Never mind, she'll be married with several kids by now.'

'Yes, but why do I think I know her? It's infuriating.'

'Stop thinking and maybe it'll come back.'

* * *

Fenwick just had time to visit Katherine Johnstone's house before a briefing from the door-to-door teams. As he walked in, the first thing he noticed was that the letters had been removed from the mat and stacked neatly on the half-table. Cursing the person who had interfered he picked them up and looked through them idly.

A muddy gas reminder, a postcard from her parents that had taken four days to arrive, the message smudged by rain, a special offer that looked to come from a clothes catalogue and a personal letter, postmarked in London the day before she died. He noticed that the envelope had been opened and the contents were missing. She had obviously stopped to take the one interesting item with her and had left the others for her return.

He walked into the empty lounge. It already felt dead. Fenwick had noticed this before in the houses of the dead or bereaved. There was an indescribable sense of loss that made the rooms feel hollow, not just empty. No one entering this room could have expected to hear a voice from the kitchen, or footsteps on the stairs, the creak of a floorboard above.

As Fenwick walked around the house he wasn't sure why he was there. Another DS and WDC Nightingale had done a thorough search. He was known in the local force for following hunches – always backing them up it was true with ruthlessly detailed police work. Guesswork smacked of a divine providence he simply did not believe in. He did believe, though, that his unconscious assimilated seemingly random bits of information, forming them into hypotheses that sprung spontaneously into his mind. He hadn't yet been proved wrong, not totally, which in part explained his excellent case record. Occasionally, he would have to adjust the direction of his intuition as further facts emerged but always there would be a link to the original 'guess'.

His track record created more room for him than for some of his peers, allowing him to indulge in complex and costly work. He always had to fight but eventually the Superintendent would find a few more men; politically it was always expedient to back a winner.

In this case, though, it wasn't resources he lacked. Fenwick's inspiration was letting him down. Eighteen hours into it he could already feel the case growing cold about him, yet he had been sure the previous evening that they had been close, very close, to the murderer. Despite the statements so far to the contrary he had expected someone to have seen the man. The extensive house-to-house – targeted to be finished within twenty-four hours – was costly in manpower but it was driven by his certainty of there being an eyewitness somewhere.

As he walked into the kitchen he instinctively checked that the muddy mark was still there. It was, but as he walked through the other rooms he increasingly felt he was wasting his time. A beam of sunlight through a rain-spattered window made him realise there was a break in the clouds after days of rain and he noticed for the first time the glorious display in the back garden.

His wife had been a keen gardener and now that she was gone he was confronted each time he went home by neglected borders and weedy paths. Begrudgingly he had started to weed and tidy up, a habit that had become compulsive during her final decline. True, the children didn't mind. Bess would play happily anywhere and Chris didn't play at all any more. Thinking of his young son brought a constriction around his heart. He wondered what the child was doing right now and guiltily thought about the lack of progress they had made with a diagnosis over the past month. Even he admitted now that there was something wrong but nobody could tell him what. He caught his breath sharply as he thought again of Monique and her decline.

She would have loved this garden and so, obviously, had Katherine Johnstone. Impulsively he went outside and sat on a drying bench, set due south against the wall. The smell of wild thyme and lavender as he brushed by relaxed him and he recognised immediately that this had been a special place for her.

A movement against his leg startled him. He looked down into the suspicious yellow eyes of an old ginger tom who, with the uncanny instinct of cats everywhere, had identified Fenwick as a cat hater and therefore someone to be rewarded with special attention. He reached down gently to push it away and was rewarded by a flash of claws that caught his fingers. Cursing, he sucked at the small drops of blood and realised at once how the murderer had come to leave his own marks on the carpet in the bedroom. The rubber must have come from the finger of his glove. There *was* more for him to learn here, he had just been looking too hard for the obvious. Determinedly more relaxed he returned to the house and set himself to amble with an open mind.

After fifteen minutes he gave up. It was nearly midday and he had to get back to the incident room. No further thoughts had struck him. Returning to the hall, he had the door open before he realised the obvious message that had been staring him in the face since he arrived. Where was the letter, the one he assumed she had opened before going to work? It wasn't on her when she died. She could have left it at the school but was that likely?

The more he thought about it, the more he realised the potential significance; the SOCO photos confirmed that the post had been on the mat when they had arrived yesterday, apparently undisturbed (he would need to check the photographs for a record of where the empty envelope had been). If the post had arrived after she'd left, and assuming she hadn't returned home for lunch (unlikely given the weather yesterday), it could only mean that someone else, probably the murderer, had taken the letter. *If* he had done, why and how had he attached any significance to it? The envelope was distinctive, the handwriting an angled black calligraphy. It had a first-class stamp and London franking mark, a dirty brown smudge ran across the front diagonally. There was nothing on the reverse and yet something about it may have made a murderer stop, open it and take the contents. Perhaps it was from the murderer himself or someone that could identify him. This might be the break they needed.

First he would need to prove with reasonable probability that the murderer had taken the letter, then he could set out to discover who had written it. He placed the empty envelope gently into an evidence wallet and left.

Fenwick knew the moment he walked into the incident room, that something had happened. The buzz and expectation on his arrival were unmistakable.

'Right let's have it – and get straight to the meat, please, I'll have the detail later.' The young detective constable assigned to boost the numbers in the team looked to Cooper for the nod and, getting it, stood to deliver her report. Nerves and pride of achievement struggled for supremacy on her face.

'Yes, sir. This morning at 10.05 I interviewed a Miss Sandy Jones, a shop assistant at Handishopper—'

'Which is where?'

'On the junction of Copse Lane and Farm View, sir. Miss Jones advised me that Miss Johnstone is, er, was a regular customer stopping by on her way home from school. On the night in question—'

'I'm not a judge, Constable, get on with it.'

Unnecessarily cruel, thought Cooper, with quickening interest. He's impatient, which means he's on to something himself.

'Last night Jones was expecting Johnstone to stop by to pick up some cat food. The later it got the more worried she was. She kept on looking out of the window. There were very few people going by because of the weather. At about six o'clock – she can't be more precise – she saw a cyclist going west along Copse Lane. She thinks it was a man; he was wearing a bright yellow cycling cape and hood – it was the colour that made her notice him.

'When I interviewed the occupants of number 20 Hedgefield, they also remembered a man in a yellow rain cape on a bike cycling up and down the road. They said it looked as if he was searching for an address. If they saw the same man, it's the only person we've found so far who's appeared more than once on the route.'

'Well done, Constable. And you can add a third sighting.'

Fenwick looked at the assembled team ruefully. 'I passed a cyclist wearing a yellow cape coming back down Elm Drive as I drove to the house. 'We need to find out where the cyclist went. He may be local, if we're lucky. Any ideas, anyone?'

The constable, in full swing now, volunteered a suggestion. 'Two ideas, sir: a reconstruction at the same time tonight and release of the information to the press and local radio – it can't do any harm.'

Fenwick thought a moment.

'Agreed. Cooper, see to the arrangements and then join me in the staff common room.'

Half an hour later, Cooper discovered Fenwick patiently going through Katherine Johnstone's papers and pigeonhole in the staff room.

'What are you looking for?'

'A letter, Cooper. A recent letter to Johnstone without its envelope.' He recounted his discovery and the conclusion he had reached while in her house.

'It's a bit of a long shot, isn't it? I agree – if you're right, it's something more to go on, but why would a letter be so important? Why open it there? And how can we be sure it wasn't thrown away?'

'But supposing it was opened by the murderer – why? It's that that bothers me and makes me think the letter *wasn't* from the murderer but from someone he knew, knew well enough to recognise the handwriting. It looks as if he was more interested in its contents than concealing its existence, which makes it important that we find out who sent it and what it said.'

'Can I see the envelope?'

Fenwick passed him a photocopy of the original which was already on its way to forensics.

'Can't tell much from this – what was it like?'

'Expensive, good-quality paper. Peculiar handwriting, I thought. Looks as if someone practised it for a long time or it's someone's best, not a natural scrawl at all.'

'It's that calligraphy writing, isn't it, written with one of those italic pens. My daughter's got one she uses for cards and invitations – things like that. Anything else at the house?'

'Not that I found, and the other stuff isn't back from forensics yet. Find the postman, Cooper, and the time he delivered yesterday's post.'

CHAPTER SIXTEEN

At six o'clock Fenwick and Cooper reported back to the Superintendent at Division. The murder of a school teacher was
sensitive, headline news; the ACC had already phoned the
Superintendent from HQ demanding a written progress report
by the next morning. Superintendent Beckitt had decided his
team should concentrate on solving the crime, not pushing
paper, so he had already written most of the one-page summary.
He just needed Fenwick to fill in the details and sign the damn
thing without getting into a semantic debate about its relevance.
Knowing Fenwick he had more chance if Cooper was there.
The man wouldn't reveal his complete lack of respect for the
ACC, and what he stood for, in front of lower ranks.

'This is stupid, sir. The case is only twenty-four hours old
and the idiot wants us pushing pens. It's bloody typical.'

'That'll do, Fenwick. It will take very little of your time and,
believe me, a fast response will count when you expect me to
go back and beg for more resources!'

'With respect, sir, even so—'

'Chief Inspector, I said enough. Leave it.'

Fenwick took the warning and Cooper started to relax.
Sometimes there was no point in wasting energy fighting the
inevitable. The report was, in any event, depressingly brief. So
far, they had no idea who the man was that had killed Katherine
Johnstone and rifled her house. From his shoe size and the
flaky eyewitness accounts of the cyclist seen on the route to
Hedgefield, they believed the murderer to be a tall man, fit

enough to have cycled away from the scene quickly, clever or lucky enough to have dropped out of sight.

'Pity you didn't surprise him at the house.'

'Yes, sir, but we cut the sirens before we were near enough for him to hear them so it was just bad luck. We were there within twenty-five minutes of the crime being reported.'

'Why so defensive all of a sudden? I wasn't accusing you!'

But the Superintendent knew why and now Fenwick knew too that the fact they had so closely missed the intruder at Johnstone's house would be put in the most positive possible light.

'Can we be sure the person at her house was the murderer, not just an opportunist thief who took her keys?'

'We can't be one hundred percent sure yet because we still haven't received the forensic report on the samples from her house, but it looks very likely. We've got bike tracks at the school that match those at her house, sightings of the same cyclist en route, footprints that are roughly the same size so far as we can tell. We'll know better tomorrow morning when we get the next reports.'

'Are you getting what you need from forensics?'

'They're doing their best but half of them seem to be away. We've got priority it's just lack of resources.'

'Much outstanding still?'

'Well, the report on her house, research on the knife – Pendlebury gave us an idea to follow up – detailed analysis of all the footprints. SOCO did a bloody good job at the scene itself, preserving prints despite the rain. Then there's hairs from her house, elimination on those once we've found out who's been there recently; the tyre tracks, like I've said. Anything else, Cooper?'

'There's the envelope, sir. They've got that.'

'The envelope?'

Fenwick had to explain about the envelope. The Superintendent looked no happier once he had finished.

'So no motive, no suspects, no theory, nothing.'

'No suspects, no, and to call it a theory would be pushing it but I have some ideas.' Fenwick hesitated.

'Well, go on then, don't stop there.'

'They're not for the report, right, sir? Not yet.'

'All right, all right.'

'Well, somebody has gone to a lot of trouble to make this look like a random killing, but I don't think it was.'

'Why not?'

'There's the hypodermic, for a start. No trace of drugs on it – and how many addicts do you know who use clean needles, let alone are stupid enough to lose them? Then there's the killing itself. Pendlebury describes the death wound as precise, almost professional, and the damage done to her after death was restricted to her clothes. There was no frenzy.'

'The photographs looked bloody frenzied to me!'

'I can understand that, sir. With that sort of death the blood is spectacular but the mess is created by the sheer pressure of the blood as it left her body. And that's another thing, we'll know more when I get more information from forensics, but I've asked them to work out how much she moved around after her throat was cut. You see, Pendlebury's view is that she was held still while she died. Not many people would do that once they'd cut someone's throat.'

'So this is someone who knew what they were doing. Had done it before, perhaps. Any matches to HOLMES?' He was referring to the Home Office computer on which data from major investigations was held.

'None at all.'

'Hmm. What about boyfriend or family?'

'No trace of the former, and the immediate family all appear to have alibis. We're checking on them now. Her father's coming in tomorrow to identify her.'

There was a silence. All the men in the room had daughters and for a moment they could think of nothing but the horror the man would face.

'Nothing more for now then?' The Superintendent spoke briskly. Fenwick and Cooper shook their heads. 'We've got to get this bastard, Fenwick. Get out there and do it, will you?'

CHAPTER SEVENTEEN

'Andrew, I don't care what case you're working on, you have to come with me to the specialist on Monday. He's your son, for heaven's sake, and there's something seriously wrong with him.'

Fenwick had had no peace since arriving home late and dejected after his meeting with the Superintendent. The case was slipping away from him. His mother had been waiting for him with a contained but palpable determination. She was a patient woman until she became fixed on an idea and she had nagged him incessantly about the importance of the appointment with the specialist. Over the previous six weeks Christopher had become more withdrawn – sliding from communicating in short sentences, to monosyllabic grunts until he had finally retreated into a silence not one of them could penetrate. And all the while he stared out at the world, confused and frightened.

Fenwick wanted to hug him and take away the awful pain he could see lurking behind his eyes but when he tried, the boy remained stiff and wooden in his arms. Or worse, only the day before Chris had screamed, a high-pitched, insistent wail, from the time his father had touched him to the point where he had given up and stepped away.

'Monday's a difficult day. I'm in the middle of a murder investigation, remember.'

'As if you'd let me forget. But this time I'm not letting go. He's only a wee boy – and he needs you there. There is

166

simply no one else to go in your place.'

Chewing and swallowing his meat pie was suddenly too much for Fenwick and he pushed his half-finished meal aside. Another delay in the detailed forensic reports meant he was already losing twelve hours, and further delays would only make matters worse.

He had few ideas left to go on. The crime had happened too late for the copy deadline for the local paper and, although the story of the man with the yellow cape would be carried by the nationals, giving the case fresh prominence, he was expecting the local coverage of the reconstruction to produce more results. But that was still a full week away.

'I'll spend a few hours with the children tomorrow before I go in; I can't take the day off because forensics will be delivering their report.'

'And Monday?'

'I'll see.'

'That's just not *good* enough, Andrew.' His mother brought the flat of her hand down sharply, making the cutlery jump and Fenwick flinch with reflex memory. 'You simply don't realise what's been happening over the last few weeks. He's a very sick boy.' She abruptly quietened her voice, which had been rising in anger. 'He really is very, very poorly, Andrew. And he needs your help. I'm not exaggerating. I know how important this case is to you, particularly after Monique's illness. I'm not daft, you know. I know you need to push yourself back into work, not least to rebuild your reputation. So I'm not asking for this lightly.'

Fenwick was taken aback by his mother's sympathy and understanding, in what was for her a surprisingly personal observation. She was a dour, hard-working and tough Scotswoman. He knew, or thought he knew, that she loved him in her own way, and he was sure of the deep affection she held for her grandchildren but not because she had ever told him. Her unexpected sympathy worked where her temper had failed.

'All right, what time's the appointment?'

'Ten o'clock, sharp, at Mount Cedar Hospital. I arranged it for as early in the morning as I could so that you'd have the rest of the day – and I appreciate you may have to go in first thing but please be prompt!'

Fenwick made a habit of looking in on his children whatever time he returned from the station. Invariably, they were asleep, innocent and unaware of his attention. But he hoped that somehow the sense of caring would last until they woke in the morning and ease the loneliness that he sensed his frequent absences brought to their lives.

As he gently pushed open the door to their bedroom, he was greeted by silence. Since the days of their birth, he'd fight down the irrational dread that he would find them cold and lifeless. He froze as he was, ears straining to catch an intake of breath, eyes pushing into the dark to follow the hoped-for rising and falling of bedclothes.

He offered up an instinctive 'thank you', to whom he was not sure, as he satisfied himself they were both breathing and sleeping in their goose-down cocoons. He walked softly to stand between their twin beds. Bess lay sprawled in an untidy, fairytale-covered nest, a loose smile on her face, a faint snore as she exhaled. He stroked her hair gently and kissed her brow. Opposite her his tiny son was curled tight as an ammonite into a foetal ball, only a few strands of fair hair showing against a plain white pillow. There was nowhere to kiss. Fenwick touched his fingertips to his lips and rested them for a moment on the covers where he assumed the boy's head to be. All that he truly loved lay in this room. If he were to lose one of them now he would fall apart. Pulling back from the brink after Monique's illness had been tough but it was achieved in silence, on his own. Only he knew how much the necessity to care for the children had carried him through.

In his own bed minutes later, a silent tear trickled icily from the corner of his eye to soak the hair above his ear, to be followed by another, and then another.

The forensic report on samples from Johnstone's house was waiting on Fenwick's desk when he arrived in a filthy temper at ten o'clock on Saturday morning.

A message on his desk, timed at 8.45 informed him that DS Cooper had taken a copy and was in the incident room at the school. Apart from the report there was little new: a few reports on possible sightings of the cyclist that had been followed up and led nowhere and a large envelope from Downside School enclosed Katherine Johnstone's personnel file. He ignored them and opened the envelope containing the report on Katherine Johnstone's house. He read it methodically, jotting down notes on a pad, referring to the set of black-and-white photographs that he spread over his desk in careful order. From left to right he set out the photographs of the hall, living room, kitchen with close-ups of the tyre marks, stairs, large bedroom, bathroom. All of these showed orderly rooms, small traces of a careful search.

Then there were the photos of her bedroom and the mess that had been left on the floor. Fenwick arranged these directly in front of him. As he came to the part of the report that covered this chaos he paused and took a deep breath then resumed his reading. Here at last was trace evidence, detailed with scientific practicality.

First there were the two dark hairs. Forensic had confirmed that they were definitely human and not the victim's, and there was an initial analysis. The hair was circular in cross section, which meant it came from the head; the colour natural; no dyes. It was short, no split ends at the tip suggesting the hair may have been cut recently. It was straight, black, with evenly distributed pigment in the cortext which made it very unlikely that it was Negroid. One of the hairs had follicular tissue attaching to the root so they were going to test for blood factors to cross-match to the blood found on the carpet. There were also promising results from neutron activation analysis as well as an attempt at a DNA profile from the root.

It would all be useful for building a case against a suspect. Fenwick's problem was, he reflected ruefully, that he had no suspects. He turned to the report on the partial fingerprints.

They were too small for forensic to estimate size or shape of finger and they had no way of telling whether it was from the right or left hand. The good news was that the prints appeared to contain a delta and the core. There was an inner terminus and part of what appeared to be a scar on one edge. No way would they be able to produce the required minimum sixteen points of resemblance that would enable Fenwick to use the print as evidence of identity in court. What they could do, and had done, was confirm that there was no match to Katherine Johnstone. It would have taken hours and hours of painstaking checking to be sure of just that one fact and Fenwick jotted a note to remind himself to call the lab.

But it was in a sombre mood that he turned the pages to the blood analysis. The SOCO team had found five drops of blood on the bedroom carpet and bedspread and they had all been analysed. There was page after page of detail, most of it over Fenwick's head and then one sentence: 'Therefore, notwith-standing the fact that full DNA analysis has yet to be completed, it is possible to state categorically, as described on pages 3, 9, 10 and 14, by reference to serology tests conducted thus far, that the semen samples from the scene and those of blood and follicular tissue found at the address set out and in the circumstances described on page 1 derived from different individuals.'

There were two people after all.

Fenwick could feel his head start to spin. He reread the key pages: even at the basic level there was no match; the semen was from a man with blood type O, the blood in the bedroom type A. And Cooper had taken the reports to the incident room! Jesus Christ, the investigation would be in turmoil by now. He had to get there and calm them down, fast. Just as he was leaving, the phone rang.

'Yes!' He yelled hard into the receiver, impatient to leave.

'Is that Detective Chief Inspector Fenwick?' It was a young girl.

'Yes, who's that?'

'It's Melanie White. You said to ring if I remembered anything. It is all right, isn't it?'

He forced himself to calm down: 'Yes, of course. Go on, what is it?'

'Well, it may be nothing but—'

'Go on, don't worry.' He was biting his tongue with impatience.

'OK. It was on Tuesday evening, as I was going into the pub.'

'The White Lion?'

'Yes, right. Well, I saw Miss Johnstone as she was walking home. She didn't see me because I hid, didn't want her to see me. But I watched her walk down Elm Drive and I think – well, I can't be sure, but I'm pretty certain – I saw a man following her. He'd been sitting on a bench by the pond on the corner opposite the pub and as soon as she'd passed him and gone a little way he got up and followed.'

'It was a man? You're sure? What did he look like?'

'He was tall, well over six foot, which is why I assumed he was a man. He was quite slim, athletic-looking and he had dark hair. That's all I saw.'

'Nothing else, not his age, his face, how he walked – anything at all.'

'No, like I said, I didn't really look at him. I was more concerned about Miss Johnstone not turning round. Is it no good then? No use?'

'It's very helpful, very helpful. Can you come in and give us a statement. We're all at the school still, the large room next to the art room. Please, come by. What you've seen is exactly what we needed.'

'OK.' She sounded doubtful.

'Melanie, really, this could be very important. And, Melanie? Thank you, for remembering and bothering to make the call. Some wouldn't.'

As he drove to the incident room Fenwick worked through the implications of the forensic results. Did this mean that the killer and the intruder were different men? Had they worked together? Had one been at the school whilst the other was at her home waiting for the key? But there had been no sighting of two men on bikes. On the other hand, was this a deliberate attempt to confuse them even more. Melanie White's call made it look almost certain that the murder had been premeditated and very carefully planned. But how could he have got semen from another man. Was he homosexual? Were there two of them involved right from the start, there in the music room – one excited, staying to do whatever it was he had to, while the other one went to the house? Which meant the other one could be a man or a woman. They had no idea what he or she looked like. In his rush to reach the incident room he hadn't finished reading the report. Did the shoe prints match the shoe sizes even?

Cooper was alone in the incident room, reading the same report that had caused Fenwick such consternation.

'Where is everyone?'

'House-to-house; interviews; talking to cycle shops in the area, you name it they're on it.'

'But what happens if something develops here?'

'Nightingale and Taylor are on a bun-run, elevenses. They'll be back soon.'

Fenwick ignored the reference to the time, glad to have Cooper to himself.

'What have you told them about that?'

'Not much. I've emphasised that it looks as if this was premeditated, well planned – and perhaps the work of two people. They're redoing the house-to-house in Hedgefield just in case, and they're to ask everyone they interview for a list of visitors to the teacher's house so we can start getting samples of hair for elimination. You can imagine the idea of a team has given them the blues but there's no panic. I played it down.'

'Well done. Spot on. I need to call forensic but I want to be sure there are no other surprises in there.'

'None that I've found. Shoe prints are different, the cast from the house is a half-size smaller than that taken from the prints in the shrubs at the school. Different tread. They're starting to try and identify type and brand. I've suggested they look at overshoes to match against the prints from the school. The rest looks pretty standard.'

'I'll make the call then.'

Morale in the investigation team was falling prematurely. Response to press articles in the nationals had been poor by any standards and the completed house-to-house had produced no further information. Fenwick sent the despondent policemen and women home early in the evening and was leaving the incident room when the telephone rang.

'Yes?'

'Hello, this is Octavia Anderson. May I speak to Detective Chief Inspector Fenwick, please?' A fluid woman's voice trickled down the line.

'Speaking, Miss Anderson.'

'Chief Inspector, you rang me yesterday and left a message on my answering machine. How may I help you?'

'Thank you for calling back so promptly. I am afraid I have some bad news for you. Were you a friend of Katherine Johnstone's?'

'Kate? Yes, I am. Why, what's the matter with her?' The voice was anxious but not overly concerned.

'Miss Anderson, I'm very sorry to tell you this, but she's dead. She died on Thursday.'

There was silence at the end of the phone.

'Miss Anderson, are you still there?'

'Yes . . . I'm here. Go on, Chief Inspector, tell me how it happened. For such a senior policeman to be involved, there must be something more to it.'

'I'm afraid there are suspicious circumstances and the likelihood is that she was murdered. We have, as yet, no idea by whom or why and at this stage we're keen to talk to anyone who knew her, including you.'

It transpired that Octavia Anderson was in the country for only two days before setting off on her next tour. She seemed shocked but controlled, and keen to help the police in any way. Mindful of his Monday morning appointment with the specialist, Fenwick arranged to see her on the Sunday. He suggested meeting at her house in London – anything to be out of the claustrophobic incident room at the school. His famous intuition failed him as he replaced the receiver. There was no tingle of anticipation, no excitement to alert him to the importance of this rendezvous.

CHAPTER EIGHTEEN

He was deeply angry. Furious. There could be no excuses for the mistakes he had made. He had taken too long, fumbled the encounter and become careless at her house. At any stage, he might have failed to complete his mission, or worse, have encountered the police.

Back in the rented house in South London the killer mentally retraced each step of the murder. The scratches on his hand and face would heal; the bruising to his groin and thigh, from her umbrella and stout walking shoes, were already turning yellow, but he still hurt inside. She had damaged his self-esteem and had struck a blow at his confident assumption that the things he wanted to do would always go to plan.

He ran through an inventory of mistakes in his mind. He had failed to kill her in his initial attack; he'd had to resort to using his knife when he wanted to avoid any trace of a weapon; he'd not locked the door on her – no excuses for that, just plain carelessness; he had ignored the threat of the cat; he had stayed too long at her house, missing the police only by minutes.

There was one consistent reason. He was losing his touch. It was months since he had left the unit, first travelling to Australia to arrange the clearance and sale of the estate, then returning, much wealthier but with few material possessions, to England. In that time, his training had slipped. Some good habits remained, and his instinct was still sound, but his reflexes were a fraction of a second slower, his judgement was just starting to blur, hesitation was creeping in.

175

Ideally, he should retrain and impose a tight discipline on himself but there was no time. The letter he had taken from Johnstone's house confirmed that he had only three months in which to complete his work – or lose the opportunity of the most important kill.

He turned the pages of the five-year diary. They were all neatly filed in order again – only one page missing. He had been sure that he would find confirmation in her house and he'd been right. Page after page of adolescent drivel had changed abruptly into guilty self-torment which went on for months. And in Johnstone's misery of self-reproach, he found all the evidence he needed to justify the verdict and sentences he had taken on himself to execute. He now knew with certainty the final names: two down, two to go.

CHAPTER NINETEEN

Fenwick arrived for his meeting with Octavia Anderson in good time; the train for once had delivered him promptly at Victoria. She had a small house in a road off Ebury Street, not far from the station. It was painted white with black railings and a colour co-ordinated window box like all the others in the terrace.

He was kept standing a few moments on the Edwardian tiles at the top of the short flight of white-painted steps, before a breathless maid answered the door.

'So sorry to keep you waiting,' she bowed. She had peach-shaded skin and dark almond eyes in a faintly Indonesian face. 'Madame, she is nearly ready. Just finishing her dressing. Please to come in.'

He was led into a small elegant sitting room, not the formal drawing room the exterior of the house had made him expect.

'Coffee, tea, a cold drink?'

'Coffee, please, black, with sugar.' The maid dipped a short bow and withdrew.

The room smelt of jasmine and his curious eyes found the plant, in full bright sunlight, on a marquetry table to one side of a window which looked on to the street. The walls had been painted a soft coral red and were covered in paintings, prints, drawings – no one larger than 2×3 feet but all arranged to create the impact of three huge abstract canvases. He found the effect disorientating and moved closer to a wall to allow himself to focus on the individual works of art.

He was following the minimalist lines of a nude torso, trying to establish whether it was male or female, when he sensed a presence behind him. He waited a moment before turning around, conscious that she would be studying him all the while, curious to know why she felt it necessary to do so, why the delay in announcing her arrival. Fenwick could feel her eyes on him, not just at the back of his neck but across his shoulders and down his spine. He was aware of her perfume, a floral spice, heavier than the jasmine in the room, but linked to it in subtle accents.

Eventually he turned round. She was stunning; five feet ten or eleven, slender, long black hair pulled back into a geometric pleat away from a face that could never be beautiful in the classical sense but was compelling in its intensity. In his mother's words, she had presence. She was used to being appraised. It was obvious that for her every act, every day would be a performance in which she would expect to be noticed. She was standing now, perfectly at ease, one hand resting lightly on the back of a chair, one long suede-trousered leg extended to the side, regarding him with interest and light amusement. She did not introduce herself.

'Is it a woman?'

'Does it matter?'

'To me, yes. I like to know what I'm dealing with.'

'It's entitled *Torso II*. No clues.' She smiled enigmatically. 'Personally, I have always thought of it as a man. The power in the shoulders, the sense of strength.'

'Funny, my first impression was of a woman.' He smiled back and extended his hand. 'I'm Detective Chief Inspector Fenwick, Miss Anderson.'

'How do you do?' The touch of fingers, a slight shock; more interest from dove-grey eyes.

'Won't you sit down?'

The coffee arrived and she spent some minutes putting on a performance of the perfect hostess.

'Miss Anderson, you know the reason I'm here?'

'Poor Kate's death. It was a big shock.'

178

'Kate? You mean Katherine Johnstone? Yes, that's right. I understand that you'd recently been in touch with her.'

'Yes, about a concert in September. It's the school's anniversary and I had, purely by chance, a short gap in my calendar so I agreed to take one of the solo parts.'

'Why did you? I mean, you're well known, famous even to someone like me who is hardly an opera buff.' She smiled at the compliment.

'Sentiment, I suppose – and gratitude. If it hadn't been for the school and its strong musical tradition, I would never have got to where I am now. You see I came from a poor family – not poverty-stricken but struggling – my mother was always ill, my father always tired. At least I was an only child but even so, I had to do my bit as soon as I was old enough to earn any money. And there certainly wasn't enough for singing lessons. It was good fortune I ended up at Downside, but virtually from day one, my life changed.'

It was a near-perfect recital. Fenwick wondered whether she had practised it for him or whether it was her standard interview opening.

'To return in September, just for one performance, is still a very generous gesture.'

'I know, but at sixteen I was awarded a music scholarship. One of the founding governors had left a bequest sufficient to finance an annual endowment, and I never looked back.'

'What prompted Miss Johnstone to contact you, do you think? Did you keep in touch? Were you friends?'

'Well no, not really, not since school. We weren't really close, and I hadn't seen her since I left – well, only once or twice at weddings of mutual friends, that sort of thing. I suppose she was egged on by others on the organising committee, someone else's idea that she followed through. That would be typical of Kate, being put upon by friends, being embarrassed into compliance.'

'And you did say yes. When did you let her know the good news?'

'Last week. I rang the school personally first but they

179

couldn't find her. Someone took a message. Then I wrote a few days ago. More coffee?'

It was a rich, dark complex blend, an embodiment of the hostess.

'Was that a hand-written letter or typed?'

'No, handwritten. I felt it ought to be a personal response to a personal request, a letter from my agent would have been all wrong, and there were no fees involved.'

'Could I see an example of your handwriting and envelopes? I just need to check for our records.'

'But surely you have the letter by now?'

'I'm not sure. We need to check. A sample, please.'

She was gone no more than a minute and returned with a stationery box and address book which she handed without a word to Fenwick. The leather-bound book was full of addresses in a neat, stylised calligraphy that matched that of the envelope photocopy in Fenwick's pocket. The stationery in the box was of heavy, expensive, cream paper, the same as the envelope that was probably being examined by forensics at that moment. He removed the photocopy from his pocket.

'Is this the envelope in which you sent her your letter?'

'Yes. I remember the stamp – an old Christmas one I had left over from the last time I was in the UK. But you should know that if you have the letter.'

'I'm afraid we only have the envelope. The letter's missing. Perhaps you could tell me what it said.'

There had been nothing remarkable in the letter, just confirmation of the engagement and good wishes. Octavia Anderson speculated for a few minutes on the fact of the missing correspondence but dismissed it lightly. Nothing she could tell Fenwick produced any insight as to why it was missing and she appeared genuinely unconcerned by its loss. She happily handed over handwriting and paper samples from her supply for comparison, smiling as Fenwick delicately placed them in thin plastic bags.

'Two things before I leave you in peace, Miss Anderson. They may seem odd but we really are looking into everything.

Firstly, your writing – is it used in any publicity? Is there anyway in which someone seeing the envelope would know it was from you?'

'Hardly. I rarely write letters and only to close friends. My signature has been used on programmes and such like but never my writing.

'It's very distinctive.'

'A sign of very strict schooling as a young child. I had a fearsome teacher for writing and spelling. Believe it or not, I had mastered that script by the age of ten – and had the bruises to show for it! Early training like that never goes. Even when I was teased at senior school, I never changed.'

'That brings me on to my second point. This may seem an odd question but did anything strange happen whilst you were at school together? Anything that might – however remotely – have a connection with Katherine Johnstone's death?'

The warmth went from her face. Cool grey eyes looked straight into his without blinking.

'You're right. That is an odd question. I can think of nothing out of the ordinary at all. We were boringly conventional – we didn't even smoke in secret because of the voice training. Now, Chief Inspector, if you have no more questions, I have another appointment shortly.' He was being politely dismissed.

It was only as he was walking briskly back to Victoria that a new explanation for the missing letter hit him. Supposing it had suggested a meeting, a time, and that Katherine Johnstone had been killed whilst she waited for her appointment. It would explain why the letter could not be found. It would also make Octavia Anderson a prime suspect and he had not asked her where she had been last Thursday night. Another point for Cooper to check.

CHAPTER TWENTY

Monday dawned slate grey and wet with a summer storm bringing a return of the unseasonably miserable weather. In homes all over Harlden, children whined over designer cereals, mothers snapped with little provocation at yet another day of damp washing, and policemen and -women donned wet-weather gear in preparation for whatever else the day would throw at them. Katherine Johnstone's murder was still the main case. A few leads had come in as a result of local radio appeals, but they merely confirmed that a yellow-caped cyclist had been seen in Harlden and had disappeared into the town's small multistorey car park. No one had seen him leave, no bike had been found abandoned. The common theory in the police team involved a car and a foldaway cycle. An even commoner theory was that the case was already growing cold. But there was still forensics. More reports on the envelope, the murder scene and response to a few detailed questions of Fenwick's were due that day.

Cooper had been astounded to receive a call from Fenwick on Sunday evening instructing him to review the latest reports himself and to follow up on any necessary actions as Fenwick would be out mid-morning until lunchtime. The behaviour was reminiscent of the DCI's withdrawal during his wife's illness and when Cooper woke gritty-eyed from a disturbed night, he immediately took the gusting, heavy rain as a metaphor of failure for the case.

Fenwick did not wake to the morning; he had lain rigidly

awake all night, unable even to find a sleep of exhaustion. He had accepted his mother's insistent demands to go with her to the doctor. As a father, he could do nothing less – as a policeman the decision ate into him like acid. There was no excuse for it professionally. He knew the case was in trouble, that the reports, due within hours, presented the last real chance for a lead to develop. And time mattered. The colder the trail the more difficult it would be for them to follow. There had been no breaks on the case. They were working steadily on routine, detailed policework in the hope that something would turn up. The search for the bike and murder weapon included local streams and rivers; they were checking back even further over known offenders' reports in case there were any similarities, reviewing unsolved cases, completing and cross-checking the interviews with family and friends in the hope of a connection somewhere.

But his son was seriously ill. Throughout the interminable, rain-soaked night, Fenwick replayed in his mind the six blighted years of his marriage, tracing them to this point. He had been a confirmed bachelor when he had met, been overwhelmed by and married Monique, all within four months. His friends, father (then still alive) and mother had all doubted his wisdom but there was no contradicting the fundamental and wonderful love he had felt for the woman. She held him spellbound in a way none of his many previous girlfriends ever had. Half French, dark-haired, black-eyed, with pure white and rose skin, she held a concentration of sensuality in her tall slender body that he had become obsessed with.

He'd had no need for children, maintaining his characteristic self-sufficiency in all respects but his love for his beautiful young wife. But Monique had been fixated with the idea of motherhood, so desperate he had no power to resist. He had been sure, too, that she would be a wonderful mother, she had so much passion and love for life. She fell pregnant on their short honeymoon and Bess was born, traumatically eight months later by Caesarean. Monique plunged immediately into a deep depression which took over six months of careful treatment to cure. Twelve months later Christopher's birth triggered a second, worse attack from which she never fully recovered.

At first Fenwick had had faith – not in any God but in the love that he and Monique felt for one another. After the second birth though it became impossible to pretend that she was well and the reason for a complete silence about her side of the family was explained. Eventually she admitted that she came from a long line of sufferers from what she chose to call '*la méloncolie*'. Her own doctor in the UK was more grave.

All her abnormal behaviour was directed at herself, not the children, nor Andrew, whom she increasingly ignored. Her first suicide attempt was almost laughably pathetic. She put her head in the gas oven but forgot to turn on the tap, but Andrew had taken it seriously and they had made some progress towards normality until she became pregnant by accident for the third time and miscarried.

Her second suicide attempt, with razors in the bath, was almost successful, prevented only by an alert neighbour who spotted Bess crying incessantly in the garden and banging on the door to be let in. They had wanted to institutionalise her then but he had refused to give up on his wife. From that point, Fenwick put aside all pretence of work and spent his time at home on extended leave. His care increased, the medication increased, more and more specialists examined his wife but she had slipped further away every day.

He was at home for the third attempt. She had knotted together a number of his ties and created a noose which she attached to the ceiling light fitting that hung above the central well of the staircase in their two-storey house. He had been making porridge for his breakfast and a cup of tea to take up to his wife. He could remember vividly the sights and smells of the kitchen. Bess being good and eating Rice Krispies in her grown-up chair, Christopher playing his favourite breakfast-time game of flicking crumbs into Bess's bowl, the porridge burping like molten lava as it simmered.

He had just turned off the gas. The hiss of the jets disappeared, the children were both miraculously quiet at the same moment so an unnatural silence had fallen on to the room. Into the silence had dropped a swishing sound, like a curtain being drawn, followed by a mucous gurgling and retching. His first thought had been that Monique had made it downstairs on her own and had been taken ill. So certain had he been that he'd run out of the kitchen and into the downstairs bathroom before his subconscious finally alerted him to what his eyes had seen but his mind had refused to accept.

He ran to the bottom of their stairs, his wife's bare feet were kicking weakly in the air whilst her hands twitched. He wasted precious seconds trying to reach her and take the weight before realising she was too far from the ground. He ran, stumbling up the stairs, tripping on the loose rod on the corner step, falling heavily on his right knee in the process.

Afterwards, in the nightmares that came every night for weeks, he would remember the tiniest details. She was naked, not uncommon, she had started taking her clothes off at odd moments and walking round the house but she had shaved her legs and painted her toenails. She was wearing every piece of jewellery she owned – the earrings attached as ghastly pendants to dozens of assorted necklaces, her fingers encrusted with rings of all types. It was probably the necklaces that delayed her suffocation. The knot had slipped so that despite the drop, her neck hadn't broken. He suspected that she must have let herself down gently as a jump over the height of their stairwell would have killed her instantly.

At the top of the stairs he used his umbrella to drag her body close and over the banister, but then it took her needlework shears to sever the noose. Her eyes were glassy and set but she was still warm and until moments before he had heard her struggling to breathe. His training took over immediately. He checked her carotid artery at the corner of her jaw – there was no pulse; her pupils were dilated and didn't react; she wasn't breathing. He started cardiac massage, pausing every five pumps to blow new air into her lungs. Time ceased to exist. At some point, shortly before he was about to deliver a sharp blow below her sternum, he checked her pulse again to find it had returned. Then his life became a continuous cycle of resuscitation.

There were no sounds from the kitchen. The last thing he had shouted as he ran out was for the children to 'stay there'. Neither of them had appeared on the stairs; they were used to obeying his strange instructions when their mother was out of bed. His mind went through a rapid routine to identify the nearest phone. It was downstairs in the hall; the mobile was in the car.

He checked his wife's vital signs. Her eyes remained unfocused; she appeared not to breathe when he paused. He needed help. The nurse wasn't due for another three-quarters of an hour – he could not go on that long.

'Bess!' Deep breath, blow out. 'Bess, come here.' Breathe, deep breath, don't forget to keep the head tilted. His right arm started to cramp. 'Bess!' he almost sobbed in desperation but could not afford the breath.

'Yes, Daddy?' A little whisper crept up the stairs to him.

'Bess, can you hear me?'

'Yes. Can I come up?'

'No! No, stay where you are but listen to me carefully.' Breathe deeply, blow out, breathe again.

'Yes? Daddy, I can't hear you.' Bess's voice was a whimper. He could tell she wanted to come up, wanted a cuddle but he was afraid the sight of her mother would panic her.

'Bess, be good. I need you to use the telephone for me.' Breathe, blow out, pause, short breath, breathe, blow out.

'I want you to pick it up and find the 9 – you know 9, don't you?'

'Yes, I know right up to one hundred now.'

Breathe, blow out, short breath, pause, breathe, blow out.

'Good girl. You're to pick up the handset, like when you talk to Nanny, and push the 9 three times – 999.' Breathe, blow out, short breath, pause. 'Can you do that?'

'Yes. Will Nanny talk to me then?'

'No someone else will. Someone nice.'

Silence.

'Bess, you still there?'

'Yes.'

Pause. 'Good girl. Now say to that person your name, your age, your address and say – wait a minute.' Breathe, blow out, short breath, pause.

'Say we need a doctor – your mummy needs a doctor, quickly. Can you do that? Repeat it to me.'

His daughter's confident voice repeated his words with barely a stumble, reciting them like a difficult lesson.

'Good girl, now do it.'

'Do it?' Pause.

'Use the phone. Do exactly as you said but use the phone.'

Beyond the drumming that was starting in his ears, he could hear her perfect, tiny voice and the click of the receiver being replaced.

'Done it, Daddy. A nice man said they were on their way.'

Fenwick didn't look up from the faint rise and fall of his wife's chest, now roughly covered by his own dressing gown after a desperate dash to the bedroom. She had been so cold.

'Very good. Good girl. Now go and wait with your brother downstairs.'

'He's not here, Daddy.'

'What . . . ?'

Fenwick looked up in frustration, straight into the eyes of his four-year-old son. The child was crouched motionless on the half-landing immediately below him, eyes fixed on his father's face. Fenwick struggled for calm and a normal voice.

'Christopher, you're in a draught there. Go downstairs and wait with your sister like a good boy.'

'No, I want to be with my mummy!' The reply was a ringing aggressive shout that brought Bess running.

'I'll stay with him, Daddy, don't worry. He'll be all right if I'm here.'

In the days and weeks that followed while his mother was moved from a life-support machine, to intensive care and finally to a long-stay ward, Christopher clung to his sister obsessively. At the time Fenwick had been glad. It was all he could do to hold himself together and make decisions on his wife's care without the preoccupation of children. His mother had come down and he made sure that he spent time with them every night but it was Bess who came for the cuddle and Christopher who sat next to her stroking her nightie constantly.

It became clear that his wife would never recover – well, not never, because the doctors refused to administer the relief of that certainty. Rather, they used phrases such as 'highly unlikely'. There had been some brain damage but they could not be certain of the degree. Monique didn't respond to any tests. It was as if she had withdrawn completely behind a wall, whether of disability or of her own making it was impossible to say. Whatever, she made no attempt to come out.

Eventually, she was moved to a long-term-care institution, over fifty miles away. At first Fenwick visited every other day, then as late winter turned the weather foul, once a week. He tried contacting her relatives in France, even travelling to the town she had come from, but could find no one. Eventually, following an inspiration born out of years of detective work, he went to the local mental hospital for the district and there found his father-in-law, senile at sixty-two. The doctors explained, although he hardly needed to be told, that there was a history of mental instability in the family.

He was furious with Monique at first, could not forgive her for the deceit and half-truths, but he was not a vindictive man. The anger wore itself out and he finally settled down to fortnightly trips that he'd maintained for the five months since.

Now there was glaring evidence that his son was seriously ill. Through the long interminable night his mind patrolled a Möbius strip of argument – starting out positively with the thought that this was the inevitable reaction of a sensitive child to his mother's illness, then sliding along to the dread that he had inherited her mental instability, before coming back around to the starting point again. At five o'clock in the morning, abandoning all thought of sleep, he rose, put on a tracksuit and went out for a run. It had been months since he had last taken his usual exercise and after five short miles he was sweating and breathless with exertion. He was not fit. Too many snack lunches and late dinners, and not enough exercise were unforgiving to a man of his age.

He made himself a healthy breakfast of fruit, wholemeal toast and decaffeinated coffee, feeling better mentally for the exercise despite the aches and pains he knew would be waiting for him the next day. His right knee already throbbed ominously. He showered and dressed, read the newspapers from cover to cover and felt ready for the day – whatever it held. His determination to beat any problem was fully restored.

Fenwick was clear what he would do. He would allow himself the pleasure of waking his daughter and giving her an early breakfast in bed and a story. Then, a change of plan, he would get to the office early, read any new reports and reread the old ones. He could have Cooper targeted on follow-up actions and be home shortly after nine o'clock on schedule to take his son and mother to the specialist clinic. After that, he would have to take things one step at a time, but at least he would be in control.

Cooper had been anticipating a good Monday morning. He would get in early, review the reports, direct the work for the day and then have time to spend testing his pet theory. Instead, he found that Fenwick had beaten him to it. There was a list of tasks that would take him two days to sort out. The only good news was that one of them added direct support to the private opinion that he was developing on the case.

Fenwick turned up at the incident room shortly after two, clipped and unapproachable. The team was relieved to see, however, that he was fully in command of himself and others. No one asked about the unexplained absence.

'Right, results, Sergeant. Where are they?'

'I'll take you through them, sir. One, you were right, the semen sample taken from the body was twelve to eighteen hours old, which means that the killer brought it with him to the scene and obviously pre-planned the whole event, even securing a sample from someone else.

'Which means he could be homosexual, or a voyeur, spying on couples in Friday Street and Pixt Lane. I've detailed PC Miller to make enquiries tonight and again on Wednesday to catch the regulars – see if they saw anything.'

Fenwick could hardly have been said to smile but the muscles in his jaw definitely relaxed and twitched.

'No matches of either samples against PNC either, sir, and no real leads on known offenders. We've sent details off to be checked against the AFR but the fingerprint sample was too small to get sufficient points of comparison to match to the PNC.

'The report on the empty envelope found at Johnstone's house just confirmed what we already knew. It was sent by Anderson; it had her fingerprints on it and the paper and ink match. They sent handwriting samples to a graphologist who has confirmed that the envelope was written by the same person who wrote out the entries in the sample of the address book you gave them.'

'And the tyre mark from the back of the envelope?'

'Ah yes. You were right on both counts. It matched the cycle-tracks at the scene and in the back garden, which means that the intruder at the house wheeled the bike over it when he entered. Also, as you suspected, if you look at the photograph taken of the post on the mat after we had arrived, there is no consistent pattern of tracks – they're all jumbled up which means that her post had been moved between the time he entered on the bike and when SOCO and the photographer arrived.'

'Forensics have got the whole lot now, to see if we can recreate the complete track – and check nothing else is missing?' Cooper nodded. 'Good, what else?'

'The detailed report on the scene has just arrived. You wanted to check whether she had been held still as she died. Well, she had. There are spurts of blood on the walls and ceilings consistent with a single wound severing her main veins and arteries. The direction of the splash marks is consistent and there was substantial pooling around the body with no signs of dragging to the position in which she died.

'The blood found at the foot of the stairs is consistent with a heavily bloodstained person standing in one spot, perhaps while changing their clothes. It's hard to say for sure.'

'There's no way this was unpremeditated or random, is there? We're up against someone who planned this meticulously, with or without an accomplice. It's time to take stock and focus. We've got too many unfinished lines of inquiry.'

Cooper hesitated before he made his next comment. They were sitting in the small screened-off cubicle where Fenwick had his desk, to one end of the incident room. The screens were only six feet high and all their conversation could be heard by the team in the room. Now he had to discuss something far more delicate, and he knew he and Fenwick would not see eye to eye. Fenwick made it worse by asking the question he was dreading.

'What about your reread of all the reports? Did you find anything significant that we had missed?'

Cooper's last chance to lie, but he was an honest man: 'Yes, but it's probably nothing. As you said, we've already got too much to worry about.'

'Well, it's either worth mentioning or it's not, make up your mind!'

Cooper passed him a copy of the report on Johnstone's house, with a small yellow Post-it note stuck to one page, pointing to an entry in a long index of items that had been analysed: *One page of A5 feint-ruled paper from a diary. Page dated May 16th, 1979.*

'So?'

'You'll recall that we found diaries for 1973 onwards but that there were no diaries for years 1977–1981; this is a page from a 1979 diary. It must have fallen out at some stage. It doesn't change anything. I thought she'd thrown them away – perhaps they fell to bits.'

'Perhaps. But it's equally likely that the intruder took it. We already know this was premeditated – which means the murderer had a motive. He took the risk of going to her house and searching it – there must be a reason. It wasn't burglary so perhaps he was looking for something. All that we know is missing so far is a letter from Octavia Anderson and this diary which happens to be for a year when Anderson and Johnstone were at school together.'

'But it doesn't say anything, sir, just drivel. I can't see the connection and the case is already too complicated, like you said.' Cooper was uncomfortably aware of the silence beyond the screens.

'So far we can find no clues in her work or private life. No secret relationships, love affairs, dark secrets – nothing. It was either random, but the planning speaks against it, or there is something we've failed to discover, or it has something to do with her past. We need to find out what.'

'With respect, sir,' Fenwick's jaw tightened visibly as he listened with hard-won patience to his sergeant, 'there is another explanation. He might have preplanned it but she could still be a random victim; he stalked her for a few days perhaps, became fixated, but that's all.'

'And the connection with Anderson? Why did the killer take the letter, Cooper?'

'We've known weirder mementoes.'

'Unlikely – why should he have opened it? Anyway, if you're right, what line of inquiry do you intend to pursue? What are you going to give this eager team to do?' A wide sweep of his hand took in the incident room and the small group of officers trying hard not to look as if they were listening to every word.

'Good point, sir,' Cooper lowered his voice, 'but we'll come under pressure soon on team size anyway.'

'Exactly; so make the most of them now and get on with it.'

DC Nightingale was a freshman detective and used to receiving the monotonous, grinding chores that fell to trainees everywhere. Hers was the unenviable task of tracking down the current whereabouts of the 'class of 1980', as Fenwick's latest bee in the bonnet had been christened. So far she had traced nine, lost one to Australian emigration, another two to Canada, and had the distressing experience of talking to a long-bereaved mother who had lost her eighteen-year-old in a car accident almost twenty years previously, but had still sobbed down the phone recounting her daughter's contemporaries' names and what had become of them. She had revealed an almost encyclopaedic knowledge of 'her Anita's' friends gleaned from an obsessive following of marriages and births in the local paper – a vicarious sharing of the life her daughter never knew.

It had saved Detective Constable Nightingale many hours' work but she'd still felt like a grave robber and had eventually cut the woman off with a promise to get back to her once they had followed up on the names given.

She looked at the nine names she had left:

Judith Richards – Canada
Amanda (Mandy) Lovell – Canada
Carol Truman – Australia
Leslie Bannister (now Smith, husband Brian)
Angela Barnet (now Jones (lives locally still) a very good friend of Anita's)
Wendi (with an i) Compton (now Russell, husband James with two 11-year-olds)
Judith Plaistow – unmarried
Mary Smith (now Heath – husband Andrew or Albert)
Deborah Waite (now Fearnside – husband Derek)

A Jones and a Smith in so short a list seemed more than unfair, so Nightingale decided to make a start on the other UK names – tracing telephone numbers, addresses, trying to arrange interviews.

Mary Heath's telephone rang unanswered. It was four o'clock, school run time, but the unmarried constable did not appreciate that. She was young and, though engaged, totally unaware of the commitments that followed marriage and family. Instead, she focused with customary single-mindedness on the job before her. No matter how tedious or unpromising she always completed the work she was given with a focused determination that could strike others, including her fiancé, as selfishly ruthless. But it was one of the characteristics that had already singled her out for the curious attention of her superiors and she was incapable of giving less than one hundred per cent to her work. Wendi Russell's answerphone obligingly took a message. As did Deborah Fearnside's – a man's voice abruptly asking the caller to leave details. There was no trace of a Judith or J. Plaistow in the local directory and no less than 35 Joneses and 26 B. Smiths.

Nightingale was working laboriously through the Joneses when a vague memory started to stir in her mind. Her subconscious was doing its best to tell her something which the tedium of the current job held at bay. In exasperation, and with a slight curse to all DCIs and DSs who could go traipsing around doing interviews, following up leads, anything other than sitting in the stuffy, overheated incident room, she went and made herself a cup of tea.

Standing, staring at the tea-bag as it begrudgingly gave up its flavour, her memory finally broke through. Tea forgotten, she literally ran back to her desk to pick up her car keys and notes, then left the incident room for the station.

Fenwick convened a review meeting on the case for Monday evening. There were still no more reported sightings of the killer. The detectives' ideas were that:

- a random nutter on a bike had stalked and murdered Katherine Johnstone but the MO matched no other cases on the computer
- an unknown friend/lover/relative for reasons as yet unclear did the same
- someone from her distant past – possibly her schooldays given the missing diary – had decided to kill her, again for reasons unknown
- Miss Johnstone's involvement in the anniversary Mass was deeply resented and had led to her death.

Four days into the case and all they had were options and no facts to discount any of them.

The bottom line was no motive, no suspects, no leads.

General consensus favoured the second hypothesis. It was obvious Fenwick had no real enthusiasm for it but as the majority of murders are committed or arranged by a person known to the victim, he deployed the majority of the team, under Cooper, to following up any connections in an attempt to establish a motive.

WDC Nightingale arrived late towards the end of the meeting and was greeted by an array of sarcastic comments. In her rush to follow up her idea, she had left no note of where she had gone – a cardinal sin, as Cooper intended to point out.

'We'll have a word after the meeting, Nightingale.' Cooper never joked on matters of discipline.

'Yes, sir. I'm sorry, sir, only something came up.'

'Of such importance that you clear off and then waltz in late? Then spit it out now.'

'Yes, sir, at least I think so, sir.'

Cooper let the silence continue.

'I was checking on the class of 1980, sir, and noticed a possible connection. Katherine Johnstone was at school with Deborah Waite, who married Derek Fearnside. She went missing in April and has never been found.'

Fenwick felt the hairs on the back of his neck rise and his mouth go dry. He stared hard at Nightingale in absolute silence as everyone else in the incident room waited expectantly, sensing his immediate interest and excitement. The Fearnside investigation had gone nowhere despite extraordinary efforts by Fenwick and Cooper to break it open. It had fallen by the wayside as other priorities took over. Lack of resources and other pressures had meant that the loose ends still remained untied. Now the victim of a grisly, premeditated, yet so far motiveless murder had been linked to Deborah Fearnside. His instincts screamed at him as his team sat and stared at his distracted face. It was not unheard of, in a small town like Harlden, for tragedy to befall two school friends within months of each other, but he felt it was more than that. The connection was too close to his own intuition, and he still lived with his feelings of guilt about the unresolved Fearnside case. However oblique the connection – and merely being at school together proved nothing – Fenwick immediately decided to follow it up.

He assigned Taylor and Nightingale to find all the old schoolgirls and interview those associated with the anniversary performance whilst he personally took on the twin task of reviewing the Fearnside file and persuading the Superintendent to leave the full team on the case. The latter would be the most difficult, but he reckoned that he would have at least another week before he came under real pressure.

CHAPTER TWENTY-ONE

Fenwick sat at home in front of the fire and thought back over an extraordinary and disturbing day. He had been true to his word and had returned home in time to take his mother and son to the specialist, despite an extended visit to the incident room to review the reports and leave instructions for Cooper. They had travelled in silence, he and his mother, because they could find no words of comfort for each other, and Christopher because he now seemed incapable of speaking at all.

The consultant they were due to meet asked to talk to Fenwick first, alone, a long probing interview he had found difficult and embarrassing. By the end of it, although the doctor has been at great pains to appear neutral throughout, Fenwick felt a complete failure as a parent. Next his mother had gone in alone, for even longer. Then finally Christopher. At the end of two hours they had been told that the little boy was seriously disturbed but there were no obvious signs of mental illness. More appointments were made – with behavioural psychologists, specialists on autism, post-traumatic stress disorders – the list was endless. And still Christopher remained totally withdrawn into his own world.

As Fenwick escaped from the uncomfortable silence at home into the Fearnside papers he tried not to think about the next few weeks. The specialist had offered little hope of immediate improvement. He had added the appointment dates his mother had given him to his diary but resolutely refused to discuss the matter in the absence of facts.

Instead he turned to the comfort of the ageing missing person's file like an old friend. He found his notations in margins, blunt comments on the scrappiness of the original investigation and a checklist of follow-up actions that had barely been started before resources had been withdrawn from the case. He read them all with new eyes, alert for links to Katherine Johnstone's murder.

By the time he went to bed, he was frustrated with his lack of new thinking but secretly reassured by the quality of his original work. His checklist of questions was resurrected with only a few adjustments, made relevant by the recent murder. He lay in bed watching the headlights of occasional passing cars send parallel beams across the ceiling. There were no obvious patterns in this case. A classroom connection was all that linked the two, and in the dark solitude he had to admit it was a tenuous link, attractive because of the lack of other leads. He decided to forget the Johnstone case for a moment and focus again on Deborah Fearnside, not the facts of her disappearance but the reasons for it.

Had she run off, lost her memory, been abducted, traded in white slavery, been killed accidentally and hidden, been murdered? Or had she been abducted and then murdered? For each of the reasons he had a question – why now? Supposing there was a link to her school days, what could be enough to kill her? There were rarely more than six reasons for murder: greed, love, hate, revenge, jealousy, fear – was there a legacy from an old school teacher or friend and one of the legatees was killing the others? Unlikely, but still worth adding a question to the interview checklist.

Love or hate – had someone had a desperate love affair that had gone wrong and for some reason waited all these years to kill the person/people that had spurned them? It didn't stack up. And why the interest in Octavia Anderson's letter about the concert? Still, questions on old boyfriends would go on the list for the morning.

Fear – was there a guilty secret? For some reason, had someone lost their nerve and decided to kill off all parties to it rather than risk disclosure? He couldn't dismiss the idea as easily as the others but it seemed far-fetched. All three women, Deborah, Kate, Octavia (assuming she was involved at all), seemed to have had normal schooling and successful lives – but then he had met too many well-brought-up, urbane wife beaters, friendly rapists and polite murderers to allow a collective display of good upbringing to deflect him.

As a motive, fear remained, linked to the guilty secret theory perhaps? Which brought his wandering mind smoothly to revenge. In all his years as a policeman he had only come across three cases where a criminal act had been motivated by revenge, and all had involved so-called neighbours 'getting their own back' on each other. One had been wilful damage (an offending fence taken down and destroyed); one a public nuisance charge (three pit bulls allowed to roam and defecate on a village cricket field were poisoned and died – a member of the second XI had been charged), and one grievous bodily harm (a brick, used as a missile had struck a convicted dangerous driver at an all-night summer barbecue, breaking his nose and fracturing his skull).

He remembered each case in detail. As a boy he had devoured Agatha Christie's books and in every other plot it had appeared that smouldering revenge lay at the heart of violent crime. Consequently, from the early days of his police career he had looked for the vengeful culprit – and had only ever succeeded in finding these three.

So he circled around the revenge motive suspiciously. It fitted neatly in with the guilty secret but he found it hard to believe that Deborah Fearnside and Katherine Johnstone had done anything worthy of their execution. He was shocked at the word his drifting mind provided, dramatic and threatening. Had the women *really* been executed for something judged by the murderer to be a crime? The idea was compelling but highly unlikely. In the dark grey hours of the early morning Fenwick finally drifted into a dream-filled, restive sleep.

Tuesday opened, a glorious sunny day; light winds and low

humidity made the heat bearable. From before breakfast everyone on the Johnstone case, with the exception of Fenwick, was calculating what time they would finish that evening and escape into summer.

The sight of DS Cooper, white-board marker in hand, awaiting their arrival, lowered everyone's spirits. The officers charged with interviewing close friends and relatives were summarily dispatched, bemused by additional questions on legacies, boyfriends and dark secrets from the past. Fenwick personally described the further tasks he had in mind for investigating the class of 1980.

DC Nightingale had arranged to meet her fiancé at the local pub and then go on for dinner with friends. It had been a slightly risky promise to make, given that she was working on a murder but there were so few developments apart from the possible link with Deborah Fearnside that she had been pretty confident her work would be finished by six at the latest. Jeff had been away on business for ten days and she was dying to see him again. But once Sergeant Cooper had finished briefing them, she had to give up any idea of meeting him early after all.

She tried unsuccessfully to call him at work and ended up leaving an apologetic message on his voicemail. Personal life reordered, she committed herself willingly to her share of the work. It had, after all, been her observation that had given this side of the investigation new life and she felt an obscure ownership. Fenwick wanted them to report back at five and decide what to do next; the day already seemed too short.

Fenwick commandeered Cooper to help him find out more about the anniversary concert. The list of organisers and participants was awesome. In addition to the school orchestra and singers, there were the county choir and orchestra and three local choirs – in total 175 names. Most interviews could be dealt with by phone. Fenwick selected the key people for himself and left the rest to Cooper to sort out.

Nine hours later hot, sweaty, dispirited members of the Sussex constabulary reconvened.

'Nothing.' Cooper's voice was flat, hoarse.

'Constables?'

'Not a lot really, sir.' DC Nightingale spoke on their behalf. She was bitterly disappointed. 'None of the school friends we've contacted so far could shed any light on the disappearance of Deborah Fearnside and the murder of her classmate. One, Leslie Smith, was a friend of Deborah Fearnside when she went missing. She had been due to go with her on the day she disappeared, in fact. She's convinced the modelling opportunity was real – she said they went through too much to be selected for it to be anything else. Oh and, sir, she says can we stop bothering her. We've apparently already called her about the choir and about Kate Johnstone so she was pretty upset.'

'I don't care what Mrs Smith thinks, I want you to chase up *all* the loose ends as soon as you've finished with the school friends.'

'Sergeant?'

Cooper was already flicking through his notes.

'Smith's a member of the county choir. Not surprising really, given the—'

'Musical tradition of the school. Yes, Sergeant – thank you.'

'And you, sir?'

'Nothing really. The various choirs and orchestras appear to rehearse separately until about three weeks before the day. Then they practice together three or four times before a dress rehearsal and the Mass itself. It's an important event for the school and county and they're delighted that Octavia Anderson will be there – because of her the other soloists they've managed to get are much better than they expected and it looks as if the city mayor is going to be there. No one's received any threats. Nothing strange has happened – except for the unfortunate murder of Katherine Johnstone – and I got the impression that her death, and my line of questioning, were an embarrassment they could do without. Oh and by the way, apparently the ACC's wife is chairwoman of the fund-raising committee. All the proceeds of the concern will go to charity. The top ticket price is going to be £100 including the reception, if you can believe it. They've raised the price because of Anderson. And I was told most have already been sold to the great and the good.'

Fenwick looked at him glumly. More politics to cope with.

'So where does that leave us?' It was almost a rhetorical question.

'Well, we've got the interviews to finish off; the disappearance of Deborah Fearnside to investigate and . . . that's about it. Oh, apart from checking Anderson's alibi, and you said you would do that.' Cooper sounded tired but there was no trace of scepticism in his voice. He still might not believe that Fenwick's primary line of enquiry was the right one but that was a conversation the two of them would have again privately – not in front of the other ranks.

'Right, well, you get on with it. I have an appointment with the Superintendent and then the press. At least I'll be able to tell them we're handling several lines of inquiry!'

In reality the case was going nowhere. Exactly one week to the day of Katherine Johnstone's death they staged a televised reconstruction – more in hope than expectation. Even the weather refused to co-operate. The sun shone brightly, making the tall dark bobby on the bike sweat profusely inside his yellow cape. The response that evening and the following day was one of the lowest experienced by the TV production company.

Several callers rang in claiming to have seen a large black Honda motor bike – some said 500cc, some said 750cc – leaving the multistorey on Thursday evening. No one recalled a number plate nor any details of the rider other than he/she was wearing a black helmet with a tinted visor.

Cooper had finally got around to voicing his opinion to Fenwick that the murderer was probably an old boyfriend and he had probably swapped his pedal bike for the motorised variety. The atmosphere between the two was distinctly cool by Friday.

All Katherine Johnstone's relatives and friends had been interviewed at least twice and tempers were starting to fray. There was no evidence of a current boy-, or for that matter, girlfriend. Two old boyfriends had been traced, both now happily married, both with water-tight alibis. Fenwick confirmed

Octavia Anderson's whereabouts for the Thursday evening. Not water-tight, but close to it. She was being driven from her home in London to Heathrow for a 7.30 p.m. flight to Amsterdam. They were still trying to trace the driver.

On the following Wednesday, the team was slightly reduced to release resources to investigate a recent string of barn fires and to find the arsonist before more than property and livestock were torched. Fenwick had fought against the reduction without success and re-planned the team's workload in a foul mood but with no less determination to pursue and resolve the case.

EMISCA

PART FOUR

INGEMISCO

Ingemisco tanquam reus,
Culpa rubet vultus meus,
Supplicanti parce, Deus.

I lament, for I am guilty:
And I blush for my wrong-doing:
I implore Thee, Saviour, spare me.

CHAPTER TWENTY-TWO

Several weeks later Fenwick, dressed in dark grey suit and black tie, promised his mother that he would be back from Katherine Johnstone's memorial in time to take Christopher for his fourth assessment in as many weeks.

He made a habit of attending the funerals or memorials of victims – both as a mark of respect and to observe the interaction of family, friends and acquaintances. It would not be pleasant. It never was and it would be made more uncomfortable by his distinct lack of progress.

Cooper would be there with him. The strain between the two had eased. Fenwick was genuinely optimistic that his sergeant's hunch about a motorcycle might be correct and he was pleased that Cooper had dropped the idea of an old boyfriend.

He was now down to a team of twelve including Cooper, with a promise of immediate additional resources as soon as a new lead came up. The detectives were still hard at work – two following up the loose ends of Deborah Fearnside's disappearance in the hope of finding a connection. One, WDC Nightingale, was almost through the list of all the old girls from 1976 to 1983, at least those she could trace.

The school term had long finished but the back rows of the church were crammed with pupils, many in school uniform as a mark of respect. Kate Johnstone had been a popular teacher. Family sat quietly in the front pews – mother, father, sister, a very elderly grandmother and various aunts, uncles and cousins. Between the two groups, more tightly packed, sat friends, colleagues and the police.

The church was full. Delicate and beautiful flower arrangements stood on pedestals by the altar, donated by the flower arranging club to which she had belonged. Readings and speeches confirmed Fenwick's impression of the woman as a well liked, friendly, local girl who had stayed loyal to her community and who had put a lot back in her teaching and musical work. There were no grand statements to be made. Her kindnesses and contributions had been measured out in small gestures, unremarked during her lifetime but weighty now, on her death.

The ceremony was poignant. There were a lot of flowers. Among them a cat shaped in white carnations stood out incongruously. Fenwick paid his respects to her parents and declined the invitation to the Sussex equivalent of a cold collation. He lingered at the church as the family led the group of mourners to their waiting cars.

'I can't actually believe she's gone.' Octavia Anderson came up behind his right shoulder. 'Of all of us, she was the one in the lead – she always knew where she was going. It didn't surprise any of us that she became a teacher, and a *good* one at that.' There was vehemence in her tone.

'Does anyone say she wasn't a good teacher?'

'Oh no. It's just that under this government, it seems to be a profession that needs defending.'

'Not from me. You said, a moment ago, "of all of us", as if you knew her very well whilst you were at school. Did you?'

'Well yes. We were quite close really. In the same gang, you know how teenage girls are – or perhaps you don't, Chief Inspector?'

On a less attractive woman, the look she gave him would have diminished into a simper, on her it was provocative.

'My memories of teenage girls come heavily tinged with embarrassment.'

'At least you're honest.'

'Who else was in the gang?'

'I'm not sure I can remember now, me, Kate . . . oh, and

Debbie. Which reminds me, I was surprised she wasn't here today. She'd stayed very close to Kate.'

Fenwick stopped walking towards his car and looked at her closely. She appeared sincere.

'You obviously don't know then. Mrs Fearnside – Debbie – disappeared about three months ago. We have no idea where she is.'

'Disappeared? My God!' Octavia paled and stretched out a hand to a nearby tombstone to steady herself. She seemed to shrink inwards on herself, forgetting she still had an audience.

'Debbie, too . . .' Her voice was barely a murmur. 'My God.'

'You said, "Debbie, too", Ms Anderson – have you reason to think there might be a connection?'

'What? I'm sorry. What did you say?' She still looked shaken, deeply disturbed. Fenwick took her elbow and guided her to a wooden bench to the side of the path which ran through the graveyard. He gave her time to recover.

The sun had reached its zenith during the service and cast short dark shadows at the foot of each gravestone. The inclined graves disappeared into the distant heat haze long before the eye could reach the boundary wall. This was an older part of the graveyard but still well tended with the attention to detail of small town churches everywhere. On the nearest grave a rose had been planted. In the long years it had grown there, well enriched in its soil, sporadic and inexpert prunings had taken their toll. Now it ran almost like a briar over the close green turf to the foot of the granite tombstone.

Octavia appeared calmer; some of the gloss had returned to her looks and gestures. 'I'm sorry Mr Fenwick.' The use of his surname sounded inappropriate from her lips. 'It was just the shock on top of the service today.'

'Don't worry. And if you're not going to call me Chief Inspector, I'd prefer Andrew.' He was rewarded with a warm smile.

'Do you think there might be a connection between Mrs Fearnside's disappearance and Kate's murder?'

Her reply was immediate. 'No, I can't think how there

could be one. It doesn't make any sense.'

'Nothing that happened to them both while you were all at school together?'

She shook her head decisively. 'I can't think of anything. We were just ordinary schoolgirls. It must just be a ghastly coincidence.'

They were still sitting on the bench, the sun burning into their dark mourning clothes. Around them, the churchyard hush was emphasised by constant humming from the bees. The colours that surrounded them were all greens and golds; even the stones in this part of the cemetery had weathered in the fifteen or twenty years since they had been planted in loving memory. From where they sat, no bright yellows, or pinks or reds of florist's ribbon decorated these graves. The flowers planted in remembrance had softened and naturalised over the years.

'Are you ready to move now?'

'Yes, I'm fine but, Andrew, I could really do with a drink! Would you think it too forward of me to ask if you'd join me?'

There was a lot he should be doing, papers on his desk crying out for attention. But it was a beautiful day, the case was going nowhere and he was with a beautiful woman.

'I'd like that, Miss Anderson.'

They walked together slowly towards the cast-iron gates, the sun, hot on their backs, casting a short linked shadow before them through the haze of green and gold.

Just before they reached the gates Fenwick caught a flash of red from the corner of his eye. To his left, set back from the path, one of the graves had been covered with dozens of crimson roses – placed directly on the cropped turf.

'Good Lord, look at that!' Even Fenwick's normally tough and unemotional heart was touched. 'I doubt anyone would do that for me long after I'm dead. "Carol Anne Truman",' he read carefully. 'I wonder who she was – and who loved her so much that they would keep putting flowers on her grave since 1980 – that's how many years? – nearly twenty! '*Dearly loved daughter of Vera and Robert, treasured niece of Alice and George –*

Requiem Aeternam. Must be the parents – she seems to have died young.'

Fenwick became aware that he was talking to himself. After a cursory glance, Octavia Anderson had walked on towards the gates.

'Sorry, I got side-tracked.' He jogged to her side.

'I've seen enough of graves for one day.' She was clipped and unamused.

'Time for that drink, then?' Fenwick took her elbow again gently and led the way, rehearsing as he did so the manner in which he would make it clear to her that he knew she had lied to him at their first meeting.

The service had touched Detective Constable Nightingale deeply. This was her first murder and it hurt. For the first few days she had been secretly so deeply affected that she had doubted her vocation. Then the thrill of the hunt took over and the pain had turned to slow, controlled anger. She no longer doubted her choice of a police career in the least but now she despaired of being any good at it.

At the church, it had been the relatives that reached her most. The body had ceased to have a significance. She had seen the photographs, read the PM reports; the physical remains now had nothing to do with Katherine Johnstone, were only so much evidence. But the family were different. They were real people, grieving people whose few consolations included the hope that justice would be done and their daughter's/sister's/niece's/friend's/teacher's killer would be caught and punished. The sight of a loving family, united even if it was in grief, affected her deeply. It was so strange, beyond her own personal experience.

Woman Detective Constable Nightingale was letting them down. She took it personally, this lack of progress. Immediately after the service, she returned to the incident room and read through all her notes and the main evidence files again. Hers had been the responsibility for checking on the school friends. It had been a disappointing task. She'd had hopes of Leslie Smith but the woman had been upset, defensive and simply wanted to be left alone. The interview had revealed little – confirmation of the strong musical tradition of the school, a few harmless reminiscences, some names of classmates remembered. An ineffectual interview that hadn't even produced an insight into Katherine Johnstone's character.

Something was niggling Detective Constable Nightingale. She read the Smith notes again but that wasn't it. Frustrated she made herself a coffee – the combination of instant caffeine and powdered milk was making her slightly sick, but it was a break. She stirred the muddy mixture vigorously, creating a mini whirlpool in the mug. Why was Smith so defensive? Why did she have so little to say? Why had she given no insight into Katherine Johnstone's character?

It dawned on her what was wrong – *why* had she not been at the service? The woman appeared to be trying to create some distance between herself and Katherine Johnstone and yet there was no logical reason for this. It could just be grief or she might not be a particularly strong person. On the other hand, she could be hiding something. Nightingale decided to call on her again. She decided not to ring first, that would only alert her. She would call round on the off-chance she was in.

The door was opened promptly by Leslie Smith herself after the first ring.

'Yes?' She kept the heavy wooden door between her body and the policewoman.

'Mrs Smith, I wonder if I might come in? I have a few more questions for you.'

'Why? Haven't I answered enough already? I've told your superior officer that I'm fed up with all this intrusion.'

'It won't take a moment, Mrs Smith; and I'm afraid it has to be today.'

The door was opened in a sulky, childish yank as Smith turned on her heel and entered the sitting room. It was left for Nightingale to close the outer door behind her.

'Mrs Smith, how close a friend to Katherine Johnstone were you?'

'I've already told you, not very.' Her hand shook as she lit a cigarette.

'Not now, when you were at school together.'

'Not really close, even then. I knew her, of course, everyone did. She was one of those people – good at games, good at maths, good at everything it seemed.'

'You said one of those, were there many like that?'

'A few.'

'Could you give me their names?'

'I can't remember after all this time. Why do you keep asking me such pointless questions anyway?'

Nightingale risked stretching the truth although her puritan soul protested loudly.

'For one reason only, Mrs Smith. We have other statements which claim you were a close friend of Katherine Johnstone at school and it seems odd that you should deny that now.'

'I *wasn't* really close,' she whined. 'Oh, I wanted to be, everyone did – the Famous Foursome attracted hangers on. I was one of the pests that hovered round them, but I was never a close friend, now do you see?'

Nightingale did, and was sympathetic. Childhood failures were always among the most painful. She suspected that rejection had left its scars on the Leslie Smith of today, but she wasn't there to sympathise.

'Who were the Famous Foursome, Mrs Smith?'

'Oh, I can't remember now.'

'Come on, Mrs Smith, that's not strictly true, is it? It obviously mattered a great deal to you – most people would have a very clear memory.'

'Perhaps I've blocked it out.'

'I don't think so.' Nightingale let the silence develop. It lasted some time.

'Why don't you just go *away* and leave me alone?'

'You know that's not an option, Mrs Smith. You obviously know something and it's my job to find out anything I can – anything at all – that may help us find Katherine Johnstone's killer. You must tell me – and you might as

213

well tell me now and save yourself the hassle.'

'Well, there was Katherine, and Debbie and Octavia Anderson. As I said, I just tagged along.'

'You said there were four in the group, that's only three. Who else?'

She hesitated then said evasively, 'Judith – Judy Plaistow, that's it, she was the fourth.'

Despite further questions that was all Detective Constable Nightingale learnt. It was hardly startling, nothing to get worked up about, so *why* had Leslie Smith become so disturbed and so defensive?

It was nearly six o'clock on a warm summer evening. Nightingale could hear distant voices from the local riverside pub calling and she hadn't seen her fiancé all week but she could not relax. Instead of turning left towards home, a decent drop of best and a chance of seeing Jeff on the way, she reluctantly turned right at the end of the Smiths' road and back to the incident room. It was almost deserted, the air stale behind closed windows. Wearily removing her jacket she toyed with the idea of letting in some fresh air but decided she would be gone in a few minutes. The name Plaistow rang a bell. She had interviewed a Judith Plaistow over the telephone weeks before – with any luck she would be able to confirm Smith's story at once.

She found her previous notes and the number. There was no indication from the interview that Plaistow was particularly close to Katherine Johnstone. Five minutes later, she knew Leslie Smith had been lying about the fourth member of the group. Plaistow had been at the school less than three terms and had formed no close attachments. Thoughts of the pub now completely forgotten, she was back on Mrs Smith's doorstep, armed with the old class lists by 6.20 p.m.

Leslie Smith tried to close the door as soon as she saw who it was but a determined size six allowed Nightingale to gain entry.

'You lied to me, Mrs Smith, and I want to know why.'

214

'Mummy, Mummy, who is this?' A boy of about five or six ran down the hall from the kitchen.

'Please, it's the children's teatime and their father will be home soon. He hates it if I've not cleared away and got them into their pyjamas.'

'Then the sooner you answer my questions, Mrs Smith, the sooner I'll be gone.'

'Mummy, who is this lady and why's she talking to you like that?'

'Go back to the kitchen, Matthew, now, and finish your beans. I want every scrap gone by the time I come in – go on.'

She watched him run back and then ushered Nightingale into the same sitting room. She looked guilty and defeated. Glancing nervously at the clock she started talking without preamble.

'I'm sorry I lied to you. I don't know why I did, it's just that talking of Carol always upsets me.'

'Carol? Carol who?'

'Carol Truman. She was the fourth person. Katherine was very fond of her, we all were. She was a lovely girl. One of the special people you meet in life, you know?'

'You say *was* a lovely girl. Why?'

Leslie Smith looked at her in surprise and paused before responding. 'God, don't you ever stop asking questions? She, she went away. Left the school. The family emigrated or something.'

'That's hardly upsetting, Mrs Smith.'

'No, well it's not just that, you see.' Mrs Smith hesitated, searching for words. 'I was a bitch to her before she went, two-timed her with her boyfriend. She nearly had a breakdown. I never forgave myself.'

'I see, and you have no idea where she went, what she is doing now? What her family did?'

'No. They were farmers, I think – her family emigrated because of money troubles. That's all I know.'

'And you've never heard from her since?'

'No,' she sighed deeply, 'how could I?'

Leslie Smith lifted sad, washed-out blue eyes to Nightingale's. Either the woman was an exceptional actress or the guilt and regret in them was real. Detective Constable Nightingale was inclined to believe her.

In the car she double-checked the class lists; Carol Truman did not appear after 1980. She had come to a dead-end for the evening. In the morning she would check with emigration to find out whether and when the Truman family had emigrated. She felt deflated and somehow cheated. Earlier in the afternoon she had been sure that she was on the trail of *something* that would take them forward. She didn't have the keen intuition of Fenwick nor the years of experience of Cooper, but she had a ruthlessly logical brain and a meticulous, structured approach to investigation that had infuriated her fellow students at Police College. That and her ability to focus, analyse, deduce and deliver had earned her top marks and a certain place in CID, despite criticisms of her 'linear approach'.

She felt Fenwick was right. The connection between Johnstone and Fearnside could not be dismissed lightly. Back in the incident room Nightingale checked her list for Carol Truman. Her heart sank when she found it. According to her notes, the Trumans had emigrated to Australia in 1980. She had already faxed Australian immigration but they had been unable to trace anyone by that name entering the country in any of the months Nightingale had suggested. They had, though, helpfully sent her the complete list of Truemans and Trumans who had arrived in 1980; there were forty-seven names. Nightingale weighed up her hunch against the daunting list, came to the logical conclusion and then carefully filed the fax.

CHAPTER TWENTY-THREE

Of the names on the killer's list, only two remained. No further information was needed – their guilt was certain. One would be dispatched simply and quickly. Her part had been trivial but one that deserved punishment nevertheless: plans for the execution were easily laid.

The last one was different. The victim's name was ringed in red ink on the page with a wreath of scrolls and loops that almost obliterated the other names listed. This one deserved to die – to be executed in public for the murderer she was. Had there been any justice, she would be hanged at the end of a rope in a public place of execution, her crime and punishment witnessed by her peers. Or better still, put up against a wall and shot, bullets ripping her apart, releasing the slime and bile beneath the deceptively attractive exterior.

The beginning of an idea entered the killer's mind. It would be daring, perhaps suicidal but it would be right. If anyone could pull off such a plan, the killer could, army trained, used to performing in almost impossible situations. Surely, the years of training and deployment in the field, the move to more discreet and deadly assignments, had been enough preparation. The killer was deeply fatalistic. The idea was right despite its risks, and it might just be accomplished without his own death being an inevitable consequence, not that even his death would be an unacceptable price.

It would take formidable planning, specialist supplies, rehearsals and finally, courage. There wasn't much time – and the other killing had to be carried out in the meantime, perhaps only a few days before the main execution in case the ultimate goal became obvious. The killer discarded the list of names and started to compile, on a clean feint-ruled pad, a checklist of supplies.

CHAPTER TWENTY-FOUR

July continued hot and dry with clear high blue skies and soft breezes. It was as perfect as an English summer could be, except to Fenwick and his team. There had been no new developments in either the Johnstone or Fearnside cases. At least the Fearnside case was now being treated as suspicious. A short but productive inquiry had established that the whole catalogue-modelling opportunity had been cleverly faked but there was no trace of the people that had been involved – interviewer, photographer, chauffeur. Consequently Fenwick had no new leads to pursue. It had been impossible for the Superintendent to ignore the failure of the original investigation into Deborah Fearnside's disappearance. Inspector Blite, the original investigating officer, was called in for a dressing down by the Superintendent but as his conviction record was the second best in the Division it meant little.

Fenwick pressed on, determined to find and interview anyone who had known Kate Johnstone or Deborah Fearnside in the past twenty years. With a smaller team it was going to take him the whole summer just to get through the names they already had.

He was making no better progress at home but at least things hadn't got worse. Christopher had been receiving gentle counselling since his visit to the specialists. Some recent improvements, though barely perceptible, encouraged Fenwick to hope he would eventually recover despite the family history.

He still wasn't speaking and continued to live in his own

little world but the specialists had ruled out autism and favoured a diagnosis of acute and severe post-traumatic stress disorder. He could recover at any time, they said, quickly or slowly, but they could not predict when. Bloody typical, was Fenwick's reaction, long words dressing up the fact that they hadn't got a clue.

His mother had booked a holiday cottage in West Dorset, a short walk from the coast. On the spur of the moment Fenwick decided to join them for a few days at a time, leaving behind for the first time in his career a serious crime unsolved. While he was with them he was determined to try to focus entirely on his family and the gentle distractions of a beach holiday.

The weather was indulgent, warm enough every day for the beach or long walks and games along the limestone cliffs. There were no calls from the investigation team, nothing to distract from the simple pleasures of each day. Fenwick relaxed, his mother occasionally succumbed to girlish giggles, and the children blossomed. With Bess it was like watching a daisy open each morning to the sun and tuck down again in the evening tired and happy. With Christopher it was different. At first he appeared unaltered but deep down a change was occurring; colour was re-entering his tight, monochrome world. It started with his conversations with Bess, then his simple pleasure in the waves and spray sprinkling his head, arms and toes. By the time Fenwick had joined them for the second time he could bear to be touched again, even briefly cuddled. Although the tension remained, keeping him closed shut, his struggle to break free was clear. It was incredibly painful to Fenwick, who observed everything, waiting for his first chance to reach out and help his son.

Two days before Fenwick was due to return to work again he found Christopher lying prone on his small bed, sobbing hard enough to jar its wooden frame. At first he was appalled, cast down, unable to think clearly what he should do. He wanted to cradle the child in his arms, hug him, comfort him and take all the pain away, but he was too scared of getting it wrong. In the end, when he could bear to watch no longer, he sat gingerly on the mattress and lifted the little boy on to his lap.

The crying grew stronger but the child remained limp, hot and damp in his arms. The awful rigidity had finally gone. Fenwick cradled the boy, stroking his hair, kissing his forehead, rocking him to and fro for long minutes. Eventually the weeping subsided enough for a white cotton hanky to be offered and then, slowly, the boy started to talk.

His words ripped into Fenwick like shrapnel, tearing at his heart, leaving him empty and raw: mixed-up memories of rejection and petty cruelties as his mother withdrew into her final breakdown, a deep guilt that it had somehow been all his fault and, worst of all, that his daddy hated him and could never forgive him.

Fenwick continued to rock the child, afraid to speak in case his choked words added to the confusion and hurt. Large, individual tears tracked down his face and soaked, one at a time, into the boy's curly blond hair where his chin rested against the child's head. Eventually, an accumulated puddle trickled down Christopher's temple and behind his ear, causing the boy to start and look up. 'Daddy, you're crying. Why are you crying? Please don't, I'm so sorry.'

For the next half-hour, father and son talked – sometimes calmly, sometimes with tears. Fenwick felt his own sense of family purpose and responsibility take root again and grow, leaving him exhausted, depleted but with returning confidence.

His son was delicate, damaged, hurt beyond any of their understandings by his mother's illness. He had witnessed more than anyone had realised and, with a child's limited comprehension, had pieced together his own twisted version of events.

The doubts and self-loathing had lain like a cancer within the boy, distorting and hardening him with the poison of guilt. He had ceased to grow and react to the world, and it would take a long time for the damage to be gently removed. Perhaps the scars from it would always remain. But that was something Fenwick could cope with. It was a real task that he, with expert help, could work on for as long as it would take.

The sun was nearing the sea as the pair of them set off for

a walk across the long beach. Other families were still around, enjoying the last real heat of the day but for the two of them the sea, shimmering like a gauze scarf into which the sealing wax sun was slowly melting, was there for them alone. Christopher occasionally let go of his father's hand and dared the molten waves, running back shrieking, breathless and elated to hug his father's knees. Fenwick alone, or with his son by his side, felt truly happy for the first time in many months.

On their way back to the cottage Fenwick bought a local paper, the first he had purchased during the holiday, and promptly set it to one side as he agreed to join the children in a final game before bed. The next day, over an excellent malt before dinner, he read the bitty local stories and felt his perspective on life restored. Not all could be wrong with the world when a feature on mischievous moorland ponies still made the front page. Sadly, a harsher reality lay in other stories.

A man in his early twenties had been arrested after threatening a publican with a knife; the ex-serviceman had become drunk and offensive and had waved 'a knife somehow retained from his service days' at the landlord. There was a lurid and detailed description of the weapon, complete with photograph of a similar blade. Despite his relaxed holiday mood, Fenwick's mind automatically logged the similarity to Katherine Johnstone's supposed murder weapon, still unrecovered. As he went to turn the page his attention was attracted by a single column entry in the bottom corner.

Mrs Trudi Swithin – Correction
The Editor would like to point out that a reference to Mrs Trudi Swithin, in connection with last week's article on the woman's body found in Dyle Copse, was by no means meant to imply that the body found was that of Mrs Swithin, who went missing some months ago. Detective Inspector Churt of Dorset CID has emphasised that he is still pursuing nationwide enquiries in order to ascertain

the identity of the dead woman. We apologise to Mrs Swithen's family for any upset or distress the reference may have caused. Story, page 3.

Inside, the paper repeated the key facts concerning the discovery of the remains of a woman in a remote copse in the north of the county. The pathologist had estimated her age at thirty to forty and, from the quality and extent of dental work, she had been wealthy enough to afford private treatment. She had also had at least one child. Police were searching local and national missing persons registers but so far had not identified the woman.

Fenwick reached Cooper in minutes and the sergeant called him back within half an hour to confirm that details of Deborah Fearnside, as well as those of other missing women in the county, had been sent and would be cross-checked in due course but as yet they had heard nothing. The divisional CID in Dorset were prioritising the matching, starting with the records of local women and gradually moving out. It would be some time before they reached West Sussex.

Fenwick's next call was to Churt. Initially the local DI was hostile, resenting the clumsy intrusion of a holidaying officer on his patch, but he agreed to meet over a pint later that evening, and after he had heard the details of the Fearnside case, he agreed to raise her name to the top of the list for the following day.

'How was this woman you've found killed?'

'It's still pretty tentative – you know Paths, until all the tests are done they won't commit – but our local boy is prepared to say her throat was cut. With some blade, too, given the marks on her spine.'

The hairs on Fenwick's arms rose and the back of his neck prickled. Adrenalin hit his stomach, souring the beer and whisky; his heart raced. He knew this was Deborah Fearnside and he knew why the two local articles held his attention. Absently he thanked Ben Churt, confirming that he would call the following day. In his mind he could hear again Pendlebury's narrative over the body of Katherine Johnstone.

Fenwick was becoming convinced that the killer was a military man. The planning and execution of Johnstone's killing suggested training and a disciplined, practical mind. Had it not been for a few drops of blood and his obsessive insistence on full SOCO treatment at her house, they could still have been pursuing a fictitious sex attacker.

If this second body was Deborah Fearnside's that meant her abduction and all the stages leading to it had also been a carefully orchestrated con. Either that, or she was an unfortunate random victim but the coincidences were too great for that. Anyway, why hide the body so far from home?

None of the team's painstaking work trying to trace the modelling catalogue company had yielded any information. There wasn't even an echo of their existence beyond a run-down address of convenience. He contemplated the idea of calling Cooper immediately to start him working on the military theory but paused with his hand on the receiver. Better to wait until the following day and call with certainty.

The indulgent summer weather broke the next day. Soft West Country rains fell in continuous sheets from sunrise. Fenwick, impatient, irascible, was up before dawn and already pacing the small cottage like a bear in a pen when the rest of the family awoke. He suggested to his mother that she take the children to a local dinosaur museum but not even the lure of prehistoric monsters would persuade Bess and Chris to leave their father's side.

In the end Fenwick played a distracted, but determinedly good-natured, game of Monopoly until the telephone rang just before lunch. It was Churt.

'Fenwick, they've completed the preliminary check. It looks as if our lady *is* your Deborah Fearnside.'

Fenwick stared into middle distance. Through the gap of the partly closed door he could see from Park Lane round to the Angel Islington, with his son's silver racing car firmly placed on the Old Kent Road. As he watched, a small hand moved the piece out of view, leaving the board bare.

He had expected elation. Instead he felt immense, heavy sadness and a real pain in his heart. She had been a beautiful and adoring mother; now she was dead. Her children would always be motherless, much as his were. Even if another woman came along, for Fearnside or himself, she would never replace their mother. The pain slowly changed to flat, unyielding anger. For his own wife there had been no tangible villain, no personification of evil, just a debilitating, degrading disease. Now there could be a legitimate focus for his fury, a way to expiate the hatred and the guilt. Nothing was going to stand between him and her killer.

He became aware of Churt's voice in his ear.

'Fenwick, are you still there? I said, do you want to come over? I'll give you directions. It'll be a while before the pathologist finishes – I'd have lunch first if I were you.'

'I'll come over now. I can wait.'

The Fearnside case was reopened officially as a murder investigation that day. Fenwick was given his extra men and Cooper put them to work at once. When Fenwick returned to the incident room he found the sergeant and Nightingale industriously reviewing and sorting files for a move back to the station, anything to take their mind off breaking the news to Fearnside. Fenwick had insisted they wait for his return. He felt he had to do it.

'Boss? You're back a day early. Did you have a good time?' Fenwick blinked hard at a question that seemed to come at him out of time.

'Yes. Yes, very good. The children loved it, until the weather broke yesterday. They were happy to come home.' His impatience to get on was palpable. 'Where are the extra resources? Why aren't they here?'

'Four started today, I've got them working. The rest arrive tomorrow morning, from HQ. The station can hardly cope but we're moving the incident room back to Division, as you asked. This isn't a good base any more, particularly in the middle of school holidays. By the way, there's been another major riot on the coast – we're going to have to fight to keep the extra men. All leave's cancelled as it is.'

Fenwick grunted a reply. Reopening a three-month-old murder investigation in the middle of summer came high up a masochist's wish list. He needed to keep the team active, both to stop them being poached back and to maintain some semblance of morale.

'I've decided to try television again, a reconstruction of her last trip; and the *Evening Standard* are usually very helpful if there's a London connection. Has anyone interviewed Leslie Smith again? Her name was coming up too often for it to be pure coincidence.'

Nightingale answered: 'I did last month but now she's on holiday in Turkey with the family, sir, for three weeks. Went two days ago. We're trying to trace her but no one's quite sure where she is. The local travel agents didn't book it.'

'Keep on it. I'm sure there's still more to come there.'

'Nightingale established a definite link to the two women, at school.'

'She claims not to have been one of the "Famous Foursome" – I think that's what they called them back in the fifth form, sir.' Nightingale consulted her notes. 'In addition to the dead woman, the others in the group were Octavia Anderson and a girl called Carol Truman.'

'Truman. Have we interviewed her yet? The name rings a bell but I don't know why.'

'Can't trace her, sir. The family emigrated to Australia. I've put in a routine request for information but there's nothing on her. I've got a list of nearly fifty other Trumans. I could try them.'

'Yes, do – it's essential we find all the group members.'

Cooper shifted uncomfortably on a school chair inadequate for the task of supporting his considerable frame. 'Is it right, sir, to make this our main line of inquiry? I mean, all we've got is the school connection. It could just be a coincidence.' Unconsciously he held his breath, waiting for the cutting tirade. It did not come.

'Of course, I haven't told you. That's my oversight. Sorry. It looks as if both women were killed in the same way, potentially the same weapon. I'm getting forensics to check. Luckily, there are definite slicing marks on Deborah Fearnside's spine. We had the same with Kate. Dorset have also agreed to allow Pendlebury to look at Fearnside's body; we'll have the report in a couple of days. Now, I suggest you two stop gassing and start working. Dig out the interviews with Anderson, would you? While you two are occupied, I'll try and talk to her again. She's been inconsistent to the point of lying about her friendship with the dead women. I'm going to find out why.'

Miss Anderson's maid politely informed Fenwick that Madame was in Montpellier and would be there for another week. He contemplated interviewing her by phone but decided against it. The woman was too much of a performer; he would need to see her face to face, try to surprise her.

In the meantime, the press conference on the discovery of Deborah Fearnside's body, *Evening Standard* feature and reconstruction took up most of his time. Fenwick pondered more than once the gradual slide of modern crime investigation from detection to media relations but decided on balance that the benefits outweighed the cost and inconvenience. As it was the silly season for news, the discovery of the body of an attractive young mother months after her disappearance, gained considerable column inches. Fenwick deliberately kept the potential link between the two murders secret. Fortunately, the two were so different that no one made the connection.

The publicity this time generated a reasonable level of response with two definite leads. One call came in from a Mr Stanisopolous, a Greek restaurateur, another from a freelance photographer.

Mr Stanisopolous, small, energetic, moustachioed, was adamant he had seen Mrs Fearnside at Victoria *and* had seen her with a man. He was a remarkably confident and observant witness. He was sure that the lady he had tried to help outside Victoria Station had been Deborah Fearnside. Why? Because she had been beautiful. She had reminded him of Marilyn Monroe.

He was sure a man had been there to meet her, by arrangement certainly. He had addressed her by name and escorted her to his car. Had they met before? He could not say, perhaps not, she had not seemed to recognise him.

His description of the man was less detailed. He had been tall, dark, he thought, but the chauffeur's cap and tinted glasses had concealed much of his features. He recalled that the man had had a 'military feel' about him. He should know; he had worked in his father's restaurant in Athens in the seventies and it was second nature to him to spot an army man. It could just have been the driver's uniform and cap, yes, and the short hair, but there had been something else too, his walk, his authority. Anyway, the woman had gone with him happily enough.

The car? He was more vague about the car than the woman. Well, it was expensive; looked good and new; black paintwork. He could not remember the make, perhaps a Mercedes saloon, or a BMW? Not British for sure – it had more style! Cooper closed the door with relief after two hours on a beaming, fulfilled Stanisopolous, delighted to have been of so much help to the authorities in his adopted country.

The photographer, by contrast, was potentially a poor witness. He sat, sweating profusely, twisting yellowed fingers and eyeing the no smoking sign on the wall with despair. For someone who was supposed to make a living observing and recording detail, he was hopeless. He turned up late, reluctant, obviously regretting his lapse into good citizenship and the stupidity of having given his real name and address.

Gradually, Fenwick and Cooper focused the hazy detail. It had been a one-off contract, arranged by phone, paid by post. No, he had long since cashed the postal order and hadn't thought it an odd way to pay – it was as good as cash in hand. He had never met a representative from the catalogue.

'Wasn't that unusual?'

'No, not really, happens all the time.' The man squirmed.

He could not recall whether it was a man or woman he had spoken to, nor what had happened to the film and proofs. It had been a well-paid, average assignment.

'For which you never met the client, got paid in cash and made no enquiries as to why your services were required? Come on!'

'There's no need to take that tone, Sergeant.' The yellow fingers were a twisted, skeletal knot.

'I'm just wondering what sort of work it is that you normally do.'

Sweat dripped on to the table. 'Now look here. I came in of my own free will. You have no cause to keep me here. I'm leaving.'

'It's all right, George, calm down. We're not interested in how you make your money, just tell us all you can about Deborah Fearnside.'

The man relaxed visibly but no further detail emerged. After a further twenty minutes of questioning they concluded the man genuinely knew nothing more, and let him go.

Fenwick sat alone in his oppressively hot office after the interview, contemplating the complexity of Deborah Fearnside's abduction. The detail and planning had been extraordinary and at no stage did the victim or her friends suspect that they were being led into a trap. Whoever was behind this was extremely intelligent and cunning – look at how long it was taking the police to pull the threads together, at how little evidence had been left behind. Fenwick realised that for the first time in his career, he could be facing a criminal with a mind at least as clever as his own.

In the days remaining before Octavia Anderson's return, whilst Cooper continued to chase dead ends and the additional quota of resources drew blanks in every direction, Fenwick went back over the school records. He tracked the four friends and Leslie Smith through each term, noting when Octavia Anderson joined the school and where Carol Truman and Octavia's names disappeared from the register at the end of the Upper Fifth.

He noted down the names of teachers who were no longer at the school and diverted Nightingale and a section of the expanded team to tracing them. Most were in retirement and continuing a habit of long summer vacations; several were dead; two were rambling together in Scotland. Nightingale was tempted to catch the next sleeper to Fort William, anything to escape the pointlessness of an old case in summer, but in the end they asked the local force to track them down and returned to the dwindling outstanding list. Nightingale had found the names of Carol's parents in school records and had contacted immigration again.

She was still waiting for a response when late on Friday afternoon, as the air grew stale in the station's unventilated incident room and she listened dully to the death rattle of bluebottles on sealed window sills, a fax chattered into life with details of the Trumans' immigration. Its routine contents prompted Nightingale to postpone yet another pub garden meeting and make her way to the offices of the local newspaper.

Cooper watched her go with mixed feelings. At least she had a lead to go on, even if it might muck up her weekend. He was having a frustrating time with Ministry of Defence officials who were proving reluctant to release details of service leavers over the previous twelve months. His request was not helped by the weakness of his argument, nor his own scepticism, which came through whenever he tried to persuade them. All they really had as a basis for their requests were Fenwick's hunch and a possible murder weapon with a services pedigree. Just moments after Nightingale had left, Cooper was handed three large, security-delivered envelopes, each one containing bulky computer printouts. Each service provided information in a different way but the content in all of them amounted to the same: name, rank and number. No addresses, telephone numbers or reasons for discharge. It was virtually useless.

Within the hour he also received the first list from a national car hire company, contacted about the rental of a black saloon. The firm was much more helpful. The printout for the key dates in April matched Cooper's priority order: London, Home Counties, South East; male, cash payment. Even so, given the description of the car involved in the Fearnside abduction, there were several hundred names. And it was a leap of faith that their 'chauffeur' had hired, not bought a car. Still, at least this time they had addresses and phone numbers. With a certain satisfaction, Cooper called the enlarged team together and divided the list up among them. Faced with at least a long evening and Saturday ahead of them, one bright trainee showed true detecting initiative and hunted down the key for the sealed unit double glazing.

Nightingale had no air to refresh her. The newspaper's library and records office were in the basement. There was no air conditioning, no window. The air fell flat and heavy on the stacks of back copies, teetering around the walls. A retired metal-press printer-turned-archivist proudly told the detective constable they were microfiching records. Unfortunately they had only worked back as far as 1984. He directed her to a stack of papers, chest high, in one of the darker corners, labelled 'January 1979 – December 1981'. Wearily and cautiously, she removed her light cotton jacket gingerly, glancing round for a clear spot on which to lay it. With resignation, she folded it inside out and brushed off a plastic canteen chair. Her hand came away black.

She lifted the top stack of papers aside until she found the start of 1980. Fenwick had said that was the year both Truman and Anderson had left school. Johnstone's diary for the year was missing as well and the fax from Australian immigration had confirmed this as the year the Truman family, *excluding Carol*, had arrived.

It was a local newspaper that made up for quality with quantity to provide value for money. Even in 1980, there had been two sections for each edition. She was tempted to concentrate on the main news pages, convinced that what she was looking for would be front-page news. But her training and her own meticulous attention to detail kept forcing her to review every page.

By eight o'clock she had worked through to the end of May 1980. Her hands were black from old newsprint, which had mysteriously found its way on to her face and hair, adding premature grey streaks to the short dark bob. The long plait had been cut off as impractical a month before. Her clothes were thick with paper dust and her eyes and throat felt as if they were lined with fine sandpaper. She had found nothing apart from a reference in February to a school choir performance in which both Octavia Anderson and Carol Truman had been singled out for glowing praise. Part of her felt she had done more than enough for one evening but the thought of returning to the room the next day was more unattractive than carrying on. She decided to keep going to the end of June – halfway – and then stop for the night.

A giant haystack occupied centre page of the first June edition, a typical example of the level of local news, and Nightingale swore in disgust. Discarding the offending paper, she bent to pick up the following week's edition from the dwindling stack. Two clear light-coloured eyes caught hers, poised in a petite oval face framed by straight blonde hair. Above the picture the sub-editor had excelled by setting a block headline in inch-high characters: 'TRAGIC DEATH OF LOCAL SCHOOL GIRL' and beneath it the subheading: 'Gifted pupil's death plunge while on school trip'.

Detective Constable Nightingale had found Carol Truman.

An end-of-term celebration ended in tragedy this week as gifted 15-year-old school girl Carol Truman plunged to her death from 200-foot-high cliffs.

A party of thirteen girls and two teachers from Downside Community School visited Durdle Door, a well-known beauty spot in Dorset, as part of an end-of-term treat that went tragically wrong last Friday. Commenting at the scene, Coastguard William Price said: 'We received a call at 15.40 and were on the scene by 15.55. A helicopter was launched at once and, sadly, we found the body of a young girl within fifteen minutes.'

It was necessary to use a winchman to reach the body as access from the cliff top was too dangerous.

The accident has raised doubts again about the safety

of teacher-supervised school trips, doubts robustly denied by Downside's headmaster Dr Boyle. 'There is no question of this trip being undersupervised. Two very experienced teachers were in charge of the party of 13 girls. All the girls are of an age and maturity to make this a more-than-adequate number for safety reasons.'

Nevertheless, a full enquiry is to be established and it is expected that both teachers will have to appear to answer questions about the ill-fated trip. In charge of the party was geography master Kenneth Jackson. Gym mistress Barbara Dicks was also in attendance.

Turn to page 2 and 3 for full story.

Inside, the full story described the accident in detail: the party of thirteen girls and two teachers had arrived at the coast just before eleven o'clock on a clear, sunny day. The party had split into three groups, one of which included both teachers – the girls being deemed old enough to look after themselves. The other two groups went their separate ways along the cliff.

The morning had passed without incident, with everyone meeting up for lunch, and the groups had split up again for the afternoon when the accident happened. The report continued: 'Schoolfriend Leslie Bannister was with Carol Truman in the group. "It all happened so suddenly," said the tearful 15-year-old. "One minute we were all together fooling about and singing, then we had a race back to the bus. I was a bit ahead of the others but suddenly somebody heard Debbie or Octavia, I think, cry out. Carol had just gone, disappeared. It was only later that we realised what had happened." '

Carol was described as 'an exceptionally talented pupil' by headmaster Dennis Boyle. He was quoted extensively. 'The whole school is deeply shocked; a number of girls have been sent home. Carol had a unique talent and this terrible accident has taken from us not only a loved and respected pupil and friend but also a musician of immense potential. An investigation has been opened into the incident and obviously we will co-operate fully.'

Detective Constable Nightingale read the remainder of the article and then re-read the whole piece. A few key facts lodged in her mind: the accident had happened *after* the date of emigration for Carol's family – where had she been living? Leslie Bannister as was, Smith now, had been 'a close friend' and virtually a witness to the accident. Why had she lied? The article went on to make clear that the accident had involved a fall from the cliffs and police were not treating it as suspicious. Could it have triggered the murders, some twenty years later, of two of Carol's friends? Or if it had not triggered the killings, what other connection was there?

Nightingale's call at eight that evening was enough for Fenwick to summon both her and Cooper to his house. As an afterthought he softened the inconvenience by serving a chilled Australian Chardonnay as they sat in the garden, away from the children's late bedtime noise.

Nightingale had found the name of an aunt and uncle of Carol Truman in later articles, Alice and George Rowland, and was immediately charged with hunting them down. As she searched further she discovered they'd had a son and added his name to her list. Cooper, to his surprise and disappointment, was tasked with arranging the cross-checking of the stack of military print-out for *any* of the names mentioned in the article or the school records of the time. As the computer output was in ID number order and he had no faith in the military connection whatsoever, his motivation hit rock bottom. The wine too was sour for his palette.

'What're you going to do then, sir?' His belligerent tone bordered on the insubordinate and never had Fenwick seen leather-patched elbows more aggressive.

'I'm going to Montpellier and then, probably, to Scotland, Sergeant. I will then return in time to meet Smith's flight from Turkey – I assume you haven't traced her? – no, quite. And, Cooper, keep the extras busy, will you? I don't want them disappearing while I'm gone.'

CHAPTER TWENTY-FIVE

Fenwick stepped from air-conditioned, dry chill into the enveloping warmth of Mediterranean summer and enjoyed the few seconds of pure sensuous pleasure that greets all northern travellers as they realise, again: Yes, this is what I was born for. Simple, heady heat on every part of his exposed skin, the sun, hot on the top of his head, a new elusive tang in the air. Then it was over. Except, inside him, the warmth did not disappear. Had he been less practical and preoccupied, he would have had the sense to recognise and guard against this growing sense of expectation. But he was not.

By the time he had collected his luggage, waited thirty minutes in line to hire a car and become immediately and hopelessly lost on leaving the airport, he was regretting the tie, the trip and his poor second language. He could feel the sweat accumulating along his collar, dripping from armpit to waistband as he struggled, sun blind in the maze that was Montpellier. Fenwick had arranged to meet Anderson at her hotel, one definitely outside his limited expense allowance. Given the delays, he had no choice but to go straight (an inappropriate description, surely) there from the airport.

He removed his tie, combed his hair, lifted a still smart sports jacket from the back seat of the parked car and entered the marbled lobby. With the aid of the freshen-up tissue from the plane, he even smelt fresh, if tangy. The uncompromising air conditioning forced him to put on his jacket at once. He put the goose-pimples on his arms and thighs, as Octavia Anderson walked towards him, down to the abrupt change in temperature.

She was with him in moments, tall, relaxed as she swayed across the floor, turning heads. Her thick black hair was loose, framing an ivory complexion untouched by sun and startling in its contrast to the bodies around her. She wore a jade silk trouser suit, casually tied around an almost too-thin waist. Fenwick tried not to notice that she was not wearing a bra and the effect on her of the frigid air conditioning. He found he was sweating despite the cold.

They made their way to a quiet palm-lined corner. 'A drink of some sort?' She assumed the role of hostess automatically, signalling a waiter on the balls of his feet, desperate to come over.

'A large soda water and lime. Thank you, Miss Anderson.'

A frown line appeared briefly between dark, shaped eyebrows at the return to surname terms.

'Make that two, Nico.'

Fenwick waited comfortably, letting the silence build. She did not break it. When the tall tumblers arrived, dripping condensation, Fenwick took the initiative.

As she looked up, half quizzical, half coy, to salute him over the rim of her glass, he said: 'I am here to talk about Carol Truman.' He was looking her straight in the eyes as he uttered his one brief sentence. Trained actress as she was, Octavia was too shocked and surprised to hide her reaction entirely. Her eyes widened, her bottom lip sagged and the sharp gasp was audible even over the hotel music. Soda water slipped over the rim of her glass and down her hand as she quickly replaced the drink on the glass table top.

She busied herself for several moments, mopping up the spill with a tiny napkin provided by the ever-attentive Nico. By the time she looked up she was in control again, face set in an expression of polite enquiry. But there had been no hiding her initial reaction and in her eyes Fenwick could see that she knew it. For the first time since they had met, she could not hold his gaze.

'I see. I'm sorry, Andrew, for my silly reaction but you have touched on a very old, and very painful, memory. One that I hadn't thought about for a long, long time.'

'Despite the deaths of Deborah Fearnside and Katherine Johnstone?'

'Deaths? I thought Debbie was only missing!' This time she let the shock and sorrow show.

'I'm afraid her body was found some days ago. But I ask you again, did you make no connection between Deborah, Katherine and Carol?

'No, none. Why should I? Carol died when we were school-children. She was a good friend of mine, Chief Inspector, but that was around twenty years ago. And Debbie and Kate – I didn't even connect what had happened to them. Kate's murder was awful, an urban nightmare brought to life. Debbie's disappearance, well, I honestly thought she might have run off.' Fenwick experienced a spurt of anger on Deborah's behalf. Why were people, even her friends, so quick to assume the worst of her when he had such a clear view of the dedicated mother?

'And now that there are two murders? In total, three deaths from the "Famous Foursome" – aren't you concerned?'

She flicked an invisible speck from the hem of her silk shirt impatiently.

'No, Andrew. I'm not. I am *not* a superstitious person and I can't think why I should suddenly become worried. They *were* my friends – of course they were – but that was a long time ago; it feels like a previous life, another country.'

'Tell me about Carol's death.'

'I genuinely can't remember much. It was horrible, I know that. One moment we were all of us larking about together – the next, she was gone. And before you ask me, I can't remember the details. I've shut it out. For weeks afterwards I withdrew from everyone I knew, friends, family, teachers. Only my music brought me alive. These days there always seem to be counsellors on hand to help the bereaved. Then, well, you were on your own. I genuinely believe I would have gone mad if it hadn't been for my music.'

'What happened after Carol's death – what did you all do?'

'You mean immediately afterwards? I can't remember. We went home straight away, I expect. I recall that later after the body had been recovered, we, that's Leslie, Kate, Debbie and I, went to see Carol's family. I don't know why, we just felt that we should. It was ghastly. They kept asking us all these questions we couldn't answer. Vic even started shouting and screaming at us, as if it had been our fault, but there was nothing we could've done. Nothing. In the end, they just went quiet and we left. They couldn't even bear to look at us. You could see them thinking why Carol and not one of us. At the time I assumed they hated us but, of course, they didn't. It was the grief.'

'Who was Vic – a brother? And I thought her family had emigrated.'

'Vic was just a friend. It was her aunt and uncle we went to see, of course. And before you ask me, I *don't* remember their names. Look, Chief Inspector, have you finished? I need to go and get ready.'

'Just one more question. What was Carol like?'

Octavia looked away from him, out across the marble foyer to the tinted automatic doors.

'She was lovely,' she murmured, 'simply lovely.'

To his surprise, Fenwick saw her eyes fill, her voice cracked. She wasn't acting this time.

'Can I go now, Andrew? I'm very late.'

He stood up and escorted her to the lift. So much emotion after such a long time baffled him. His eyes were full of questions as he waited with her.

Before he could say more, the deputy hotel manager, badge glittering in the crystal light, trotted up to them, his arms full of crimson roses.

'Mademoiselle Anderson, these have just been delivered for you.'

'Oh how lovely, Jean-Luc. Did the delivery boy say from whom?'

'No, mademoiselle. Sadly no.'

238

'And there doesn't appear to be a card. Never mind! Thank you.'

'Does this happen often, unknown admirers sending flowers?'

'Not as often as you might expect, but this is about the third bouquet of red roses I've received during the festival, so I'm not complaining!' She smiled at him, lips matching perfectly the blood-red blooms.

'Shall I be seeing you tonight? I know it's a fringe festival but they gave me my first real break and I'm sentimental. Still, it'll be my last year; it's just too inconvenient now.'

'I doubt that I'll see you. I don't have a ticket and I imagine they've sold out.'

'Poor Chief Inspector! All this way and no fun. We shall have to see. *Au revoir.*'

Fenwick was disturbed, during a brief nap in his small, comfortable but unfortunately non-air-conditioned room, by the arrival of a single red rose, attached to which was a dress circle ticket for the evening's performance. There was no note.

CHAPTER TWENTY-SIX

In England, in a muggy, thunder-bug-ridden evening, Nightingale cursed the lack of a national identity system. She had had little luck in tracing Carol Truman's aunt, uncle and cousin. They were not on the electoral roll in Sussex, Surrey, Kent or Hampshire.

She took a break from the incident room and walked out into the breathless August day. The fumes were terrible and the park too far away. Out of habit she walked the pavements as far as the churchyard in which Kate Johnstone was finally to be buried in a few weeks. She paced the Tarmacked paths, noticed with sadness and disgust a used hypodermic in the grass by a flat-topped tomb, and felt her mood grow sombre.

She was still a trainee detective, painfully aware that her accelerated programme annoyed old hands and contemporaries alike, and frustrated by her lack of progress on the case. Cooper was a stalwart. He did not agree with most of Fenwick's lines of inquiry but you could never tell, and he drove the expanded team hard, with no room for excuses. He tolerated her with wise amusement, tickled by her initiative, appalled at her cheek.

Going back to Leslie Smith had been a lucky break, but the wretched woman had escaped to Turkey. Tracing poor Carol Truman had been the type of slog that earned silent praise but the poor girl was dead. Now she had to find the aunt and uncle. She started her third circle of the graveyard, wondering at the mess of dead flowers on one of the far graves and casually, naturally, as she was walking towards it, she found George and Alice Rowland. They weren't going to run away.

George Henry Rowland and his wife Alice Mary
Beloved parents of Victor.
In life we are in death.
Taken from us 6th and 7th August 1983
RIP.

The double plot was marked by an open granite book. A recent arrangement of white and yellow chrysanthemums was expiring on the closely mown mound. The vase was dry and the flowers drooped. Nightingale carefully poured the remainder of a her warm can of Coke into the container, hoping it would be enough to freshen them for at least one more day. A lot of money had been spent, some would say wasted, on the arrangement, destined to last a few days at most in the flat summer heat.

Another dead end. She sat on a nearby bench and let the detective in her take over. Why spend all that money on flowers, and who had spent it? There was no card but the Cellophane backing had the name of a local florist printed on it in white lettering. It was her only lead in tracing Carol's living relatives.

She walked back along the path towards the gate, and noticed again the mound of desiccated flowers on a distant grave. Dead roses, dozens of them, had been spread all over the plot. They were lying flat on the ground, sacrificed to the heat of summer. All the other graves were dry, grey-brown in the heat. The extravagance and waste were the more shocking in contrast.

She walked over out of curiosity and felt a premonitory shiver down her spine as she made out the name: Carol Anne Truman. It had to be more than a coincidence, this singling out of the dead to receive grotesque floral tributes at a time when their names had worked their way to the centre of a murder investigation. Or perhaps there had always been flowers. She could find out.

The florist was shut, early closing. Nightingale pushed a note through the door. When she returned to Division a message was waiting for her on her desk. 'Australian Immig called while you were out taking the air!!!' Cooper's leathery patience was not weathering the heat well.

His mood had deteriorated to the point where he was communicating in short, grunting sentences; the smell of his tangy sweat and spicy aftershave occupied the room. All the windows had been forced open but the air hung sullenly, refusing to circulate, sticking in sulky clouds around each of the occupied desks.

'What did they say, Sergeant?'

'I'm not your answering service, Nightingale; I left the number on your desk.'

'Thank you.'

He looked up from a portion of the thick computer printout and gave a smile.

'I thought you'd delegated that lot, Sarge.'

'I have – well, most of it – but I've nothing better to do while we wait for DCI Fenwick to come back from his jaunt in Europe.'

The other constables in the room shifted uneasily. Things were not going well and there was a sense of frustration in the team that was getting the sergeant down. It had not yet flipped into failure but it was not far away. Sensing the tension the other officers variously buried their heads in the files or made yet another phone call in an attempt to match ex-servicemen and women to the names from 1980. At least they were keeping the search focused locally – to start with.

'Seriously, Nightingale. There wasn't much of a message – not good either. Both Carol's parents are dead. The mother passed away shortly after they emigrated; the father died last year. They've no record of any other family.'

Nightingale, at Cooper's suggestion, wrote out a fax to the Melbourne Police Department stressing the importance of tracing any friends and relatives and asking for the name of the lawyers that had handled Carol's father's estate to track down any trustees.

She was explaining to Cooper about the graves when the

florist rang. She had gone in to water the stock with all the heat and had found the note. Yes, she recalled the roses well. The customer – a man – had rung a few days before to make sure she had sufficient stock – three dozen crimson. He had come to the shop briefly on Monday to pay for the orders, cash, and had insisted they deliver to the cemetery as he could not go. Odd that, but he had a little map showing where the graves were and the names. No. That was gone with the rubbish that Monday evening.

Despite the value of the orders she had questioned the sense of leaving the roses loose, no water, but he had been insistent. It was the oddest order she had ever taken. He'd never bought from her before.

'Can you describe him?'

'A bit. He was tall, well over six foot, I'd say. Dark – short black hair; quite thick hair, it was. He wore sunglasses. And he was tanned, really sunburnt dark.'

'Anything else?'

'Well, he was fit, very fit I'd say – you know, athletic. He had a thin white cotton shirt on, and you could see the muscles – a hunk, if you know what I mean.'

'Sounds to me like you noticed quite a bit about him.'

'Well, he was a dish – he hasn't done anything wrong, has he? I mean—'

'We just want to try and talk to him, that's all.'

'Oh, eliminate him, like, from your inquiries!'

'Something like that, yes. You were saying, he was a dish.' She tried hard to ignore Cooper's eyebrows, which were performing a disconcerting dance across his corrugated forehead.

'Well, yes. I quite fancied him. There was something about him, you know. Nice clothes, lovely shape, but not flash. No gold. No jewellery of any kind, come to think of it. Nice watch though. Big, expensive-looking, like a diver's watch – all dials and knobs. And he was a bit out of the ordinary, you know. When he was in the shop he filled it.'

'He had presence, you mean?'

'Yes, that's a good word for it. He had *presence*.'

'Could you spare us a bit of time, to work with a police artist? We'd like to work up a likeness.'

'I'm not sure. I don't know. What's he done? I don't want to get involved in any trouble.'

'As I said, we just need to trace him, that's all. It's quite important that we talk to him and it sounds as if you could help a lot.'

The woman eventually agreed to come down early the next morning, before opening hours.

No sooner had Nightingale replaced the receiver and given a thumbs-up to Cooper than the phone rang again. It was the florist.

'There's one other thing – thought I'd better ring you in case I forget it again. I don't know if it's important but I was wrong when I said he hadn't any jewellery. He had some sort of chain round his neck, not gold, silver-coloured, with something on the end of it, I couldn't see what.'

'Like an identity tag, perhaps?'

'Could've been. I only caught a brief look. And he had a small scar on his face, on his cheek – like you see in them German films.'

'I see. Thank you, every little helps. See you in the morning.' Nightingale turned to Cooper thoughtfully.

'Sarge, our short list of people leaving the army – have you come across a Rowland?'

'Let's look.' Cooper and Nightingale checked all the lists. 'We've got two. One is a Linda – she's in the clear, and a A. R. V. Rowland. Haven't traced him yet. Why?'

'I think I've worked out why Carol was in this country, and where she was staying. Supposing her parents had to emigrate when they did for job reasons – no choice. She'd have been studying for her exams and they wouldn't have wanted to interrupt those. So she stays behind with Auntie and Uncle.'

'Seems reasonable. And you're saying she had a cousin – that he might be connected in some way.'

'Could be. It's another name to look for in the lists.'

Cooper grunted.

'Oh, and by the way, our man in the florist could've been wearing a dog tag.'

Cooper groaned aloud.

'Just thought I'd cheer you up!'

The beep of the fax machine interrupted their conversation. Constable Taylor went over and picked the flimsy sausage of paper from the floor.

'It's from the boss. He's flying to Scotland tomorrow. Couldn't get through on our phones! It says . . .' Taylor read it silently: 'Here, Sarge, you'd better read it yourself. Perhaps France wasn't a complete jaunt after all.'

The fax was brief and to the point.

Cooper,

Inconclusive trip in France but check out:

- 'Victor': have we come across someone of this name? I think he was a friend or relative of Carol Truman's.
- Truman's death: find out *precisely* who was where at the time, particularly the girls. Who was with her? I want to be able to re-enact it by the time I'm back – Friday.
- Roses: who's been buying roses back home? Lots of them, dozens, and where are they being sent?

A. F.

P.S. And get some more phone lines!

'Right, Victor's mine. These records and reports are yours, Nightingale – you seem to get on so well with old files. You,' he singled out Taylor, who had made the mistake of looking up, 'the remainder of these files are yours. All of you, we're looking for Victors now. And you, check out all the other florists locally, will you, see if they've had rose orders too.'

He hid his smile at the growing dismay in the room at the extra work. For the first time in two weeks he felt they had something real to focus on. He had been down many blind alleys working with Fenwick in the past, but he was just starting to remember that they had always found the road in the end. He felt they could be just about to start off in the right direction again. He might even forgive Fenwick France.

He would not have done so if he had seen Fenwick at that moment, in a hired white evening jacket and black tie, settling into the front row of the dress circle.

It had been years since he had been to the opera. It had never been a favourite of Monique's. He wondered if he could remember how to enjoy it. But as soon as Octavia Anderson came on, he was hooked again.

Sipping a cool glass of local Viognier during the interval Fenwick started a private game of spot the tourist. It was depressingly easy and by the time the warning bell for the Second Act sounded, he felt thoroughly belittled. All resentment evaporated though in the white heat of the performance.

The curtain fell at the end of the Second Act to a standing ovation. Fenwick was carried out into the foyer on a wave of euphoria. He ordered his third glass of wine with a return to his natural authority, flicked his jacket casually over his shoulder and was delighted to be mistaken for a family friend by a charming French lady of a certain age.

When he returned to his seat he found a square white envelope neatly perched on the upturned edge, his name written in a distinctive calligraphy: *If you have nothing to do this evening, meet me at Chez Gerard, at 11.30. They'll have a table for supper, booked in my name. O.*

Fenwick arrived at the restaurant early and was greeted with an indifference that changed to respect as soon as he gave his name.

'Ah, yes. The *ami* de Mademoiselle Anderson. *Bien sûr*. This way, monsieur.' It was obviously the best table. A complimentary glass of champagne arrived as he studied the menu; an almost affable wine waiter explained the finer points of the wine list in heavily accented but fortunately slow French.

Octavia arrived at nearly a quarter to twelve, as pale as ever but lit by an inner radiance and energy that charged the air around her. The restaurant was filled with affluent opera-goers, replete with the rich performance. As she made her quiet but unavoidably obvious entrance they turned to her, tapping their neighbours' arms to draw their attention. She smiled, pleased but modest, paused to shake proffered hands, received the maître d's arm in escort and made her way resolutely to Fenwick's side. As he reached his table, the room filled with muttered, then shouted cries of '*Brava!*' By the time she reached his side nearly all the diners were on their feet, applauding her.

She deliberately kissed him on both cheeks, warm lips touching flesh not air. Even before she was fully seated, a bottle of complimentary champagne appeared and *petites bouchées* were placed on the table.

'*Brava.*' Fenwick raised his glass, meeting her eyes over the rim.

'Thank you, Andrew. I'm glad you came, and I'm so glad you're here.' She reached over and touched his arm.

Over the champagne, the chilled soup, the fresh trout and the dessert she forbade him to talk about the performance. She wanted, she said, to talk about anything but that.

He told her about his career and his children By the time they were nibbling on champagne sorbet from a spun-sugar basket he had even told her about Monique.

'Hence your French.'

'My French? No. It's not very good, I did very little at school.'

'I disagree. The accent is good, the vocabulary too – and as for the grammar, I'm sure it is better than you think. That is one of the problems of being a perfectionist.'

She had deftly lightened the subject, saved him from a mournful introspection he would later have regretted, but once his mood had revived she returned to the subject of Monique as he ordered two *digestifs*.

'How long has Monique been in hospital?'

'Several months.'

'And before that she'd been very ill for a year? More?'

He nodded.

'It's a long time for you to have been on your own, Andrew.'

'Oh, my mother's been very good.'

'That's not what I meant.'

He saw her back to her hotel in the dark hours of the morning. The spent air of the previous day was still hanging exhausted in the streets. They walked over tarmac, cobbles, dry grass in a slow, lazy return to her icy, air-conditioned palace. The white of her skin reflected the moonlight. Despite the smothering, hot air, he shivered.

The champagne, the wines, the armagnac affected them both. As she stumbled, delicately, he steadied her. In the end it was easier to put an arm around her shoulders. They walked more slowly, paused more often, talked less, laughed less until they reached her hotel. The question went unasked. In the end it was easier not to answer.

CHAPTER TWENTY-SEVEN

Fenwick arranged a case conference in Dorset for the Friday followed by a reconstruction of the accident in which Carol Truman had died. Nightingale had faxed her information to him, catching him during his brief visit to Scotland. They gathered at the local police station before setting off in an ill-assorted convoy to Durdle Door. Fenwick had with him a trim, agile woman who looked to be in her seventies, whom he introduced as Miss Dicks. She wore heather tweed and carried a substantial leather shoulder bag.

On the cliff top he assigned roles for the re-enactment and handed out a précis of Nightingale's information to all the participants. He took Octavia's part. Miss Dicks was to play herself.

'I was one of the two teachers in charge of the group,' she explained to the assembled police. 'Mr Jackson is dead now. I was here in the car park waiting with Ken – Mr Jackson – and the rest of the girls. It was about three in the afternoon, after lunch. The Famous Foursome were always the last back. We had no concerns as we waited.'

'But, Miss Dicks, there were five girls.' Nightingale was unsure whether to interrupt but it was an important point.

'Yes, little Leslie. I remember them all very clearly, even now. She always tagged along but she was never part of the group.'

Following Nightingale's summary of the original notes and reports, all the police made their way west from the car park along a footpath leaving Miss Dicks behind. The precise route had changed a little over almost twenty years; meandering to limit the erosion from thousands of tourists' feet, but the broad direction was the same. The girls had walked about a mile and a half along the track, which dropped and rose with the swell of the cliffs.

They had found a spot to sunbathe and, typically according to their statements, had forgotten the time. Just before three, Kate Johnstone had noticed her watch, leapt up and told the others to hurry. As they shuffled to comply she started to jog back. All the statements agreed on this point. The detective constable playing the part of Kate obediently jogged away at a pace he judged consistent with that of an athletic teenage girl, timing himself as he went.

According to Deborah Fearnside's statement at the time she followed shortly afterwards, first stopping to put on her shoes. A WPC left in her place. Cooper was taking the part of Leslie Smith. She claimed to have set off with Deborah and to have kept pace with her the whole way. Cooper paced off, leaving Fenwick as Octavia and Nightingale as Carol.

Octavia's statement had been brief. She and Carol had been together. They had not run for the first part of the way but had been engrossed in conversation as they walked. The footpath had followed a sharp decline down into a dip, levelling out at the bottom for ten or twelve yards before rising steeply on the other side. Seeing the sharp dip and climb the other side, Octavia had decided to run down the slope and gather momentum to carry her up the other side.

Fenwick set off, noticing that clumps of gorse and broom bordered the path, thickening at the base of the cliff. At the bottom of the dip the chalk had broken into a loose scree that slithered as he slipped the last few yards.

Without pausing, he focused the momentum of his run on the climb the other side and was more than halfway up before he had to break his stride. He noticed that Cooper and the other two constables were out of sight, beyond the crest of the next hill. Looking back he could see no sign of Nightingale, the gorse obscuring his view of the dip. Octavia claimed that she had paused before the top to catch her breath. Fenwick did the same. Then he climbed to the top of the slope. He could now see the three others making a slow descent to the distant car park. After a quick glance behind, still no Nightingale, he set off at a trot to join them.

After he arrived they waited a good five minutes before becoming concerned. Miss Dicks had indicated that she had a number of important observations to make about the reconstruction but preferred to wait until all five of them were together.

'How long was it before you became concerned about Carol?' Cooper asked, killing time.

'Not long – I cannot remember exactly, no more than five or ten minutes I think, certainly.'

'In your signed statement you said "less than five minutes after Octavia's return" '.

'As I said, Sergeant. Not long.' Miss Dicks had dealt with far too many opinionated school children to be put off by Cooper's normal style of interrogation.

'If it was about five minutes, we should be heading back.' Fenwick looked worried. 'Nightingale should have been here by now. We agreed to meet back here. Even walking we'd have seen her coming down the slope by now.'

'Still in role I see, Chief Inspector. That's almost exactly what Octavia said.'

'You have the most remarkable recall of events, Miss Dicks.'

'I shall never forget a moment of that dreadful day, Chief Inspector, although I pray nightly that I might.' She roused herself and picked up the stout bag, refusing all offers for it to be carried.

'Come along, you may take my arm.'

The five of them followed the narrow path in a slow climb from the car park to the first ridge, then down into the gully with its flat oval bottom surrounded by gorse bushes on all sides, except that facing out to sea. There was no sign of Nightingale.

Now seriously concerned Fenwick sent one constable on to the sunbathing spot, another to the top of the ridge. Both returned shaking their heads, stones spinning out from their heels to ricochet off the bristled turf that ran from the chalk circle to the cliff edge. Miss Dicks stood by calmly as they searched in the thick bushes through which the path cut from east to west.

Despite his own preoccupation, Fenwick was forced to help Miss Dicks down the sharply inclined path. As soon as she was on level ground he left her and went off to search the south side of the clearing. There was a clear view out to sea. The chalk extended to the point at which the slope of the cliffs began. At first it was gentle, covered by sea grass and the rustling heads of thrift. After about five foot, the angle steepened sharply and the slope ran at forty-five degrees before being sliced off by a precipitous drop down bare-sided cliffs to the rocks and sea below.

He peered out gingerly and found his view of the rocks obscured by a green carpeted overhang less than ten feet below. There was no sign of Nightingale. As he turned back he caught sight of tufts of dark hair poking up over the edge of the cliff. He let out a shout.

'Over here.'

At the sound of his voice Nightingale's face rose into view.

'What the bloody hell do you think you've been playing at? We've been searching all over for you.'

'Just as they would have done for Carol, sir. What did you find?'

'Get back up here and don't be so damned cheeky.' He offered his hand but she scrambled up easily. Apart from a few chalk marks on her dark jeans she appeared unscathed.

'Don't be too hard on her, Chief Inspector. You wanted a reconstruction and you have been given a most authentic one, if I may say so.'

Miss Dicks joined their group, choosing to ignore the rich variety of expletives that had welcomed Nightingale's return.

'I will wait whilst you compare the findings from your

reconstructions with the original reports. As I said earlier, I have some observations of my own which I think may be relevant but I'll speak later.'

She walked back and found a reasonably comfortable rock. Taking a small cushion from her capacious bag, she placed it neatly on the stone, sat down comfortably and proceeded to open a large Thermos. 'Coffee, anyone?'

Fenwick reflected, grudgingly, that her calm, authoritative, eminently sensible style would have made her an excellent teacher. The reconstruction must have been traumatic for her but so far she was the least upset of them all by the afternoon's events. They reviewed the main conclusions of their little play and confirmed that the gorse-bordered chalk circle at the base of the two paths was completely screened from view anywhere along the route; no one could have seen Carol's fall from the circle to the rocks below. The reconstruction was in danger of becoming an expensive waste of time and manpower.

'I think you might be interested in something I have to say.' Faces turned expectantly to Miss Dicks. 'Something about your re-enactment has disturbed me this afternoon and I have been trying to determine what it was.'

'Go on.' Fenwick settled himself on a rock next to the elderly teacher and sipped excellent fresh roast coffee from one of her picnic mugs.

'It was the arrival of the first three officers in a rush. It simply didn't happen like that. I can remember. I was furious with the girls, they had been late back from lunch and they were doing it again. I had a PTA meeting for which I needed to return and I do so loathe being late. And these wretched girls were letting me down.'

'Why is this relevant to our inquiries, Miss Dicks?' Cooper was still smarting from her earlier put-down.

'I'm coming to that, Sergeant. It was *your* reminder about my original statement that prompted me to identify a discrepancy. You see, I was watching the clock, as they say, from before three – hoping to be able to leave early. All the other girls were on the coach in good time and I was checking my watch minute by minute. I can assure you we waited *much* longer than five minutes past three.'

'Perhaps they all started to return later than they stated. It would be natural to underestimate.' Fenwick, though more polite than Cooper, was struggling to find the relevance in her statement.

'Perhaps you should let me finish! It wasn't just that they took longer returning, it was also that the delay between the first of them returning and the last was considerably longer than that in your re-enactment, which I think could be significant.' She paused. 'Shall I go on? Katherine *did* arrive shortly after three and I can remember being relieved; where she was, the others were usually close behind. I can recall looking up at the path behind her and seeing Deborah, some way off, she never could run as fast as Kate. *But there was no Leslie.* In your reconstruction, the three of you arrived in a staggered group. Even allowing for the fact that you ran at a different pace from those poor girls, you were inaccurate.'

'We followed each of the statements carefully. Leslie Smith clearly stated she was in a group with Katherine and Deborah.'

'Well, Chief Inspector, she was not. Either she was confused or she was lying. I am quite sure. I was more worried about her, you see, than the other two. I thought that Carol and Octavia would be together but it was just like that gang to forget Leslie and leave her behind. And she wasn't nearly as bright as the others. To be honest, I can't place precisely when Leslie arrived but it was not within five minutes of Katherine and Deborah. I can assure you, I was watching that path like a hawk. I stood by the coach until a quarter past three. Katherine and Deborah were seated inside with the other girls. Leslie, Octavia and Carol were still missing.

'At 3.15, I set off up the track, slowly because I was looking around the whole time, expecting to see them at any minute. I reached the top of that slope and looked down into this hollow. Of course, I could see nothing. I returned to the coach and shortly afterwards I noticed that Leslie was sitting on the bus.'

'And you're sure Leslie hadn't been there before?'

'Completely, Sergeant. Mr Jackson had counted heads as I set off. All three were still missing at that time.'

'You didn't see any trace of her on the path?'

'No.'

'Constable, work back the way we came. Find out how feasible it would be for someone to make their way back to the coach unseen from the path.' Fenwick turned to Miss Dicks.

'Why didn't you come forward with this information at the time?'

'Oh, but I believe I did, Chief Inspector. If you check my statement, I doubt you will find any significant inconsistencies.'

Fenwick turned to Cooper and Nightingale, who had been rereading the statements as Miss Dicks had confronted them with her story.

'It's broadly in line, sir,' admitted Cooper. 'The inconsistency was here in the statements but they'd been taken by different officers. No one spotted it. At the time there seemed no doubt that it had been an accident.'

'What did Leslie Smith's statement say?'

'She claims to have been at the tail end of Katherine Johnstone's group, sir. She says they were in sight ahead of her all the way.'

'What did Octavia Anderson say?'

Nightingale read out the words from the original interview: ' "Carol and I started back last. We had been deep in conversation – about our future careers as it happens. God, isn't that ironic? The others were way ahead of us. At first we walked. Then we realised that we were very late and I said, 'Let's run.' I started off. I thought Carol was right behind me. I was singing as I ran – down the dip and up the other side. Halfway up I stopped, took a breath and looked back. There was no sign of Carol but I wasn't worried, you couldn't see the hollow from where I stood. I shouted: 'Come on, Carol,' but I didn't wait, I was too keen to get back. If only I had. If only I'd gone back for her. But I didn't, I carried on.

' "I ran the rest of the way to the car park. I told Miss Dicks and Jacko – that's Mr Jackson – that Carol was just behind me.

They were furious. We all waited but Carol didn't come. In the end, Miss Dicks went off after her. I waited a few minutes with the others but I was getting worried – I couldn't just sit there, so I went off too. Jacko shouted after me but I ignored him, pretended I couldn't hear.

' "About halfway back I saw Miss Dicks ahead of me on a slope, walking fast. I ran after her but then I saw Carol's jumper. She'd taken it off because it was so hot. It was lying on the grass, near the cliff top. I don't know how Miss Dicks had missed it. I went over to it and called Carol's name. Miss Dicks looked round—" '

'That is true.'

' "I went down the slope carefully, hanging on. It was a bit steep. I didn't really think I'd find Carol, I was just trying to work out how her jumper had got there. There was a ledge, hidden from the path and I saw something on it. It was a hairband. The ledge wasn't very deep but when I looked out over it I couldn't see anything – it sort of jutted out. I lay down and peered over the edge." ' Nightingale broke her narrative to remark: 'There's quite a delay before the statement is concluded; Anderson probably became very upset at this point.'

' "I lay down and looked out over the ledge. I had to lean out a long way. I could see something fluttering or flapping on the rocks but I couldn't make out what it was. I tried to lean out even further but it was no good and Miss Dicks started calling out behind me. I told her that I thought something was down there. Well, you know what happened next." '

'What did happen next, Miss Dicks?'

'First, I made sure Octavia returned to the path. I then looked out over the ledge but could see nothing. Nevertheless, I was very worried and Octavia was sure that she had seen something. We returned to the coach. Mr Jackson went for some help whilst I tried to keep the girls calm.

'The police arrived before the ambulance and they had already alerted the coastguard. There was a lot of consternation at this point and the police agreed that the girls could all return home after they had taken details of their names, addresses and phone numbers. They took a very brief statement from Octavia, I think, but that was all.

'I was rather shaken so Mr Jackson drove the minibus back whilst I stayed with the rescue services. You know the rest from your records. The coastguard found the body shortly afterwards.'

'Thank you, Miss Dicks. Cooper, when is Leslie Smith back?'

'Monday. Flight's due in the evening.'

'Have a car waiting at the airport. I want her picked up and brought in immediately.'

'She'll have the kids with her, sir, and they'll be dog tired after their journey.'

'Even better. She's been lying to us and I want to find out why. If she's tired and worried about her children, it won't do any harm. Come on, we might as well head back.'

'Excuse me, sir, don't you want my report?' Detective Constable Nightingale struggled to her feet.

'What report?'

'I went climbing for a purpose sir, not just exercise!'

Cooper winced and squinted up at Fenwick to see if she'd got away with it; the rest of the team suddenly rediscovered the view. But Fenwick had only partly heard her and nodded disinterestedly as he helped Miss Dicks repack her bag and come gently to her feet once again.

'The reason I went down on the ledge was because I was trying to work out just how Carol could have fallen to her death here.' She walked over to the edge and looked down. 'It looks fairly steep, but really it isn't. And even if she did slip from here, the ledge below is big enough to break her fall.' The rest of the group moved to stand beside her.

'She's right, we know from the survey records that the cliff hasn't changed dramatically in twenty years. It would be very difficult to fall from here, and you'd have to be unlucky to avoid the ledge.' Cooper scrambled down as he spoke, surprisingly agile despite his large frame. 'So, she either scrambled down here, which seems unlikely as they were already late, or she jumped deliberately...'

'Or she was pushed.' Fenwick scrutinised the bushes around them again. 'Whatever happened to her, these bushes provide a complete screen. There could have been no witnesses.'

'That was the second thing I wanted to mention, sir.' Nightingale stooped to give Cooper a hand back up the slope. 'When I was down there, I could see you all as you came back to search for me. The ledge juts out so that it could be seen from the path. If someone had been up there, looking back, they could have seen *everything* that happened on the ledge.'

CHAPTER TWENTY-EIGHT

An energised Fenwick set his team to confirming in detail the erosion patterns of the cliffs and to tracing and interviewing the original accident investigation and rescue team. Meanwhile he and Cooper awaited the arrival of the Smiths in the nightmare that was Gatwick Airport on a late-summer night. The flight was delayed, and when it did land, it was an hour before they realised that they and the airport police had missed the Smith family in the crush of exhausted brown faces.

They called in and arranged for a car to pick her up from home. She was taken into the interview room, claustrophobic at the best of times but almost unbearable in that hot, thick soup of an evening. The time was 10.05 p.m. Her husband had had no option but to stay with the children and try frantically to contact the family solicitor. It was as close to harassment as Fenwick had ever gone, symptomatic of the anger and frustration he felt with the woman.

Fenwick decided to let her stew for a short time while Cooper finished the phone call from her increasingly irate husband. His office was almost as hot as the interview room, windows open ineffectively although psychologically comforting. The air was completely still, humidity reminiscent of a Florida swamp rather than West Sussex downland. Reluctantly he replaced his crumpled jacket and then banished all trace of sympathy from his mind.

They entered the interview room at 10.10 p.m. It had been a long five minutes for Leslie Smith. She raised a grubby, perspiring face to the policemen, her tan yellow in the fluorescent light. Fenwick looked at her properly for the first time. Every feature of her face was almost pretty, a fraction off attractive. Her eyes were a pale blue but slightly too close together for comfort; her nose short, almost snubbed, without a point of distinction. Her mouth was fully shaped; in a face with better bone structure it would have been voluptuous, even beautiful. On her it created a fleeting resemblance to a wide-mouthed frog, a similarity encouraged by her weak jaw.

She had narrow, sloping shoulders, long bony arms and hands, nails grubby now from over twelve hours of travelling. She looked desperately miserable – and frightened. She stared at Fenwick as if he were a deadly snake, waiting to strike.

The WPC on duty left to collect the coldest drinks she could find for them and Fenwick and Cooper sat down. A tape recorder was turned on. Fenwick dispensed with the formalities quickly and moved on.

'Mrs Smith, we have asked you in here because we have urgent questions to ask you regarding your relationship with Deborah Fearnside and Katherine Johnstone.' He intended to hold their knowledge of Carol Truman's death in reserve.

'Is this all really necessary? What's going on? Why have you dragged me down here at this time of night? I'm needed at home.' She paused for a moment, then asked the question that was obviously troubling her. 'I'm not under arrest, am I?'

'No, Mrs Smith, you are not at this time. You have been asked to the station to help us with our inquiries into the deaths of Mrs Fearnside and Miss Johnstone. We have interviewed you before but we have reason to believe you have been withholding information from us which is relevant to our enquiries and . . .'

He stopped. Leslie Smith's face had turned from yellow to a sickening greenish white. Her bloodshot eyes stared at him in horror as she chewed at her bottom lip.

'Deborah? Debbie's dead? Oh my God, I didn't know. When? How did it happen?'

'Mrs Fearnside's body was found a few weeks ago.' He spoke a little more gently; her distress was obvious and genuine.

Several moments passed in which all that would be heard on the tape were muffled sobs. The WPC returned with drink machine water and left again in search of tissues. Fenwick gave Smith a few more minutes.

'I am sure you can understand that the discovery of Deborah's body has added a new dimension to our inquiries, Mrs Smith. In particular, it's led us to review again the circumstances of Carol Truman's death.'

Smith's head jerked upwards. She tried to avoid his eyes but kept sneaking sideways checks, as if she was compelled to confirm he was still there. Her bottom lip was red raw as she worried at it.

'Now perhaps you'll tell us why you have been less than open with us. Tell us what you know.'

Smith clamped her lips shut and unexpectedly folded her arms. Fear or guilt had suddenly provided her with an unexpected hidden strength. She glared at Fenwick as she spoke.

'Before we go on, I've changed my mind about a solicitor. I want one here. Now!'

After a number of fruitless telephone calls, Leslie Smith had to be allowed home. She was adamant that she wanted her own solicitor – not one from legal aid, and when the police eventually reached him by phone, he was equally adamant that the police were being unreasonable in seeking to continue the interview at that hour. He strongly advised his client to terminate the interview and rearrange it for a time *mutually convenient to them both*. No amount of muttering about 'withholding evidence' would make him shift. He remained unconvinced and so did his client. Either the police charged Smith or they let her go home.

To make matters worse, Smith was categoric that she would not be able to return to the station until late in the morning, claiming her rehearsal with the Oxlea Singers for the Requiem Mass as an excuse. The solicitor was also unavailable, in court with a client. Short of arresting Smith, for which he had insufficient grounds, Fenwick was forced to accept an 11.30 appointment the next day, before Smith stalked off into the oppressive night. As she left, the first faint breath of breeze stirred the window blinds.

'Fancy a pint?' Fenwick was trying to arrange the tumbled piles of paper on his desk into neat parallel stacks, with little success. There was just so much – and so many bulldog clips, wallets and plastic folders, that each one cascaded gently on to his blotter or to the floor the moment his hands left them.

Cooper paused in the act of lifting his latest tweed jacket to his shoulder, this one a Prince of Wales check in deference to the season. It must have been less than five years old as the elbows were still in their original, unpatched state. He hid his surprise. It was unusual, these days, for Fenwick to suggest a drink.

'It's closing time nearly. Y'sure you don't need to go home, sir?'

'Not tonight, not yet.' Fenwick was restless, irritated. The thought of shutting the door on the day depressed him. If they hurried, they'd just make last orders. 'Come on, if you fancy one that is – and drop the sir; we're off duty as of now.'

They walked together to the pub at the end of the road from the station, entering as the bell was rung. It was virtually empty, but they still took their pints out of the smoky, stuffy atmosphere into the small garden, where the car park lights lit up a few tables. They were on their own except for a smooching couple literally wrapped up in themselves. Half their pints disappeared in long, satisfying draughts. It was Cooper that broke the thoughtful silence.

'Things are better now – at home, I mean – now that Mrs Fenwick . . . I mean, well, now . . . Sorry, I don't know how to ask.'

'That's all right. I understand. Things are getting better, yes. The children are more settled and my mother's a marvel. How are things with you?'

'Surviving. Ellen's got one more year at university, she's reading Geography. Seems to love every minute, though heaven knows what good it will do her. We rarely see her now – but that's to be expected, I suppose. 'Course Janey's same as always. Lives in the next road and is very good. We see quite a bit of her and the nipper. The lad's not going to university. I've got him an apprenticeship at the local garage. He nearly missed out there, till they found out who his dad was.' Cooper grinned. 'Always helps, that. It's not what I'd expected of him but it's a job and he's taken to it straight away. Works harder than I've ever seen 'im before, and his mother's pleased. He's good with his hands too. My motor's never run better.'

Fenwick's pint had gone. Cooper picked up the glasses without asking and went inside. The landlord was another one who remembered who he was. Moments later, he was back with full tankards.

'On the house.'

Fenwick started to protest.

'Seriously, he was just closing the till, said he'd rather not have the hassle of cashing up again.' Fenwick took a huge swallow and ignored the half-truth. His mind inevitably had returned to work.

'What's happening on Victor Rowland? Have you traced him yet?'

'Not a chance. I'm being stonewalled by ministry bureaucrats.' Cooper sounded exasperated. 'He was on the list all right. He left in February this year, but I can't find him. He's not local and the army's not letting on where he's gone – if they know.'

'Do we know what regiment he was in? Perhaps we could trace him through friends still in the service.'

'Thought of that one. They're not budging, tell me the files are not in the public domain. Public domain, my arse. Bloody civil servants. I told them, we're talking about a double murder investigation here but they didn't want to know.'

'Is it time to roll in the ACC? He'd do it if we asked him.'

'P'raps. I'd hate to do it, though – it's such an admission of defeat. But we need to find Rowland, particularly now Leslie Smith's back in the country.'

'What?' Fenwick looked at him closely. Cooper was usually

phlegmatic, calm. He seemed worried and if he had doubts about Leslie Smith's safety, Fenwick was concerned.

Cooper was embarrassed. 'Well, sir. About twenty years ago, five young girls set off for a walk on a school trip. One died and we don't know how. Now, two more are dead, within months of each other, and we know all too well how they died! Two are left. One of them knows more'n she's telling, which makes her a potential suspect or potential victim. The other's famous, charming,' he looked sidelong at Fenwick, 'and has an alibi that we discover, on cross-checking, is a little dodgy. Into the picture comes a mysterious cousin of the dead girl. Discharged from the army in February and untraceable since.'

'But you're the sceptic. We have nothing stronger than my hunch that all this is connected to the past, the possibility that the killer used a service knife and unexplained roses!'

'I know, sir, but there's enough here to make me suspicious – *and* concerned. I know I started sceptical like, but I'm not now. And, frankly, I reckon I'm more convinced than you are at present. I'm worried about little Mrs Smith. Don't ask me why. Thumb's pricking I s'pose.'

It was a long speech for Cooper, a man of few opinions and fewer words but he was a good policeman. Fenwick turned over what he had said and his own anxiety grew. It had been his, Fenwick's, instinct, that had sent them off down a tortuous path into the past but recently he had deliberately tuned out his feelings about the case to concentrate on the facts. He knew why.

He had become too close to Octavia Anderson and he was scared of his emotions obscuring his judgement. So he had shut them off and in consequence risked damaging his handling of the case anyway. It had been left to his unimaginative, solid sergeant to show him how close he was to making a big mistake. Even at the reconstruction he had been wrong. He had been concentrating so hard on the timings and the routes, the minutiae of events, that he had missed the obvious. Carol Truman could not possibly have fallen accidentally from the main path.

Now that he had uncaged his instinct again, Fenwick was

worried too. Octavia was still out of the country, villainess or victim, and there was not much he could do about her until she returned at the end of August. But he could set someone to watch Smith. As Cooper sat patiently in the buggy, clammy darkness, Fenwick rose abruptly.

'I'm heading back to the station. I'll arrange for someone to watch Smith's house tonight and for surveillance tomorrow. It's late, and I'll have to bribe Ralph somehow to find someone, but you're right. We can't leave her.'

'But your pint!'

'You have it, Cooper, you're the one who's earned it!'

CHAPTER TWENTY-NINE

Surveillance is a grand term for a tedious, monotonous, sleep-inducing job. DC Charles Watkins was still new enough to the force to be keen. When he heard that Detective Chief Inspector Fenwick needed a favour, he was the first to volunteer, before he had even found out what it was. Now, at 3.20 a.m., as his colleague left to stretch his legs and relieve himself, he struggled vainly against an overwhelming desire to sleep as he sat in the least uncomfortable position in the passenger seat of their unmarked car. By 3.22 a.m. he was asleep.

A black Ford Scorpio with tinted windows cruised slowly to the end of the street and paused. For long moments the two cars rested motionless, less than a hundred yards apart. Then the Scorpio inched forward and drove past at a steady 30 m.p.h. Moments later there was a soft thump of a car door being closed quietly and a shadow slid between the fence and car in the Smiths' driveway. Two minutes later it was gone. DC Watkins stirred but did not wake up until a distant roll of thunder disturbed the night and his colleague made an urgent return to the car.

Life was hell in the Smith household on Tuesday morning. A violent thunderstorm before dawn had woken the children and dog, all of whom had insisted on shelter in the parental bed. Leslie and Brian, besieged by sharp elbows and importunate knees, legs pinned down with the bulk of frisky retriever, had abandoned their pretence at sleep by six o'clock.

Leslie rose to tackle the first load of holiday washing with a sinking heart. The torrential rain, battering the westerly windows of the house, brought with it the prospect of sagging racks of damp laundry too delicate for the tumble dryer.

Brian left early for his first day back at work, routinely patting the children's heads and pecking his wife on the cheek. The dog, returned from their obliging next-door neighbour, received a genuinely affectionate farewell. Brian was glad to get out of the house, away from the children, already bored and playing their PC games too loud as a consequence.

It was with relief that Leslie bundled the children and dog into the car two hours later. Mavis Dean had agreed to look after them while she attended choir practice. It was likely to be a long session as there were only three further rehearsals before the full dress rehearsal. She was conscious that her own performance was below the required standard. Her worry about being shown up almost put the dread of her visit to the police out of her mind. Almost. Leslie Smith was a deeply confused and disturbed woman.

Just running from the house to the car left them all soaked. Moving into the storm was like standing under a huge power shower. By the time Leslie had secured the dog safely in the back of the estate the windows were already steamed up, with childish drawings appearing in the condensation. She turned the key in the ignition and the engine coughed apologetically. She turned it again and it whirred in protest but failed to catch.

The third-hand car, left standing in a heat wave for three weeks and now drenched since before dawn, appeared to have selected that Tuesday as one of its non-performance days. They were rare, admittedly, usually triggered by the damp, but regular trips to the local garage had failed to produce either diagnosis or cure. From bitter experience, Leslie knew they had no option but to walk. Across the road, PC Adams, who had replaced Watkins and colleague at eight o'clock, was praying for the car to start too and his spirits sank as he watched the family step out into the rain. What a day to have to follow on foot.

'Right, out you lot. Matthew, put up your hood *before* you

leave the car. Jamie, put your raincoat back on.' She just had time to walk to Mavis's and reach the school in time for the practice; her early start meant that she was ahead of her schedule.

The children's wellingtons were in the back of the estate along with the dog. Within minutes they were happily finding puddles and enjoying the walk, oblivious to the following policeman and the grey shapes of cars crawling by on the flooding roads. Leslie, in her grey-green mac and hood became resigned to arriving as a wet mop at the rehearsal and began to have fun with the children too.

She turned down Mavis's offer of a lift. She was already wet to her skin and the school was less than ten minutes away. She kissed the children goodbye and set off again at a brisk pace.

The persistent drumming of the rain on her hood was deafening, blocking out all noise from the few passing pedestrians and swishing traffic. She walked on quickly, head down, peripheral vision obscured by the jutting square cut of the hood. Her mind flitted between immediate concerns about the second soprano chorus and her meeting later with the police. She was scared but silence, and the blank spaces in her story that were tantamount to lies, had become reality for her over the years. Not even Brian knew the truth, nor had Debbie. Why, oh why had she decided to confide in Kate? It had been an extraordinary, daring lapse, quite out of character, but she told herself she had nothing to fear. She had made Kate promise, on the Bible, never to go to the authorities and she knew Kate would not break her word.

Which meant that now there were just the two of them left alive who knew the full truth. Her heart skipped a beat on the image of the other as the killer – but that could not be. Why now? After all these years? The deaths could not be connected. It had to be chance, a coincidence, coming so long after the other death. Yet she knew that the 'accident' had been a killing. Would that other person really kill to preserve the silence?

Leslie shuddered again inside her coat. She *would* tell the police all she knew – just the facts, not her suspicions as to why. Then there would be a confrontation of her own making and she would find out the truth, once and for all. Thoughts of September turned her mind again to the Requiem and she started humming the 'Libera me' as she walked. She had less than ten minutes to complete the journey and decided she had to cut across to the back entrance of the school, down Hays Road. The streets were almost deserted, traffic passing by slowly, cautiously skirting deep puddles that were fast joining up to transform roads into streams.

At the zebra crossing on Osborne Road Leslie paused carefully on the curve, turning her head deliberately, conscious of her restricted vision. Behind her, Constable Adams hovered in a shop doorway, keeping his distance. She looked carefully right, left and right again, mentally repeating the words as she had done since childhood. The road was clear. In the distance a black saloon car was cruising slowly towards the crossing, far enough away to give her plenty of time to make the other side.

Leslie stepped out on to the black and white stripes, head down, guiding her feet to avoid the puddles in the tarmac. Mercifully she did not hear the sound of the engine accelerating savagely, nor Adams' shout as he saw the black bonnet bear down on her. Only a sense of closeness, of bulk, and a rushing of air ahead of the car, made her raise her head at the last moment. Too late to move, too late for anything other than a last, sharp intake of breath as the bumper caught her shins a fraction of a second before the radiator grille and right headlight smashed into her pelvis and thighs.

She was thrown up on to the bonnet, head smashing the windscreen, creating a star-burst of cracks from the point of impact. The momentum of the blow carried her on, up and over the roof of the car to fall off to one side. The rear tyres passed within inches of her head as she lay, face down, across the far lane.

The car screeched to a halt and its reversing lights came on as Adams ran into the road. After a second's hesitation the car changed gear and launched forward, tyres squealing as it took the corner expertly despite the flooding road.

Adams was radioing for backup, calling an ambulance and shouting the registration number of the Scorpio into his radio as he reached Leslie's side. He had instinctively dashed forward to try to pull her back but had too far to go. Now, he knelt by the woman, feeling for a pulse. There was the faintest movement in the carotid artery, so slight and irregular that he could not be sure. Gently, he made sure her airways were clear, and lifted her head above the puddles of water.

She had fallen almost exactly into the recovery position, thus releasing him from living through the reality of one of his recurrent nightmares – having to decide whether or not to turn a badly injured person with the risk of doing more harm than good. She looked in a very bad way. Her right leg was extended at an unnatural angle away from her body, with a bloody compound fracture above the knee. Luckily, the bone had pierced forward, missing the femoral artery. Several motorists stopped and he set two of them to warning traffic on both sides. In the distance, behind the hissing of the rain, he thought he could hear the first faint sounds of the sirens.

Blood was slowly mixing in the puddle under her chest and stomach. He dare not move her to try to stop it, fearful of inflicting more internal injuries. The water made it impossible to tell how badly she was bleeding anyway. Worst of all was her head; the right side of her face had been smashed in, blood trickled from her ear, the top of her head was a crimson mess. He took off his waterproof and laid it over her gently. He had done all he could.

CHAPTER THIRTY

Fenwick paced the short length of his office like a penned animal. The news from the hospital was grim. Leslie Smith was on life-support in intensive care, her prognosis was poor. If she did survive, and the doctors refused to extend any real hope, it was highly unlikely that she would recover fully. Her skull had been fractured in two places, with a strong probability of permanent brain damage; her pelvis had been broken and the right leg had been shattered; given her poorly condition, surgeons had not even started to consider its repair. Her only piece of good fortune was the relatively minor internal injuries she had suffered.

In his frustration that morning, he had visited the hospital as the operations centre co-ordinated a massive search for the car. One look at her had convinced him she was beyond helping them. Her husband, ripped apart by his own sense of helplessness, turned his anger on the police, but eventually agreed to the search of their house, bewildered as to how the accident could be anything other than a random hit-and-run. So far, the search team there had found nothing.

The team on the case had risen at once to a full-time thirty-five. Constable Adams' eye-witness account supported their theory that the incident had been deliberate. His immediate calling in of the car details had led them to the abandoned vehicle within twenty minutes of the attack. An obviously rushed attempt to set fire to the car had been doused by the rain, leaving plenty for forensics to work on. Their minute scrutiny would take days.

The owner of the car had been traced. It had been stolen from a station car park twenty miles away, at some time on the previous evening. There were plenty of prints, and the owners and their friends were being co-operative, but Fenwick doubted any would belong to their attacker. So far, one witness had come forward who claimed to have seen someone running away from the abandoned vehicle into a nearby park. The rain had prevented a clear view and he could not even say whether it had been a man or a woman.

Deeply indented running footprints had been found across the sodden cricket pitch and the groundsman was certain they had not been there the previous afternoon. Casts were being matched to the ones left at the school where Katherine Johnstone had been killed and to those in her back garden. The length of stride indicated someone tall, running at full speed. They had no luck lifting prints from the park gates or railings. Fenwick was treating the case as attempted murder with a constant guard at the hospital. It was deeply embarrassing, inevitably harmful to their case. Fenwick had spent an hour with the Superintendent, preparing a full report for the ACC, and a further, deeply uncomfortable thirty minutes, confirming the bald facts directly on the phone. Fenwick had suspected a connection; had failed to obtain a statement; had let her go home; and had established surveillance which failed to prevent the attack. That he was left in charge of the case – now two unsolved murders and one attempted murder – said a lot for both Fenwick's persuasive skills and the Superintendent's support, but it was clear there were doubts as to whether Fenwick was the detective he had once been. Fenwick had undertaken to provide personal, daily reports to the Superintendent.

It was not only Brian Smith that was eaten up by guilt. Every policeman and -woman on the case felt a failure. Fenwick knew this and took on himself the overall responsibility when they met the following day, explaining that there was nothing, personally, they could have done. What they had to do now was to find the perpetrator and stop them. Cooper noticed that he had stopped using the masculine pronoun again.

He singled out Constable Adams for praise, commending his behaviour. He had undoubtedly saved Smith from death under reversing wheels. His words missed their mark. Adams, a long-serving, loyal, county-born policeman loved his job, lived for the force. He no longer had the idealism, but he was diligent, straight and knew his duty. Leslie Smith had been his responsibility and he had let her be run down when he was only yards away. It was unlikely he would ever forgive himself. Rather than send him home, Fenwick arranged to move him on to the case full time. The constable's gratitude had been a brief bright spot in a long, grim day.

A full team meeting was called for seven that evening. Leslie Smith was still alive, still unconscious, dependent on life support. Nothing had been found at her house; no one had seen the black Scorpio between the time it was first parked by its owner and when Smith was attacked.

Priorities were agreed, responsibilities confirmed. House-to-house and local enquiries around the station from which the car had been stolen would have top priority, together with those along the route from Smith's house to the zebra crossing, and on across to the park and the site on which the car had been abandoned.

In the meantime, Fenwick was incensed at the lack of progress in tracing Victor Rowland and elected to take on the ministry himself. He set Cooper to tracing Octavia Anderson; first to confirm her alibi (although that did not eliminate conspiracy) then to warn her to be on guard.

273

CHAPTER THIRTY-ONE

The office of Major Anthony West was immaculate – discreetly but well furnished with burgundy and racing green tartan and old creaking leather chairs. It was empty, save for Fenwick and Nightingale, and had been so for over twenty minutes. The Chief Inspector was angry. He had rarely had to deal with the armed services in the past but had always found them to be efficient, polite but, most of all, punctual. He had never before been kept waiting. He had already resorted to asking the Assistant Chief Constable to intervene to make the appointment and he was in no mood for further insult.

The door opened and a man entered. He was tall, well over six foot, one of the few people whom Fenwick could look directly in the eye. The word that most adequately described him was grey: silver-grey hair, ice-grey eyes, dark grey suit, pallid grey complexion. Fenwick immediately assumed this stylish room could not be his office.

There was no smile of greeting and no trace of apology for his late arrival. Fenwick allowed a silence to develop. Beside him, Nightingale fought a desperate need to fidget.

'Mr Fenwick.' West was clearly irritated by Fenwick's poise.

'Detective Chief Inspector Fenwick, Major West. And this is Woman Detective Constable Nightingale.' Fenwick's tone made it clear that he considered himself to be the senior officer present.

'I see. Well, look here, Fenwick, you've caused a most unnecessary stink by dragging your Assistant Chief Constable in on this. There are protocols, you know, and it simply doesn't do to upset relationships with these local difficulties.'

Fenwick's expression did not change. Nightingale would have stated on oath that not a muscle moved, no twitch showed and yet the intensity about him grew. He radiated anger.

West clearly felt something too. He broke eye contact and motioned them to sit down. Nightingale obeyed reflexively and instantly regretted it. Fenwick remained standing.

'Here's the file on A. R. V. Rowland.' West flipped a slim brown folder over the table and Nightingale stretched to pick it up. She read the three short pages in a minute, then turned to Fenwick.

'It's not the Rowland we want, sir.'

Fenwick glanced at the papers. 'What's the game, Major West? We gave the full name, place and date of birth of the Rowland we are looking for. None of it matches this file.'

'I can assure you, A. R. V. Rowland was the *only* Rowland on the list we sent you.'

'That's as maybe, but he's not the only Rowland that left the service this year, irrespective of whether he was on your list or not.'

'Well, if it is a different man you'll have to reapply for information and I'll see what we can do. Follow the protocols, Chief Inspector. It's always easier in the end.'

'Several weeks ago my sergeant made routine enquiries, following the correct procedures and observing the proper formalities. At daily intervals since then we have repeated our requests for more information. We have received precisely three computer printouts, incomplete, unsupported, almost useless, on which we have proceeded to expend hundreds of hours of police time. I suggest you make up your mind to answer my questions now.' Fenwick's voice was quiet, but it seemed to pin West to his chair.

Nightingale felt the hairs on her arm rise.

'Now look here, Fenwick, you can't simply come in here and demand confidential information. Personal details of officers are protected and can only be divulged under special circumstances.' West was blustering. It was a ludicrous argument, completely inaccurate. The protocols he referred to allowed for a full exchange of information. Still, Fenwick's expression remained fixed, except perhaps for the fractional tightening of muscles around his jaw.

'West, you're talking rubbish and you know it. I'm dealing with two murders, one attempted murder and an accident so suspicious it was probably murder too. Three families have been ruined. And you sit there and think you can trade banal excuses with me.' Fenwick paused, clearly now struggling to remain in control and to keep the upper hand. Words flowed unchecked in a menacing monotone: 'Rowland is the prime suspect in our enquiries. Bluntly, just so that you understand exactly what I mean, he is suspected of multiple murders and attempted murder, as well as more trivial charges of abduction, possibly rape, robbery and car theft. You are standing between me and my prime suspect, West, and if you can't help me, I suggest you butt out now and find me someone who can.'

He was, by now, at West's desk, leaning forward on his hands, his face inches away from the grey major. West stood up and with a whispered 'excuse me' left the room.

The two waited silently in West's office. There was nothing to say and, in any event, Fenwick's mind was far away. In his imagination, he was crouching again at the top of the stairs, trying to breathe new life into Monique, looking up into the astonished, frightened eyes of his young son. Disease had nearly destroyed his family when it took her from them. He had not been able to fight it and the professionals to whom he had turned had, in truth, been powerless. Now there was a killer out there, ripping the hearts out of families like his own, and this time *he* was the professional to whom the distraught husbands and fathers were turning. So far, he was failing them too.

Until the confrontation with West he had considered the services enquiry as one of several. His accusation of Rowland had flowed straight from his subconscious, out of his mouth without reasoning intervention. But the words, once spoken, had become truth. He knew it, and so as he had seen in the major's eyes, did West.

A tea tray, laid for four, arrived within a few minutes. There were garibaldi biscuits.

Nightingale was on her second cup when the door opened for the third time. West was there again but he was accompanied by another man. He was about five foot six, and wore a broad pinstripe suit with waistcoat over a rounded, plump body. He smiled at them, displaying strong, straight, slightly yellow teeth within full lips.

The smile worked his face well but did not warm his close-set eyes.

'Detective Constable Nightingale, Detective Chief Inspector Fenwick,' he turned his attention to the policeman. 'Sorry I kept you waiting. Anthony had a devil of a job tracking me down and then extracting me from a meeting. Do sit down. Tony, arrange for a fresh pot and more cups, would you, old boy?'

West nearly ruined the act of familiar geniality but remembered just in time not to salute as he executed a 180-degree turn and left.

'And you are?'

'Er, George, Alan George. Call me George, Andrew please, everyone does.'

He settled comfortably into the chair previously vacated by West. Fresh tea arrived and the major returned.

'Ah, good. Don't disturb yourself, my dear; I'll be mother.' Nightingale had not stirred.

There was silence as he fussed over the cups. No one touched the garibaldis.

'Now. To business. You want to know where Victor Rowland is. Well, embarrassing for us to admit it but, frankly, we don't know.' Fenwick drew breath. George raised a staying hand.

'I know. I know, but it's *not* a smoke screen. He left the service on January 14th and, after spending a few weeks in Australia, we believe he returned to this country.'

' "Believe?" Surely, there are ways of checking, of being sure?'

'Yes, of course. I meant that he *did* return to this country but we are not sure to where.'

'Why was he in Australia?' Nightingale spoke for the first time.

'I believe a relative died. He received a small legacy and he had to sort out affairs down there.'

'That would have been his uncle then, in Sydney?'

'Yes, I believe I did hear word of that.'

'Why did he leave the service?' Fenwick's question was blunt.

'I'm not really sure. People do, you know. All the time, even the most unlikely people. And there are reasonable incentives to do so, you know.'

'Was he an unlikely person to leave then?'

'I'm not really sure; I didn't know him.'

'So why do you know so much about him now? And why do you know he left for Australia; and,' Fenwick walked over to the desk again and leant on it, 'why do you "believe" he returned? Is it usual to keep such close checks on all ex-servicemen?'

'On some yes, it is quite usual.'

'Which ones?'

'Special cases. Hardship, invalid – you know, where we want to make sure they have as good a start as possible.'

'Touching. And one reads such critical stories in the press. They obviously don't realise how much you care. But Rowland wasn't, isn't, a hardship case. You said yourself he had a legacy . . .'

George weighed his words carefully. 'He became ill a few months before he left and never quite recovered his health.'

'How ill? What illness?'

'I hardly think it's relevant to this case.'

'Everything about Rowland is relevant. You've obviously been well briefed in your few minutes between meetings.' A thought occurred to Fenwick. 'Unless you already *knew* of the case, of course. There will be a file somewhere; look up what you don't know.'

'Not even the police have automatic access to medical

records, Chief Inspector, you know that. Some things are, thank God, private.'

'Was his illness triggered by work-related stress?' Nightingale again paused in her note-taking to ask a question.

'I don't believe so.'

She rephrased her question more precisely. 'Did he suffer from any form of mental instability?'

'What a strange question, Constable. Why do you ask?'

'The person we are looking for is physically very fit, hardly an invalid. Many people do suffer mental illness, and it's more common than average in some occupations, the services being one.'

'And the police, and police families, being another.' George snapped back at her. 'But I don't think we need tread too far in that direction, do we, Fenwick?'

It was quite the wrong move and finally broke Fenwick's precarious self-control. He leant over the complete width of George's desk, his six-foot-three-inch, broad-shouldered frame dwarfing the portly beaurocrat.

'Now listen here, George, if that *is* your name. You're snowballing us and you think you're being very clever, pretending this is minor, routine. But it's not and you're shit-scared, aren't you? It's clear you know a lot more about Rowland than you're saying. That means something's wrong. And you don't want a bunch of civilian flat-foots traipsing about on your turf, do you? Well, I've got news for you. Just because you've got some highly trained weirdo out there, *don't* think he's all yours. Because he's not. If he is *in any way* connected with the murders of these women, he's mine and I intend to find him.' His hand went to the phone on the desk. 'You have a simple choice: help me or move aside. But *don't* think you can stand in my way because after I call the Assistant Chief Constable, and whilst his superior is calling the Home Office, the next number I dial will be that of our press office.'

Behind him, West gulped above a minor rattling of cups. It was a tiny noise but enough to reassure Nightingale that Fenwick's bluff speculation was close to the truth.

George glared at the major and returned his attention to Fenwick. He was in no way intimidated but his face looked suddenly tired. 'You won't find him.'

'Oh, I'll find him. You forget, I can use tactics beyond your reach. A murder is good press, good television. All I need to do is whisper "serial killer" and I'll have hundreds of thousands of pounds worth of air time and press space. So far, I haven't done so because it will create a circus – which will be costly to feed and hard to control. But now, you are leaving me no choice.' He turned to leave.

'Fenwick! A moment.' All the urbanity had dropped from George's demeanour, revealing the hard, intelligent, political survivor beneath. 'Be very careful. That's not just a threat from me. This is a *very* dangerous situation and you are proposing to blunder through it in public. I will try and stop you, though I doubt I can succeed at this stage. I repeat, this is very dangerous – and potentially damaging.'

'Danger from Rowland or from you?'

George said nothing.

'But you have left us no choice.'

CHAPTER THIRTY-TWO

Fenwick got his press briefing, backed by the Assistant Chief Constable even though the ACC was unhappy. He'd had to call in too many favours and his political sixth sense was sending him constant warning signals.

'Be careful,' he had said. 'I've backed you this far, and we need a result, but I had to go all the way to the top to bring this in. Don't waste it.'

They were working hard on the press briefing when a call came through from Cooper.

'Cooper; where are you?'

'London, sir.'

'I thought I told you to find Anderson!'

'That's what I'm trying to do. I called to speak to her in Montpellier only to be told she wasn't there.'

'What?'

'She's not there. She missed her last performance two days ago because of a throat infection but, *get this*, she actually flew out of France on Saturday. She took a flight to Amsterdam and then on to Gatwick, despite the fact she could have taken a direct route home. She's not arrived at her London home, nor at her place in the country. The maid says she hasn't heard from her in days.'

'Damn. We need her, and her story.'

'It's more than that now. She was in the country on Tuesday, when Smith was knocked down. This is the second time she's got a dodgy alibi!'

'Well, find her, Cooper. Take the men you need from the other teams. This is your number-one priority – and check again where she was when Deborah Fearnside disappeared.'

Fenwick slammed the phone down. 'Damn.'

'Problem, sir?'

'Maybe, Nightingale, maybe. I might just be about to make the biggest bloody cock-up this force has ever seen. I'm staking the lot on Rowland – and I could be ignoring a more obvious candidate.'

'Octavia Anderson?'

'Yes.'

'It's perhaps the stronger possibility, sir, you've got to admit.'

'Yes, but I just don't see her as the killer, do you?'

'That's irrelevant, isn't it, sir, with respect? It's a matter of evidence and probability. The least likely people can turn out to be guilty. It happens all the time.'

Fenwick thought for a long time, pacing the length of the stuffy room.

'We'll proceed as we are now. There's no other logic for the red roses.'

'Roses, sir?'

'Why send herself red roses? That's the bit that just doesn't stack up.'

The press conference went like a dream. The BBC snatched up the opportunity to do a reconstruction of Smith's hit-and-run and to repeat the one they had screened on Katherine Johnstone.

Fenwick's one problem was that he had no photograph of Rowland and no real description other than the florist's. Even for the television broadcast he had to make do with a video fit based on her vague recollections.

By ten in the evening, as the programme was going out live, they had heard from only two people who claimed to have known Rowland: one from school days, who was surprised at the degree of police interest in his tentative call; the other was from a man in Watford who claimed to have known Rowland in the army. Fenwick dispatched Cooper at once, with instructions to phone in his report that night. The school friend, now in Newcastle, would be dealt with by local CID. He waited by the phones in the studio, desperate for further calls.

The continued low response was very disappointing and highly unusual given the *Crimewatch* coverage. There had been no wives, ex-wives, mothers-in-law, girlfriends, colleagues, old drinking pals or relatives. And the military silence was strange. Not everyone that knew him could have been warned off.

'Sir,' one of the constables manning the lines called him over, 'there's a man here claims to know Rowland but insists on speaking to you.'

'DCI Fenwick here. Who is this?'

'These telephones, are they the ones in the studio?'

'Yes.'

'Then I'll call you back in your office. Be there, it's important.'

The line went dead; the call had lasted less than a minute. Fenwick hung on at the studio but there were few other calls. After a brief consultation with the programme hosts, Fenwick thanked the team and left.

His office was stale and unwelcoming. The waste-paper basket sat unemptied from the day, two mugs, encrusted with the remains of the day's supply of coffee, weighed down an overflowing in-tray, in which the insistent memoranda of bureaucracy clamoured for attention.

He rang his mother briefly to check on the children and was amused to hear that she had taped his television appearance, but not the reconstruction, to share with them the next day. Then he sat back to wait. To keep himself awake, and to stop his mind from worrying at the edges of the case, he started to work on the in-tray.

The tray was empty and the waste bin had disappeared under a paper mountain when his phone shrilled into life. He started up from a dozing slouch and grabbed the receiver. His watch showed 2.45 a.m.

'Yes?'

'Detective Chief Inspector Fenwick?' It was a man's voice, smooth, accentless.

'Yes. Who else would be stupid enough to be here at this time of night?'

'OK, calm down. It's important you listen carefully. I haven't long. Do you have pen and paper?'

'Er, yes. Who is this?' His question was ignored.

'I want you to go to the east corner of Market Square. Be there by three. I'll call you at the phone box there.'

'What? Hey, hang on!' Fenwick was speaking to the echo of an empty line. 'Bugger, he's gone again!'

Fenwick replaced the receiver and rubbed his chin in thought, the black stubble rasping against his fingers. He must look a sight. He would probably be arrested for loitering if he went into town at this hour. Still, he had a choice. He could ignore the man and go home or, having waited this long, he could give him one last chance. Fenwick looked at his watch again, it was already ten to three. He hadn't been given long to make up his mind. The rational, safe move was to go home. On impulse, he picked up his keys and left.

The call came at three exactly. Fenwick was in no mood to play further games. He spoke into the handset as soon as he picked it up.

'Now listen, whoever you are, this is your last chance. You can tell me who you are and what you have to say now, or forget it.'

'I'll speak to you now, Fenwick. There's no way this line could be tapped.' Fenwick refused to react to the melodramatic remark.

'Your office line undoubtedly is, Fenwick, and I couldn't be sure about the studio.'

'Then why not meet in my office?'

'Oh, that will definitely be wired – and your home too, so watch what you discuss there. You've no idea who or what you're up against.'

'And you do? Who are you?'

'I'll perhaps give you a name later – but first, I want to be sure we need to talk at all. Tell me about the murders and why you need to find Vic.'

The man still had all the cards. If he was to make anything of the call, Fenwick had no choice but to give him a brief account of the two murders and Smith's hit-and-run, dwelling on the vulnerability and innocence of the women and the viciousness of the attacks.

He was acutely conscious that he could be talking to the killer rather than a potential witness, so he played down the connections, repeating nothing that hadn't already been mentioned in the press. 'All the evidence so far points to Rowland – I can't tell you more until I know who you are and why you're being so evasive.'

'I'm sorry but I shouldn't be talking to you at all. At the least I could lose my job for this. But it was your description of the women. We all discussed it and the other two were determined to keep quiet but I decided I couldn't have another death on my conscience. I have enough of those as it is. I've got kids, you see – about the same age as that woman's. It brings matters very close.'

'Tell me your name, and those of the other two. How do you know Vic and why have you decided to talk to me now?'

'My name's Jim Bayliss, but I'd prefer you not to use it. My rank's an irrelevance. Vic and I were in the same unit before he left. We were also mates, which makes this hard. But Vic is not a murderer, not by nature. He's ill, very sick and he needs help. Seeing you on TV I decided he probably stood more chance if he was found by you than by anybody else – and I think he needs to be found soon for everyone's sake.'

'Right. I'll need to see you, interview you. I must know everything you know about Vic and what's going on. When can we meet? I'll come to wherever you say.'

'Won't the phone do? I'm not sure we should meet.'

'Listen, it's gone three in the morning. I'm standing in an open kiosk and it's starting to rain. I know you must be nearby and I need to meet you. For all I know you could be Rowland, or a hoaxer, or a member of the press. I can't base the rest of my investigation on one suspect phone call.' There was a short pause. Fenwick could feel the man weighing up the odds.

'OK, we'll meet. Wait, don't say *anything*, just listen.' The man's tone grew more insistent. 'You might be being watched. Don't scoff, you don't know these people. Just in case they are following you, I want you to play to the gallery. In a minute, I want you to act as if I were refusing to meet you or to say anything. We can see each other tomorrow, first thing, 0630 hours. Do you know Beckett's Farm, out near Cuckfield? Good. I'm calling from the phone box in the lane opposite. I can see a barn to the right as I look at it, near the road. It's big enough to drive a car into and it's screened from the main farm building. I'll meet you there. Needless to say, come alone. I'll leave you to do your Olivier now. Good night, Fenwick.'

The line went dead. Fenwick felt a fool standing there, pretending to listen and an even bigger fool about the charade he then kept up for several minutes before slamming the phone down and storming off to his car. It was nearly 3.30 in the morning but he needed to call Cooper. Hazarding a guess that he would have gone home after interviewing the man in Watford, however late, he rang the number from his car.

'Cooper?'

'Uh?'

'It's Fenwick. I need to see you. Meet me at my house in half an hour.'

He let himself into the still house quietly. By the time Cooper arrived he had showered, shaved and changed. A full grill of sausage, bacon and tomato was sizzling gently, a frying pan stood ready for the eggs and a warm dinner plate groaned under a mound of white and brown toast.

The mixed aromas of strong fresh coffee, hickory smoke, and sage and onion made Cooper's mouth water as he walked down the hall to the kitchen. His stomach was wide awake. He eyed the DCI suspiciously. He doubted the man had slept, yet he was clear-eyed and looking at least ten years younger.

'I thought we'd need a good breakfast, a farmer's breakfast, before we start the day. I suspect it's going to be a long one.'

'You're on to something.' It was a statement, not a question.

'I think so. Yes, I think I am, if we're lucky. Come with me.'

He left the grill gently bubbling and took Cooper into the downstairs shower room. The sergeant regarded him with grave concern.

Behind the camouflaging rush of the shower he relayed, word for word his conversation with Bayliss. It took a matter of minutes only but by the end of it Cooper was pink and damp inside his summer-weight tweed.

'It could be a hoax, of course, but I don't think so. Anyway we'll find out in a couple of hours. We're meeting at 6.30. He want's me to go alone . . .'

'You're not going to, surely?'

'Of course not. We're going to leave a note at the station with the duty sergeant and you're going to come with me – stay under cover and make sure the station knows exactly where we are. If I'm not out of the barn within fifteen minutes you're to ring for backup. *Don't* come in on your own. And make sure we get fingerprints from the phone box. Now, I need to know what happened in Watford. Is it innocuous enough to tell me over breakfast?'

Cooper thought and then nodded – there was only so much steam a man could take.

'Lenny Dilks was in the army, with Rowland, in the Fusiliers. He now acts as a gamekeeper at a commercial shoot. He remembers Rowland from then, remembers him because he says he was an exceptional soldier with an excellent reputation. Dilks was a young lad, only eighteen, and he clearly hero-worshipped the man. He didn't have a bad word to say for him and was keen to see us to "set the record straight." '

'So no rumours, dark stories about him?'

'None. The opposite. Apparently Rowland was decorated while Dilks was serving under him. He saved the life of someone when they were on a training exercise. The man fell from a mountain in Snowdonia and the weather turned, preventing a full search. Rowland carried on looking in sub-zero temperatures and found him – carried him back. To hear Dilks speak you'd think it was a one-man rescue mission.'

'So what happened to our hero then?'

'Apparently he was commended later, for bravery in the Gulf. Dilks was cagey on the details. After that he was posted from the regiment. Dilks doesn't know where but knew he'd gone for selection to the SAS.'

'So a decorated war hero who maybe joined the SAS. That could start to explain some of the reticence and concern, but the SAS isn't a secret society, for God's sake!'

Over strong coffee, they outlined plans for a purely fictitious day. Both felt stupid and out of place but they persisted long enough to excuse the early start. Much of the discussion was rooted in truth anyway, as both men had growing concerns, for different reasons, about Octavia Anderson's disappearance.

It was just after five o'clock when Fenwick closed the door carefully behind Cooper and prepared to leave the house. He wanted to check out the site of the meeting before six and make sure that Cooper was well concealed. As he picked up his car keys he heard a whisper from the top of the stairs behind him.

'Daddy, where're you going?'

All he could see of Bess was two brown shins and the frilly hem of her nightie. He crept back to the bottom of the stairs and smiled up at her.

'I'm going to work. What are you doing out of bed? Go on, back upstairs with you!'

'But it's early and I heard talking.'

Fenwick ran up the tread lightly and scooped her up in his arms. Her hands immediately clasped his neck in a hug and he had to prise them away as he tucked her up in bed. She looked up at him with huge solemn eyes.

'I don't like this, Daddy. I'm frightened.'

'My big girl? Frightened? No you're not. Snuggle down now.' He was acutely conscious of the minutes ticking away and his desire to arrive at the barn early. He had almost reached the door when she sat up in bed again.

'Daddy! Don't do anything dangerous! I love you!'

He dashed back and kissed her once more, confused by her insight and worried by her warning.

Fenwick pulled his car into the barn out of sight of both road and farm. He completed a detailed and methodical search, checking potential exits in case he needed to leave in a hurry. It was a rickety, rectangular structure twenty-four feet by thirty-six with a stack of old straw bales in the far right corner and a wide, open entrance.

He had satisfied himself that he knew all there was to know about the building, and was returning to his car, when he sensed a change in the atmosphere behind him, emanating from the back of the barn. There had been no noise, just a thickening in the air that suggested he was not alone. He became intensely conscious of the vulnerability of his spine; the exposed gap between his shoulder blades itched. He had no weapon of any kind; there was a tyre lever in the boot but that was half a dozen paces away.

For a split second he saw again the wound in Katherine Johnstone's throat and remembered their speculations about the weapon that could inflict such an injury. He started walking casually towards his car.

'That's probably far enough, Chief Inspector.' The voice was less cultured than it had sounded on the phone but was just as deep. Fenwick turned around slowly, consciously working on an expression of confidence. The man was standing about four yards away. He was just under six foot, stocky, deep-chested with a baked-in tan that suggested recent, extensive work out of doors. His hair was a mass of grizzled grey-brown curls, too old for the square face of hard, flat angles. Fenwick put him in his thirties but he could have been younger – the grey was deceptive. He held a handgun in his left hand which he used to motion Fenwick away from the car.

'Some identification, please, Chief Inspector.'

'I must ask the same of you.' He reached into his jacket and pulled out his warrant card.

'Throw it over.'

'No. You should know better than that. You can read it from where you are.' Fenwick extended his hand toward the gunman who stepped forward to study more closely. He was now less than nine feet away.

'All right.'

'Now you, Mr Bayliss, if you don't mind.' His dry, official tone made Bayliss smile as he put his gun away. He passed over ID and driving licence which bore the name James Aubrey Bayliss.

'Are you on your own?'

'In here, yes. My sergeant's outside. You don't need to worry, I wasn't followed but I've made sure a few of my people know where I am and why.'

'You're early.'

'So are you.'

The two men appraised each other in silence. Bayliss was shorter than Fenwick but solid and fit enough to go fifteen rounds with someone much larger. He was alert, no longer overtly threatening, but Fenwick was sure his hand would find the gun again before he could reach him. Even without it, he was at a disadvantage.

'You said you could tell me about Victor Rowland.'

'Yes, we worked together for a while.'

'In the SAS?'

Bayliss shook his head then shrugged. 'If you say so.'

'Why did you decide to see me?'

'I need to tell you that I think you're bloody right to be looking for Vic but I had to see you first.'

'How can seeing me make a difference?'

'I had to see whether you were up to it.' He paused, his stare intent on Fenwick. 'I think you are. It's hard to say. I would have known immediately if you weren't. But I think you could do it. I bloody hope so.'

'Why such drama? This might be a tough case but I don't see it as impossible.'

'Then you're fucking stupid and that could be fatal. I mean that. For you to imagine that this was just another case – Jesus! Vic Rowland is, was, a very special soldier. You've got to start thinking differently. He was a cut above. Right from the start, he was singled out because of his ability. Trained, tested and proved himself time and again.'

The man was talking in short half-sentences, reluctant to say anything one minute, gabbling away the next. Fenwick kept quiet, letting him go on in his own way. He described Rowland's gift for languages, his strength and how he kept himself in peak condition. What distinguished Vic was his fuck-you mental attitude.

'But you've got to understand that he was able to keep his emotions under complete control, to focus on what he had to do completely, whatever the circumstances.' Bayliss walked over to the car and leant heavily on the boot.

'You make him sound like some character from a Schwarzenegger movie!'

'Listen, Fenwick, I knew him, off and on, for about fifteen years, and I *never* saw him out of control. He just didn't have the emotions the rest of us had, or if he did he wasn't bothered by them. And Vic was a fucking star with potential. He was the man that was rolled out to impress the bloody politicians. He was known in very high places.'

'You make him sound a hero.'

'Do I? That's not what I meant at all. He was one of us. Special but no more nor less heroic. I think the difference with him was his emotions; he was so bloody balanced and controlled.'

'What about women? Are you saying he was celibate?'

'Get real! He wasn't married, didn't have a regular girl-friend. He needed sex but it was just something else physical that he enjoyed, nothing more.'

'So we are up against a highly efficient, clever and fit man. From what you've said, someone that has killed in the past?'

'You make it sound so bloody dry, Fenwick. Christ, all of that's true but you still haven't grasped *him*. I genuinely don't think he has *any* memories of the people he's killed; they were just part of a problem to be solved. And he never failed, however shitty the assignment.'

'I see.'

291

'I haven't finished yet. I've just described the mate I worked with for years. I trusted him absolutely. I was the closest thing he had to a good friend.'

'And you're betraying him now? Or are you setting me up?'

Bayliss stared into the middle distance, his eyes unfocused, a deep frown line between them.

'I hope to God I'm not, Fenwick.' He turned to the detective and drew in his gaze. His concentrated stare was so powerful Fenwick could imagine cross-hairs neatly targeted on his forehead. 'I think you're his only hope. You see, the bloke I've just described to you doesn't really exist any more.'

Fenwick's mouth twisted in disbelief.

'No. Believe me. It started last November. We'd had a particularly tough series of assignments throughout the year and we were all fucking exhausted. Post, letters from home had been stacked up waiting for us in . . .' he hesitated, 'it's irrelevant where. Vic rarely received letters – he didn't seem to have relatives or close friends. On the day we got back though, he had several. I can remember them well. I used to take the stamps back for my boy so all my mates gave me their envelopes. Vic had three; two letters and a large brown envelope that had been under-stamped. They'd all been sent from Sydney.'

'You've got a good memory.'

'I saved the stamps, as I said, and later I looked at them again, trying to make some fucking sense of what was happening around me. I was curious about the letters – so many – and asked him about them that evening. He mentioned that his uncle had died; said that the letters were legal, said he had a legacy. He was quiet, withdrawn but I didn't remark on it. He never was a gabby man.

'But I'm sure it was from that day that he started to change. We didn't really notice at first but we began to realise that he wasn't saying anything. He avoided us and I noticed he wasn't eating much. He started to lose weight.' Bayliss took a deep breath. 'Then the nightmares started. Two, three times some nights he'd wake up in a sweat and shouting. I couldn't make out many words – he kept screaming "NO! NO! NO!" again and again. And once there was a name, "Carol." '

'You're sure it was Carol?'

'Yes. Positive. I was already wide awake and I heard it clearly. I talked about it with him the next morning, and that's when I realised he was in a terrible state. It bloody creeps up on you, when you're with someone every fucking day. You assume you know them so well. But really, they're changing, sickening, before your eyes and you don't even notice.'

'Yes, I know.' Something in Fenwick's voice brought Bayliss back to the present and he looked at him keenly.

'You do, don't you? So you know how I felt that morning, realising how fucking bad it all was suddenly. I went up to him first thing and challenged him to tell me what was wrong. He was becoming a danger to us, but he was also a mate, and I was bloody angry with him for putting me, us, in an unacceptable position. I couldn't shop him, but he needed help. He looked awful. Not eating, lack of sleep – he'd aged then, fifteen years – and his skin had a sallow, dead look to it. Vic just stared through me as I spoke to him, he didn't say a word. It was as if he was completely fucking disconnected.' Bayliss drew another deep breath. 'His silence made me furious. I was losing sleep too; we were due to go out again within days and our preparation was suffering. He could end up getting us killed. He just moved to walk past me and I grabbed his arm. He was on me, in an instant. One second I was standing talking to him, the next I was on my chest in the dirt, his knees in my back and on my arms, left hand gripped under my jaw. I was powerless. I twisted round to look up into his face, trying to smile, joke it off, but I could hardly move and my mouth was clamped shut. I couldn't breathe to get the words out; his whole weight was bearing down on my chest. His eyes were dead, flat like a shark's, no fucking expression in them. I'd thought we were mates, but I couldn't see the man I knew there, just a stranger prepared to fucking kill me! I didn't know what he was going to do. I'll never know. Another bloke from our patrol came on us just then – thought we were larking about. Vic just got up, dusted himself down and walked away.'

Bayliss was silent for a long time, then he pulled himself together and described how he'd told the CO and about how they took Rowland off active duty for a while. All had seemed normal until just before Christmas.

'A few of us joined in a small combined exercise. It was unusual, involving us in something like that, but some bright fuck somewhere decided it was our turn. We shared a camp with another Regiment. All right really, most of them. Except that there was this couple of arseholes, real big mouths after a couple of pints. They were bigoted, racist pricks but the racist bit stopped soon enough when they met our Jimmy Ray, black as the ace of spades and a fucking big lad! So that left them with religion and women as topics for abuse. Religion was out – they could tell they weren't going to upset us with that one – but women remained fair game. We all like a bloody good joke but they went way beyond that. They resented us being there and it pissed them off that we refused to get worked up.

'Vic didn't really notice them. He was still unsociable and he rarely hung around in the bar. But we had an evening's break in the exercise and went to this local pub. Vic joined us in the bar and these two pricks were there, well oiled. They just wouldn't let up that night. A few of their mates egged them on and eventually things got out of hand.

'There'd been a rape locally – two seventeen-year-old girls on their way home, no escorts. Our two comedians started making remarks about these girls, how they'd been asking for it; and it got worse. Their mates tried to calm them down but they'd fuckin' lost it by then. They came over to us. We were about to leave but they grabbed my arm. Vic was still with us. I tried to take the heat out of things but they weren't having any of it. They kept on about these bloody girls and then started asking if we had sisters, girlfriends, wives, and were they having fun in our absence; they were very explicit as to the fun. It was juvenile stuff, petty, nasty, and they did it quietly, no shouting or raving any more, just in our face. Another mate was standing next to me and I could feel him tense up. He was fucking furious. I learnt later that his aunt had been raped and it had

294

virtually finished her off. Anyway, he starts forward, and I grab his arm. I'm concentrating on him, you see, holding him back.

'Next thing I know, one of them, the cockier of the two, says something and he's on the floor. He just went down, smashed his head on a big table on the way, and he's lying there. I look round and Vic is standing on my other side, just behind me, rubbing his right hand. And everyone else is looking at him. The man on the floor isn't moving. There's blood coming from his nose; you can tell it's broken. Then I notice his eyes are open, just staring up at the ceiling. I bend down and feel his carotid artery – no fucking pulse. His eyes are turned back in his head so that only half the pupil is showing – there's no reaction there. I put a glass that's on the table to his mouth and nose – no condensation.

'We continued with AR and cardiac massage until the medics arrived. It seemed fucking for ever but it was only ten minutes. When they took him away I noticed that Vic had gone; apparently the MPs had arrived while we were trying to resuscitate the man.

'I didn't see the blow that had killed him – oh, he was dead by the way, killed instantly. Apparently it was just one punch, so fast no one saw it start or finish.' Bayliss took another deep breath. 'It's affected me like no other death! He was on our fucking side, you see, a prick and a bully but one of ours.'

'And of course, a few days before it could have been you.'

Bayliss checked Fenwick out for sarcasm. He found only concern.

'Yes, it could have been me. I was interviewed by the MPs, but they were in a fuckin' difficult position – trying to decide what case to put together, and against somebody who was marked out for higher things. Vic was held in custody at first, but opinion started to swing round in his favour and eventually he was allowed out until the inquest, provided he stayed on the base. No one wanted to rush in and get the charge wrong. They were still working on a case when he disappeared a few days later.'

Bayliss suddenly stopped talking and his head snapped up.

He ran silently to the front of the building, gun in hand. He flattened his back against the bare wooden wall by the cart-wide entrance. Seconds later, Cooper peered in cautiously. Bayliss had him in an arm-lock, gun to his head, smashed against the wall, before Fenwick had time to speak.

'It's my sergeant. Let him go, Bayliss.'

Cooper turned round slowly, straightening the badly crushed tweed jacket; there was a tear in one elbow where it had snagged on a nail. He viewed it glumly. He looked every bit his age.

'I came to make sure you were all right, sir.' His sombre attempt at dignity was laughable in the circumstances but Fenwick kept a completely straight face.

'Quite right, Sergeant. I had warned Mr Bayliss to expect you but it seems he has a little bit of a problem controlling his finely tuned reflexes. I'm sure he's waiting to apologise.'

Bayliss muttered an embarrassed apology and extended his hand. After a moment's hesitation, Cooper accepted it, pumping it once. Then Bayliss went on with his story.

'It was early January but I didn't know for sure he'd gone. They tried bloody hard to keep it quiet.'

'Then why was his name on the computer printouts we were given?'

'It shouldn't have been. Are you sure?'

Cooper flicked back through his notebook. 'Here we are, Rowland, A.R.V.'

'That's not him. His initials are V. R. – Victor Robert – that's another man.'

'No wonder Major West prevaricated; he had no idea how we'd found the man's name and made the link! Go on.'

'There's not much more to say. He was gone; so was his passport, full kit, clothes.'

'What about money?'

Bayliss snorted: 'First that's what gave them comfort – his chequebook and cards had been left behind – but they'd forgotten the legacy, over a million.'

'A million!' Both Cooper and Fenwick looked shocked and

worried; a man with that amount of ready money was dangerous.

'When his uncle died he was the only heir. Over the years the old man had made a bloody packet.'

'So, he had passport, clothes, money and promptly disappeared after killing a man in an unprovoked attack! No wonder the military authorities are touchy!'

'Yes and if the press put the story together it will be *very* embarrassing. And that's not the worst of it. When I said that he'd taken his kit, I meant everything, weapons and all.'

'How the hell did he manage to take weapons with him?'

'I don't know. No one knows. The procedures are bloody tight – particularly given the range of weapons we have. The log shows he handed his equipment in, right down to his personal pistol and knife, but rumour has it that they're not there now.'

'So what is his standard kit?' Cooper's question was edged with contempt and Bayliss looked uncomfortable for the first time.

'I don't know, but I can tell you what he favoured.' The list was frightening: a Browning High-Power – 9 mm calibre, magazine fed, 10 rounds, reliable and accurate up to 50 metres; an Ingram MAC 10 submachine pistol, 11.4 mm calibre, a short-barrel weapon with very high rate of fire; survival knife.

'Anything else?'

'I can't say; all those would be easy to conceal – tuck one into a cross-draw holster, the other into a long pocket. Other weapons would be more difficult to hide.'

'But if he had, say, been able to walk out with what he wanted, what else would he have taken?'

'Just about anything! As well as the others, an assault rifle, perhaps a sniper's rifle, explosives, grenades – the list's endless. As for the assault rifle, he preferred the old NATO 7.62 mm; he'd have gone for that. Very accurate.'

'And the sniper's rifle?'

'It would depend what was there – and he'd need matched ammunition and telescopic sights. But, if he'd had a choice? The Accuracy International PM – the L96A1. It takes 7.62 mm calibre ammo. The magazine gives him ten rounds, more than enough to take out key targets and a range of up to 1000 metres. That comes with a Schmidt & Bender PM6 × 42 sight. It's my favourite and it's good in poor light. Vic's had all the special training he needs – not just the marksmanship but in camouflage and concealment, just as important. As for explosives and how much ammunition, that's bloody hard to tell but, *if* he'd had free rein, you should assume he had TNT or C3/C4; blasting caps, fuses of some sort – safety or Detcord primers, detonators, perhaps timers and electrics as well.'

'He's a one-man frigging army!' Cooper could no longer contain himself.

'That, as I've been trying to fucking tell you, is *exactly* what he is! It really doesn't matter what weapons he actually took, I've told you his favourites but he'd use whatever'll get the job done, basically. He's done the sniper training, of course, that's very special.'

'And he's had it all?'

'Oh yes, he had it fucking all.'

Time was passing, and with every minute Fenwick became more frantic to be moving, to be *doing* something to stop the menace Bayliss had described, but he knew that to rush off would be disastrous. There was still more that he didn't know about Rowland than he did, and Bayliss had to be good for some of it.

'Let me see your knife.' Fenwick could still envisage the long wound across Katherine's neck like a grotesque, second smile.

Bayliss twisted away suddenly and when he turned again, he had an unsheathed hunting knife in his hand.

'Sergeant, take this and ask forensics to match it against Katherine Johnstone's injury.' It went straight into a plastic evidence bag.

'Now,' he walked towards Bayliss, ending up inches away from him, 'is there anything else you need to tell me that you think I should know?'

'I think you know it all already.' Bayliss looked tired and

very sad. 'Vic was a fucking great guy, Fenwick, one of the best. And a friend. If I thought . . .' He paused and squeezed the bridge of his nose tight. 'If I thought there was a hope of finding the old Vic and bringing him home, I'd do it myself. But that's a pipe dream. Something's happened to him and it's flipped him over the line.'

'The line?'

'Between the killing that produces heroes and the kind that creates the murderers you have to find – and you'd better find him. You have to stop him.'

'Why us?'

'Now it's my turn to get personal, Chief Inspector. Not just "why us." Why *you*? I could try and track him down, sure I could, but then what would I *do* with him? I think he's fixated, you see. Heaven help anyone that stands between him and his goal.'

'Thanks!' For the first time there was sarcasm in Fenwick's voice.

'It's true. The military powers-that-be could find him – will probably find him thanks to your help – but they're not going to take any prisoners! Vic's slipped from the legion of honour to the legion of the damned. To everyone else, he's now the fucking target.'

Fenwick studied the man carefully. Behind the bluster – the only way he appeared able to cope with the personal dilemma in which he had found himself – there was genuine concern for his old friend. He voiced the obvious question: 'Why turn him in?'

'Because he's going to kill again – I know it. He's building up to something grand. There's too much of the showman in him to end on a hit-and-run.' He paused. 'And because if you find him he stands a chance of trial – and treatment for the sick man he's become.'

'Meaning that that won't happen if military intelligence find him first? Is that what you're saying?'

'You're a big boy, Chief Inspector. Work it out for yourself.'

'If you're serious about helping us, Bayliss, you'll have to tell us everything you know. So far all you've done is confirm his name and rank and work on our suspicions. I need more – like where he might be right now.'

'There's no knowing. He's got money, remember.'

'His targets have all been in Sussex so far – is he likely to have a base here, say Brighton?'

'Possibly. It's got the advantage of the coast. You could try there, but I'd also look to London. It would be my guess. The first abduction happened there, didn't it? And the body was discovered in the west. He'd have more flexibility if he was in London – South London with good access to the M25. He may be in a hotel, but I doubt it. More likely a short-term let. He'll need to plan – be able to leave his kit and materials out – so he won't want a serviced place.' Cooper was scribbling furiously.

'And transport?'

'He'll keep changing that.' Bayliss thought. 'Rented – by cash, I reckon, from different firms. He *might* have bought something fucking fast, as a backup in case he needed to get away in a hurry.'

'In which case he'd need a garage. Perhaps it's a maisonette or mews. Even something with covered parking. What name might he be using?'

'Well, it won't be his own and we don't exactly disclose aliases much in our work! But as to what it might be, I haven't a clue! This is a man who's used to blending in whatever the circumstances. He could have any identity, and change it as easily as you do your jacket.' He inevitably looked to Cooper as he said this, thought of a smart remark but then swallowed it.

'All this is adding up, even for a man with a million. Are there any other places he might have kept money?'

'Not that I know of; all his accounts have been frozen, and he wouldn't be able to sell his house. I suppose he might sell the old man's, though, if he was running low.'

'I'll alert the Australian authorities.'

'No, not in Australia, here. The uncle kept his house here – rented it to Vic's parents when he emigrated.'

Fenwick and Cooper shouted out simultaneously:

'House?'

'Where?'

'It's somewhere local, where he grew up. But you can be bloody sure he won't be there!'

'But he might visit it, for old times' sake.'

'Unlikely. Very unlikely, Chief Inspector – this man's a professional.'

'Yes, and a sick professional, according to you and on his own. It will be interesting to see if he's keeping his judgement.'

'I'll get on to it straight away, sir. We know the old man's name. We'll find it soon enough.'

'How? He emigrated twenty years ago.' Bayliss regarded the portly, middle-aged detective with doubt. Cooper couldn't resist a moment of bravado – honour demanded it.

'There are many ways. Council records, Land Registry, old electoral rolls. It won't take us long.'

'And the old school records, Sergeant. Don't forget we still have those. When that house is found, I want you to give it the full treatment, OK?' Cooper almost stood to attention.

Fenwick quickly ran through the remaining practicalities. Bayliss took a lot of persuading but he finally agreed to make a formal statement, help with the video fit of Rowland and have his fingerprints taken for elimination purposes – all provided it could be in a neutral setting where there was no chance he could be identified by anyone watching Fenwick.

At the last moment, as he was about to leave, Bayliss hovered, reluctant to go.

'Be careful, Chief Inspector. Vic is brilliant at his job. If he's going to kill again, he'll already have his plans in place – he's a meticulous planner.' Fenwick nodded and turned to walk away but Bayliss grabbed his arm, his face filled with doubt.

'Go armed, Fenwick. He will be. Don't put your boys up against him with wooden sticks; he would cut them down without a fucking thought.' Fenwick nodded once in acknowledgement, and then finally turned away.

CHAPTER THIRTY-THREE

The air was thick and heavy as he made his way unobtrusively down South Street, through Canon Gate and down Canon Lane into the cloisters. Bunches of tourists loitered in the cool-banded shadows, idly reading plaques and memorials. Young girls wedged themselves into the arched gaps that faced on to the green lawn called Paradise to catch the sharply angled sun on arms and faces already burnt brown by the summer.

He walked steadily, but not so purposefully as to draw attention to himself, and passed into the hush of the cathedral. It was busy inside, which suited his purpose. He smiled at one of the willing lady helpers and went to sit on a wooden chair in the long narrow nave. Scaffolding from restoration work spoilt the perspective but he noted it was already being dismantled.

Behind him was the main west door, to his right the south aisle with small chapels beyond. The sun shone through the south-facing windows, casting aqueous ripples of pink, blue and green light on the stone floor. On his left the north aisle ran straight, dull and shadowed. He craned his neck upwards past the Purbeck marble shafts to the simple stone vaulting. He noticed none of the fine Norman architecture and considered only the nuisance value of the delicate stone pulpitum that stretched in perfect balance across the nave in front of the choir.

He started to pace slowly along the north aisle, passed Holst's tomb without a glance and continued to the lady chapel at the eastern extreme of the cathedral. There were few obvious places of concealment and none that would afford him a view down into the nave. His progress back along the south aisle was impatient but he forced himself to keep to the same measured pace.

He ignored the Romanesque carved stone panels, the cathedral's most astonishing treasure in nearly nine hundred years of artistic patronage. He was completely preoccupied with his need to find the right vantage point, and disappointed by the openness of the tombs and chapels that he passed. A large group of tourists walked by him, following a guide providing a commentary in English, despite their mixed nationalities. The man joined them, careful to avoid being noticed as he completed a circuit of the cathedral for a second time.

Half an hour later he was no further forward and he decided to have lunch in the Bishop Bell gardens tucked against the south face of the cathedral. As he sat on his own, eating a salad, three men and a woman seated themselves at a nearby table to drink their tea. Their conversation washed over him unnoticed until he caught a reference to 'the performance'.

'It's going to be difficult to fit them all in, particularly as you've decided to increase the size of the choir and orchestra.'

'Yes, Dean. I appreciate that but we must be able to do something. Is there a gallery we can use? Or what about the aisles?'

'Fire regulations prevent us from using the aisles and we don't have a gallery. We can't have people standing on the Bell Arundel screen either.'

'What about putting some of the girls in the choir? They wouldn't be able to see, of course, but they should still be able to hear.'

'Yes, that would be feasible, as long as they were well supervised.'

'Well of course!' The woman sounded offended.

The first man spoke again. From the corner of his eye the eavesdropper could see him pot-bellied and anxious, sitting primly in his jacket and tie despite the heat. 'But we still need to find somewhere for the trumpeters. The trumpeters, you see, for the Tuba mirum.'

'If there aren't many, you could use part of the triforium. It would need cleaning up but that wouldn't be too difficult.'

'The triforium – where's that?'

'It's an arcade that runs all the way along the nave, above the aisles. It's quite narrow, and access is restricted so you'd have to limit the numbers but it would work.'

The man left the remainder of his salad and went back to the cathedral. Inside, he looked up above the arches of the nave and saw the wooden platform running all the way along above the aisles. The Dean might have been too pompous to call it a gallery but that's exactly what it looked like. He walked quickly along the south aisle, looking for steps. He found a flight, curving upwards, and climbed.

It was dusty and cramped, and there were wires snaking across the floor, but it gave a perfect view down into the nave. There was an old chest tucked against the wall. Thick layers of dust in its worn carvings suggested it was little used. It would be perfect for his needs. He had already devised his excuse for being here for the performance. Now all he needed to do was start his early preparations.

PART FIVE

LIBERA ME

Libera me, Domine, de morte aeterna, in die
  illa tremenda,
quando coeli movendi sunt et terra.
Dum veneris judicare saeculum per ignem.

Lord, deliver me out of everlasting death,
Oh Lord, upon that day of terror, when the
  earth and the heavens shall be shaken.
When thou shalt come and the whole world
  know the fire of judgement.

CHAPTER THIRTY-FOUR

There was a full team meeting in the evening with the Assistant Chief Constable in attendance. Fenwick was still in charge but Alistair Harper-Brown, the ACC, was now taking a personal interest in the case.

The team had been expanded again and the meeting was part briefing, part council of war. Fenwick pulled no punches as he told them all bluntly that they were dealing with a serial killer who would kill again. He told them enough about Rowland to make them proceed with extreme caution, but not enough to panic them. The details of the likely weapons the man could be carrying he saved for the authorised firearms officers who had joined the team.

The ACC had refused to issue firearms straight away. There was no immediate danger to the team and Rowland's whereabouts was still unknown. If and when they found the uncle's house the investigating team would be armed, but otherwise Harper-Brown was concerned about escalation too early. Fenwick accepted his judgement reluctantly.

Individual areas of investigation were placed under the direction of a number of detective sergeants and inspectors. There was now a real risk of the case pulling apart as each section of the team pursued its own inquiries. Fenwick decided to keep Cooper as his right-hand man, available to investigate new areas quickly but also to help him co-ordinate the work. Nightingale had almost fallen into the role of a glorified PA – available to do whatever, whenever it was necessary, but neither she nor Fenwick was complaining. She realised that as the new girl she had a unique chance to stay at the heart of their inquiry rather than being relegated to the role of foot soldier on the periphery. If that involved menial tasks, so be it.

Lines of inquiry were agreed, with strict instructions given to report in regularly and for the heads of the teams to attend all progress meetings. Fenwick was sure the case would be solved by working the connections. He handed Cooper and Nightingale a list of activities and who was heading up what:

1) Trace Anderson – recheck alibis – Newgent
   – when found Fenwick/Cooper to interview.
2) Find Rowland's uncle's house – Ball.
   – A.F.O.s in attendance. Full SOCO treatment.
3) Interview all traced school friends and teachers – Parmiter.
4) Prepare press statements and field enquiries – Fenwick + P. R. officer
5) Trace car rental for April – and subsequently – Hurst.
6) Letting Agents – find Rowland's current whereabouts – Russell.
7) Circulate information/new picture to all stations – Nightingale.

'Right, let's run through it one more time.' Fenwick's voice betrayed his weariness, a hard lump of stress in his throat. Everyone except he, Cooper and Nightingale had already gone home but he was desperate to ensure nothing had been over-looked. He took a gulp of tepid machine brew and felt his stomach twinge; he missed the secretary's special filter coffee.

'Cooper, as soon as we find Anderson, you and I visit, and we don't leave until we have the full story. If necessary, we charge her with wasting police time and take her into custody.'

Cooper and Nightingale looked at each other and winced.

'Ball is looking for the house,' Fenwick continued. 'Cooper, watch that one. Next, Nightingale, you've drawn a blank on any new information from old school friends. It's probably a waste of time doing too much more but I've given Parmiter two days and a good-size team. Make sure that Rowland's picture is distributed across the country, with a briefing. I'll help you draft that. Most importantly, I want regular reports on all developments. Wherever I am you're to make sure I get them. I've got the press off my back for a few hours but we'll need another briefing ready. They've smelt blood. Next, Bayliss' knife. We've got forensic's report. They state "both wounds could have been inflicted by weapons of similar shape, weight and design." That's as close as they'll come to confirmation and it's good enough for me—'

Cooper interrupted: 'Bayliss has solid alibis for all three attacks and there's no match at all between his fingerprints and the fragment we have from Johnstone's house. It looks as if he's clear.'

'Good. That makes things easier. The Met have got teams trying to trace the car used in the April abduction, and, with luck, the car he'll be using now. They're going to focus on South London first; I think we should back Bayliss' instinct there. I want to be available to become involved in that as soon as there's anything solid to follow up. So wherever I am, you'll have to find me if we get a lead. OK?'

'Yes, sir. I've already said yes.'

'Right, good, yes. Now. We've a PC at Smith's bedside and we've authorised armed protection. We've got to keep that up. I know it's unlikely we'll get anything from her but she is improving—'

'She's still in intensive care! They've only just taken her off life support!'

'Yes, but at least her improvement will help morale. Now, what are we going to do about covering all the letting agencies and car rentals? I'm worried that there are just too many. We'll never get through them in time.'

Cooper was reassuring. 'Russell has had the bright idea of using faxes and Hurst is following suit. They're working their way through Yellow Pages, local directories, even *Exchange and Mart* – they're fresh, keen and convinced they'll get a result. Leave it to them, sir, and relax. You've got us the resources we need. It's time to regroup and for you to ease up, ready for whatever happens next.'

Cooper just managed to keep his tone from being patronising. Fenwick was too tired to notice in any case.

'Yes, you're right – it's just that we've been pushing this along on our own for so long now, I keep forgetting. Go on home, the pair of you, you look exhausted.'

Cooper and Nightingale left gratefully but it was another two hours before the lights were finally switched off in Fenwick's office.

He eased his key into the front door lock and pushed it open gently. The house was in darkness. Without switching on the hall light he found his way by touch to the kitchen where the oven light cast a weak welcoming glow. Now he could turn the light on. A note from his mother was propped against the salt and pepper to the side of a single laid place. He picked it up with trepidation.

Your dinner is in the oven. There's fresh gravy in the fridge door if it's too dried out. Chris had a little bit of a wobble today but he's all right. Try to make some time for them this weekend, you're becoming a stranger again.

He took the covered plate from the oven with a double thickness of tea towel. Beneath the saucepan lid the chicken had stuck to the plate and the cabbage and carrots had dried into reduced hard lumps. Only the baked potato remained edible. He added a knob of butter, ate it quickly, scalding his mouth, and poured himself a whisky and water as a nightcap.

Fifteen minutes later, showered, hair still damp, he crept into the children's bedroom. Both were fast asleep, breathing noisily. He kissed each smooth brow and stroked Chris's hair gently, hoping he would be aware of the love he felt, in his dreams. Then, after needlessly tucking their quilts around them, he turned and made his way silently to bed.

CHAPTER THIRTY-FIVE

Fenwick and Cooper were shown into the same sitting room in which Fenwick had first met Octavia Anderson. Early morning sunlight slanted in from the window overlooking the street, banding vases of lilies, white, pink, pale yellow, clustered at different heights on occasional tables and the ornate marble mantle. The room was filled with their cloying perfume, like stale scent in a woman's closet.

Neither policeman sat down but stood side by side with their backs to the empty fireplace. The maid brought in a cafetière of coffee and an icy jug of freshly squeezed orange juice. They watched her serve in silence. Within a few minutes Octavia entered the room, a smile ready for Fenwick.

'Chief Inspector, how nice to see you. To what do I owe this pleasure?' There were to be no power games of silence this time; instead she was the relaxed friend. Fenwick yearned to meet her halfway, to keep the smile on her face a little longer, but he had arrived in the role of policeman and it left no room for any other.

'Miss Anderson, I believe you've spoken to Sergeant Cooper before.'

'Ma'am.' Cooper dipped his head briefly.

'Won't you sit down, gentlemen?' The smile was still in place, slightly quizzical but untroubled.

'We're comfortable as we are, thank you. But please take a seat if you wish. This may be a lengthy conversation.' Fenwick's whole manner was awkward, stilted. Anderson sat down and

311

lifted a chilled glass of fruit juice to perfectly made-up lips.

Cooper and Fenwick had agreed the opening and their roles beforehand. It was easy to fall into the practised routine.

'Miss Anderson, as you know, we are investigating the murders of Deborah Fearnside and Katherine Johnstone.' Cooper's voice was a flat recital of facts. 'We have reason to believe that the shared motive for these crimes may be the death of Carol Truman.'

'But—'

'Let me *finish* please, Miss Anderson. You appear to be the only surviving member of the party that accompanied Miss Truman on her last walk. So far, you have avoided or ignored our enquiries, underplayed the closeness of the friendship you had with both dead women and have gone so far as to disappear for a crucial ten days. We are now expecting your full co-operation. Alternatively we may consider charges of wasting police time.'

'But, you can't—'

'In a moment, Miss Anderson. Let me finish. We intend today to obtain a full account of Carol Truman's death – and other matters. You may wish to have a lawyer present but, I must warn you, given the delays and inconvenience to which you have already put us, and the urgency of our enquiries, we will *not* put up with further unnecessary time-wasting. Now,' Cooper's voice was emotionless, 'you may speak.'

Octavia Anderson regarded him open-mouthed, speechless. She turned once to Fenwick, only to flinch visibly from his unrelenting face. The police let her silence develop. With new eyes Fenwick was sensitive enough, and belatedly objective enough, to see despite her apparent shock the rapid calculation in her eyes. Where once he would have assumed that she was hurt and bewildered, he could now see the iron control she applied to her emotions. He was a fool ever to have believed that she needed him. She would never have climbed so far in her career without ruthless determination, no matter how great her talent.

He was aware of a small, insistent pain inside him. This was going to hurt him more than he had expected. But he too could apply rigid control, and he had had too much practice at managing his feelings to fail now. The first flutter of pity died before it could draw breath.

'This is all somewhat of a surprise, Sergeant. I – I really don't know what to do. I . . . should I perhaps call my lawyer? I'm not really sure.'

'It's entirely up to you, miss, but make your mind up, we're in a hurry.'

She tried confusion once more, then became tearful, before recognising that she was on her own.

It was time for Fenwick to play his part. 'Octavia.' He tried to find the right tone; avuncular but firm seemed appropriate. He felt he achieved a reasonable approximation. 'It's been a bit of a shock, I know, but you must talk to us. It's very important and if you don't, we really will have to consider taking you to the station.'

His intervention confused her. She searched his face for signs of calculation but found none.

'All right. But please, won't you sit down? This will be a long story.'

She related the events leading to Carol's death. Her account matched, almost exactly, her original statement. Sometimes whole phrases reappeared that had previously been used twenty years before.

'What did you talk about on your walk?' Cooper used the first of their preprepared interruptions.

'I can't remember, Sergeant. I expect all sorts of things – music, plans for the holidays, mutual friends.'

'Plans for the future?'

'Possibly, I really can't recall. Would you be able to after all these years?'

'I might, if it had been my last conversation with my best friend.'

His barb drew a sharp gasp from Anderson:

'That was unnecessary, Sergeant. Why?'

'Because I don't like you playing games with me, Miss

Anderson. Others in the party clearly recall you in heated debate with Carol Truman – an argument even – on the subject of her chosen career.'

'I . . . I don't recall that fully, no. It's all a very painful memory for me.' Tears were back in her voice as she apparently struggled to recollect. 'You're right, I think we did have a small argument but it's not the sort of thing one wants as a final recollection. I think we argued about music. Yes, and her plans to become a musician. It was a stupid, stupid idea. She was very clever – the best brain in the class – and to throw it all away for music; it was crazy!'

'But you did.' Fenwick's voice was a whisper.

'Yes, but I have talent and stamina *and* the determination to succeed. Carol had none of that. She was a lovely, gentle person with a pretty voice but it wasn't a great voice.'

'Whereas yours was – is?'

'Ask your Chief Inspector, Sergeant. He can tell you!'

Fenwick sketched a brief gesture with his hand and Cooper moved on.

'Did you see anyone else on the walk – anyone at all?'

'No.'

'Was there anyone who might have had a grudge against Carol, any enemies?'

'No one.'

'What about boyfriends, lovers even? How sexually active was she?'

Unexpectedly, Anderson blushed and looked away, her composure momentarily defeated.

'Well?'

'There was no one. You don't understand. Carol wasn't that type of girl.'

She could not meet their eyes.

'How well did you know Victor Rowland?'

Anderson's face lost its flush and her skin paled to an unbecoming grey.

'Not well.' Her voice was a hoarse whisper as she looked down at her hands, fingers twisted together painfully around the glass of orange juice held in her lap.

Fenwick was reminded of Leslie Smith on the night before she was struck down and with a shock recognised fear in Octavia for the first time.

'Was he close to Carol?'

She glanced at him quickly then shook her head hesitantly, not daring to speak. It was an obvious lie. Why?

'Who was closest to her?'

'Apart from me? Her aunt and uncle. She was living with them, until she finished her exams, then she was meant to go to Australia. Carol was very excited about it.'

'There was no suggestion of her staying on at school?'

'No. That wasn't the plan at all; she was going to a sixth form college in Melbourne, one of the best. She was expected to gain excellent grades. That's why it was all so stupid, her thinking of giving it all up for music.'

Cooper marched on through their questions but to Fenwick they were increasingly pointless. They were learning little more and Octavia was regaining her composure and control. He indicated to Cooper that it was time to change tack.

'I think that concludes our first set of questions. Now, if we could turn to the next.' Cooper passively turned over to a clean page in his notebook.

'The next! I have morning appointments, Sergeant!' She bent to sip from her orange juice but it had become tepid in the heat of the room. 'What on earth do you want to cover now?'

'Your whereabouts on August 24th.'

'What? How should I know? And why do you need to know? This really is ridiculous.'

'Miss Anderson, on the morning of August 24th, Leslie Smith was the victim of a serious hit-and-run attack. We need to know where you were at the time.'

At the mention of Smith's name, Anderson's composure finally shattered. Tears started suddenly and dripped from her chin to stain her peach skirt and spray the ivory silk blouse with droplets as they fell. Her face didn't crumple, and she made no noise beyond a low moan, but the sight of her fixed face weeping

315

huge tears moved Fenwick more than hysteria would have done. This wasn't normal grief or mourning for a lost friend, it was rigid, almost catatonic shock. He sat down beside her and gently prised her rigid fingers from the glass of orange juice she still clutched.

'Cooper, would you go and ask Miss Anderson's maid for some fresh coffee and tea? Thank you.' As he was left alone in the room he turned his face to the woman.

'Octavia, you've had a shock but you must talk to me. You are in a very serious position.'

'I . . . I didn't know. I simply didn't know. Is she dead?'

Fenwick shook his head but explained how serious her condition was.

'This is terrible, just awful. Leslie? Why Leslie of all people? God, how? When did it happen?'

Fenwick sketched out the facts, searching her face for signs of guilt behind the show of grief and fear.

'Will she be all right? Will she survive?' Was it the care of a friend or concern of a would-be killer? Fenwick couldn't tell and remained noncommittal.

'Octavia, you must understand, you must realise, that this looks bad for you.' He saw fear in her eyes but she remained silent. 'Your alibi for one of the previous murders is weak and you returned to the UK in time for Leslie's attack – with no explanation.'

For a split second, relief dawned on Anderson's face and then she started to laugh – an awful, sustained high-pitched cackle.

'You think . . .' she gulped air, 'you think that *I* did it? That I'm behind these awful things? Oh shit!' She laughed even harder. 'This is too much. It's pathetic.'

Her hysteria changed abruptly to anger and she turned on Fenwick, eyes blazing, her voice flat and ugly. 'You fool, you bloody fool. I'm not the murderer, I'm not the killer of those poor stupid bitches. I'm the *target*! Don't you realise? He's just warming up! You ask why I left France, why I didn't tell anyone where I was going. Because I was scared witless. He had found

316

me there, I was sure of it. And you, you dear pathetic boys in blue, charge around searching for me because you think *I'm* the killer! My God, if it weren't so sad I'd still be laughing.'

Her anger was searing, her scorn devastating. Any affection that had been struggling to survive between them withered in her stare. Fenwick suddenly felt desperately tired. He heard his voice, from somewhere outside himself, continuing the conversation as if nothing had happened.

'Why are you a potential victim?'

There was a long pause; Anderson stood up and walked away to the window.

'Why me? Yes, that's a good question, why me?' The momentary hysteria had evaporated.

Fenwick watched her back, seeing the tension in her shoulders. He sensed an immense struggle within her. Finally, she raised a hand to massage her neck and turned to face him with a return to her customary relaxed grace. 'You have to understand the whole story, Andrew, from the beginning.' She sat down again beside him and started the staccato sentences of her long narrative.

'I've done well, Andrew. Not at first, of course, oh no. I was born into a snivelling, narrow-minded family – I was the disappointment of a daughter who arrived during the wait for a son who was never born. My father never forgave me, my mother ceased to care. I hoped – oh I hoped *so* much – that they would love me, forget about the might-have-been boy. But they never did. They started to accept me, though, gradually. As I grew up long and bony, thin and undernourished, I worked at my exercises, the sports, stealing extra milk from doorsteps and fruit from lunch boxes at school to build myself up. I made my own luck. I tried anything, everything, that would make them notice me, make them realise that they didn't need a son. The crime was always minor, the gifts never questioned when I took them home. And then the sports and games. My medals and cups always stayed on the mantelpiece for exactly one week, then they'd be gone, I never knew where.

'But things started to change as I grew older; adolescence

and women's rights! I rebelled – but in secret. I was a closet feminist, a secret new-age suffragette. Craving their affection at home, damning their stupidity outside.' A stranger looked at Fenwick from Octavia's eyes. 'Hate is incredibly liberating – did you know that? And it forgives one any deficiencies. Suddenly, you're allowed to be as you are. It was wonderful. I found other women, other girls, who hated too, and suddenly it wasn't really hate any more but a cause! And the power was wonderful. At fourteen, I looked nineteen and felt fifty. But I started to believe in myself as a person, as a woman, not as a butt for crude sarcasm and a foil for other people's disappointments.' She took a deep breath; telling the truth at last was an obvious relief but even now there was hesitation. She searched Fenwick's face again as her hand gently rubbed her neck.

'And then there was Julia. She was in her early twenties, worldly wise to me, a helper at the youth club. We ... we became lovers. It was the first time for me and she loved me so much. She told me I was beautiful! Made me *feel* beautiful, as if I belonged in the world at last.'

She looked at Fenwick through slanted eyes. 'And she made me feel so good. The pleasure. You wouldn't understand; you don't know what it's like to have a woman's body, to live in it day by day, month by month. But she did. Julia did.

'It was all very secret, exciting, but it became too much. I was only just fourteen. I began to feel trapped, restricted, and I had this voice, growing inside me. At first Julia encouraged me. She helped me to practise, even arranged youth club events to give me an opportunity to perform. But I kept on growing. They became trite and trivial, all of them – the club, my friends, even Julia. Their appreciation wasn't enough. I wanted to break away.

'Then, a miracle happened. There was a county competition for under fifteens; Julia persuaded me to enter. She coached me, trained me – I was receiving proper tuition by then but Julia seemed to have a gift for stage craft – she knew how to help me *be* on stage. I chose to sing a piece from *The Mikado* – 'The sun, whose rays' – that was ambitious enough but for my second I insisted on 'Je veux vivre dans ce rêve', you know, from Gounod's *Roméo et Juliette*? It's deceptively difficult but for that one performance I knew I could do it!' She paused for a long time remembering.

'Julia was against it, said my programme was too big, but I knew I could do it. My life became one long rehearsal, everything else disappeared. The voice, *my* voice grew. I was very nervous but then, on the day of the competition, I woke up and I knew what I was, what I could become. As I practised my exercises I could feel the power in me build. I floated through the journey to the concert hall – the first proper hall I'd ever entered. Julia took me; neither of my parents wanted to waste the time. Julia said I was distant and remote. She put it down to nerves but she was wrong. I was being carried by an amazing power. It was there inside me, an incredible feeling. She wanted me to practise with the accompanist just once, 'to loosen up' – I refused. I didn't even open my mouth; I daren't, I was afraid to let that incredible feeling escape.

'When I was called – I was second to last in my class – I glided up on to the stage, all her training giving me an assurance I was unaware of. I can remember the pianist looking at me with concern but I turned to him, nodded my head and said, 'Now' – and I could see him feel my power. He obeyed. He started to play, right tempo, and I started to sing. Only once since then have I given such a performance. That sounds incredible, I know, but it's true. I had the joy of creation – freedom, liberation – in me. I could do anything I wanted with my life – and I would. I was finally in charge.'

Octavia shook herself free of the reverie. 'There was a standing ovation. Of course I won. It was quite a sensation. I had two immediate offers to go to leading music schools but my parents refused to consider it; my place was at home. That's when my only piece of real 'luck' came in. I received an offer to go to Downside; it was local, it had an excellent music facility and it was free. What's more, there was the potential to gain an endowment at sixteen for a scholarship to the Royal Academy with specialist tuition. It wasn't awarded every year and one of the conditions was that candidates had to stay on to do 'O' levels and contribute to the musical life of the school. I didn't mind though; I would only have to wait two years.'

'What about Julia?'

'Julia? Oh I don't know. I hardly saw her again after the concert. She tried to hang on to me but I had power, you see. She didn't stand a chance!'

'And your parents?'

'Oh they loved it – at least my father did for a while – whilst the novelty lasted. He was a celebrity. Down at the club people asked him about his famous daughter, bought him drinks, told him he must be proud of me. And so he became; all the time other people made something of me he was happy to own me. Unfortunately.

'Within six months, even local fame had changed to acceptance and expectation. I didn't care. I had a timetable by then and I was going to show them all.'

'And Carol, what did she make of it all?'

'I hadn't met her then. Carol was already at Downside. As I got to know her she was happy for me, of course. We became good friends.'

'You suggested earlier she was much more than a friend. Who took Julia's place? I can't see you giving up all those newly discovered pleasures.'

Anderson remained silent, avoiding his eyes.

'Come on, Octavia, there's no point in stopping now.'

'For God's sake, why the puerile interest in my sex life all of a sudden? Just let me be!'

'Stop stalling and tell me; were you or were you not Carol Truman's lover?'

'Yes, yes, yes, all right! I *was* her lover. For one glorious year.'

Cooper, returning at that moment with a laden tea tray, quietly backed out again into the hall, unnoticed.

'No one knew. No one suspected even, not really. I was her first. All the things I'd learnt from Julia I taught her. She was very nervous at first; she thought it was a sin. Carol was a young fourteen, growing up on her own. She'd never had a boyfriend, no brothers, although her cousin doted on her, of course, but he was much older. I persuaded her it was natural, just part of growing up.'

'Why? Why did you . . . ?' Fenwick paused, trying to find the right word, his tongue drawing back from 'seduce' as too lascivious. 'How did you become lovers? Is it common for girls of that age? I don't understand.'

'No, you wouldn't understand, Andrew, and I'm not sure I can explain. I'm not an expert, you know. Julia and Carol were the only two. But why I chose Carol is an easy one to answer. Carol was so lovely. She was absolutely beautiful to look at – slight, small for her age but still growing even at fourteen, long legs, masses of blonde hair. And her eyes, they'd call them almond-shaped in books but that's not enough – they were a soft animal's eyes, huge in her face, always gentle. And she came from the most ordinary of families; she must have been like a jewel to them. I could see it when I visited, how they looked at her almost with awe, as if they couldn't believe they had produced something so beautiful. But she wasn't precocious. She was shy, natural, quite unsure of herself in new things. I'd always thought that she was lonely at school – she had lots of friends but no one really close. But when I got to know her better I found I was wrong. She wasn't lonely, she just liked everybody equally well and she somehow expected them to like her in the same way.

'It was a challenge, to make her like me *more*, and I succeeded because of my music. My singing would charm her; she would creep close to listen. When I first arrived at school, we would play singing games – she'd join in, she had a sweet voice, light but pretty. Then, later, we would disappear to the music loft and sing and play the piano together. She was a good pianist, her parents gave her every encouragement; they had very little money but she'd had lessons since she was four.'

'Was she going to be a musician too?'

'No! Of course not. She had brains – one of those rare people who are good at most things. No, she thought she might try to be a doctor – if her grades were good enough.'

'And you became lovers when?'

'In the winter, just before Christmas in the fifth form. It happened quite naturally.'

'And were you still lovers at the time of her death?'

'Yes, although we'd seen less of each other. We were looking forward to the summer holidays – it was to have been our final time together before I went to the Academy.'

'What happened on the last day you were together?'

'I've already told you, twice.'

'Tell me again.'

She repeated her story, almost word for word the same as her previous statements, as Cooper entered with a cooling pot of tea. When she had finished Fenwick returned to the present and asked his final question.

'Where were you on the 24th August at eleven o'clock?'

'I was in Wiltshire, at a retreat. I can give you the address and the name of the General Manager.'

Cooper looked sceptical. There was something about this woman he didn't like and it went beyond his distaste for what he regarded as her sexual perversion. He simply didn't trust her and despite the increasing unlikelihood that she was the murderer he couldn't help considering her as a suspect rather than a target.

Fenwick was more worried but after a lengthy discussion, Octavia declined police protection but did accept the offer of a police patrol outside her house.

Fenwick and Cooper left to pursue their separate inquiries; Cooper among the pampered and privileged in Wiltshire, Fenwick to the letting agencies and car hire firms of South London.

Octavia Anderson was preparing to leave for a relaxing few hours' shopping in the company of a comforting and unattractive acquaintance. She didn't hear the ring at the front door as she put the finishing touches to her make-up.

As she left her bedroom, she walked straight into her delighted maid, arms laden with three dozen regimented crimson roses that she was convinced would cheer up her mistress. To her dismay, Miss Anderson took one look at the flowers and with a whispered 'Oh no', fell to the ground in a dead faint.

CHAPTER THIRTY-SIX

Cooper had an excellent day despite the unpromising start. He travelled to Wiltshire, determined to break Anderson's alibi, but he ran out of luck. The proprietor of the exclusive health farm confirmed in minute detail Anderson's presence for the critical times. She was one of their more famous guests and not easily ignored. Cooper lingered two hours, long enough to test out details with the staff, but after all his questioning, there could be no doubt that Anderson's alibi for August 24th was solid.

It was after one o'clock by the time he'd finished. He bought an egg and bacon sandwich at the first service station he came to on the M4 back to London and was fighting his two o'clock biorhythmic low when the radio squawked into life. Rowland's uncle's house had been located – a small semi on the outskirts of Harlden. A SOCO team was on its way.

By the time Cooper was back in Sussex, they had finished much of their work and he had a good look round. Half an hour later he was called again: Mr Stanisopolous, the Greek restaurateur from Victoria, had positively identified Rowland from Bayliss' description and E-fit, and Fenwick was on his way to interview him again. Things were looking up.

Mr Stanisopolous was delighted to have a senior plain-clothes policeman call on him. Fenwick didn't disillusion him by explaining that he had only been a few miles away at the time. Keeping the copy of the restauranteur's original statement concealed, Fenwick carefully questioned him again about his encounter with Deborah Fearnside and Victor Rowland in April, breaking the news as he did so that she was dead.

'Oh no! Then it is all my fault. I knew, you see, that she was in trouble, but that man – and the lady – they both tell me 'go away'. Now she dead!'

Patiently, Fenwick listened as Stanisopolous went through his memory of the brief encounter again: the day had been hot and sunny; the lady flustered; the man had been in uniform; he had sunglasses; he was forceful, authoritative; and the car was definitely a new BMW. The colour? It had been a bright day – he could remember the sun on the metallic paint. Perhaps silver grey?

Fenwick recalled his earlier description of the car, circulating at that moment in hundreds of rental offices – 'black BMW, Mercedes saloon or similar, probably new' – and silently cursed the inconsistency in the Greek's retold story. He pushed, but the man would not change from his new recollection of the colour of the car.

The revised information was faxed, again, to all the rental agencies on the list, starting with South-East London and working outwards. Within three hours, Fenwick was sitting at a comfortable office of the Richmond branch of a national car rental firm, opposite the florally dressed manageress, whom he estimated to be a well-preserved fifty. She had insisted on helping the police directly and dismissed her attractive twenty-something assistant with a peremptory wave of her hand.

'I can handle this thank you, Maureen.' Her smile, on full beam, fixed Fenwick where he sat. 'Now, Inspector, where were we? You are interested in this man,' she tapped the fax with a heavily glossed nail – Fenwick estimated that it had more coats of paint than a standard saloon – 'and you believe he hired a silver-grey BMW in April this year. What would you like to know?' The capped teeth flashed again.

With a depressing sense of *déjà vu*, Fenwick recognised a rare but persistent make of public in the woman – those that use the opportunity of a police inquiry as another of life's occasions to assume centre stage, despite Providential casting to a bit part. The woman was already mentally in the spotlights, dry ice tickling her feet, and all she had done was extract a card index from her wooden filing cabinet and organise tea for Fenwick and the young constable relegated to the back of the room to take notes.

'As I believe the constable has already explained, madam, we are interested in tracing the man in the picture there, and the car we believe he hired in April this year – a new BMW, metallic paint, perhaps silver grey.'

'Of course, Inspector. And it's Mrs Court, Marjory Court; please do call me Marjory.'

Fenwick merely waited expectantly. She took the hint.

'Right, well, now, during April both Maureen and I are convinced we saw this man whom you are seeking of in this office! We hired BMWs out quite a lot in April – nearly fifty separate contracts. Of course, as I'm sure *you* realise, this is hardly the typical pattern of rentals one would find in most branches, but we do cater for a most *particular* type of client here.' Again the dramatic pause as her foot tapped rhythmically on an imaginary brake.

Fenwick gave bare acknowledgement to her exclusivity.

'Right, well of those, ten were in a metallic finish, so let's put the others aside, shall we? Of those ten, we have credit card payments for seven and cash for three.' The brown index cards were flicked expertly in her plump little hands.

She settled more comfortably on her well-upholstered rump and pulled towards her three files that had been sitting to the side of her pink blotter since the beginning of the interview.

'Now let me *see*. Mrs Emily Kenn rented a BMW 5 Series for three days – a business trip. No? No, right, moving on; Mr J.A. Smith. He rented the same car for two weeks – paid in cash – brought the car back four days later. We gave him a refund by cheque. Yes, our accounts people at Head Office could find out where it was cashed. Finally, Mr Arthur Bain; one week's hire. Cash. No further details. Right. There we are then.' She handed over the neatly stacked index cards with a flourish. Fenwick experienced a deep stirring of anticipation as he read the two names.

'Can you give us more information on these customers?'

'*More* information, Inspector? What more information could you want? You have it all: name, address, daytime telephone number, make and age of car – yes, there, that little code is my own invention. I've suggested to the company that they adopt it nationally. They're giving it very serious consideration too. It would be a major step – and you'll see there too, the mileage, state of car on return, whether there were any damage deductions . . .'

Fenwick's impatience grew. 'I'm interested in the driving licence details – DVLC number, the address on that, and the home phone number, anything helpful, plus a copy of the rental agreement, the signature.'

'Well, I can't see why, but in *that* case, you will need to see the computer record, but I can assure you my, rather these, cards are far more efficient and effective – and they never "go down" like that wretched machine does.'

Without rising from her desk, the woman executed a neat three-point turn in her chair and called through the door sharply: 'Maureen. These gentlemen need your help. For heaven's sake get a move on. And don't take all day about it, we have an office to run.' She turned belatedly to Fenwick: 'I would do it myself but as you can see I'm terribly busy. Please *do* come back to me with any queries, and to return the cards.'

The mix of coy and arch was, thought Fenwick, quite repellent.

Maureen was brisk, businesslike but not above a remark at her employer's expense. 'Mrs Court? Use the computer? I'd be more likely to marry Bernie first.' The heavy sarcasm made it quite clear that Bernie was to remain a disappointed man. Her accent was studiedly East London; her looks – honey skin, pencil-sharp cheekbones and liquid black eyes – reminded Fenwick of the model who had married that singer; he was never very good on names. But as she rapidly clicked through screen after screen, the mouse jerking to her commands in tiny obedient movements, Fenwick realised that it was for her efficiency, not her looks, that she had been employed.

She soon called up the two records – Bain's first, complete with home telephone number. They called the daytime number and Bain's secretary answered. She confirmed, after a brief consultation with the diary, that she had organised the booking but that Mr Bain had arranged to pay himself. Why, she had no idea. It was clear though that she had made her own assumptions when she suggested to the constable that Mr Bain would much prefer to be contacted at the office about the matter. Fenwick had little doubt that Arthur Bain was shortly to be eliminated from his enquiry.

Which left Mr J. A. Smith. First name, John. There were three hundred and thirty-two Smith's in the telephone directory – and over thirty J. Smiths. After a lengthy check against the index card details the constable handed it back to Fenwick with a sigh of disgust. 'There's no J. A. or J. Smith of that address in this directory.'

'Try enquiries – leave me that.' He compared the card with the details on Maureen's PC screen. While he waited for printed copies he remarked, with slight apology, that there was a typographical error.

'The postcode is completely wrong, here look.'

'Ooh – tha' shouldn't 'appen – here, don't let 'er know, she's a stickler for accuracy. Lemmee see.' She studied the card and positioned the little arrow on the screen over the postcode. A few clicks later she turned to Fenwick, a frown marring the milk chocolate perfection of her brow. 'That's odd. With this new system it shouldn't 'appen – see. It's got what we call this "Quick Address" facility, everso good, saves me a lot of work.'

'Show me.' Fenwick was asked for his postcode, which Maureen entered into a new client record on the computer. A click later and his whole address, minus only the house number, magically appeared in the blank boxes on the screen.

'Just tell me your house name or number and I've got your full address. Brilliant init? Works the other way round too, for people who can't remember their postcodes.'

'So, with Mr Smith's record, you would have entered his name, and just the postcode?'

'Let's see. No look, you can see the postcode's been entered on the card in different ink. That'll mean that Mrs Court took the detail from a copy of his driving licence later on because he couldn't remember his code when he filled in the form. Like I was saying, happens all the time, amazing in this day and age.'

'When you came to enter the details then—'

'The postcode wouldn't 'ave been there; the machine would have filled it in for me. Mrs Court often stays behind at the end of the day to complete her cards, particularly when we're busy – and she wouldn't consider using the computer to fill the gaps. She likes her manual system; "our back up" she calls it but really,' her voice dropped, 'it's because she invented it years ago and she won't give it up. We have files of them going back donkey's.'

Fenwick was intrigued by her changing voice. As she relaxed she was losing her carefully protected East End accent and diction. He was becoming fascinated by the consonants creeping back into her voice.

'It's a pity you don't keep the rest of the paperwork; I'd like to see Mr Smith's original application form.'

'Well you can, of course, here on the system.'

'What?'

'Yes, we're a pilot office for this new Document Imaging – does away with all our old files and those terrible microfiches.'

'And the cards?'

'Not yet,' she chuckled, 'but it won't be long, not now. It means that for any forms or correspondence this year all I need do is look on the computer. Do you want me to find it? I'll try; I hardly ever use it but it'd be fun to have a go.'

Mrs Court's voice enquired querulously why they were taking so long but sight of the computer in operation kept her at a safe distance. Moments later, Fenwick was staring at a screen image of Mr John A. Smith's forms.

'Is this his handwriting?'

'No, that's mine. Client's often ask me to do their forms for them. But it's his signature.'

'So you must have met him as well as Mrs Court.'

'Must 'ave but it was her recognised his picture. Anyway, look, you wanted his driving licence number – there it is.'

The attending constable was on to it in moments.

'Maureen, this is very important. I want you to cast your mind back to April – to the day you filled this form in. Try to remember anything you can about this man.'

'What's he done?'

Fenwick hesitated only a moment before deciding that the truth would work best, she was a sensible girl. As he explained she looked at Rowland's picture again with mixed horror and fascination, willing herself to remember but her face remained blank.

'Think, Maureen, he'd have been a tall, dark-haired man – probably dressed smartly. Ignore the hair, we might have got that wrong.'

She took the likeness from Fenwick and started doodling at the edges with a pencil. Suddenly, she filled in the army crew cut in the picture with a few smart, sculpted layers – still short but now stylish. Then she sketched in sunglasses and the outline of an open neck shirt below the neck. She'd obviously studied art and there was no trace of embarrassment or caution as she changed Fenwick's E-fit copy. She spoke to him as she worked, filling in details.

'It was a bad image you see, sir. I have a good memory but this just wasn't good enough. But I've got him now – I remember him very well.' She became excited as the memory caught; the consonants were back with a vengeance. 'His hair was more stylish, still short but a nice expensive cut, a proper salon job. And he had sunglasses on; not too fancy, Ray-Ban I think. It was April but I remember we had some glorious days; it was my brother's wedding that weekend and it was lovely. You were right, he was a dish – I mean really. Tall, really fit, a bit of a tan. He had these incredible muscles in his arms.' As she talked she continued to sketch on to a clean bit of paper below the E-fit: a short-sleeved shirt, powerful, long arms, the beginnings of a scar or mark on one forearm. 'And I think he had a tattoo – I can't remember it, but it wasn't hearts, or "Mum" or a girl's name – it was masculine but I didn't really see it.'

Within minutes Fenwick had asked Maureen to arrange for the car hired by Mr J. A. Smith to be returned and delivered to the forensic laboratory in the vain hope that it might still reveal something after five months of constant use and valeting. Within two hours, the DVLC confirmed that the licence was false; the Post Office that the postcode was fictitious; and the owners of the house at the address on the licence were prepared to swear in court no John A. Smith had ever lived there.

High-quality photographs of the car and Maureen's sketch had been added to the file of information circulated to other forces and the press. Fenwick knew that he shouldn't feel dejected. The afternoon had neatly bound up one loose end and the invisible man was taking shape before him. Fenwick had met two people who had seen and spoken with him. The hunt was on for his base. It would only be a matter of time now before they finally tracked him down. The team on the case were delighted, hungry, sure now of their target. But their surge of enthusiasm did nothing for Fenwick as he phoned the hospital again to check Leslie Smith's condition.

It took Cooper two hours to find and reach Rowland's property inheritance. The SOCOs had finished and the constable on duty behind the plastic police tape was leaving as Cooper let himself in through the grimy sunburst front door. He walked down a narrow dusty hall; to his left a thin blank party wall. To his right, cheap panelled doors with frosted glass that would fail any modern building standard, led into the mean front room, a back room with tiled fireplace and straight ahead, past the foot of the stairs, the kitchen. Mummified flies and wasps crunched gently under his feet.

The house reeked of sadness. He could smell it in the rising damp and peeling plaster, see it lurking behind the grey walls encrusted by years of neglect. Some furniture was still there in the kitchen – an old table and stool, an aluminium sink dulled by age and scouring. Cooper forgot he was a policeman and why he was there. He stood in the kitchen puzzling over what had happened to reduce the house from a home to this prefabricated mausoleum.

This was where Carol Truman had grown up – by all accounts a happy, gifted child in a kind, straightforward family, each comfortable in the love and respect of the other. Then came the decision to emigrate. How simple it must have seemed for Carol's parents to go early – 'only two months, come out as soon as you've finished your exams' – and how easy to rent the house out cheaply to Carol's aunt, uncle and cousin, allowing them to leave the council estate.

But two months became a lifetime. A family man, Cooper could not begin to imagine the Trumans' pain when they heard of their daughter's death. They had made no public comment, no appeals, their suffering had been in silence. Carol's mother had died within months; her aunt wasted away with cancer within two years. The womenfolk, ripped from the heart of two families leaving three grieving, embittered men: a father, living alone to die alone in a foreign country years later; an uncle who committed suicide after his wife's death; the young cousin, abandoned three times within two years, to be left utterly alone at the age of nineteen – and now suspected of multiple murder.

One small accident, local paper news; one small pebble tripping a landslide of deaths over the years. Cooper was not an imaginative or sentimental man but the weight of suffering pressed down on him as he stood in the decaying kitchen, crushing his spirit.

His mournful contemplation was broken by a sudden flash of light and colour. The setting sun had finally fallen below the low cloud to brighten the room, pushing the obstinate shadows back to the walls. A blackbird, cheered by the warmth, started singing as she perched on the ledge beyond the broken window, a persistent requiem for the departed.

CHAPTER THIRTY-SEVEN

Rowland had taken temporary lodgings in a rooming house on the wrong side of Chichester. He paid cash in advance and looked clean and respectable. The landlady accepted his rent with equanimity and then thought no more of him. She had no objection to him parking his J-registration Ford Escort in the yard at the back of the house.

Unlike many of her type, his landlady had no interest in her tenants and even less in their belongings. Even if she had poked a nose into his room she would have found it perfectly tidy but otherwise unexciting. He had a penchant for black clothes and worked for a firm of contract cleaners – or so the overall and security pass he carried implied. The bag for his cleaning materials was, perhaps, a little curious. It was long and very well made, with clips and compartments inside to hold a range of curiously shaped items. But she didn't snoop and so all her lodger's careful precautions to establish a low-key, unobtrusive presence were unnecessary.

When the Escort left and its owner had explained that he would be away for a few days, she was indifferent. Even that incurious woman, however, would have been somewhat startled to see her lodger drive to a lock-up garage two miles away and exchange the rusting two-door excuse for a car, for a sleek black 1200cc Triumph Trophy which he then rode off, never breaking the speed limit, towards London.

The ACC asked Fenwick for a meeting to review progress on

Monday evening. It had been an extraordinary day. Over fifty people from three forces had been allocated to the case within the past week, despite his initial misgivings. News of Rowland's arsenal had tipped the balance.

'We've found his car and his uncle's house, confirmed his link with Carol and eliminated, finally, Anderson as a suspect.' The ACC nodded slowly. This was becoming a high-profile, not to say expensive, case and he had become directly involved in supporting Fenwick in cross-force coordination. If it went well it would reflect positively on him; if it went badly ... it was an uncomfortable thought. He still had his doubts about Fenwick and stared at the man intently as he made his report. Fenwick interpreted his look from years of practice. 'We're going to get him.'

'Make sure that you do.'

Fenwick asked Cooper and Nightingale to join him for a quick drink after the meeting. They had stood by him from the beginning, always giving more than was asked. It was small enough thanks. He had shrugged off his gloom of the day, determined to support the huge team with the confidence and leadership it needed. As he met his two colleagues he smiled for the first time in many days.

'Have you got the press briefing organised?'

'Yes, 8.30 tomorrow morning. All of them are coming. We've got a new E-fit, the car details and photograph and a copy of the press release that's going out. Nightingale's done the summary you asked for.'

'We need to keep the bulk of the men on a search for Rowland's base. I'm sticking with the London focus. Bayliss was right about the car, let's hope his instincts are good all the way. We've faxed as far out as Croydon – and with luck we'll get another burst of press and TV coverage tomorrow. Then we'll have the forensic reports on the uncle's house and the car. It's highly unlikely they'll help but who knows? So that's it.' As he ran through the plan Fenwick sounded confident. 'We are going to find him, you know. And it's a relief that we don't have to worry about Anderson as suspect any more – life becomes far less complicated!' He smiled, and the others hid their expressions behind their beer glasses.

Despite the intensity of the investigation, Monday night was a quiet interlude of recreation and relaxation for all but the forensics teams. Fenwick was home in time to play with Bess and Chris. His mother was touring southern Germany on a coaching holiday and an agency nanny had managed to captivate his children with her energy and imagination.

Cooper and Nightingale, in their own ways, enjoyed leisurely evenings. Cooper with his wife and television; Nightingale in the quiet of her tidy flat, puzzling over why she was so unconcerned that her fiancé had decided to go on their long-arranged holiday rather than cancel it when she had refused even to consider asking for leave.

But the calm did little to settle Cooper's nerves. Woken by an owl in the early hours of Tuesday morning, he lay thinking about Octavia Anderson; he could not put her from his mind. She was involved somehow and the boss was blind to it. She was in the clear on Smith's attack; clear too at the time of Katherine Johnstone's murder. But she had lied about her relationships with them and with Carol. If she wasn't involved, why lie for so long?

He fidgeted on damp sheets until a grunt from his wife warned him he was about to wake her up, with all the consequences that would bring. He eventually fell asleep as dawn was breaking, cuddled against his wife's ample behind.

Octavia Anderson did not sleep. Her eyes were open, fixed on the ceiling. She had recovered quickly from her faint, excusing herself as her concerned maid arranged the huge bouquet in two large crystal vases in the drawing room. Octavia avoided the room all day.

There had been no card with the flowers but she knew who was sending them, remembering the wilted, decaying extravagance on Carol's grave on the day of Kate's memorial service.

She was afraid now that if she closed her eyes, even for a moment, his face would appear before her. Her fear was a real thing, a cold, clawing animal with scrabbling appetite.

Carol's face was before her eyes, open or closed all day. In the past she had become accustomed to it; she would even talk to her dead friend in moments of stress. Now she was dumb. She couldn't talk to Carol about him – she could talk to no one about him, not even the police.

Octavia had no doubt that she was next; she was the last of the four survivors and the flowers confirmed it. He was playing with her, delighting in the knowledge of her fear and she knew why. As she lay sleepless, Octavia planned her escape. She had only one appearance in the UK, that sentimental school recital, after which she would be abroad for four months. Then, she intended to go to ground. She had her first major recording contract but she needn't return to complete that. It was an international label and they'd be happy to co-operate. She would not return to England until he had been caught. Just seven days to go and then she could leave and be safe.

CHAPTER THIRTY-EIGHT

Tuesday dawned another hot and muggy day. Commuters struggling back into London after the August Bank Holiday cursed the rail operators' propensity to leave rolling stock, tight closed, in the long weekend sun.

Minerva Tate suffered in her short journey from her un-fashionable address to work at Wiggenshall's Property Services. Miss Tate never referred to herself as working in an estate agents; Wiggenshall's was far too select for that. Established after the Second World War, it had achieved in Fulham sufficient status that would-be movers aspired to a Wiggenshall board outside their house, proof that they had arrived even if they were, shortly, to move on. If anyone asked, she was a property investment consultant.

The Wiggenshall office *never* opened at weekends, and certainly not on a Bank Holiday Monday. There was, therefore, a substantial amount of mail and a stack of faxes awaiting the sound of Minerva's Yale key. Having set up the coffee filter to send strong wafts of Colombian's finest around the office, Minerva sorted the post briskly. The fax from a provincial police force provided a stimulating moment. She read it avidly, curious to learn of the crime behind the request for help and was about to throw it away when the photograph caught her attention.

The man was familiar. He had the sort of minor celebrity good looks that might mean she was confusing him with one of their other clients but the more she stared, the more she thought she might have seen him before. He was not a client of hers, of that she was certain, but Mr Oliver, the Manager's – or Jane Simmonds, the other Property Consultant's? When he arrived, Mr Oliver thought the face was vaguely familiar too and they both agreed they should hold on to the fax until Jane returned from holiday on Friday.

For the police, Tuesday was an anticlimax. The team working hotels had no luck and retired home footsore and sweaty, reluctant to start another thankless trek the following day. Faxing, phoning and visiting letting agencies continued at a relentless pace, driven by Fenwick's certainty that they would and could find Rowland's base, but Tuesday produced no results.

Ominously, the ACC was active on the case for most of the day, co-ordinating efforts across the forces involved. At five o'clock he called Fenwick and asked casually (it was always casual the first time) whether he felt they had the right balance of effort across the various lines of inquiry. When he left half an hour later to 'liaise' in private with the MOD he had made no significant changes. But they were coming. Fenwick could sense them.

The forensic reports on the uncle's UK house were due in the afternoon. They were late – the messenger had a bad sense of direction – and it was after five when they arrived. Cooper was studying them as Fenwick joined him in the incident room.

'Ah!' It was all Cooper said, but Fenwick's pulse quickened. 'Report on the house.' He threw it across. 'There was a broken window in the kitchen, quite recent. They found traces of blood on the glass and back of the sink. It could be the same as that found on the bedroom carpet in Katherine Johnstone's house.'

'Definitely?'

'Come on! The original sample size was tiny, conditions in the house less than ideal et cetera, et cetera. You know, it's never "definite" but it's as positive as forensics ever get. They're sending it on for DNA testing. Anyway, read on.'

'Yes!' This time it was quiet satisfaction from Fenwick. 'The partial fingerprint from Johnstone's diary – it could match those found at the house; over twelve points of similarity, even in the partial print.'

'He's our man then, sir. On at least one murder he's our man.'

'Of course he is, but we haven't enough evidence yet to prove it. The fingerprint is too small to provide enough points of similarity and the blood may yet be inconclusive in court. So would be the two IDs from the photograph, which link him conclusively to Deborah Fearnside's abduction. Forensic evidence suggests that he was in Johnstone's house – but nothing to tie him to her murder at the school. And no links to the attempted murder of Leslie Smith. We know it's him, but it's too circumstantial. We need more, and we need to find him.'

In a quiet mews house in a select area of South West London, the lights stayed on until the early hours of Wednesday morning. A shadow could be seen moving behind drawn curtains, apparently carrying packages from all over the house to one room, blind to view. A casual observer, although there were none, might have concluded that the resident was preparing to move out.

CHAPTER THIRTY-NINE

The weather started to break on Wednesday. Nothing dramatic, just a little cloud, a few drops of rain, an increasing breeze. Gardeners looked forward to a respite from watering gardens under hose-pipe-ban conditions. The police team on what was becoming known now as the Rowland, not the Johnstone, enquiry welcomed the cooler air.

Foot-slogging across South London, North London and Central London had produced no further results. At Wiggenshall's, no one had thought to call the police and the fax waited amongst a small pile of mail, on Jane Simmonds' desk. She was expected back on Friday but Minerva wasn't sure she could hold out that long. A nagging sore throat had developed into a streaming nose, hacking cough and sore, red eyes. She was feeling decidedly under the weather and already in danger of exceeding the stated maximum Lemsip dose.

The inside of Chichester Cathedral resembled a disturbed termite mound. Scaffolding for renovation work was being dismantled and replaced with slender stick constructions for lights and sound. The nave and triforium above swarmed with cleaners and technicians, each cursing the other for incompetence, clumsiness and undoing the work that had just carefully been completed. A blunder in the cleaners' contract had led to both firms starting on the same day and the chaos was proving spectacular.

By the end of the day, the organisers had agreed that the

lighting technicians should restart work on Thursday evening and that the cleaners would be paid overtime rates to be finished by then. They had briefly considered abandoning the idea of using the triforium that ran the whole length of the nave, it was in a terrible state, but decided not to. Chichester's was a small cathedral and they needed every square metre of space.

The change in plans didn't suit one particular cleaner, who had been planning on unchallenged access to the cathedral, at least until the Saturday. After a short break at lunchtime, however, he was able to stow his specialist equipment in a chest in the triforium, above the bustle below. He finished his 'work' by four o'clock. In the confusion, no one had questioned yet another new face.

The florist on the ring road was still open as he drove back to his digs. He hesitated a moment before parking and going into the tiny overpriced shop. The gesture was almost irrelevant now, but it was calming, still satisfying. The assistant had had more various and unlikely orders than that made by the tall, scruffy individual with several days' growth of beard but she still smiled to herself at the discovery of romance in the most unlikely of men.

The crime programme on Wednesday evening featured 'the Rowland case'. It was still the gruesome murder of the school teacher that captured the headlines even though, on this occasion, there was more to tell on Deborah Fearnside. The programme producers were keen to feature Fenwick again – continuity around a constant (and photogenic) personality pleased the viewers. The ACC was miffed but too shrewd to let it show.

DCI Fenwick quickly brought the watching public up to date on developments since his last appearance. He kept it all firmly in the present; there was no mention of Carol Truman, or the real connection among the women. But he did share with millions of viewers photographs of the BMW, a pedal bike and variations of the latest pictures of Rowland. All the emphasis was still on the need to 'question' him in relation to their enquiries but Fenwick did admit in interview that Rowland was the man the police were most keen to talk to and that he should not be approached by the general public.

Reactions to the broadcast varied around the country. Fenwick's mother videoed the second appearance even though the content was unsuitable for the children; half a dozen policemen including Nightingale, waited by phones, in the incident room. Leslie Smith's husband watched the portable in her private room at the hospital, feeling the menace in the dark outside the window and the inadequacy of the single armed constable outside the door. He reached out instinctively for his wife's limp hand as tears of anger and helplessness dropped on to the white candlewick blanket.

Octavia Anderson had the television on as background noise as she walked from room to room in her designer-decorated house. She had not slept properly since Sunday; her eyes were purple shadows set in a skin resembling uncooked pastry. For once, she looked older than her years. There was a small supply of sleeping tablets in the bathroom that could grant fragments of peace had she had the courage to take them.

His photograph caught her attention and she fumbled with the remote control to raise the volume. His face was left there for a long time as they talked. He hadn't really changed; the neck was thicker, the angles of the face sharper, and the eyes were those of a dead man – flat, hard, expressionless. In her fearful and feverish state she thought them merciless, looking out of the screen; looking for her.

He had found her, the constant flowers proved that. Now he was playing with her, cat and mouse, deciding when to pounce. There had been a time, she reflected, when she would have relished his attention – they all would. Debbie, Kate, even silly little Leslie – all of them except Carol, who didn't notice, which was ironic really. After all these years he had finally turned his mind to them – first Debbie, then Kate and Leslie. She was the only one left.

Octavia shivered involuntarily. She was last but why was he taking so long? Debbie had been killed in April. It was nearly

September. With a shock she realised that it was the first the next day. Only five more days to go and she could get out of this country for a long, long time. Rowland's face was too well known for him to be able to follow easily. The police would catch him; she would be free.

The simplistic thoughts circled in her head, as if repetition would make them real. Fenwick's face appeared on the screen. She muted the sound and stared at him coldly. Could he do it? Could he do it in time? He was clever enough, hard despite his weaknesses. He had made all, well nearly all, the connections by now and gave the impression that real progress was being made. Or was that simply good PR?

She had given him no clues, he had worked for all the answers. Why not just go the final step – fill in the remaining piece for him? Immediately she shied away from the prospect and, switching off the television, resumed her compulsive pacing and checking of empty rooms. As she walked, she forced herself to practise a few exercises and scales.

It was important, essential, that she be in top form for Monday. Compared with her latest achievements, the anniversary concert was nothing, a small-scale, local affair. But it was her opportunity to show them all that she had made it. All the people from the past that had doubted her ability, or had favoured others, would see that she had been right.

She was returning as a star, *the* star, at their request. Kate Johnstone had been amazed when she had accepted the invitation, but Kate had never understood her. Returning home would be final proof that the sacrifices, the impossible decisions that had nevertheless been made, the lack of friendships and loneliness, had all been justified. In childhood she had coloured her dreams with fantasies such as this. Again, the moment of triumph in the cathedral was a picture before her.

In that instant she knew, with absolute certainty, why he was waiting so long, why she had been kept until last. He had an opportunity for public display and he was not going to waste it. In the cathedral he would have the right occasion, the best moment, to kill her. No, to execute her for what he believed she had done.

Octavia clung to the wall, shaking violently. She abandoned the checking of the locks; he wouldn't be coming that night, nor the next. He would wait until Monday and strike in the cathedral. She clawed her way upstairs like an old woman and fell fully clothed on her bed. There was a clear choice in front of her, to cancel her performance or go on; neither was acceptable. Wide awake, for yet another night, she twisted within her dilemma, searching for a way out.

Miss Purbright would tell anyone who cared to ask her that she *never* watched television, her life being so full and varied. Unexpected visitors (of whom there were sadly few) would, however, inexplicably find the set in her large farmhouse kitchen switched on, whatever time they called. She had a number of ready-made excuses for this phenomenon – she needed the weather for the sheep; there was an important news bulletin to catch; her favourite programme had just finished.

The truth was that she was addicted to television. Although she had lived alone since her father died she was not cut from the happy hermit mould. She yearned for coffee mornings and bingo, whistdrives and cosy chats, but she had never admitted this, least of all to herself. Instead, she cultivated a surprisingly effective façade of eccentricity and a passionate involvement in hill farming and country pursuits.

Thus it was that Miss Purbright came to be watching the crime programme whilst absently mending her socks in front of the large kitchen range. She loved crime programmes and liked nothing better than a good murder reconstruction. She was aware of the Johnstone case because the woman had been a teacher, which had been her ambition once, and she was mildly surprised to find it still unsolved. He was a nice-looking policeman, though, realistically handsome. She felt confident he would find the killer.

The picture of the BMW tweaked her memory but she

ignored it. Then the three photographs came up slowly in turn and her stomach flipped. She had seen this man, the man on the television that they were saying was wanted in connection with no less than three serious crimes. But *where* had she seen him? Her mind ran over recent encounters, unable to find the face on the television among them.

She continued to puzzle over it until bedtime when, letting her overweight Labrador out, she remembered that she had to pay a visit to the new couple holidaying in the cottage. The memory triggered full recollection. That man had rented the cottage – she couldn't remember when or what they had said to each other – but she had seen him there. She could picture him standing in the doorway, blocking her view down the hall. He had seemed much fatter than the man they described on the television but she was sure she was right.

Miss Purbright called the dog back in early and the bemused but tractable animal obeyed. With an unsteady hand she reached for the *Radio Times*, as always, tucked out of direct sight down the side of her chair. The telephone number for the crime programme was there and with excited nervousness she dialled.

There was one potentially important viewer who missed the *Crimewatch* programme and later had significant cause to regret it. But he was too preoccupied with preparation and with cleaning up behind himself. He was also far too confident in his continuing anonymity to bother checking TV, radio or newspapers for news, which was another, serious mistake.

Over fifty full-time police were deployed on the case on Thursday morning, now across four counties. The search for Rowland's South London base was continuing without success. Extensive inquiries of businesses and shops around Victoria had produced no further clues.

Fenwick stayed at the operation's centre, which had been moved to HQ as soon as the ACC had taken real interest in the case. Although it was no longer part of his job to read all the papers on the case, he read and reread reports and files, looking

345

for clues and connections others might have missed. There was nothing.

At 10.30 he was surprised to receive a call from Octavia Anderson. Her beautiful voice was dry and faded with an unexpressed tension behind each word. She needed to speak with him urgently, she said, and would be with him in just over an hour.

The news made Fenwick even more restless. He took a long walk to the cemetery, passing the school on the way. There was silence behind the thick walls and railings as the building awaited the rush of the new school year. The cemetery was similarly dry and silent in the flat September light. There had been no real rain since the day of Leslie Smith's attack and the grass, shorn weeks before, had turned to a dull powdery khaki clotted with pale green splashes where graves had been lovingly watered or were shaded thickly by trees.

He walked automatically towards Carol's grave. As he approached he could see the bright crimson splash against the desiccated grass. Her grave was a mass of red flowers. The florists had finally run out of red roses and had made up the order with carnations, deep-blooded chrysanthemums smelling of funeral parlours, and panting lilies. Fenwick doubted that Rowland would have wanted or appreciated the mournful effect. Far from being a defiant expression of love, the flowers stood for what they were, a memorial for a long-dead girl.

The blooms were still fresh. Some, still in the shade of the headstone, had drops of water on their perfect leaves – dew from that morning or perhaps even the florist's spray. There was no card, no indication of where they had come from. Fenwick bent down and picked up one of the few perfect red roses, tucked into the margin of the grave and still damp. He snapped the long stem three inches from the bud and gently threaded the end through his buttonhole, before turning his back on the grave and retracing his steps.

Activity in the cathedral had quietened down from its earlier frenzy. The cleaning had finished and the echoing spaces were left to the lighting technicians. A tall, dark-haired man moved among them with a quiet assurance and competence. His long, unkempt hair and straggly beard were an unintentional camouflage, the result of a casual neglect of personal appearance rather than deliberate disguise. Still, they were sufficient enough to allow him to walk about unchallenged.

Rowland made several trips to the triforium carrying his custom-built toolbox. Each time he carefully placed certain pieces of equipment, superficially disguised, into the oak chest, covering them again with old clothes and bell ropes, and making sure that everything looked as it had when he found it. By eleven o'clock on Thursday everything was ready. He had timed his escape routes and confirmed his line of sight, allowing for the trumpeters who would be in place by his side.

Returning to his digs he showered, shaved and trimmed his hair, feeling refreshed and relaxed for the first time in months. He decided to go out and enjoy a prelunch pint of hand-drawn beer in a pub on the outskirts of the city. Rowland was impervious to the landlord's curious stare and the muttering of the bar maid. Preparing the cathedral had been tense, painstaking work, with constant risk of discovery. He felt he could relax this once before the final countdown started.

He took his pint jug into the beer garden and sat in a narrow angle of sun with his back towards a rough-cast wall against which brilliant red berries sucked in the late summer heat. Bees were droning on a few tardy lavender blooms, the city traffic was a distant buzz. He dozed.

A cat, rubbing itself against his leg, woke him with a start and he reached instinctively for the knife concealed in his belt. His untouched beer had grown stale and warm in the thick glass. He threw it out on the border behind him and decided on a quick half-pint to refresh himself.

It was instinctive to walk silently, to carry the box with him. Relaxed as he was, he still opened the door with caution. A drift of one-sided conversation carried from behind the bar. He was fully three steps into the passage between the door and the saloon before he froze.

'. . . well no, I can't be sure it's him but it looks like him . . . About six foot two, yes, and dark . . . no younger-looking than your photos.'

Rowland drew back against the passage wall, breathing deeply and steadily. He suddenly realised that he had been a fool to assume that the police didn't know who he was, that he could walk around unnoticed – to doze off in public and allow the fat landlord time to pluck up courage to call the police. In absolute silence he reversed his steps, eyes and ears concentrated on the bar hidden beyond the passage and the monologue that drifted towards him.

'. . . Yes, still here, in the garden.' He could sense the man turn towards the passage and held himself rigid, acutely aware that the sun streaming through the glass panels in the outer door was throwing a shadow of the box and his leg down the passage into the saloon. It cast an abstract, inhuman shape. If he was still it might pass unnoticed. If it did not, he would have no choice but to kill the man as he came to investigate. He flexed his free hand in the shadow in preparation for the blow.

The moment passed. He heard the man turn back, his voice become muffled. Rowland slipped into the garden, bent to put his glass down, thought better of it and placed it in the near-empty toolbox. He scuffed the rough wooden seat and table with his sleeve. Returning to the back door, he wiped the paintwork and handle swiftly on both sides. He could not recall leaning on the bar but the front latch would definitely bear his prints.

He risked circling to the front and wiping the door; he would have to hope that the inside was clear. Glancing through the window he saw the landlord replace the receiver and head for the passage. Rowland sprinted to the Escort and drove off. The car would have to go. He would wreck and burn it somewhere far away and rent another one. His funds were dropping alarmingly but he had more than enough to see him through the next few days and no plans after that for which he needed money. His immediate concern was to collect the last of his equipment and supplies from London and go to ground.

In Richmond, at Wiggenshall's, Minerva struggled through the morning but by lunchtime was hopelessly unwell and on her own in the agency. She could hardly speak and had a fever that turned her complexion plum red. There were visitors in the agency all morning and appointments arranged for the afternoon; she couldn't simply shut up and go home.

In desperation, she rang Jane's number. Although she wasn't due back at work until Friday there was a chance that she might be spending the last day at home. To her relief Jane was there. She took a little persuading but the state of Minerva's voice alone convinced her to come in. Minerva blessed her and started counting the minutes to her arrival.

CHAPTER FORTY

Fenwick had just welcomed Octavia Anderson at HQ when he was interrupted by news of the landlord's call from Chichester. The local force had already dispatched a team and he gave the inspector in charge a brief description of Rowland and impressed on him how dangerous the man was. He was confused that Rowland might be so far south and inevitably dreaded the political fallout for the wasted man-hours searching in London. If the person in the pub was Rowland he would have to reconfigure the search and brief the local force urgently. He would not be popular.

He returned to Octavia. She looked awful – tense, tired and desperately frightened. He tried a smile but she ignored it.

'Andrew, I had to see you. I couldn't speak on the phone; it might be tapped.'

Fenwick raised his eyebrows in reply but decided not to tell her that he'd had his office, home and car swept for bugs regularly for over a month.

'I mean it. You don't know him. He's very good at what he does.'

'I didn't think you knew him either – not recently.'

'I don't but I've bumped into him over the years – twice – by pure accident. I recognise competence and power when I see them.'

'What do you need to tell me?'

She stared at him, lips frozen apart, unable to speak. Now that the moment had arrived, she couldn't say the words that would make it all real.

'He's going to try and kill me. I know . . . I . . .'

'We've discussed this before. Only two days ago you were determined to be independent! Why are you here now?'

'Well, I'm not here for debate, Andrew! This is serious. He's going to kill me and I know when and where.' She paused, hand raised in a mixed gesture of appeal and emphasis. She had her audience.

'He's going to try and kill me on Monday, in the cathedral at Chichester.'

Fenwick looked down at the message on his desk from Chichester police. They were on their way routinely to the pub. He doubted they were armed.

'Excuse me a moment.' He left the interview room, called Cooper and urged him to drive to Chichester quickly and when there, move with extreme caution. Bayliss' words came back to him: Don't put your boys up against him with wooden sticks.'

It took him twenty minutes to find and persuade the ACC to intervene to arrange for the authorisation of firearms in Chichester. Then he returned to the interview room.

'How *dare* you!' Anderson exploded as soon as he walked in. 'I tell you my life's in danger and you just walk out and leave me sitting here like a bloody fool.' She had worked herself into a spectacular rage but Fenwick had finally had enough of her melodrama and compulsion to be centre stage.

'Be quiet, Octavia. Your life isn't in danger at this moment whereas others' might be. They are my immediate priority, not you.'

She was stunned into silence by his tone.

'Within the last hour we've received news of Rowland in Chichester. We had been treating it just as we have all the other reports which have turned out to be false alarms. Your information turned it from possibility to probability and I had to warn them. Now we can come back to you. Why are you so sure it's Monday – and the cathedral of all places?'

With cold assurance, Octavia went through her thinking of the night before. It sounded improbable and far-fetched to Fenwick, just the sort of idea that would appeal to her sense of life as a constant performance. Would Rowland deliberately put himself in such danger just to attack Anderson in public? Then he recalled Bayliss describing Rowland as a man who wouldn't finish his killings on a hit-and-run. She might just have stumbled on the truth!

'How quickly can you cancel your performance? There are only four days to go, that won't give the organisers much time to find a replacement.'

'I'm not going to cancel – I'm going ahead. I've thought it all through, Andrew. Cancelling my performance doesn't make me safe. He'll still be out there, waiting, and he wants me. If it's not this performance, he'll try to kill me at the next, or the one after that. My professional life is built on public appearances. Do you want me to spend my life cooped up in recording studios – and how do you think I'll promote my work? I've just signed my first big recording contract – the longer I've left it the more valuable I've become. My plan is to have a high-profile autumn season and record in the New Year. After the public acclaim I'll receive I will be *the* hot property. My agent and I have it all planned: massive, high-quality public performances for the next three months and absolutely *no* recordings – it's a condition of all my contracts.'

She was completely mercenary. The immediate fear had evaporated to be replaced with ice-hard calculation. On one level, the real threat to her life was merely an inconvenience to be managed. And to do that she needed Fenwick. For an instant, Fenwick witnessed in full the raw manipulation, cunning and ruthlessness that had characterised her success.

They debated for a long time the risks and merits of her continuing with her performance. Fenwick was adamant she should not but had to concede there was no way he could prevent her, and if he denied her police protection and she went ahead and was killed – it did not bear thinking about.

He went to check with the ACC to see what appetite the man had to have the performance cancelled.

'Preposterous, Fenwick! He'll never stage an attack in such a public place. All his other crimes have been planned with stealth and secrecy. He's struck without trace and with no chance of capture. Why place himself in jeopardy by going public? It's nonsense – the woman's got an overactive imagination; they're like that, these arty types. I grant you that she could be the next target and it's *your* job,' he jabbed his finger at Fenwick, 'to keep her alive. But if she wants to go ahead with the performance let her. It's the last place he'll choose. She's going to be safer whilst she's there than anywhere else, you mark my words. And the embarrassment of the police calling off the performance when even she's happy to go ahead . . . No. This is pure fancy.'

Fenwick argued long and hard. He could sympathise with the ACC's rationale – logic said Anderson was wrong – but his instinct, and the growing insight he had into Rowland's behaviour, led him to agree with her.

The discussion became more and more heated until the ACC finally shouted at him: 'No! Not unless she insists it's cancelled, d'you hear me? You can bloody well put your reservations on file and get back to tracing Rowland. It's time you started thinking like a policeman again and not a theatrical agent.'

It was only as Fenwick made his way down the bare stairs to rejoin Anderson that he recalled the ACC's wife was on the organising committee for both the concert and the charity that was to benefit so handsomely from the performance proceeds. He pushed the idea that this would in any way influence the ACC to the back of his mind as unworthy.

Back in the interview room Anderson pressed the advantages of going ahead: it would be a carefully planned trap; she would be the bait. They were ahead of Rowland now. They could outwit and capture him.

'I can't live with him out there, Andrew. Every time I walked on to the stage or stood up to sing, I would be wondering, waiting. I want this over.'

Fenwick was silent. Eventually, he moved to Octavia's chair and took both her hands in his. Her touch still had the power to make him shiver and he experienced a thrill of remembered pleasure as her long white fingers brushed the inside of his wrist.

'Are you sure? I can offer you no guarantees. We could have a hundred men and he'd still be dangerous.'

'I'm sure.' There was a light of anticipation in her eyes.

In all his years of policing Fenwick had never had to arrange safe accommodation but the ACC, after a sharp reminder to Fenwick about the relative costs of police cover versus the rental Anderson would pay anyway, organised it all smoothly. Anderson was sent on her way in a police car. She had had the presence of mind to bring a suitcase with her. Nightingale was ordered to the secure house to stay with her. The ACC was torn between enjoying the increasing complexity of the case, as it would show off his undeniable organisation skills to the full, and worries about the huge build-up of costs. After a brief exchange, he agreed to allow the searches in South London to continue for twenty-four hours but Fenwick knew it was his last chance, and where the blame for the hundreds of wasted man hours would fall.

He was tucking into an avocado and bacon sandwich in the incident room when he noticed excitement around one of the desks. Before he could call out, a young officer dashed up to him waving a flimsy sheet of paper.

'From Richmond. They think they've found Rowland's digs. They've interviewed the girl from the letting agency – Wiggenshall's – and she's certain she let a property to a man of Rowland's description four months ago.'

'The girl' – Jane – had ignored the telephone number on the fax and had rung an old friend in the Met. After protracted transfers, she had ended up speaking to a detective who realised at once the significance of her story. Fenwick agreed with the Metropolitan CID how they would proceed. A Detective Inspector Harrington was put in charge in Richmond and Fenwick managed to speak to him before the ACC, advised of the breakthrough, and took over cross-divisional co-ordination.

'Harrington? It's DCI Fenwick here. What's the situation?'

'We've just finished interviewing her but we've asked her to stay – assuming you'll want someone to speak to her directly. She is absolutely positive the tenant is Rowland, no doubts at all. I was about to send two cars to the address – don't worry, surveillance, that's all.'

'Tell them to proceed with extreme caution. If this is his London base you'll need an armed stakeout. This man is highly dangerous – he'd think nothing of taking out any or all of them. And we don't want him alerted.'

'Our Assistant Commissioner is talking to your ACC now. I get the impression that they're agreeing a major operation – to be run from here. Hang on . . .'

Fenwick could hear muffled conversation in the background.

'Yes. I'm instructed just to do the basics, set up surveillance, clear the area, no uniforms, all to be done very quietly.'

'I'm on my way now. With luck I'll be there in one, one and a half hours. Try not to start without me!'

The surveillance team was in position just after 1.30 p.m. Two officers stayed in an unmarked car opposite the smart mews house identified by the letting agents. The other two split up; one commandeered a street-facing function room above a corner pub which provided a view of the road leading to the house and front door. The other took a pint of beer and sat at one of the trestle tables on the pavement. The pub was busy, groups of afternoon drinkers lounging against the walls and blocking the pavement. Quietly, as the watching officer sipped at his pint, his plain-clothed colleagues encouraged the customers to leave as they cleared the street.

Shortly after two a man approached on foot and entered the house by the front door. The unit radioed in and was told to stay put until armed backup arrived. A complete force of specialist-trained firearm officers were on their way from the Met and should arrive within twenty minutes. Fenwick's driver, already averaging a reckless forty m.p.h. on the outskirts of London, put his foot down. In the back, PC Douglas Adams, attached to the case since he witnessed the attack on Leslie Smith, closed his eyes and gripped the passenger bar as the car rocked round yet another corner against a red light.

The firearms unit was late. Tension was mounting in the surveillance team, the urge to take action battling the fear they all felt sitting unarmed a few yards away from a suspected serial killer and his arsenal. The instructions from the operations centre were blunt and explicit: stay where you are; no heroics on any account. Minutes ticked past. A call came that the armed unit was nearly there, directed by the operations centre to the delivery yard at the back of the pub. There were no signs of movement from the house as the four watchers grew sticky in the late summer heat.

Rowland moved methodically through the house, dividing his belongings into two groups – take or destroy. He was disgusted with himself for his carelessness. His focus on preparing for each murder had been so absolute he had forgotten the danger that police investigations might pose. To his surprise he had underestimated them, assuming that his careful planning and subterfuge would allow him to remain anonymous until it was all over. He hadn't even bothered with disguise but that would all have to change now. At least he'd had the foresight to bring supplies. Somehow, the police had identified him and, to his astonishment when he finally bought and read a newspaper, had linked his three attacks. That changed everything. He had cleared out of his Chichester digs, trashed the car and forced himself to calm down and rent a new one, a Cavalier, that had moved unnoticed through the thankfully light midday traffic.

He had to assume the worst; if his identity was known there was a chance that the police would know his London address. On the journey back to London, he had briefly considered abandoning everything in the house but there was too much that he needed, despite what he had in the lock-up. It was risky but if the approach looked clear he would go in.

He had dumped the Cavalier in a busy NCP car park, confident there were no prints, and had approached the house on foot. He'd circled it once, checking all the exits, making sure that the inconspicuous Triumph Trophy he had concealed was still there. In front of the house the far side of the road was lined bumper to bumper with parked cars. Only two had people in them. A man in painters' overalls appeared to be waiting for his mate to buy cigarettes at the newsagents. In the other car a man and woman were engaged in earnest conversation.

He moved through the house efficiently, gathering essentials, discarding the rest in a growing pile in the kitchen. Every few minutes he checked the street outside; the pub was almost deserted, there was no passing traffic. Across the road the painter's van had gone but the couple were still there, just sitting watching his house. His pulse quickened and he moved even more rapidly. There was no time to clear the house properly, which made his next decision even easier. On the kitchen table he quickly assembled an array of plastic, tape and wires into a surreal bird's nest. Then, picking up a large holdall, and arranging a rucksack between his broad, padded shoulders, he prepared to leave the house.

Fenwick and the firearms unit arrived silently within moments of each other in the yard at the back of the pub. DI Harrington was already there. The firearms officers were immediately deployed along the rooftops and in the pub, with a group sent to watch the road at the back of the mews. Road-blocks had been set up out of sight at either end of the street. Fenwick watched, trying to find comfort in their certainty and efficiency, the silence with which they moved into position. He tried hard to forget Bayliss' warning.

Fenwick could never recall later what happened next but he read and reread the reports and eyewitness accounts until it became impossible for him to distinguish the elements of personal memory from official record.

They had just called to the unarmed officers to leave the scene, and the last of the armed officers had radioed that they were in position when order dissolved into chaos. There was a roar of throttle from behind the row of mews houses. A black 1200cc motorbike stormed out of a narrow alley, panniers sending sparks from the brick walls, the driver crouched low over the handle bars.

The AFOs hesitated, a shouted order to 'hold their fire' echoing in their earpieces. The biker headed straight at the roadblock across the street ahead. Two cars and six officers were unable to stop him. He drove at the tape that stretched across the pavement. It broke like a paper chain as the 235 kilogram bike slammed into it.

There could be no mistaking him now. They were ordered to open fire at their own discretion. Six rounds were fired as he cleared the roadblock; three sent sparks from the tarmac, one perforated the exhaust pipe, another punctured the back pack but the final one appeared to hit the rider as he drove on regardless, the noise from the bike now deafening. The unmarked car screeched into pursuit, paused while those blocking the road moved and then all three raced off. Harrington shouted into the radio and the operations centre confirmed that patrol cars and bikes had been mobilised. Fenwick suggested helicopter support and demanded urgent SOCO attendance at the scene.

There was nothing he could do to help the search for Rowland. It wasn't his patch, so he decided, with Harrington's approval, to stay and join the search at the house.

The head of the firearms unit turned to him.

'Shit! We couldn't risk hitting the others, sorry. Is he likely to have been on his own? Do you want backup to enter the house?'

'We've no reason to suspect he has an accomplice but yes, I'd appreciate it if you could do a quick sweep of the house before SOCO arrives.'

Fenwick called PC Douglas Adams to him. The man was tense, distraught that Rowland had got away. His capture had become personal to Adams.

'They're going to check the house, Doug. Then we can go in and have a look around. SOCO are on their way. He had to leave in a hurry so there could be plenty to see.'

'He got away, though. And we were so close.'

'They've got everything out looking for him – and I think we know where he'll be heading if he slips through. Let it go, Doug, our job is here.'

Constable Adams turned away, every one of his fifty years showing in stooped shoulders, every one of his sleepless nights since the attack on Smith showing in his eyes.

The house was given the all clear – no one else was in there. Harrington fed back the news to Fenwick.

'But there's some nasty-looking stuff left behind, I think we're going to need some expert support here. I'll make the arrangements.'

Two SOCOs arrived, civilian employees, expert in their craft. The older of the two, Dan Crabbott, shook Fenwick's hand while the young woman with him, Heather Coals, unpacked their gear. Fenwick put on an overall, cap, shoe-covers and thin gloves, and followed them into the house. Doug Adams, without waiting to be asked, did the same and went inside. The SOCOs immediately went into their routine, a photographer dodging round them as they worked. They started from the front door – one on the door itself, the other in the hall.

Fenwick looked around the small sitting room at the front of the house. There was a guidebook to Chichester on a small table, with several pages turned down, other places marked with slips of paper. He gently turned the pages with his gloved fingers, noting the heavy underscorings and marks in the margin. The pull-out plan of the cathedral had been squared and measured, with red lines drawn from the west door to various points in the apse and nave. Fenwick guessed they were entry and escape routes.

From the hall there was a brief exchange between Crabbott and Adams as they walked towards the back of the house:

'There's so much stuff in here, I've run out of bags already!'

'You wait till you see the kitchen!' Doug's voice was jubilant.

It was the last thing that Fenwick heard for some time.

A blinding flash filled the hall and seemed to flow into the room as a huge compression of boiling air. He saw one of the white-suited SOCOs blown past the door and then forgot everything in an effort to breath. Bolts of pain were driven into his skull through his ears, a huge weight crushed his chest, forcing his mouth wide in a desperate attempt to gulp oxygen into his straining lungs.

Despite the weight, he felt as if the top of his head was lifting off, carrying with it his shoulders and arms that flew up into the air, beyond his control. He could see the wall of the sitting room bulge as if a giant hand was pushing against it. Then the old lath and plaster gave way and flew towards him, over him, pinning him down. There was a sharp pain on his temple and the sound in his skull of a cricket ball on willow. Consciousness ebbed away as darkness closed around him.

CHAPTER FORTY-ONE

Rumour of the explosion reached Cooper in Chichester, as did the fact that, despite a continuing massive search, the London team had lost all trace of Rowland. It was a little after three and from the pub they had moved to start a search in the cathedral on Fenwick's previous instructions. They had been there less than an hour and Cooper was torn. He had no idea how Fenwick was, only that he had been rushed to hospital. Nightingale was on her way to act as minder for Anderson, which left him as the only officer on the case with the full history – and he had been committed to helping the Chichester police with their search and inquiries. They hadn't got a clue what they were looking for or where to start, just anything that Rowland might have left there. He paced the cathedral close, undecided whether to return or stay. If he went they might ignore Anderson's fears and leave quickly. He elected to stay, suppressing his concerns for Fenwick with frenetic activity.

He left a message for the ACC, hoping he would have the latest information on Fenwick's condition, but when the man called him back all he would do was confirm Cooper's decision to stay. He had no more news about Fenwick or the other officers in the house at the time of the explosion. He had taken personal charge of the whole operation.

Jason MacDonald bristled at the world 'hack'. He hadn't completed two years' hard graft on the local paper to end up in a profession undermined by pejorative terms. But neither was he the idealist he had been at nineteen, with the ink hardly dry on his Media Studies A level certificate. He had lost count of the dog shows, proud mums, car accidents, bereaved relatives and other local paraphernalia that he had covered while waiting for his big break and fame.

On Thursday afternoon, he was stuck in another typical mess, one he had christened 'mixing the filler'. The subeditor had come up with the bright idea that he should collect background material on preparations at the cathedral in anticipation of Octavia Anderson's performance on Monday night. He had already filed a 'local schoolgirl made good' profile, complete with old photographs and quotations from friends and teachers, and had hoped to be on standby for last-minute news. Instead he was loitering in cloisters, bored and uninspired.

The cathedral was busy, tourists navigating through the last remaining stacks of scaffolding poles, dismantled in honour of the performance. MacDonald had completed an interview on the subject of the latest restoration project, secured a few indignant quotations on the nonsense and costs of removing the scaffolding just for one night's performance and he was now tempted by a cup of tea and slice of fruit cake in the Refectory Garden Restaurant.

As he made his way slowly around the covered cloister, a worried-looking middle-aged man in a tweed jacket brushed past him in a rush for the nearest exit, obviously keen to improve the reception on his mobile phone. Naturally curious, MacDonald followed and lingered. He could make out little from the one-sided conversation but the whole incident seemed out of place and sufficiently interesting for him to postpone his cup of tea and return to the cathedral when the man did.

MacDonald listened as the man in the patched tweed jacket conferred with one of the seated tourists. Their heads were close together but he could make out the words 'casualties', 'hospital' and possibly even 'bomb'. His lingering became purposeful. From a vantage point in a chair at the rear of the nave MacDonald watched the man's progress. In the following five minutes he had talked with another five 'tourists', each of whom was paying particular attention to a different part of the cathedral.

At first he had assumed they were enthusiasts, studying the masonry or some of the many works of art. After further observation he realised they were not students but searchers. Each, as discreetly as possible, was looking for something. His thumbs pricked. Fascinated and excited he started tracking the searchers. He noticed that they kept to a strict patch and searched it thoroughly before moving on to the next. They were working in a grid. Something was happening and the middle-aged man in tweed was at the middle of it all.

At exactly 3.15, the man left the building again and MacDonald followed, discreetly this time, pausing to read his guidebook in a pool of shade as the man dialled.

'Hello? Yes, it's Cooper. Put me through, would you?'

He started to pace as he waited. 'Yes? Hello . . . hello. Sir, yes it's Cooper.' His voice, raised because of poor reception, carried clearly to MacDonald standing stock-still in the shadow.

'What news?' There was a long pause. MacDonald saw the man's shoulders sag, his knees almost fold. His free hand flew to his head. 'Dead? Oh no . . . dear God! He was only eighteen months from retirement. My missus knows his wife – they were devoted to each other. We've got to get this bastard, sir. . . . I'm sorry. Yes, yes, I'm all right now. And Fenwick. He's not . . .' The man's voice tailed off. 'Thank God. But they're keeping him in? . . . I see. And the others?'

There was another long pause. MacDonald strained to hear the murmur from Cooper but failed. The man covered his eyes and leant heavily against the stone wall. 'Dear Lord. Sorry, sir . . . Yes, I think it would be right for you to go yourself but take a WPC. Doris, Doug's wife, was never strong . . . No, I'll stay here as we discussed; no nothing yet. Sir, give Fenwick my best, could you, if you see him? Thank you.' The man broke the connection and stood, eyes shaded for several moments before returning slowly to the cathedral.

MacDonald could not believe his luck. The man was obviously security, or police, and whatever was going on was tied up with a bombing somewhere that had only just happened. The journalist couldn't decide whether to follow Cooper or call in and find out what was going on.

He ran back to the cathedral. The searchers were all there, huddled around the font listening to Cooper. There were about half a dozen of them. MacDonald knew enough about local police budgets to realise that six men in one place meant something significant was underway – and linked to a bombing elsewhere!

He risked a dash outside to call in and find out what was happening. Within five minutes he had learnt of the bomb in South London; no names yet but police had been involved, perhaps among the victims. One fatality, others in hospital. There was talk of Arab extremists but it was all vague. MacDonald asked for any further information to be called in to him at once. It would be; the secretary in the paper office had a crush on him and would do anything he wanted.

A gaggle of young mums with a miscellany of children in pushchairs and on reins crossed his path on the way to the café, calling to two older children straggling behind. 'Debbie! Tom! Come on, hurry up.' For some reason MacDonald thought of the name Cooper had mentioned: Fenwick. Why did he know that? And why had these mothers made him think of the name again. MacDonald was good at crosswords, loved puzzles, aspired to put his own definition of 'investigative' into journalism. There was a connection to be made and he was missing it. He walked back to the nave and sat down. The searchers were still searching. Nothing appeared to be happening.

He took out his notebook and put key words down randomly, as he would with anagram letters: 'Fenwick'; 'mothers'; 'police'; 'bomb'. Then he added 'cathedral'; 'Debbie'; 'Doug'; 'Tom'. He stared at it hard for ten minutes. Then he remembered who Fenwick was, the case, the publicity. With three unsolved serious crimes the man would not have been involved in another big case – which made yet another connection. But what had it to do with the activity in the cathedral and the killing of a man called Doug?

He remembered the station where Fenwick was based and dialled directory enquiries. He reached the station switchboard, his years in local journalism making prying easy.

'Oh hello, yes. This is Jason MacDonald, I'm new to the local paper. I'm doing a piece on long-serving public servants in our community. Who handles local press? Could you put me through?' He oozed naïvety. 'Hello?' He repeated his fabrication to the girl at the end of the phone, who tried to explain that the press officer was in an urgent conference and could not be disturbed. She sounded flustered, nervous because her boss couldn't take the call.

'Oh, but I can't wait – I've got a copy deadline and I've only got a couple of very simple questions. Please?' He made himself sound young, keen and nervous of failure on his first assignment. 'I was sure that you'd have the names of a few long-serving officers.' He let her rattle on, ask him questions, check his credentials – yes, she would do some research and call him back.

Jason MacDonald was very plausible, very cunning. He had done so many similar pieces and people were always obliging. He let her think she was in control and then – an afterthought. 'Oh, I've just thought, there was a great chap I used to know – came to our school, saw him around town. Now, what was his name? Don? Doug? – Yes that's it, Doug somebody. He'd be excellent.' He heard her intake of breath, knew he had struck home. 'Yes, Doug. He's a real community policeman, very rare breed. And he reads our newspaper. I'm sure he'd love to see his name in it.'

'No, not PC Adams, he's . . . he's not available.'

'But he'd be perfect, good old Doug.' Was that a stifled sob? Yes, she was crying!

'Are you OK? What's up, love? Come on, Doug would be ideal.'

'No, I'm sorry. You can't . . . not now. Please, I have to go.'

The phone went down but MacDonald didn't mind. If his hunch was right he now knew the name of the victim: PC Douglas Adams. He still had to work out the connections. Time was passing. If he wanted to call the nationals and get in first he would have to take a few risks. If he hurried, he could even push the name to the London *Evening Standard* for an item of late news in the West End Final.

He rang their news desk and got through to a hard-nosed subeditor. He was highly sceptical at first but MacDonald didn't shift from his story. He had the names of two of the victims in the bombing and believed that it was linked to the murder inquiries that had kept press and TV going over a dull summer. How did he know? A little bit of luck and the balls to make something of it. The men at each end of the phone sized each other up. Both were taking a risk; MacDonald that he would get some credit, the sub that this was not a hoax. Both bit the bullet and the sub agreed to check it out. Jason listened disinterestedly to the payment details, *if* the information was used. He wanted his name as a contributor on the feature. He was told that if he was right it might be.

He returned to the cathedral in the mood to take another risk. With his new confidence he found it easy to call the local paper and demand a photographer, Dave. He had worked with him before on burning ricks, wrecks and baby shows. He was free and willing to oblige. In the cathedral, a couple of men had started searching the long gallery above the nave, while others continued below as MacDonald waited impatiently.

Dave arrived and sat down unobtrusively in a pew; Jason could see his camera was set. Time passed. Four o'clock rang out, then quarter past. There was a small commotion near a door in the nave from which steps led to the gallery above. Several of the searchers went over. Jason's thumbs pricked again; they had found whatever it was they had been looking for. Dave was on his feet. The door to the gallery was open and unguarded as the searchers crowded up the narrow stairs.

The two newsmen followed, pausing at the top to assess the scene. A tight group was looking at something on the ground. There were six men, plus the middle-aged one in tweed, looking into what appeared to be an old chest. It was impossible to see what was in it. Jason nodded to Dave and the photographer sprinted forward. He shot off twelve to fifteen exposures in rapid succession, aiming wildly over their heads into the box, snapping startled faces, retreating to take a general view. Then he was gone.

The police tried to follow but MacDonald blocked their path to the stairs. Below he saw Dave sprint out of the cathedral before anyone could stop him. He relaxed and smiled.

'What the bloody hell do you think you're doing?'

He had been right, the tweedy policeman seemed to be in charge.

'My name's Jason MacDonald and I'm a journalist with the *Chichester Times*. I'd like to ask you gentlemen a few questions concerning your find this afternoon.'

'No comment. Now get out of our way.'

'Perhaps you could tell me what this has to do with the bomb explosion in Richmond this afternoon, which injured DCI Fenwick and killed Constable Adams.'

'How do you . . . ?' The man's face changed from red to crimson to grey and back to red in seconds as he recovered from the shock of MacDonald's words. Behind him the others looked aghast as they heard him blurt out the story.

'Clear off, MacDonald. You've been told, *'no comment'*. Get out of our bloody way or I'll charge you with obstruction.'

MacDonald left, dictating ideas into a Dictaphone as he drove precariously, one-handed back to the office. He still couldn't be sure what they had found in the cathedral but the rest came together beautifully. At his desk later he was trying to decide which paper to contact with the exclusive when the call from his editor came through. The whole afternoon had been a waste of his and Dave's time. The police were insisting on a complete news blackout about the cathedral, and all the facts about the bombing were already being broadcast on the early evening news.

Fenwick came round to agony, the pain of a hammerdrill pushed behind his eyes. His first thought, as the white walls and ceiling assumed crazy, half-focused perspectives, was that it was exactly like the shots they show in films. A woman's face zoomed in and out of view, a giant's hand touched his forehead. He closed his eyes, trying to ignore the pain. He tried to raise his hand to touch his head but passed out again before he could remember how to do it.

The next time he came round he could see more clearly. It was dark beyond the uncurtained window. There were two or three people by the side of his bed, just out of view. He turned his head slightly to see them better and a shaft of pain split his skull from ear to ear, making him sweat and retch. One of the bodies moved closer to the bed. It was Cooper. Fenwick was worried by his appearance; he looked old and grey.

Cooper's lips were moving but there was no sound. He must have lost his voice. Fenwick tried to tell him to shout but no words came out into the silence. Cooper looked worried now as well as old. Fenwick closed his eyes and drifted into a light sleep.

He woke again, conscious of movement by his side. He gradually became aware of the lack of background noise around him. He was obviously in a hospital; there should be noises – the rattle of trolleys, the squeak of a medicine cart, visitors' voices, a television in a dayroom somewhere. There was nothing. Cooper was still there wearing his mask of concern. He was calling a nurse over and the girl talking to Fenwick. He struggled to speak. He thought he was saying, 'I can't hear you', but even within his own head, the words made no sound.

CHAPTER FORTY-TWO

The Friday papers all carried extensive coverage of the bombing, with names and photographs of the four victims. In the *Mirror* there was a small contribution from J. MacDonald, speculating in two short paragraphs that the missing link had something to do with beautiful opera star Octavia Anderson. There was no word about the cathedral, nor photograph of whatever had been found in the oak chest. Dave had been forced to hand the film over undeveloped.

Rowland read the papers, all of them, whilst he listened to the *Today* programme. A television was on silently in the corner of the room. His photograph was everywhere; his name appeared freely in all the articles, as did that of DCI Fenwick. The police were making no secret of their urgent desire to interview him, whilst warning the public not to approach him. He had been so confident that the police would miss the connections that he hadn't bothered to disguise himself. It had been a serious mistake and one that he had corrected already. He got up and looked at himself in the small, chipped mirror. A stranger stared back, even without the padding he would put in his cheeks before he went out in public.

He folded the papers neatly and started to work through his daily exercise routine, the radio on in the background. A report came on about the murders, his name referred to constantly. He worked harder and faster as the report went on. Sweat rolled down his face, soaked his T-shirt, dripped to the floor, his muscles bunched tighter in exertion, the burn obvious in his face as he forced himself on. He ignored the pain from his shoulder where a bruise was growing from the bullet that had hit his padded vest. His breathing was faster but remained steady and controlled. He worked on through the report and up to the hourly forecast for the second time. As the pips for eight o'clock ended he moved into a slow, relaxation routine before taking a shower.

He had to assume that his preparations in the cathedral were worthless. They must have found the rifle and special ammunition he had hidden there. Although they had been careful to make no mention of it to the press, Rowland was determined not to underestimate the police again. As needles of water drummed on to his head and shoulders, pricking his face and scalp, his mind started to work. The initial anger, both at himself and the police, had been replaced by a purposelessness that he had never experienced before. Now, refreshed by the stimulation of exercise, he started to think methodically again at last.

He was safe where he was – a final bolt hole, arranged out of habit, that he had never expected to use, except perhaps to regroup after his escape from the cathedral. There were provisions in the cellar and freezer that could last him weeks, plenty of fresh water and no neighbours. There was a brand-new bike locked in the outhouse, emergency clothes and theatrical make-up and dyes that he had already put to good use. He looked down at the water swirling around his feet; it ran clear, the dye having set completely.

Rowland flicked water from his eyes and towelled down, unconsciously massaging shoulder muscles and kneading his calves. He had four choices: abandon the attempt on Anderson; postpone it to an unknown future date; bring it forward, which meant an attack on her home; or continue with a variation of the cathedral plan.

He could not abandon her. Justice cried out for her death, her execution. All the other deaths were meaningless without hers. To delay was the most sensible solution but it was hard to accept. He had come too close to her to make it easy to let go now. Besides, her plans beyond Monday were unknown to him.

Delay meant starting from scratch. It would never be his preferred choice.

Dry now, dressed only in a loose towelling robe, he considered and made his choice. He would remake his plans for Monday. Deep in his loin a beast turned over as he decided. He imagined Anderson's face, eyes wide in fright, a slender neck in his hands which he could snap or slash. The prospect was deeply, disgustingly exciting. Killing had never aroused him before and he was amused to see the effect of her imagined execution on his body. He wanted, needed to kill her more than he had ever needed to do anything before.

Carol's face smiled at him from the fading photograph beside the bed. The old forgotten longing for her hit him. With a groan he threw himself back across the coverlet, reaching for the picture with one hand, compulsively holding and stroking himself with the other. He needed Carol more than ever. All his senses, controlled and restrained for years, broke out clamouring at him as he stared into her eyes. He was sweating again, his breath rasping loudly in his throat. Pictures of Anderson dead, mutilated, slashed, flashed across Carol's face, confusing him, tormenting him. He heard himself rhythmically groaning, calling out her name, as his hand worked harder and harder and the photograph crackled in his fist. He arched his back in an exquisite agony of pain, hate and passion, shrieking out as he climaxed, unaware, unable to recall, whether he had cried out Carol or Anderson's name at the last.

There was silence. Gradually sounds returned. From the kitchen, the radio introduced the 8.30 news; suggestive, gurgling noises swirled in the pipes as they filled. His head cleared. There was no walking away. She had to die soon, before his grip on control was gone. It was now merely a question of how and when.

With a flicker of disgust he threw the twisted, damp robe and coverlet in a musty heap on the floor and walked back to the shower.

CHAPTER FORTY-THREE

Fenwick was both infuriated and reassured to learn that his deafness was the result of shock, not physical injury and that his hearing could return at any time. He checked himself out of hospital at Friday lunchtime. It was against the doctor's advice, and he had to sign two separate forms accepting that any serious consequences were of his own doing. They gave him an outpatient's appointment for the following Monday. He looked at it stupidly and dropped it in the nearest litterbin. He was desperate to get home and see the children. The nanny, very sensibly, had played down his injuries, kept Bess and Chris away from the hospital and summoned Fenwick's mother home from holiday. But despite her calm, steady caring both Bess and Chris had burst into tears as he walked in, painfully trying not to limp. He knew he looked a mess, and his deafness confused them, but an hour or two of watching cartoons together had calmed them down sufficiently to allow him a brief nap. When he woke he found them both, fast asleep, on the coverlet beside him, Chris's hand tucked protectively on top of his own.

Mid-afternoon, an irritating clicking started in his right ear to be followed by suckling and popping noises, like the sound of tiny bubbles tickling and bursting on the hull of a yacht. His left ear played dead. The afternoon was a misery. He insisted on visiting Doug's widow and spent a long half-hour with her, feeling inadequate as he allowed the poor woman to make him tea and pity his deafness. Her sister and daughter-in-law were there but in his state of heightened sensitivity, Fenwick could feel the emptiness in the room and see the black pool of bereavement that was isolating Doris for ever from the only human comfort she really needed.

His office was barred to him. The Assistant Chief Constable had insisted on complete rest and had been canny enough to extract a promise from Fenwick to that effect. He was left to his own devices. He prowled around at home, ineffectually attempting to catch up on dusty repairs, reassuring the children, trying to ignore the constant static in his right ear.

Cooper called in at suppertime, with two suspicious brown paper packages under his arm. From one he extracted a bottle of twelve-year-old single malt, from the other a stack of reports. He stared into the flames of the small fire in Fenwick's sitting room, lit in an attempt at cheerfulness, not warmth, as the Chief Inspector worked steadily through the contents of the bottle and the detail of the reports.

'What's he going to do next?' he finally asked Cooper. Both knew he was referring to Rowland. Cooper spoke slowly, economically, moving his mouth to shape every word.

'He won't give up. He will try again.'

'I agree. He's put too much into this. I assume Anderson's London house is being watched?'

Cooper nodded.

'Any activity?'

Cooper shook his head.

There was a long pause, oiled by gentle sipping. 'He's going to try for the cathedral again, isn't he?' It was more statement than question.

Cooper shrugged, then shook his head: 'The ACC disagrees. I don't see it. There's only three days left and we found his arms cache – too short a time and too dangerous now to prepare all over again.'

Fenwick was staring intently at Cooper's lips but he ignored the sergeant's words.

'He's going to try again, I know this man now. Something's driving him on; I don't know what but it's there. He's not going to let go. You've got to work on the assumption he'll try to kill

Anderson on Monday if he can't find her before.'

Cooper shook his head again: 'That's not the ACC's view. There's a huge search going on to find him. He's sure we'll get him before the performance starts.'

'We won't. He's wrong and it's not the first time. He should stick to politics – it's what he's good at – and leave the real police work to those that bloody well know how to do it!' The blast of Fenwick's anger reached Cooper where he sat across the room. He didn't even flinch; he knew it was directed elsewhere. Fenwick stood up and poured another two fingers of whisky into both of their glasses. They sipped again in silence; it was too good a malt to treat with disrespect. Cooper watched his boss stare into the flames as he stood before the fire, saw frustration and despair take over from the anger.

Cooper got up and laid a firm hand on Fenwick's shoulder, placing his face firmly in front of Fenwick's, holding his eyes. The flush that had suffused Fenwick's cheeks had receded, leaving him tired and grey. For the first time Cooper noticed the strain in his face, eyes sunk in deep purple shadows, hard lines of weariness running from nostrils to the corners of his mouth. The cuts, scratches, and bruises from the explosion peppered his skin, paper stitches holding closed gouges on his brow and jaw. His whole face was forced into a grimace – whether of disgust, pain or failure, Cooper couldn't tell.

'Andrew,' he muttered gently then recalled that no attempt at the right tone would count, plain words would have to do. 'You need to rest.'

'Rest? How can I rest?' Fenwick's voice was filled with anguish. 'I saw Doug's wife today – widow, I mean. I haven't yet found the guts to go and visit Heather Coals. She lost that leg, you know; they couldn't save it. They had to amputate this afternoon. I can't rest. It's my fault. I was warned, Bayliss told me – you heard him. "Don't put your boys up against him with wooden sticks," he said. That's precisely what I *did* do and now Doug's dead and there's a young girl crippled for life . . .' His voice caught.

Cooper shouted his reply, desperate to be heard. 'And you

374

nearly got yourself killed too! Yes, you did go in . . . yes, they went in with you, doing *their* jobs . . . but *no* it was not your fault. You had firearms there. Harrington cleared you to go in. How could anyone have anticipated a bomb?'

Fenwick turned his head away in disgust. Cooper couldn't tell whether anything he'd said had been understood or accepted. He turned Fenwick back to face him.

'The most important thing is what you decide to do now, sir. Do you understand what I'm saying?'

Fenwick nodded.

'You believe you know this man's thinking, perhaps you do. But,' he moved his lips very carefully, even more slowly, 'if you think he'll attack Monday, we need you back. Fit, and well, not tired and so eaten up with guilt you can't think straight. Go to bed, sleep – and drop the self-pity.'

The ACC planned to call the whole home team together on Saturday morning. Fenwick spent half an hour with him privately beforehand, trying to convince him of the real threat to Octavia on Monday. Straining to hear past the bubbling in his right ear, he hoped that some of what he said had an impact. Octavia's growing fame and public profile probably did more to worry his politically sensitive boss than all his arguments, and he had to accept that logic was not on his side. It would be madness for Rowland to attack in the cathedral when they were clearly on to him, and far more likely that he would try and strike outside. But then Fenwick was quite convinced that their target *was* mad.

But the ACC again dismissed the idea of an attack at the cathedral. He had been disconcerted by the gun and ammunition found in the old chest which suggested that his earlier assumption – that Octavia wouldn't have been in any danger – was wrong. But he was even more convinced now that Rowland would stay away. He would see that the police were on to him and had to expect that the arms would have been removed, despite the news blackout. And anyway, Anderson was still insisting that the performance should go ahead. For the police to press for its cancellation would be a political nightmare.

By the time the meeting was due to start, Fenwick was in dread of entering the room – the looks of blame he anticipated, no one meeting his eye. The ACC was still in charge and it grated on him that he would have to sit dumb as well as deaf while the man directed the case.

It was normal for the sounds of a large gathering in the incident room to bubble over into the surrounding offices but the ACC noticed there was silence as he and Fenwick made their way there. As they opened the door the soft, grumbling murmur within died at once. Fenwick forced himself to look individuals in the eye as he took in the scene. To his surprise, he looked out on sympathy, pity, understanding. No one turned away from his scrutiny and the undoubted anger he felt in the room was not being directed at him. A DS from his own force extended a hand and slapped him gently on the shoulder; Fenwick couldn't hear his words but the gesture spoke to him loudly. He started to relax.

Nightingale was at the meeting, which worried Fenwick. Who was looking after Anderson? She intercepted his frown and smiled reassuringly.

The ACC went straight to business. For five minutes Fenwick watched his lips avidly, trying to follow his arguments, to see what plans were being set for Monday. It was impossible and disconcerting to watch a wave of frowns cross the room, or a sudden brief outbreak of smiles, without knowing why. The questions and answers baffled him completely. His head turned from speaker to speaker in a delayed random pattern. In the end he abandoned his attempt to follow the meeting and gazed around the room.

He had never noticed before how grey the white paint was, how it peeled around the windows and radiators. The door had been scraped back to bare wood in parts by countless boots, and thick dusty cobwebs hung from the cornice. It was a dismal symbol for the case, for modern-day policing. The cleaning resources never reached the corners, their work undone before they had a chance to start again. His performance appraisals used to be full of praise for his 'results orientation'; more recently they had bemoaned his lack of pragmatism, though there were still those on high, unbeknownst to him, who felt that Fenwick was 'just the breath of fresh air we need in the management team'.

Movement around him brought him back to the present and immediate concern that adequate plans for Monday had been put in place. He looked at Cooper; the sergeant shrugged enigmatically.

'Well?' The room was emptying behind them except for a hovering Nightingale.

'A compromise. There will be a team at the cathedral from Sunday. You'll be pleased to know that there was an embarrassment of volunteers for it. Meanwhile, the search continues.'

'That's some consolation.' He turned to face Nightingale, who was looking remarkably fit and well. 'How are things with you?'

She smiled and gave him the thumbs-up, then mouthed: 'Bored but OK.'

'How is she?' It was a bluff, blunt question but neither Cooper nor Nightingale was taken in.

'Fine; very well considering the pressure. She's a true professional. I admire her.'

'I have to speak to her about Monday. I'll come round sometime this weekend.' He turned back to Cooper: 'You'll never find him before Monday, you know.'

'What makes you think I'll be looking? I'm with you, sir.'

The ACC must be furious, thought Fenwick. How many others had displayed the same lack of confidence in his plan and borne the considerable brunt of his displeasure? Looking into Cooper's face, he realised that the man didn't care. From now on, he was going to be in the cathedral, where he wanted to be.

Cooper never told Fenwick, although he did admit to Nightingale in an unusual moment of candour, the precise details of his conversation with the ACC. He was not an eloquent man but he was resourceful under pressure and his argument had been compelling.

'Look, sir,' he had said deferentially, 'just between us, I think it's essential I shadow DCI Fenwick. It'll only be for two and a half days – until after the performance – and there's no knowing yet how well he is. We don't want him inadvertently spoiling the main investigation.'

The ACC gave Cooper what his mother would once have called an old-fashioned look.

'Very well, Sergeant, stay with him. But make no mistake, I remain in charge of the whole investigation – and that includes the team at the cathedral, which, by the way, I intend to staff with supplementary resources. The main search teams will be kept intact.'

As Cooper left, he had thought nothing of the fact that he overheard the ACC ask his secretary to call the MOD, nor did he mention the fact to Nightingale or Fenwick.

CHAPTER FORTY-FOUR

Fenwick woke with a start and switched off his alarm clock. The digital face told him it was five o'clock. Something was wrong. He lay in bed, his mind still fogged with sleep, and slowly tried to identify what was troubling him. There was a constant background noise, a gentle susuration of sound that came as a welcome change to the constant popping and squeaking of the day before. Otherwise all was quiet.

Suddenly he sat up in bed and slammed his hand against the headboard. He heard the hard slap of his palm against the wood. He could hear again; the clock had woken him, the bedclothes rustled as he moved, the gentle hissing was nothing more than the noise of rain outside. At some point in the night, the hearing in his right ear had returned.

It was early Sunday morning; there were less than forty hours to go before Octavia's recital.

The small house was overshadowed by old sticky lime trees, dripping disconsolately in the unseasonably cold September rain. No attempt had been made to prune back their growth and now they sucked all light and goodness from the handkerchief garden, devoid of vegetation except for a perky daisy growing in a jagged crack across the asphalt path.

The house was still curtained as Fenwick stooped to open the rudimentary wooden gate set in a crumbling low brick wall. He squeezed past grasping branches to reach the door and depress the yellow nipple of a bell. He leant heavily on his left leg, trying to ignore the insistent pain in his right knee.

After a long minute's wait a curtain was drawn back from the small glass pane in the door and he heard a succession of locks and bolts shift. Nightingale stood before him in a towelling robe; no make-up, hair spiked in all directions. She looked sixteen.

'What's the matter, sir?'

'I've come to talk with Anderson.'

'At 6.30 in the morning?'

'Why not?'

Anderson appeared ten minutes later wrapped in a soft pink silk robe. The skin across her collar bones glowed like fine alabaster even in the unforgiving harshness of the 100 watt bulb that lit the room. Her hair was down, thick blue-black waves, rolling over her shoulders and down on to gently swinging breasts. She shivered slightly beneath the silk and Fenwick couldn't help but see her nipples pucker. He switched on the electric fire in the hearth.

'You've lost weight.'

'A little, but Louise is doing her best to fatten me up again before Monday. I haven't been fed so well in a long time.' Her voice was light, relaxed, gently amused.

'This isn't the best of houses.'

'It'll do. Louise arranged a piano and is good company; there's a decent bathroom; and new mattresses on the beds.'

Fenwick suddenly realised that Louise was Nightingale; he had never used her first name.

'Are you well?'

'I'm fine. I'm keeping really well. What have you done to your face and hands?' Fenwick touched the stitches self-consciously. She obviously didn't know about the bomb and he was not about to tell her.

'A small accident. It looks more dramatic than it is. Where's your maid?'

'I gave her a holiday until Monday. She only moped around getting on our nerves. It's a small house, we really didn't need her.'

Nightingale, hurriedly dressed in jeans and cotton shirt, came in with a tray of tea. There were three mugs, one with a Snoopy cartoon on the side – the little yellow bird was twittering in the dog's water bowl. She stirred the light brown liquid and handed it to Octavia. The singer grinned.

'My mug,' she said, lifting it vaguely in Fenwick's direction. 'Rather different from my bone china at home. We thought the singing bird appropriate.'

'I would've thought that should have been Nightingale's.'

Neither of the women appeared to see the joke. There was silence.

'I want to talk to you about Monday.'

'We've been through this before, Andrew. I'm going to sing.'

'Yes, I know.' He was irritated by her use of his Christian name in front of the policewoman. 'We need to discuss safety measures.'

'You think he's still going to make an attempt? I had heard differently.'

The ACC's wife must have been talking to the organising committee.

'Yes I do.'

She stared moodily at the glowing electric bar. 'I agree with you. He won't give up.'

'Which is why we must discuss security. Firstly, I want you to wear a vest.'

Anderson burst out laughing, her body quivering gently beneath the thin robe.

'I mean a bullet-proof vest.'

'I know what you mean, Andrew, but I can't do that. I'm there to sing, to perform. My voice has to fill the cathedral, reach into their hearts. I can't have it trapped inside a vest!' She laughed again.

'You must reconsider. You have to realise, there is no way we can guarantee your safety.'

'I know that.' There was no laughter now. 'I know you can't. But – and I don't mean this as a burden, Andrew – I trust you. If anyone can stop this man, you can.'

Fenwick's stomach twisted painfully even as he admired her ability to manipulate. They talked for another half-hour, touching on security arrangements, how they would handle the rehearsal and her journey to the cathedral. Fenwick felt a fraud. He was not even in charge any more. They had only accepted him back in an 'advisory capacity' and here he was making commitments, planning, giving reassurances. He would have to pass it all on to Cooper to follow up.

'He was planning on using the triforium, the gallery over the nave. We'll have people up there all the time. Cooper, Nightingale and I will all be there.'

'Sir, I've been thinking about my role, where I should be. I could sit close by Octavia, just below the platform or even in the choir. I could be looking out over the audience and be right on hand if anything starts to happen.'

Octavia reached over and touched Nightingale's hand gently.

'It should be an armed officer, not you.'

'There will be AFOs around too; I'm talking about acting like a personal assistant or something.'

Fenwick thought hard. Wherever she was there could be danger and she was right, there would be plenty of firepower around.

'Very well then, but you wear a vest.'

CHAPTER FORTY-FIVE

The long Sunday passed in a blur of activity. Police weaving among contractors and tourists were taken aback by the religious services and dedicated worshippers in the cathedral, surprised to see the historical monument assume an older purpose.

Airport-style security gates were being set up at the main entrances; other doors were locked and guarded. A tiny office was turned over to the police. The ACC visited, conferred and went, leaving behind Inspector Blite as his local 'anchorman'. Fenwick stayed, tacking large-scale plans of the cathedral and close to the walls of the office. Constant supplies of good coffee and fruit cake were delivered to the police team by a small army of ladies, 'friends' of the cathedral, all of whom seemed to share the common expression of an old, anxious hamster startled out of a comfy snooze.

Rehearsals started in the afternoon; first choirs and orchestra separately, and then together. The air crackled with tension, the sounds distorted and marred by the occasional barks of sniffer dogs or calls from the police. There were tears in the youth choir sopranos and a highly uncharacteristic expletive from the leader.

Fenwick left for home late in the evening. He was hungry and tired, and his stomach growled from an excess of strong coffee and sweet cake. He missed Bess and Chris; wanted more than anything to cuddle them and enjoy their simple health and innocence. Chris was so much better and Bess, as always, a treasure.

But his mind wouldn't settle. Everything that could have been done in preparation had been done. There had been no sightings of Rowland. The ACC was working the search teams twenty-four hours a day with no results. Rowland had simply disappeared.

Fenwick knew that his mother, refreshed from her holiday, would have a meal ready, and that the children would still be up awaiting his return, but even so, for some reason he could not face home. As he drove his car like a robot back from the cathedral, his mind worried through endless lists of things that had or had not been done. He felt guilty for leaving the cathedral, sure that his place should be there, but logic told him he was a spare part, kidding himself. His head ached badly and his joints and back had stiffened as bruises came out. His wrist had been bandaged by one of the old ladies and it throbbed intolerably. He needed a break. It would be more important to be thinking straight in the morning, and anyway, the team at the cathedral only had so much tolerance for an 'adviser' and he had exhausted it all.

Anderson's words came back to him: 'I trust you. If anyone can stop this man, you can.' He saw her calm face, oval eyes looking at him with complete trust, with none of the shadows that had aged and haunted her the week before. He felt sick.

He drew up in front of the towering limes. Their dense shadows screened the streetlamps' light from the tiny house. Nightingale answered the door. He had forgotten she would be there.

'Have you been cooped up here all day?'

'Er, yes . . . of course.'

'How do you expect to be at your best tomorrow? Go out and get some fresh air, go to the pub, have a drink.'

'What?' Her eyes narrowed in anger at his implied criticism and pre-emptory advice; he was too tense for it to sound avuncular. She felt like telling him that thanks to his investigation, she had no one to go out for a drink with that evening. Her fiancé was still away on what should have been their shared vacation. He hadn't called and there had been no card. She felt sick whenever she thought about what he might be doing, and with whom, and even worse when she contemplated his return. No one knew about her automatic sacrifice but suddenly, childishly, she wanted them to and to make a fuss of her about it. She swallowed the thought but couldn't prevent her reply being made bitter by its taste.

'I'm fine; I don't need fresh air. I'm perfectly relaxed and rested.'

'You need a change of scene. I'm telling you.'

'But—'

'No buts. Go and get a jacket. I'll hang on here for a couple of hours. Off you go.'

Nightingale opened her mouth to speak but bit down hard on the inside of her bottom lip instead. Her jacket was hanging on a hook in the hall; she grabbed it and was gone.

'What was all that about?' Octavia appeared at the door to the tiny lounge, lamplight behind her. She was wearing a black cashmere sweater and leopard-print leggings. Fenwick caught his breath.

'I've sent young Nightingale out for a breath of fresh air.'

'Oh.'

He stood stupidly in the hall, waiting for her move. She just stared back, an unfathomable smile on her face. The urge that had driven him to her became caught up in a mixture of embarrassment and resentment. Struggling free he turned to go.

'This is stupid. I don't know why I came . . . I'll see myself out.'

'Wait, you can't. I'm on my own. Where's my protection?' She laughed.

His arms were around her, his lips bruising hers, his tongue searched her mouth desperately. She responded at once, a low gurgle in her throat that could have been passion or triumph. He didn't care. Her hands were running painfully down his back, moving from a trace of fingertips on his neck to kneading, urgent palms, pushing their hips together. She was tall. They stood almost shoulder to shoulder, chest to breast, thigh to thigh.

In her bedroom they kept the light off and the curtains open. A half-moon had risen over the trees to show fitfully between high clouds, throwing a silver-blue twilight on to the bed. Her skin shone pure white, blood-red nipples black in the moon's fire, counterpoints to the rich luxuriously curling hair between her thighs. He stood above her, fixed by her beauty again, as he had been in France.

Thoughts of her body and their love-making had filled his dreams since the high summer. Now he could not escape the feeling of being caught up in another hopeless dream – Octavia transformed from the glowing queen of Mediterranean suns to an ice maiden, pure, deadly and utterly desirable. In his confusion he expected to wake up sweating, so painfully erect that the ache would last into the day.

He fell on her with a groan, penetrating her at once. She cried out briefly in pain and surprise but was immediately carried on by his remorseless rhythm.

Her long red fingernails dug into his back, leaving deep welts. Slim elastic legs wrapped around his hips, locking him in a compulsive embrace. They fused into one pulsing animal, cries, grunts, gasps for breath forced out as their passion became intense. Fenwick could not stop; a tiny pinpoint in his brain was trying to shout at him that this was wrong – she was wrong – but it was drowned out by his own cries and her crude shouts of encouragement.

A pressure was building inside him, starting at the base of his spine, pushing into all his muscles, squeezing his heart, filling his head as it grew, culminating in an urgent, incessant swelling in his groin. He felt the explosion as it happened, travelling up, through, out of him into her at the same time as her own climax rushed to meet him, overflow him. He looked down into her wide-eyed staring face as she howled silently at the moon.

They remained locked, rocking for long moments, bodies impossibly entwined. Fenwick looked into Octavia's face, so close to his own that he could feel her breath tickle his cheek. Her eyes had closed, the lids pure white, fringed by dark hemispheres of lashes. Her mouth was open, a black hole in the flatness of her face. The cloud in front of the moon shifted suddenly, its light creating a ghost of the warm, living flesh beneath him. The effect was enough to make him shudder.

'Cold?' She was looking at him again steadily from dark, expressionless pools.

'Just a little. How about you?'

'Mmm, a bit.' She unwrapped endless limbs from around him and stretched. They were still joined firmly at the hips and she raised hers suggestively against his. He winced from the pain in his back.

'You needed that.'

'Didn't you?' His voice was husky, broken.

The sphinx looked back at him and smiled.

Nightingale returned as the late news was finishing, banging the front door and bringing with her the seductive aroma of fish and chips.

'Supper?'

'Mmm, yummy; I'm starved.' Octavia jumped up and switched off the television. She followed Nightingale into the fluorescence of the kitchen, their joint laughter echoing back into the room.

'Do you want some, Andrew? There's plenty,' she called out above the clink of cutlery, the sounds of a table being laid.

'No, thank you. I'll be going.'

'Are you sure?' She returned to find him in the hall.

'Yes. I'll see you tomorrow.' He tried to make the words sound normal.

She gave him her everyday smile as she showed him out. As he walked down the sticky, gloomy path, he could still hear their laughter from the kitchen and wondered if he was their subject.

CHAPTER FORTY-SIX

Monday, September 6th was the seventy-fifth anniversary of the founding of Downside School. A charity school, it had been established in a burst of optimistic determination by Counsellor De Weir, a local businessman too old to have been sent to war but too young not to fear the consequences for the nation of the destruction of so many gifted adolescents.

The school originally had one teacher, one class of fourteen pupils of mixed ages, and met in a converted coach house. Miss Saunders, the first teacher, had been in her early thirties. Like many of her age and class, she faced a future of spinsterhood brightly and bravely, having lost her fiancé in 1916. School became her family, the class her children, and she devoted to their general and specific education a determination and imagination that won over the largely agricultural parents and pupils it was her lot to improve.

By chance, Miss Saunders was a proficient pianist whose skill had become increasingly accomplished in long hours of practice since the August of 1916. It was also coincidence that two of her pupils, the Mason twins, turned out to have perfect pitch and delightful tenor voices. Thus the Christmas school concerts attracted audiences well beyond the village. Mr De Weir, not a musical man, was happy to accept the congratulations and his career in local politics blossomed. When he became mayor he bestowed a musical endowment on the school, and a further award to be made available to support the artistic development of any truly exceptional pupil. The school's place in local musical education was secured.

The school had a heritage and one of which the governors were both jealous and proud. Octavia Anderson was their greatest achievement and on their anniversary they had been determined to show, or rather show off to, the world. Selecting Verdi's *Requiem* was daring, a few said foolhardy. It was a challenging work for orchestra, choir and all the four soloists – soprano, mezzo-soprano, tenor and bass. Attracting Octavia Anderson to sing had been a coup, worth all the uncertainty of whether she would, finally, turn up.

All the choirs and orchestras had been rehearsing separately, helped along by the lead conductor and the director who had the unenviable task of co-ordinating the voices. The first rehearsals as one group had been on Sunday; it had not quite been a total disaster. Monday was to be a challenging day.

The cathedral had been closed to tourists and worshippers since Evensong and overnight the electronic sensors at the entrances had been wired up, forcing musicians and technicians to walk through metal doorways on their way to the dais. Some members of the choir and orchestra were intimidated by the extensive security, with members of the brass section defending their instruments from dismantling police hands; searching became less intrusive after a trombonist nearly came to blows with a plain-clothes policeman.

The smallness of the nave restricted the combined orchestra size, but nevertheless the area before the choir was bristling with music stands and chairs. In the triforium above the nave the trumpeters settled on to small stools, crammed into the narrow space. A decision had been taken to intersperse the youth orchestra with select members of the local professional chamber orchestra.

The first full run-through on Monday morning was ragged. The conductor had a real problem with the brass section and an over-enthusiastic timpanist. Police searches and sniffer dogs in the aisles didn't help but by mid-morning there was a renewed sense of cohesion and purpose. The lunch break, spent indoors avoiding the drizzle outside, was almost cheerful. There was only one rehearsal left before the soloists arrived and the conductor decided he was ready to do a complete run-through. The effect was electrifying for choir and orchestra alike. For the first time since the rehearsals began, many of the seasoned performers felt their hairs prickle and rise in the thrill that only great music can provide. The conductor felt ready to face the soloists.

Police checks were becoming more urgent. All members of the orchestra and choir had given their names, addresses and telephone numbers to a team of six uniformed police, who were using every available phone to confirm their identities. Cooper was feeling quietly confident that they would finish their work before the main performance when Fenwick upset everyone by suggesting that all the organisers, friends of the cathedral and technicians would need to be checked out too. Blite had no option but to agree. As people were constantly moving around the cathedral, Cooper resorted to marking the backs of their hands with pink felt-tip pen, as they took their details, to keep tabs on them all.

Finally: 'All done, sir. We've got all their names down now.'

'Who's that up there?' Cooper followed Fenwick's out-stretched hand up to the triforium above the nave.

'The trumpeters, sir; they're done.'

'No, next to them – with the microphone.'

'That's a sound technician, Chief Inspector.' The chairman of the organising committee came up to him smiling.

'I've heard nothing about a sound recording.'

'I thought you'd been told. Look, I have a letter here confirming the final details.'

'It's dated only last month.'

'I know. Poor Katherine Johnstone had been organising it and, to tell you the truth, we'd all forgotten about it. But they confirmed arrangements out of the blue; wrote to me direct when they couldn't reach Kate. And it's an excellent deal. The charity receives a down payment for the recording rights and a percentage on the royalties.'

Fenwick studied the letter. It was written on the letterhead of a well-known recording company and looked authentic. Attached to the back was a photocopy of Katherine Johnstone's original letter, badly smudged at the top. It was chatty, not as businesslike as he would have expected. He started to hand it back; he was being too cautious now, doubting everyone.

'Do you want that checked as well then, sir?'

'You might as well, Cooper. See if you can confirm who signed the letter and that the technician up there works for the company.'

Cooper approached the sound recordist as he went to make a final check on the microphones by the choir. They could hardly make themselves heard over the din of the brass from above. One trumpet was still badly off key.

The sound man looked tall, even bending down, but seemed far too old to be Rowland. What little hair there was left on his head was grey, as was an incongruous goatee that straggled from his jaw. He had a letter of authorisation on him, an ID card from the same firm and a driving licence. He was tolerant but bemused by Cooper's questions and as time passed, became impatient to move on.

'Are you here by yourself?'

'Now, yes. There were others here during the week and Alec should be here any time, he helps. But mainly it's me. I'm testing levels right now and I need to finish these adjustments before the soloists arrive.'

'Do you have your boss's home phone number?'

'Course not! Why should I? We hardly know each other socially.' He had an indistinct Midland's accent that grew stronger as he became irritated.

'All right, but don't run away. I might need to talk to you again.'

Cooper reported back; the man seemed genuine but they were trying to find someone senior in the company anyway. Virtually all the trumpeters had been cleared as well and Fenwick was running out of suspects. He couldn't believe Rowland would simply turn up in the audience. He suggested another sweep for explosives and went to confer with Cooper.

391

Jason MacDonald was on the case. More correctly, he couldn't leave the cathedral story alone. Despite the suppression of his earlier piece, he was drawn by the sense of a major story about to break and agonisingly aware that he was the only journalist close enough to know it was happening.

It had been easy to use the confusion of the choir's arrival to enter the cathedral, and as the police fretted their time away to lunch, he had lain hidden in a patch of deep shadow in a narrow gap behind a restored tomb, occasionally dozing, only to jerk awake to check the time.

Harper-Brown, the ACC, arrived unannounced shortly before the full afternoon rehearsal. His anxiety at being in the front line of a dangerous and complex operation was thinly concealed beneath a veneer of ill-timed bonhomie. It irritated Fenwick to note that the stance appeared to work with police and organisers alike when it was so transparent to him. The ACC was caught in a trap of his own making, unable to acknowledge the full danger because of his earlier rejection of Fenwick's theory, but equally unable to deny that the probable next target of a serial killer, of whom he had lost all trace since the bombing, was appearing in public in less than six hours, in front of three hundred people. On top of which, Fenwick made him uncomfortable with his knowing, clever expression that he was still too stupid to conceal. Harper-Brown spent some time talking to two men, Blite and someone Fenwick didn't recognise, and when he moved towards the Chief Inspector, he was visibly more relaxed.

'How do you think it's going, Andrew?'

The use of his Christian name put Fenwick on immediate alert.

'I think you've done all you can do in the circumstances, sir. It hasn't helped having almost a couple of hundred musicians swarming all over the place, leaving bags and coats everywhere, but the local team seem to have them in order now. I haven't spoken much to the other man working with Blite – he keeps himself to himself – but I guess he's given you the briefing you need.'

The ACC looked uncomfortable. 'Yes, yes, he's quietly confident.'

Fenwick looked at the impressive figure of the ACC in his uniform and added, with regret, 'It was a little tense at times with the musicians. It would help if you could go and thank the conductor, director and chairman of the organising committee for their co-operation, sir.'

'Of course, happy to do what I can.' There was a pause in which Fenwick could not bring himself to meet the ACC's eye. 'Oh, by the way, as we haven't found Rowland, I've pulled in some more men; they're being deployed now. Any thoughts on where they'd best be put? Campbell, the, er, local man, and Blite have it all under control but your advice is always welcome.'

Campbell and Blite had made the exact opposite clear to Fenwick when he had arrived and it was only the loyalty of Cooper and his West Sussex CID friends that had enabled him to exert any influence over the arrangements in the cathedral at all. One hundred smart remarks fought for the privilege of being spoken but they remained on the tip of his tongue. The ACC had to be treated as an ally if they were to save Octavia's life.

'It would be difficult to assimilate a lot more at this stage, sir. But perhaps Campbell could deploy another six or eight inside and use the rest to throw a wide cordon around the cathedral, close enough in to give us full back-up in case anything happens.'

The ACC regarded Fenwick with renewed respect; there hadn't even been a hint of 'I told you so' in his reply and no obvious rancour at not being in charge.

'The AFOs, and vests for every attending officer, are arriving at any moment. I've authorised release of weapons to all qualified fire arms officers, by the way. I expect you'll be wanting one?'

'No, not me, sir.'

The ACC looked around the massive building. Sniffer dogs were on the last lap of a final sweep; police officers stood at every door, even those locked and bolted; some AFOs were already in position at key points along the nave, in the choir and in the triforium above, as were the specialists supplied by the Ministry of Defence about whom only the ACC, Campbell and Blite were aware. He had been delighted when they had been offered by an old school friend now well placed in the Ministry. Co-operation these days always went down well, and it was a useful complication if things did go wrong. Besides, they were not on his budget. He knew that Fenwick wouldn't approve and hadn't told him. Fortunately they were so well disguised that they blended in perfectly. Even now, he couldn't distinguish them from the musicians and their helpers. Blite had been very co-operative about the specialists, recognising the advantages at once. There were eight of them at strategic points. They could cover all the potential sniper positions from where they stood, as well as a large portion of the audience and orchestra. They were in touch with each other and Campbell through discreet radios and concealed receivers.

A flurry of activity at the main door announced the arrival of the soloists. Octavia Anderson came in shaking rain from a large golf umbrella. She was laughing; Nightingale was with her. She was dressed warmly in fine black, woollen trousers and a fluffy cashmere sweater the colour of fire, from which her compelling ivory face rose surrounded by a mist of black hair. Raindrops sparkled in delicate curls as she moved forward under the bright spotlights that lit the nave and dais. Her height and strange beauty made her an imposing figure despite her deceptive slenderness. But what held and captivated every person in the building, as she walked the long length of the aisle, was her presence. The artist in her made even this small progression a performance that reached out to capture her impromptu audience. Octavia went straight to the conductor and greeted him like an old friend. He, honoured and flattered, fussed around her, kissing her hand, holding her delicate long fingers in his own podgy fists as he introduced her to the leader and the choir director, his standing immediately enhanced in their eyes. There was a flutter of welcoming applause from the choir and then, as the other soloists filed in and took their places, an expectant hush.

'I didn't know she was so beautiful.' The ACC addressed no one in particular. Fenwick, choking on memories of moonlight and fire, could not bring himself to answer.

The full rehearsal got underway with relatively little fuss, each soloist conveying a professional confidence that helped calm amateur nerves. Next to Octavia the mezzo-soprano looked impossibly tiny – five foot two, with a cherubic face and wicked grin. Her light brown curls looked flat and dull beside the soprano's. It was difficult to believe that she could produce a cathedral-size voice but her opening lines in the 'Kyrie' were magnificent.

The tenor was clean-shaven, Germanic, expressionless until he started to sing and then his pale blue eyes were incandescent. Beside him the bass redressed the balance of the quartet, a fitting counterpoint to Octavia, standing shoulders above the others on the conductor's right as he faced the choir. Well over six foot, African-American, the bass's powerful face and barrel chest hinted at a voice to command armies. Like Octavia, he barely referred to the music he held incidentally before him. Instead he gazed out over the empty chairs, obviously impatient for the full performance to begin.

Fenwick noticed that the ACC had unconsciously sat down in front of a tight group of police officers and was listening intently to the music. The chairman of the organising committee bustled up to him with two libretti, one of which he thrust at Fenwick, the other at his superior.

'Here, have a libretto. It'll help you to appreciate the music,' he whispered. The expression on Fenwick's face must have told its own story for he added: 'Don't worry if you can't read music, the words will give you enough clues – and you need to understand what they're saying to appreciate it fully.' A crescendo from orchestra and choir drowned out Fenwick's answer; the ACC was surreptitiously flailing through the pages, hoping to guess at his place.

'It seems almost operatic in style.' The ACC was now ignoring the libretto and had discarded it beneath his chair.

'Oh, it is, yes,' replied the chairman. 'Not really a sacred piece at all. It's true Verdi bel canto, a real challenge for the soloists.'

Fenwick could see the ACC struggling for a reply and enjoyed the moment.

'Bel canto?'

'Yes, you know. How can I put it? It means that somehow the voices are above and beyond the orchestra; they are more than just a vocal instrument, they become the heart of the piece.'

Another loud interlude from the choir drowned out the chairman's hushed tones but he chatted on. Fenwick tuned out, leaving the ACC to nod occasionally as an indication of shared understanding. He tuned in again at the mention of Octavia's name. The chairman's repetitive style of conversation made it easy to follow what he had been saying.

'. . . yes, very lucky. It's amazing that she said yes, amazing. Worth all the last-minute hassle and worry. It's such a challenging soprano part, very challenging; so few performers can manage it, particularly the "Libera Me", with any credibility . . .'

'Excuse me?' If it concerned Octavia, he wanted to know.

'Here, I'll show you. Page . . . 192; there, see that octave jump to a top B flat – and *pianissimo* too. Amazing, *pianissimo*. It's worth listening out for.'

Fenwick scanned the page, following the man's stubby finger. There was a line marked 'SOP' which he guessed was Octavia's, the soprano soloist. It looked very simple. Elsewhere the musical notes dashed across the pages like swarms of ants, scurrying up and down an orderly grid that strained to impose structure on apparent chaos.

'A Requiem Mass, what is it?'

'A mass for the dead really.'

Could Rowland have known the relevance of this piece or was it simply a macabre coincidence? The chairman's chilling words provided yet further confirmation of his own belief that the killer would use the performance to strike.

'And what exactly is a mass for the dead?'

'Well. They vary but they tend to beg for God's mercy and the forgiveness of our sins. Some tend to be more optimistic than others.'

'And this one?'

'Not very hopeful at all, I'm afraid. Tremendously powerful, of course – very powerful – and the music is so glorious one tends to forget the words at times. But it starts with a prayer for eternal rest and ends with, what I think is, a desperate plea for mercy. It's moving, very moving.'

Fenwick turned to the last few pages, tracing the chorus's final lines. At the last, only the soprano was left, singing a pitiable solo as the music died. The chairman smiled at him.

'Yes, it's that soprano part again. She voices all our hopes and fears throughout. It ends on her final prayer.'

The conductor tapped his baton on his music stand and, without hesitation, launched choirs, orchestra and soloists into their first full rehearsal of the whole piece. Staring down half the length of the nave, Fenwick winced at Anderson's vulnerability; her bright red jumper marking the bull's-eye in the middle of a massed human target. Nightingale had moved to sit just below the dais, facing out over the rows of empty seats. She looked heavier than usual, a puffer jacket emphasising the bulk of the bullet-proof vest he guessed she was wearing.

He tried to assess, yet again, the points of maximum risk for Octavia. He thought it unlikely she would be attacked while sitting down. Even though the soloists were positioned at the front of the raised platform, from most angles, other than directly to her right, she was partially screened by the others whilst sitting.

There was the remaining possibility of a bomb or a grenade, of course, but he doubted it. Too many others would die, the structural impact would be impossible to estimate – meaning such an attack would be potentially hazardous for the bomber – and most of all, it was just too clumsy. It lacked style. The most likely weapons were a knife or gun.

A knife was consistent with the early deaths. Anderson could be stabbed as she walked to or from the platform, or as she arrived outside. But Rowland would have to sneak up close to her, to work his way through the massive security cordon. He couldn't be sure that he would reach her, and capture would be inevitable. Fenwick dismissed the idea of a knife attack.

A gun then. He had assumed all along that this was most likely. Rowland was a marksman, familiar and expert with most types of personal hand gun and rifle. There were dozens of places he could site himself to have a clear shot whilst she was standing. The triforium was favourite but that had been checked and triple-checked. And Rowland's cache of guns had been discovered, which meant that he'd need to bring his weapon with him. There were armed policemen on both sides, three trumpeters and the sound man. Their instruments and equipment had all been searched and nothing looked suspicious.

Fenwick remembered that he still hadn't heard whether they had confirmed the credentials of the remaining musicians and technicians, and signalled Cooper over to chase it up. The ACC had moved off to discuss tactics again with Blite and Campbell, and to agree the last round of checks.

The rehearsal was in full swing; the peaceful opening of Verdi's *Requiem* had finished. Fenwick sensed a tension in the choir sufficient to make him concerned. He was starting to move forward towards the dais when a wall of sound from the 'Dies Irae' hit him. Unified sound from over a hundred voices and a weight of sheer musical power rolled across the cathedral. The hair on his arms, legs and neck rose in the unearthly charge. He found that he was holding his breath.

The music echoed up to the vaulted roof, rolling back down the walls, swirling around pillars. And Fenwick stood in the midst of it surrounded, all senses drowning in the unearthly sound. He had never had an experience like it. He felt vulnerable yet elated and somehow wildly excited. Through the music around him he felt connected to life, part of something massive of which he could only perceive a tiny fraction.

The sound moved on and the sensation passed. Repeats of

the chorus were small aftershocks and merely lapped his senses as he opened the libretto he had rolled tightly in one hand. Stunned, he fumbled through the pages to find the words that had inspired such creative genius.

From the sheer density and excitement of notes on the page he guessed where they might be. Eventually he found the chorus line and the words in the original Latin with a faint translation underneath: '*dies irae* ... day of wrath'. He was chilled by the coincidence. Had Rowland known his music, he could not have chosen a more appropriate piece in which to attempt his murder.

As the music moved on, he found more and more relevance in the words: '*What a trembling shall possess them, when the Judge shall come to judgement, searching all the souls before Him!*' First the bass, then the mezzo-soprano stood up to sing of death, terror and anger, before the repeat of the 'Dies Irae', just as loud and terrifying filled the hollows and tombs of that holy place again.

The frail mezzo-soprano stood again, on her own as the chorus seated themselves. Her beautiful, mellow voice reached even the distant walls. Used now to the way music and words were written down, Fenwick followed her solo with little difficulty. '*What shall I plead in my anguish? Who will help me ...*' Beside her to her right, now standing, Octavia's face went from ivory to bone white as she joined in: '*Who will help me?*' she sang, her voice rich, velvety, pure. Even the chattering police officers turned to listen. She stared out, over the empty seating, never glancing at the music in her hands. The terror in her was obvious as she stood in her blazing red and black. Below her, Nightingale's tension was palpable as her hands locked together and her knuckles showed white as she tried to stop them shaking.

Then the chorus stood and the tension was broken again as Octavia and listeners lost themselves in the music. Around him Fenwick felt everyone return to the tasks they had left moments before. The rehearsal went on and on; the chorus stood then sat; the soloists as a quartet or singly rose and settled as the waves of music carried them forward. At no other point did Octavia again appear so isolated and vulnerable and they all, bar Fenwick and Nightingale, started to relax.

Fenwick took a walk outside in the damp afternoon, too taut still to eat or focus, frustrated that Blite and Campbell clearly found him superfluous. He had become so accustomed to the background noise of the rehearsal from the cathedral that the silence outside disconcerted him. He walked back inside, assuming that the rehearsal was over.

He had been mistaken. Within the cathedral the chorus was standing, singing softly with the orchestra whispering accompaniment. A single soloist stood before them, her brightness a glowing contrast to their blacks and blues.

The chairman beckoned him over and, in a barely audible voice, told him: 'This is the part I told you about, the "Libera Me". Here, look, they're on page 178.'

Octavia was barely breathing the words: '*Trembling, frightened, full of despair am I, full of terror and great fear, I am trembling with terror.*' She was staring straight at Fenwick as she sang, her eyes dark and wet even at this great distance. Then, one final time, the chorus slammed into the silence with the 'Dies Irae', beating out the terrible warning as Octavia simply stood there transfixed and waiting. Fenwick started forward, to be closer to her, to show her he was there closeby, but the chairman grabbed his arm, his podgy hand surprisingly strong:

'Wait. She has more yet. And that top B flat I told you about. It'll come any minute.'

Sure enough the music died and Octavia's solo filled the ancient cathedral again. Poignant, heartfelt, a prayer for peace repeated again. Hers was the single voice, pleading forgiveness for the frailty and failures of man, begging God for another chance and understanding. To the audience, Fenwick knew, she would be giving the performance of their lives; to the unseen slaughterer, her would-be assassin, she was pleading for her life.

The rehearsal ended in complete silence. Then the the choir and orchestra started laughing and clapping the soloists, praising themselves, idolising Octavia. She had been magnificent, not only her voice but also the emotional quality of her singing had stirred them all. She stepped down from the dais and looked solemnly at Nightingale, who still sat, immobile in her chair, transfixed by the performance.

The man who ran at Octavia from behind a knight's tomb was a blur in her peripheral vision. Nightingale was on her feet, leaping across the few short yards to intercept him before anyone else had even turned around. She caught him in a flying rugby tackle, pinning his legs and throwing him to the ground with the force of her momentum. The long black object he had been holding outstretched toward Octavia slithered across the marble floor to rest against the platform.

There were shouts from all around her as she felt the thud of feet vibrating through the floor and into her prone body where she lay across him. She grabbed the man's arms, pinning them behind his shoulders, and rested her weight on her knee wedged into his back. No matter how hard she tried, she could not stop it shaking violently in the long seconds before the others reached her.

Three officers appeared, guns drawn and primed, all pointing at the skull of the spread-eagled man. He was trying to shout but his face was pressed hard into the unyielding floor, muffling and twisting his words.

One of the policemen fumbled in the man's jacket and withdrew his wallet. 'It says he's Jason MacDonald, Press. What have you got to say for yourself?'

Two pairs of hands dragged him ungently to his feet. There was a trace of blood at the corner of his mouth which he wiped away gingerly with the back of his hand.

'For God's sake! What the bloody hell are you doing? I only wanted a photograph!'

'Then why were you hiding away like that?'

'I wanted a bloody exclusive!'

'You wanted to frighten her!' Nightingale was enraged. 'You wanted to scare her into saying something that would give you a headline.' MacDonald's eyes shifted sideways.

'Jason MacDonald? You're the one who tried to release the story about our search here last week.' A musty tweed jacket heralded the arrival of Cooper on the scene. He advanced to within inches of MacDonald's shoulder, closely followed by Blite and Campbell.

'Yes, hello. We meet again.'

'Either this is a very elaborate cover, sir. Or he is who he says he is. I met MacDonald here last week.'

After a brief consultation with the editor of the *Chichester Times*, Blite was reasonably certain that the man was insignificant but he needed the distraction cleared out of the way. He also wanted to find out how the searchers had missed him.

'Constable, call the local station. Warn them we're bringing a suspect in for questioning. Ask them to hold him until we get there this evening.'

'What!? You can't do that. I'm a member of the Press. I have my rights.'

'Indeed you do, Mr MacDonald. And I have mine. You are being arrested for breach of the peace and will be held pending release by the magistrate tomorrow morning. Thank you, Constable. Please take him away.'

A further, vigorous sweep of the cathedral and precinct found nothing. But for Fenwick it failed to remove the memory of Octavia's petrified face turning helplessly from her 'assailant', to Nightingale, and back to him. She was resting now before dressing for the evening. It was five o'clock. Nightingale was with her.

CHAPTER FORTY-SEVEN

It had been a struggle to eat even a spoonful of the smoked salmon, lightly creamed tagliatelle and spinach purée that her maid had prepared for her but Octavia literally forced the food down. Experience had taught her that a sustaining meal was essential before a performance. Others starved themselves, claiming that food depressed their voice but she knew that a little of the right food, a few hours before she sang, added power and gave her stamina.

Now she was resting, pink and tingling from an excellent shower, wrapped in Nightingale's warm dressing gown, her own being too light for the miserable evening. There was a constant drizzle outside bringing an early dusk. She had to be in the cathedral in a tiny room they had put aside for her, by six o'clock. The performance was due to start at seven and the police wanted her safely installed before the crowds arrived. The journey from the hotel she was staying in would take less than ten minutes.

She couldn't make herself think about the afternoon. She had had a superstitious faith in Fenwick, believing he could protect her from Rowland, whatever the odds. Their animal couplings had all been part of her sacrifice to that belief; if they did this together he could not possibly let her die. Now she knew differently. He was no longer in charge. Despite all his personal efforts and the dozens of police, someone had got through. And where one had been another could follow. Still she had been insistent that the performance should go on, and the ACC had agreed. Life had to go on and he still seemed to judge the threat as small. He just couldn't believe that Rowland could or would strike in such a public and well-guarded place.

Anderson shuddered and wrapped the warm gown more closely around her bare, white shoulders. It was time to dress – to prepare for the evening. Her maid had set her hair exquisitely and it was cushioned as her head rested above the pillows. The mass of blue-black waves had been disciplined into glistening coils that perched securely on top of her head, elongating her white neck and accentuating the porcelain fineness of her neck and jaw.

She always did her own make-up, knowing precisely how to enhance her startling eyes – widening them, creating infinitive opportunities for dramatic expression. Normally she needed no cosmetics on her skin for a simple recital, but tonight she had to resort to light rose blusher along her cheekbones and a faint brush of powder to eliminate the awful pallor she saw in the mirror.

She was ready to dress. A long mirror had been placed in the bedroom to help her. Standing, she let Nightingale's turquoise robe fall to her feet and stood naked before her own reflection. Delicately, curiously, she ran her fingers over her shoulders, gently over her breasts, stopping to cup them and brush the nipples before tracing the tips of her fingernails down her flat stomach to her thighs.

She opened her legs slightly, fascinated to see her own red-tipped fingers stroke and tease. One hand slipped between her thighs, but then she stopped herself. She wanted to trap the sexual energy and tension inside to release later in her performance. From experience, she knew the tension would add a passion that communicated beyond her voice.

Octavia started to lay out the clothes she would wear. Each item was pressed to perfection. It occurred to her briefly as she pulled gull's-egg-grey silk camiknickers up to her waist that the next hands to remove them could be a pathologist's. Memories of a primary school teacher's voice came back to her – 'remember to wear clean knickers, you never know what might

404

happen to you.' The memory of her early childhood made her smile, not shiver. Her life had been one long performance, why should it not continue beyond her death?

Her slip matched the knickers. She wore no stockings, preferring to feel the raw silk against her waxed legs. There was a tap at the door. 'Ten minutes, madam.'

'Right. I'm nearly ready.'

She stepped into her dress. It was a shocking, flaming red hourglass; wide, structured wings fanned out from her waist curving above long, skin-tight sleeves at her shoulders. The front was cut low and straight across the rise of her breasts; the skirts flared from a waist that was sculpted to look tiny but allowed a deceptively large room for breath. A wide train fell from her shoulders, beneath the stiffened raised collar formed by the wings as they joined at the back.

The effect was stunning. Her white neck rose in a slender marble column from the stiff red petals, her head poised centrally above the architecture of her costume like the curving stamen of a hibiscus. She elected to wear no necklace but spiked ruby and diamond drops into her ears before finally placing a matching ring on the third finger of her left hand. Without a further glance, she extinguished the blaze of material beneath a heavy black opera cloak and left the room.

Jason MacDonald had been an unwelcome and unnecessary diversion for Blite's team and the subsequent inch-by-inch search of the cathedral stretched nerves to breaking point. Up in the gallery, the trumpeters and sound man, who had been engaged in a silent territorial battle from the beginning, vented their combined spleen on the backs of the unfortunate officers endeavouring to crawl all over them. When they attempted to dismantle the music stands for the third time that day Cooper had to step in to quell a small riot.

Rowland, watching the débâcle in relative comfort, found it all amusing. True, he had yet to assemble his weapon; true, it was a far less fine instrument than his original; true, he would be under the curious gaze of several players for most of the time which would make manoeuvring difficult. But he remained confident. He was an excellent shot; his escape route was planned and, above all, he had thus far escaped detection for five hours. With the time left to the performance counted in minutes, there was little risk the police would now discover him.

His final problem was to decide when to strike. He thumbed through the score in his hands casually, looking for the soprano line all the time. He was amazed at the appropriateness of her words which spelt out her guilt for all to hear. There was a strong temptation to leave it all to the end – so pathetic were her closing moments – but then, that was too high a risk. He flicked back, looking for the moment – then his eyes found the words, saw she would be standing proud in front of the choir, and it was decided.

Fenwick was running through his own final checklist with Cooper; there were minutes to go before Octavia and the other soloists arrived. Already, early birds in the audience were taking their places. They would have a longer wait than they anticipated as the start time would be pushed back to allow for the impact of greater security.

His men were scrutinising faces as they passed, keeping the admissions in orderly rows. It didn't comfort Fenwick. He was certain that Rowland had already arrived.

'Have we cross-checked the names and addresses of all the choir and orchestra yet?'

'We're still twenty short. You wouldn't believe how many are ex-directory or have no driving licences.'

'Well get on with it.' Fenwick caught his sergeant's fleeting look. 'I know it's probably redundant but it gives the ACC's extra men something to do. Right, what else? The recording company; what about them? Have you checked the sound man's credentials?'

'The letterhead's OK and Dalton, the bloke that signed it, works for them, but we can't trace him. He's been uncontactable all day. But we've found his secretary and she says it looks like his signature.'

'Well keep on it – tell whoever you're got in the gallery to keep their eyes on him and the trumpeters, they're ideally placed.'

'Yes, sir. But we've been over their equipment time and again. There's nothing remotely resembling a gun up there or bullets – believe me.'

'How about a blow pipe?' With a sinking heart Cooper realised Fenwick was only half joking and set off once more to order a final check in the triforium. It would not be pleasant.

Fortunately, the rain had eased and few of the audience had brought umbrellas. However, there were still enough to challenge the rudimentary raffle ticket system that had been set up to manage their collection and it looked as if it would be a lottery when the time came to return the right accessories to their owners at the end of the performance.

The chairman of the organising committee bustled up to Fenwick. 'Chief Inspector, I've reserved you a seat right at the front. Here's your special edition programme.'

'Thank you, sir, but I won't be sitting there. Some of the ACC's officers are in the front row already. I'll be keeping an eye on things from back here.'

'You really won't enjoy the performance as much from there, you know.'

'Unfortunately, I'm not here to enjoy the performance, sir.'

Rowland settled comfortably to wait. The performance was delayed but he had expected that, given the security. All his equipment was to hand; he could assemble his weapon in less than ninety seconds and only in the final fifteen would even the most diligent observer recognise it for what it was. It would take him no more than a further fifteen seconds to aim and fire; a danger time of half a minute maximum.

If necessary, he would disable or kill anyone who got in his way quickly and quietly, just using his hands.

His escape route was simple but it would expose him to any hostile fire there might be for about fifteen seconds. There was no other option, though. The triforium provided an excellent vantage point but the stairs leading to it were narrow and easy to block off. He had no choice but to use a rope over the rail down into the nave. In the field it would have been suicidal but here, with surprise to his advantage and the reluctance of the police to open fire, he stood a chance. They were not used to bold, experienced and above all fast protagonists; he had found that out in London. And if they did succeed in blocking the exit, he would simply take a hostage. On balance, he felt the odds of a clean escape were fair given the confusion he would be leaving behind and police hesitation to pull a trigger.

In the cathedral, the audience was unsure whether to applaud the arrival of the conductor and then the soloists. No one started to clap and instead, the vast nave settled into silence. The choir stood, children in the front rows. Fenwick sat down.

The opening bars were so quiet that the sound crept up on him before he had noticed. '*Requiem, requiem aeternam.*'

It had started – so normally and peacefully he was, for a moment, taken by surprise. He saw Octavia, dressed as a target again, sitting on the raised dais at the front of the choir. What he took for Nightingale's head, rested beside her at knee height. Around the cathedral he could see officers, watching the watchers. By craning his neck upwards he made out the truncated shapes of uniformed and armed police side by side around the triforium. Immediately above him, their faces obscured by the wooden railings of the gallery, he could see the trumpeters resting their instruments on their knees.

The body of the sound recordist was hidden but he could see his feet and the woolly microphone peeking out of the woodwork to capture the music. It all appeared quite normal. In the cathedral, the first solo concluded without incident. He looked down and found he had twisted his programme into a tight, sweaty paper baton. He forced himself to smooth it out and flicked through the pages with a nervous twitch. He noticed Octavia's picture appearing two or three times.

There was an interview with Octavia at the front of the programme – looking backwards to her schooldays, looking forwards to her next tour and recording contract. Above him, the trumpeters responded to their cue from the bass and, in the words of the libretto, called the dead from slumber. Nothing else happened. She still sat there, calm, stunning the audience with her presence and the power of her voice every time she sang.

As the performance continued smoothly, with no interruptions or suspicious developments, Fenwick tasted relief and defeat and started to anticipate the sharp barbs of ridicule that would be his when the performance concluded and over one hundred officers made their way home. He made a quick calculation and estimated the probable cost of the police effort over the weekend; it was enough to blow their budget for the quarter and he would undoubtedly be held responsible. And yet he had been so sure that Rowland would strike today and he was tormented by the idea that he was still missing some vital clue to the man's whereabouts.

Pushing the growing prospect of failure to one side, Fenwick went back over the events of the past few days – his conversations with Octavia, the checks they had done on all the musicians, the endless searches of the cathedral. Instinct told him that Rowland should be in the building. To have avoided the performance completely suggested a caution and infinite patience he doubted the killer still possessed. Despite his army training Rowland was a hunter working solo for nearly nine months. He had positioned himself close enough to smell his prey; it was unlikely that he would turn away now. Above all, Fenwick's sixth sense for danger told him that Rowland was there, that something would happen.

Octavia was standing in front of him again now, a perfect target, but nothing happened. Around him thirty trained pairs of eyes scanned performers and audience constantly for signs of threat but obviously could see nothing unusual. The conviction that he had missed something vital grew as the seconds stretched to minutes. He went over in his mind every report that he could remember, silently replaying Octavia's statements. Something was out of balance, a small fact was sitting out of true and it pricked his brain each time he passed over it, but he could not see it.

A slight grating noise from above irritated Fenwick as he tried to concentrate. Octavia's voice was echoing back from the high vaulted roof. He turned over the pages in his programme to find her photograph. His sweat had stained the paper and there was black ink on his palms. One page had to be peeled away from his right hand where he'd gripped it so tightly it had stuck fast. As he focused on the programme notes, Octavia's photograph looked up at him, her smudged words strung out beside it: 'I'm particularly looking forward to my next tour. It will be the most demanding I've done. And of course, when I return, I shall be starting on a major recording contract. As it will be the very first personal compilation, I'm obviously being careful about choosing the right company . . .'

A memory of a forgotten conversation with Octavia unfolded in Fenwick's mind. They had been talking about her career and she had mentioned the recording contract. She had emphasised how important it was, the money it could mean. Would she have sanctioned a one-off recording of this concert right now? What was it she had said? Something about exclusivity. Fenwick looked around desperately for the chairman but he was in the front row. Could he risk complete disruption and potential disgrace on a hunch?

Above in the triforium, Rowland removed the five simple parts of the weapon smoothly from their casings and felt wrappings, his movements screened by a stack of equipment studded with meaningless flashing lights. People expected there to be odd bits of metal and lengths of wire around a sound technician; each individual element was innocent enough. The long sound boom that peeked from the wooden railing provided a basis for medium-range sights, perfectly aligned on the soprano's chest based on measurements he had gathered during the rehearsal and week before. It had been very helpful to be able to insist on knowing precisely where each soloist would stand as part of his preparations. The far sight extended by millimetres from the fluffy wool muffler; the other appeared to be a random lump of solder on the boom itself.

His hands worked smoothly by touch, his eyes continuing their playful charade of checking dial readings and sound levels. Only when the last piece clicked into place did he dare check that all was ready. He looked down and pulled back the wire, setting it in place to be released by a hair trigger. The bolt lay at the bottom of a tobacco tin cushioned by Old Virginia and Green Rizlas. The tin had never been searched.

Rowland prized off the lid, annoyed by the slight 'pluck' as the air-tight seal broke. One of the trumpeters turned and glared at him swiftly. His fingers rummaged in the moist tobacco, found the smooth metal shank and traced along to the hardened steel tip. There were two bolts in the tin. He removed the first and laid it gently on the discarded felt by his side, the other he left on top of the tin by his hand. It was unlikely that he would have need of or time to use the second but he was always careful.

Rowland looked around him. There were six other people within immediate sight in the gallery; three trumpeters and three policemen – one by the door on his far right, one behind the musicians that were seated between him and the door and the other to his left at the end of the gallery. No one noticed his covert gaze although the police were looking around constantly, trying to keep alert during the performance. Despite their firearms training Rowland could tell that not one of them had come under fire before. It was his biggest advantage. Their inexperience would make them hesitate before pulling a trigger no matter what their training. He would have a significant tactical advantage.

Below him the mezzo-soprano began another solo; Rowland checked his score, it was the 'Liber scriptus'. It was all so macabrely appropriate: '*Open lies the book before them, where all records have been written.*' It had been the diary that had finally confirmed his suspicion – aroused by that awful letter from the past, his uncle's dying words laying on him a doom far worse than any he could have imagined. He had sought revenge and in his first blind hatred, Deborah Fearnside had died. Hers had been the most difficult death, perhaps the least justified. Her guilty memories babbled out in a desperate attempt to save her life only hinted, didn't prove, what had happened.

And then Katherine Johnstone had died. He had been lucky, finding her diaries. Lucky that she had revealed so much in her adolescent scribblings. Three pages had told him all that he needed to know. He had kept them folded tight in his wallet, taking them out occasionally in moments of compulsive curiosity and disgust. Unconsciously, his hand moved to press them against his chest.

The mezzo-soprano sang on: '*What was hidden is uncovered. Naught forgotten, naught unpunished.*' They were nearly all punished now. Leslie Smith was as good as dead. He had mistimed his acceleration, skidding slightly in the rain, but it didn't matter. She had been a bit player, guilty only by association. Now there was only Anderson left. He could feel his anger grow again, blossoming in his chest. It was so fierce he wondered that it did not show, angry, red, glowing from the gallery.

There were only moments left before he would strike. Below him the chorus whispered the awful 'Dies Irae' with growing menace and the orchestra echoed their theme. He had the timings from the rehearsals noted on every page. In seconds they would storm in again in a sudden crescendo, before all sound died and they left the four soloists standing alone at the front of the dais.

Fenwick pushed his way to the side-room that had become the police centre of operations. There was no one there that he knew and Campbell turned his shoulder to whisper more closely into a hand-held radio mike. Fenwick ignored him and whispered urgently to the plain-clothes man huddled over the screens.

'The letter from the recording company, has it been validated yet?'

The man looked bemused, then indifferent. He shrugged.

'For God's sake man, this is urgent. Where is it?' Something of his near panic communicated itself.

'All the checklists and paperwork's on the desk over there.' He pointed to an old deal table in the corner, covered with forms, two laptop computers and a stack of hymn books. Fenwick nearly despaired but then he realised there was simple order in the chaos. A list of names, heavily scored through, was attached to a clipboard – letters, faxes and returned phone calls in a wire tray beside it. Fenwick found the letter from the recording company in moments. There was no indication that the director who had sent it had returned their calls. He looked down the list. On the second page he found the sound man's name – it had not been ticked off, but then neither had several others.

He stood irresolute in the small room. Beyond the walls a woman's voice sounded pure and distant.

Fenwick couldn't work out where they were in the piece, whether it was Octavia singing or not. He stepped outside. A small figure in blue was standing alone in front of the choir. Relief flooded through him but was then washed away in turn by a wave of fear. His instincts were screaming at him to do something but he was confused. Was it just his screwed up emotions towards the woman destroying his judgement? All around him people were calm, sitting listening to a glowing performance, oblivious to everything but the glory of the music and the magnificence of the surrounding architecture. He could see police officers standing quietly to the sides of and above the nave. They appeared calm, alert yes, but not disturbed.

And then the quiet rumble of the 'Dies Irae' hit him, like distant thunder warning of a storm of gigantic proportions. He had no view of the triforium from where he was standing, as the narrow passage ran directly above his head. He risked audience displeasure and stepped out into the walkway that had been created halfway across the nave to allow access to the tightly packed seats.

There was a muffled 'pop' from above him. A woman tutted as he craned his neck upwards until he could see the sound boom and a man's foot and calf. The technician had changed his position. He looked down at the letter of authority still clenched in his hand and tried to remember Octavia's words. It had been something about her tour, the importance of the recording contract that would follow it.

As the 'Dies Irae' rose to crash around him, he suddenly remembered: 'My agent and I have it all planned: massive high-quality public performances for the next three months and absolutely *no* recordings – it's a condition of all my contracts.'

There was no way she would have agreed to a recording of this performance and Katherine Johnstone would have been experienced enough not to organise it without her permission. There could be no recording deal – even the chairman of the organising committee had been unsure as to how it had been arranged, and surprised when the letter turned up.

Fear became certainty as Fenwick started running towards the staircase that led to the triforium, the sound of his feet lost in the noise from the chorus. But the sudden movement caught the eyes of the hidden watchers and they immediately became alert, tracing his every move, guns trained.

He reached the stairs as the music died behind him. He could hear the rustle as the choir sat, the expectant murmur as the soloists stood. The steep spiral staircase slowed him down, breaking his rhythm. At the top, the policeman by the door turned and tried to stop him even as Fenwick thrust his warrant card into the man's face. He stumbled, half caught by the man who still insisted on blocking his path.

Octavia was standing proud at the front of the platform. Even at this distance her presence could be felt. Rowland slipped the crossbow bolt into the runner and eased the weapon into position. For a few brief seconds, he would be exposed as he took careful aim. The commotion at the door worried him not at all, his only focus now the woman in red before him. He aligned the sights and took up the pressure on the trigger. In a casual, smooth movement he found his mark and fired.

A huge weight fell on his shoulders. At first he thought a piece of equipment had overbalanced on top of him, then he realised it was a man. Below him he heard screams and cries and despite his extreme jeopardy he smiled. He had no handgun, the searches had made that impossible, but there were always his knives. The man pinned his arms to his sides from behind. From the corner of his eye he could see his uniform. With all his strength he thrust his elbow into the man's midriff and felt the gust of air from his injured lungs on the back of his neck. He found the flick knife strapped to his chest. It was small but sufficient. With casual elegance he drove it upwards under the man's ribcage, avoiding bone and twisting as he went. The bullet-proof vest offered no protection for a blade and the young officer, who less than a minute before had been standing bored and tired behind the trumpeters, died instantly.

Rowland tried to pull the knife from the dead man as he fell but it held fast. It was useless, he needed the other. Crouching in the shelter of railings, grateful for the useless panic of the musicians to his right, he spared a few seconds to think and plan. To his left an armed officer was almost on him, prevented from firing because of the danger to the civilians around him.

By the doorway, another armed policeman had drawn his weapon and was desperately trying to aim across the heads of the trumpeters. Beside him another man was fighting his way through the crush to reach him. Rowland recognised Fenwick immediately. He mouthed the man's name across the space, meeting his eyes for the first time.

Rowland's route to the stairs was blocked, he could run the gauntlet of the long gallery but already others were running to block it off. He had this throwing knife left but couldn't waste that. He glanced down below into the terrified audience. If he could find time to skim down the rope he had ready, he could pick one of them for a hostage.

The armed policeman to his right was on him, gun held close for a body shot. So casually that it could almost have been in slow motion, Rowland ducked, reached out and broke the man's arm with an audible crack. Standing he lifted the agonised man and threw him heavily into the path of the others that were fast closing on him. He lurched for the rope tied to a thick wooden pillar and pushed the length of it over the edge. Still crouched he swung his body over the railing ready to grab hold of the rope with his spare hand.

Rowland never quite made it. As his fingers brushed the rough cord there was a sharp retort from behind him, followed immediately by two more. Pain flared across his back and into his arms. His fingers refused to close on the rope and he fell, in a clumsy half-open somersault on to the chairs below.

It was an unlucky fall. The iron-framed chairs, vacated moments before, were rigid and unyielding, putting yet more strain on his spine as he landed hard across them. His back snapped. The last feeling he had was a sickening pop as he felt his legs and pelvis drift away from him and his body became entangled in the metal legs and spars as he lay on the marble floor. Within seconds he was surrounded by armed police.

Rowland could see his hands twitching uncontrollably and his own blood washing across the floor in a delicate stream. The pain was fading as he lay there and that worried him. Pain was a friend to the living. It's alternative, the intense icy cold and blackness that threatened to engulf him, were the harbingers of death. He tried to say something and heard the air rattle in his throat. The sound was familiar. He knew with certainty now that he was dying. Still he struggled to remain conscious and to speak.

'Fenwick.' The name came out as a hiss. The barrel at his head jabbed into his skull and he was told to 'shut the fuck up'. He looked up into the faces above him and recognised them at once. These were not beat bobbies deluded by flack jackets and intensive training into the belief that they could handle guns. These were professionals. Someone, somewhere had wanted him dead, not arrested, and they were succeeding. Still, he had to speak to Fenwick, to know before he died whether he had succeeded and that Octavia was dead.

'Fenwick!' The word died in a gurgle as the sole of a boot found his throat, the pressure choked the air from his lungs. He didn't take it personally; someone was just following orders. Black spots were breaking before his eyes and muffled static filled his ears so that he didn't hear the argument or struggle as e man fought through the armed ring to reach him.

'Let me through. Get the paramedics in here. For God's ke, he's not going to attack you now, he needs medical tention.' Fenwick knelt carefully beside the dying man, trying avoid the spreading puddle of blood around him. Slowly, owland's eyes focused for the last time, finding Fenwick's ce. When he spoke his voice was a ghastly bubbling whisper.

'Is she dead . . . ? I must know, is she dead?'

Fenwick's eyes gave him his answer.

'Listen.' He struggled to continue. 'It isn't murder . . . It's stice . . . You'll see . . . In my pocket.'

Pink froth bubbled at the corner of his mouth. He struggled find his final words. 'It's up to you now, to finish it.'

Rowland's head lolled sideways and his eyes glazed as his ody was gripped by a final seizure.

Gingerly, Fenwick lifted the bloodied jacket from the dead an's chest, millimetre by millimetre, half expecting some ooby trap to take his hand. In an inside pocket he found a slim eather wallet and four carefully folded pieces of paper. Both vere soaked with thick blood from an exit wound below Rowland's shoulder. He removed them carefully by their corners nd placed them in an evidence bag. He saw Cooper in the rowd and called him over. There was no way he was going to rust this evidence to these sudden strangers in the cathedral.

'Here, get these over to forensics. And Cooper, *I* want the eport on them both.'

Fenwick rose slowly, noticing the bloodstains on the knee of is trousers and jacket cuffs. Rowland lay in a twisted back flip n the floor, his arms flung out to either side, legs at impossible ngles. He was a big man grotesquely feeble in death. Fenwick urned his back on him without a second look.

He walked down the long aisle in the nave towards the dais vhere a small crowd had gathered. The ambulance had just irrived and Nightingale was being helped outside towards it. She was grey-faced with pain but calm. She tried to smile as Fenwick approached her but it didn't quite come off. He wanted o reach out and touch her – in comfort, sympathy, respect.

Instead he smiled back, gently touching the back of her han
Nightingale recognised the unfinished gesture.

'It's all right. I'm all right. Don't worry.'

'It was a very, very brave thing that you did. You're lucky
be alive.' He walked beside her to the open ambulance door
The paramedics had applied an emergency dressing to the dee
wound in her upper left arm but he could still see the tip of t
bolt sticking out through her jacket. She had been lucky; it ha
missed the main brachial artery by millimetres.

'I'll stop in at the hospital later. Take care.'

He walked back towards the cathedral. Inside, witnesses ha
been arranged into orderly groups and there was the characte
istic low buzz that came from organised mass interview
Octavia was nowhere to be seen. To his right he could see the
taking a stretcher up the twisting stairs of the triforium
retrieve the body of the dead constable. He was momentari
overcome by guilt, appalled at the thought of facing anoth
widow or mother at another service funeral. The operation ha
come close to embarrassingly public failure. Well, the AC
was the one who would have to do the explaining.

There was nothing he could do in the cathedral excep
commiserate with the ACC and Blite, which would be a
insensitive and stupid thing to do. The questions and recrimina
tions would start soon enough. A policeman was dead, tw
others injured, and the suspect killed – all in front of hundred
of traumatised witnesses. He was hugely relieved that th
operation had not been his, and then cursed himself for ever b
acknowledging that if it had been, perhaps they would all b
alive and uninjured right now.

Outside, the sky was on fire in the west as the sun finally se
Glowing embers flickered across dying vapour trails as the su
sank into deep ash-grey banks of cloud on the horizon. Flare
of crimson, red and orange ripped through the black thunde
heads into the dome of a royal-blue sky above. Within minute
the colours died leaving a flat, two-dimensional canvas, acros
which a strong wind was already dragging grubby fingers t
blur all traces of the sunset performance.

PART SIX

REQUIEM

Requiem aeternam dona eis,
Domine, et lux perpetua luceat eis.

*Rest and peace for ever, grant them rest and
  peace eternal,
And light for evermore shine down upon them,
  Lord Our God.*

CHAPTER FORTY-EIGHT

The enquiry into operation Knight Capture – as the efforts to catch Rowland in the aftermath of the London bombing had been named – was indeed bloody. There was a full internal inquiry and the press, relishing every moment of it, hounded police and investigators relentlessly. Fenwick was ordered to resume his sick leave immediately and banned from both Division and HQ until certified fit to return. He was interviewed at home early on and then again at regular intervals over the following weeks.

They pushed him hard on the details of the operation, almost begging him to criticise the ACC and DI Blite, but Fenwick held his silence. In the seemingly endless wait for the first interview he had gone over and over again in his mind the two questions that plagued him: if he had been in charge would things have been different? And if asked, how critical should he be of the officers who were in charge? The answers to both were intertwined.

If he had been left in charge the threat at the cathedral would have been taken far more seriously right from the beginning and every single person, bag, box and instrument would have been searched without exception. There would have been more men on the triforium and the credentials and identities of every person would have been checked and double-checked. And Rowland would still be alive. He wouldn't have relied on what he realised now was secret support from the MOD; he would have put his faith in his own men.

And therein lay the criticisms he could have levied at the ACC and Blite. They had both been cocky, overconfident and in his opinion, foolishly reliant on the specialists 'helpfully' provided by the Ministry. The extra police resources arrived far too late to be useful and the whole operation had been overcomplicated. But Fenwick decided to say none of this to the investigators as they conducted their post-mortem.

They never once asked him how and why he had made the connections between the murders, Carol Truman, Octavia Anderson and Victor Rowland. When he'd started to explain, assuming that they were curious to know all about Rowland's obsessive love for his young cousin and ever-consuming rage over her death, they brushed his words to one side. He was still unclear why Rowland had suddenly started out on a murderous rampage. The letter from his uncle had triggered it somehow but exactly why remained a mystery. But he was so used to the randomness of mental illness and its bizarre, tragic consequences, that the break in his chain of understanding didn't trouble him over much.

With the investigators, he stuck to the facts, never lied and limited his opinion to a point at which they once accused him of deliberately obstructing their inquiries. They clearly had a problem placing him in the order of events and were reluctant to exonerate him entirely.

An awkward compromise was achieved when they included a general criticism in their report of the decision to use 'unofficial advisers' with the consequence that their activities 'introduced additional areas of complexity to an operation that was already overengineered'.

The ACC was not, in the final report, censured, although there were times during the inquiry when it had appeared inevitable that he would be. In the end, the involvement of the military was held to blame by the police and the ACC's role in involving them obscured. Too many people wanted the ACC's career to flourish for too many different reasons and he survived. Although it was clear that he would have to work hard to re-create his image, the ACC was quietly relieved by the outcome.

Consequently, there was little odour to pass on and down to Fenwick.

The pinboard opposite Fenwick's desk had been emptied, its contents stacked in neat piles on a side table for sorting. Wearily he sat down to resume the task, his mind engaged elsewhere. Nightingale was making a good recovery. She was going to carry a nasty scar for the rest of her life but it looked as if there would be no permanent serious disability. Cooper had left for his annual leave; two weeks in Florida at his wife's insistence.

Fenwick hadn't seen Octavia since the night at the cathedral. He knew that she had cancelled the start of her tour on doctor's orders but other than that it was as if she had dropped out of his life. Everybody was treating the case as closed bar the recriminations. Even Fenwick had forgotten Rowland's dying instructions. His enforced home leave, the guilt that wouldn't leave him and the tension of walking the tight-rope of the inquiry had driven everything else about the case from his mind. He had retreated into the simple pleasures of his children's company and the reassuring chores of his home and garden.

Anne, the ever-efficient secretary, bustled in with a depressingly thick bundle of post, and a mug of excellent fresh coffee extracted with much patience and persuasion from the antiquated machine by her desk.

'Your post, Chief Inspector. There's a report from forensics in here, the usual internal circulars and memos and a great stack of papers from some legal firm in London; they've been screened.'

Fenwick picked up the forensic report with mild curiosity. It was an analysis of the contents of Rowland's pockets which had been given very low priority and he hadn't chased it. At the back there were photographs and a full transcript of the missing pages from Katherine Johnstone's diary that Rowland had kept in his wallet. He decided that he deserved a few minutes off to enjoy his coffee and, with the intention of creating a mild diversion, he started to read the transcription.

... June 19th ... so Frost told her off a real strip. I escaped! THANK GOD!! That's all I needed. Tomorrow we are off to sunny Dorset – the famous five on the trail again, with Les as Timmy the dog, of course, to follow us everywhere. Saw J. at the bus stop. I'm sure he smiled at me. S. was with me. I think he was jealous.

... June 22nd ... Octavia came round. I'm off school. Police *again*. I can't do this.

... June 27th ... I haven't written anything for days. I don't know if I can now but I've got to try. I have to let this all out *somewhere*, and, God knows, I can't tell anyone. Carol's dead. There, I've said it. Lovely, lovely Carol is dead. It's so unfair. Why *her* of all people?? She was so good. She never hurt anyone, she was so kind. Now she's gone and I never had a chance to tell her how special she was, how much she meant to me, to all of us.

The writing became more tiny and cramped as she squeezed her thoughts onto the small page in margins and corners.

God, if you're listening, I hate you right now and I don't know how to cope with that either. It was an accident. It must have been but I can't see how it happened. One minute they were together – Octavia and Carol – I saw them; the next Carol was gone. The police are coming round tomorrow – Mummy said there was no way they could talk to me again today. But I still don't know what to say.

... June 28th ... God I don't hate you any more but I need your help. I don't know what to do. Octavia's lying. I don't know why she is but I'm caught up in it now. She doesn't want them to know – says it would be misunderstood. But *I* don't understand and Leslie's lying too. We could all simply have told the truth – the police could've worked it out, they're not stupid. I've got a stinking cold but at least it means I'm not going to school tomorrow. S. came round. It was nice of him but it didn't help.

. . . July 2nd . . . I have decided to write here what really happened. I must say it somewhere and going to the police now after all this time is impossible. Anyway 'the truth is all relative' as Octavia would say, and what Leslie saw could be taken so wrong. For the record, this is my account of what happened before Carol died.

It was all normal until we were heading back to the coach in the afternoon. I was running ahead with the others. I've got long legs, I run better than them – Leslie was tagging along as always. Then she realised she'd lost her bracelet, the silver one that was a birthday present. She decided to go back along the path to try and find it. Leslie says she was going along in a sort of crouch. When she got to the top of the rise, she could see Carol and Octavia coming down the other side. She waved to them but they didn't see her. They seemed to be arguing – Carol kept running ahead and Octavia kept pulling her back, grabbing her by the arm. Leslie wasn't sure what to do so she walked down the path slowly – looking at each side among the bushes in case the bracelet had flown off as she ran.

As she got to the bottom of the slope, Leslie could hear raised voices. Carol was saying, 'Leave me alone, just leave me alone.' She could hear Octavia shouting at her, something like, 'You can't, you can't – it's mine!' It was embarrassing when she told me she'd been eavesdropping, the whole thing. She decided to head back to the bus – it was really late anyway. As she turned to go she heard them arguing still. Carol was saying something like, 'Let go, let me go. Don't be so stupid.' She might have been crying. Octavia sounded really angry, she was sort of like snarling and shouting at Carol, swearing at her, telling her she wouldn't let her ruin her life, not now she'd come that far. Leslie wondered if she should go back, Octavia isn't someone to argue with – and Carol sounded really upset. But she didn't. She just sort of stayed where she was. Perhaps if she'd gone back things would've been different but Octavia says not, that this sort of guilt is natural.

Leslie was still trying to work out what to do when there was a horrible noise – not a scream just an awful barking cry. She says it sounded like an animal being hurt. She started down the path at a run but then heard Octavia laughing, proper laughter, and there were footsteps on the path. She started running as fast as she could to be out of sight before they came up. Leslie says she thought it was all right. She honestly thought Carol was there, that they'd made up. But she wasn't of course. And she might have still been alive as I was running back to the coach – Octavia says she was – I'll never know.

I can't sleep at night. I'm ill. I think I may even be mad. Octavia's been wonderful. So calm and gentle. She's explained it all, said Leslie's not to blame, neither am I; there was nothing she or anyone could've done. Octavia has come round every day begging me not to blame her, not to blame myself. But I don't understand the laugh. When I mention it, she just looks at me as if I'm mad, says Leslie was imagining things. She heard it, though, I know she did. I just can't work out why Octavia was laughing.

Fenwick could remember every detail of the chalk bowl from which Carol Truman had fallen to her death. How the ledges fell away in tiers ready to break the most violent of falls. He recalled the debate they had had, their assumption that Carol had been climbing down as a prank when she had slipped and fallen to her death.

Anderson's statement was clear in his memory – she had been nowhere near Carol, she had said. It was lies. She had been with her friend seconds before her death, had left her on her own and had returned to the coach party with ready lies. Why?

He rehearsed again his thinking of the four alternative ways by which Carol had come to die: accident; suicide; murder by a stranger; murder by someone she had known. The more he'd learnt of Carol the more he'd suspected accident, before he had read Katherine's diary. Suicide was a possibility; Leslie had heard her crying but that appeared to be in argument not despair. And everyone spoke of her promise and her new plans.

That left murder. He was so close to murder, its smell, like that of formaldehyde, lurked in his hair and in the folds of his clothes. He felt it everywhere. Murder as a possibility existed after the elimination of the other alternatives. Over fifteen years on he couldn't eliminate them categorically and in the absence of clear motive there was no case in the bloody diary pages.

His coffee was cold and, as if in anticipation, the obliging secretary brought him in a new mug, freshly made from the antiquated coffee-maker she clung onto possessively by the side of her desk. He picked up the large brown envelope; it had been fully screened but he still tensed as he lifted the flap. Inside, there was a brief covering letter from a firm of London solicitors he had never heard of, explaining that they had been asked to forward to him the enclosures, unopened, in the event of their client's death.

Fenwick opened the inner envelope and removed the thick elastic band from around the bundled contents. On the top there was a sealed envelope addressed to him by title and name in a long sloping hand. The note inside was brief.

Fenwick, if you are reading this, then I am dead but if I am dead and you are still alive, there is a chance that she still has to be brought to justice.

These papers are my legacy to you. Use them as you will. I do not ask for, nor need, your understanding but I demand your judgement so that the dead may rest in peace.

Victor Rowland.

Fenwick pulled out the remaining contents, loosely tied together with old post office string, from an envelope post-marked from Melbourne and addressed to Rowland the previous year. The stamps had been removed. He sorted the papers into date order, most recent first. It was a letter from Rowland's uncle, Carol's father, dated September of the previous year, almost a year to the day of Rowland's death. He read it slowly, sipping his scalding coffee as he read and reread its tragic contents.

Dear Victor,

I write as I am dying. The priest here is taking down my words and once we have done and he swears on the Bible he has dispatched this to you, I will have only my confession left to say.

You are the last remaining relative and so must assume the burden of truth that I have carried alone for so many years. It is a curse. It killed my wife and has more slowly poisoned me. Had I been a stronger man, I would have ended it sooner but now, thank God, my torment will end soon enough.

It concerns your cousin Carol. My only, lovely daughter, my single child. So perfect and lovely we thought she was a gift from God. Too good for us, too beautiful to have been ours. But I drift. I do not have time to write of her life, merely the manner in which she met her death.

When you have read my words, and the papers I am sending you, you will wonder why I have kept silent for so many years. In truth, I am not sure. At first, when I knew, I was consumed by revenge. I wanted to return to England and fight for justice, but then my wife began to die and all my energy and money went in futile attempts to save her. Futile because she wanted to die and my ravings did her no good.

And then, after she was dead, I waited to die too. I was penniless, I drifted, waiting for the end. I assumed that it was inevitable but it wasn't. I kept on living. I thought of going back to the police in England so I found a job to pay for my fare. As I worked, though, I thought of what going to the authorities would mean, of what it might do to Carol's memory. All that talk about her and Octavia, it was nonsense but what if the police took it seriously?

In the end I did nothing. I put all my energy and guilt into my work. I was reckless; I speculated; took crazy risks. The less it mattered the more money I made. I would do anything to be tired senseless at the end of the day. The Devil was laughing at me. The less I cared the more I prospered but at least my money will give you what you need to finish it. All my assets here are liquidated, everything is to be yours. Even after tax, you need never work again.

Again, I am wandering and I must finish quickly now. Two years ago that woman, Octavia Anderson, came to Sydney. The fuss, the bother, it was sickening. The real hatred started then. There was that woman, prancing around as a budding celebrity, in the limelight, when it should have been Carol. I went to a performance. She was good but not as Carol would have been, she didn't have the soul. Afterwards, I tried to reach her. I would have killed her then if I had found her and, God forgive me, I still wish I had.

I started to plan how I could kill her but then I became ill and she left the country. I hoped, at first, that I would recover so I could follow her. I haven't, and here I am trading favours with a priest so that he passes this information to you.

It is my bequest. There is money too, but this is what I am really leaving you – the knowledge that your cousin, whom I know you loved more than life itself, was murdered. And the murderess, thanks to the collusion and silence of Carol's supposed friends, parades today in her place on this earth.

What you do, I leave to you. Whatever you do, you do with my blessing so long as it brings justice and we may all rest in peace.

Richard Truman.

The priest had added a hasty postscript:

> Dear Mr Rowland, I am bound to send this under oath. I have prayed constantly these last few days and I know I must send this, I have given my word. But *please* do not listen to your uncle. He is an old and dying man, in agony as he refuses the morphine that would help him. I do not know what is in this package you will receive with this letter but do not be beguiled and misled by its contents as your poor uncle has been. It is the Devil's work he bids you do, not our Lord's. I will pray for you both.

Fenwick sat with his face in his hands, head bowed, trying to resist the tentacles of hate and anger that struggled to reach out from the pages before him. Slowly, reluctantly, he opened the final two letters. The first was from Katherine Johnstone, dated six months after Carol's death. It was a letter of condolence written carefully, with obvious affection for the dead girl. It stopped short of revealing everything she had poured out in her diaries but the girl's inherent honesty forced her to say more than she had ever done at the inquest. Enough to reveal that Octavia had been with Carol just before she died and that Octavia had lied.

Her final words were:

> I am telling you this because I thought you should know. I am convinced that there is a sensible explanation and that Octavia would convince you, as she has us, of her innocence ... Katherine Johnstone.

Thus had she signed her own death warrant for execution twenty years later.

Finally, there was a letter of condolence from Carol's music teacher. One paragraph stood out.

> I am sure you realise how gifted a child Carol was. This cruel accident has robbed not just the school but, I am

convinced, the world of a great musical talent. I hope that she told you we were considering her for the De Weir scholarship. It is a rare honour, and not one awarded every year but it is one I personally believe she would have fully deserved, even in the face of tough competition from another candidate . . .

Fenwick had his motive.

The ACC gave Fenwick five minutes before rushing to a charity function. They had spent virtually no time together since the murder in the cathedral and the atmosphere was brittle.

'The answer is no.' The ACC was implacable. 'You have no case, just gossip from the letters of dead people. This whole affair has been damaging enough without you raking up twenty-year-old allegations of murder and conspiracy. The case is closed.'

'But sir, we know that Anderson was desperate for the scholarship. Her whole future depended on it and it's clear now that it was going to Carol. That's what they quarrelled about. We have *motive*.'

'Tenuous at best – and nothing else. Thanks to Rowland all the others are dead, or as good as, that Smith woman isn't going to recover. And even if she was, you have no evidence but hearsay. No, Fenwick, let it go.'

The ACC smoothed down his hair and checked the lie of his jacket. The interview was over.

He had to ring the doorbell three times before the maid peered through the safety-chained crack into the late afternoon.

'Is she in? I must see her. It's important.' The chain was let fall.

There were three large suitcases and a trunk in the hall, ready labelled for an American tour. Octavia was in the small red drawing room, standing facing a glowing fire with her back to the door. Fenwick watched her for a long moment, confused by the power of her attraction even now. She turned slightly and muscles rippled on her slender body, stretching the cashmere sweater taut.

Music was playing softly in the background. He recognised *Faust*. It had been one of Monique's favourites. The glow from the fire and a small Edwardian lamp were the only illumination, throwing flickering ogress shadows on to the ceiling and walls.

'Why?' Octavia turned fully and addressed him. She was wearing no make-up, her eyes feral and bright in a pale angled face. An antique, garnet-encrusted crucifix lay on the soft wool above her breast, threaded on a thin black ribbon. 'Why come now? Why no word? Why no *apology*?' She spat out the word. 'I nearly *died*. Had it not been for Nightingale, it would be my funeral tomorrow, not his.'

Her anger was palpable. Fenwick saw again the animal inside her, naked and hungry, a wild cat vicious in defence, pitiless in attack. Up until that point he had kept alive the hope that his growing suspicions were false. Seeing her now like this, her narrow, feline face contorted in fury as she faced him, all doubt left him. This woman could kill, would kill to protect what she had clawed out for herself. Worse, she would enjoy revenge. She had probably understood Rowland better than any of them, enjoying the trap that would be closing in on him as she stood as bait, her ultimate prize to watch him die as she triumphed.

Revulsion must have shown on his face. She took a step back from him and sat down on a chair next to the fire. The light glinted off the garnets on her chest, sprinkling crimson droplets around the room that shifted with each breath. Still Fenwick said nothing. He could think of no suitable words with which to start what he had to say. Instead he tossed a sealed packet towards her. She let it fall at her feet then slowly bent to pick it up. She ripped it open and started to read, crushing each page in one hand as she finished reading before throwing it carelessly into the fire. Chemical green and yellow flames spurted out from between the coals as the fire found and consumed the inks.

As she finished the last page, she crumpled and dropped it in the hearth where it lay like a desiccated dung ball at her feet.

Neither spoke; the *Faust* had finished long before.

'What are you going to do?'

'Is it true?'

'What do you think?'

The silence gave her answer.

'Why come here on your own then? Where are your gallant boys – or are they waiting outside?' She paused and studied him intently. 'No, you haven't got a case, have you? Are you hoping for a confession, is that it? Are you wired, Chief Inspector?'

'No, no tape recorders and yes, I am on my own.'

Her smile was long and slow. Ice formed down Fenwick's spine and he added, for no reason, 'But I have shared this information with others.'

Octavia bent down and in quiet ritual dropped the last paper ball into the fire.

'It was a copy.'

'I know.'

The last page flared a sickly blue and was gone. She dusted her hands practically and stood up.

'You have no case, Andrew. If you had, you would have been here now to arrest me, not to stage a melodramatic confrontation. It's time you left. I have a difficult journey tomorrow and a lot still to do this evening. I shall be away some time – I doubt we shall meet on my return.'

'Why? Why did you do it? She was your best friend!'

At first it appeared that she wouldn't answer then, with a shrug, she replied.

'Don't be ridiculous. I *had* no friends, I never *have had*, nor do I want them. You should realise that, Andrew; you have come closer than most.' She stood up and moved to his side.

She drew her finger slowly across the back of his hand. He tried to pull it away sharply in disgust but the nail bit deep, drawing blood in a long welt.

'Get out, Andrew, you're pathetic. Just like the rest of them. Take your sticky sentimentality and go.'

As the maid closed the door on him, he thought he could hear laughter from inside.

Fenwick abandoned his car askew in the church car park and walked to Carol's grave. He was aware that he was being sentimental. He added his small bunch of yellow roses to the dozen that were already there, arranged in a new funeral ornament. His had not been the only legacy then, just the most difficult.

He bent and casually removed weeds and small stones from the smooth turf of her mound. He felt dirty, betrayed, deeply ashamed of his past with Octavia. It occurred to him, belatedly, that he was still a married man. He needed to pray.

The church was locked; a typed note tacked to the door apologised, blaming vandalism. Anyone seeking access for prayer was welcome to pick up the key from the vicarage; there was a helpful little map. Fenwick needed the anonymity of the church not the challenge of a personal request or unwelcome sympathy. He sat on a bench in the small stone porch. It would do.

No words came. His mind slithered over facts like feet slipping on oily stones. He could find no safe point of purchase from which to regain his balance. The whole case was a parody of justice. He had dedicated his efforts, risked his life, *given* the lives of others to protect the woman from whose original sin the whole tragedy had grown. She had not even bothered to deny her guilt. Worse, she had had no compulsion to confess. In Fenwick's experience the guilty always had a hidden need to tell the truth and to be praised or blamed accordingly. Not Octavia.

He regretted, but had no guilt over, Rowland's death. The man had been a calculating killer. The widows of two policemen and the memories of three wrecked families justified his death. It was Anderson's rottenness that made him gag, that and her complete lack of remorse. She deserved punishment, she should suffer as everyone else had done for her crime. For a brief moment, he almost understood Rowland.

There was a figure by Carol's grave, stooping and peering at the flowers. Fenwick felt a surge of possessive anger and leapt up.

'What the hell are you doing? Leave it alone!'

Jason MacDonald turned to face him, his scowl transforming into a malicious grin as he recognised Fenwick.

'Well, well, if it isn't Mr Plod. One of the "gentlemen" I have to thank for four hours unnecessary incarceration. I'm considering suing, you know – wrongful arrest.'

Fenwick dismissed him with a weary wave and turned towards his car.

MacDonald followed him.

'I am, you know.'

'It was not wrongful arrest, Mr MacDonald.'

'I'm going to make a complaint, though. Anyway, what are you doing here? Case is closed, isn't it?'

'I could ask the same of you.'

'This is a closing piece. I'm turning in a human-interest story – you know: two beautiful women, one life cut short by tragedy, the other going on to become a famous star.'

'Two women?'

'Yes, Carol and Octavia Anderson. School friends parted in death, nearly reunited by revenge, that sort of thing.'

'So you still think there's a connection.'

'Don't look so innocent – I've done my homework, I know who Rowland was. And I've interviewed Leslie Smith. Did an exclusive deal with her husband. He gave me all her schooldays stuff. She won't exactly be needing it any more.'

'I didn't know Smith had recovered!' Fenwick looked at MacDonald hopefully but his spirits sank when he saw the lie in his eyes. 'She hasn't, has she?'

'Weeell, recovered is a strong word. I had to help her, of course, but she could indicate if I was right or wrong.'

Fenwick's disgust showed.

'Don't act superior. You know there's a link between Carol's killer cousin and the schoolgirl slaying.' Alliteration was obviously habit-forming. 'What is it? Is Rowland Anderson's lover from the past? Is that it? With a celebrity, and a pretty one at that, this story will sell. Or did he kill Carol in a tragic triangle of love and hate, acted out on the windy cliffs of Devon.'

'Dorset.'

The beginnings of an idea began to form in Fenwick's mind. It was repugnant, and he was appalled that he had even thought of it, but he was a man confounded by an old injustice with recourse to few, if any, legitimate means of redress. The solution started to shape itself. It would be difficult not to cross the line into disloyalty or betrayal but perhaps there was a way.

'I suppose you've hit the big time now, have you – national tabloids?'

'They take my stories, yes. We have an arrangement.'

'Ah, you've turned freelance.'

'Freelance with a look-in – it makes a big difference.'

'After this piece, what's your next story?'

'Wrongful arrests, I think – with an insider's perspective. My complaint will be the perfect start of the story and I'm sure I'll find plenty of others who feel your force has treated them badly. You just wait. I'll want to see you personally!'

Fenwick laughed. It would be so simple.

'Thank you!'

'What?'

'That's my first laugh for a long time.'

'What's so funny? If you think you're going to get away with this . . . I've got my contacts at the nationals now, you know.' The man prattled on but Fenwick was no longer listening. He could picture his office perfectly. The old, slow coffee machine outside by the secretary's desk, his own desk and table covered with papers, and on the top the open forensic report on Katherine's diaries lying next to the letters from Rowland and his uncle. All the evidence he had but still not enough to prove to the system that a murder had taken place some twenty years before. It would never go to trial in law but there were other instruments of a rougher justice. He looked at MacDonald again; yes even parasites were useful in cleaning up after the dead.

'Mr MacDonald, why don't you come back to my office with me and make that complaint now?'

'I haven't time. I've pre-sold this story and there's a deadline,' he consulted his watch, 'and I've still got to come up with a punchy conclusion.'

'Perfect.'

'Pardon?'

'Nothing. I suppose you're aiming for the nationals?'

'This is hardly front-page stuff.'

'No, exactly.'

Something in Fenwick's tone made MacDonald stop and look at him hard and the policeman gripped his arm.

'As you say, Mr MacDonald, it's hardly front-page stuff, which means that you do have time to come in to my office and make that complaint.'

Fenwick turned to face him again and smiled. 'I really think you should. I'll even take the time to make you a cup of coffee myself.'